THE LIBRARY OF LITERATURE
UNDER THE GENERAL EDITORSHIP OF
JOHN HENRY RALEIGH AND IAN WATT

The Confidence-Man:

HIS MASQUERADE

THE LIBRARY OF LITERATURE

The Confidence-Man:

HIS MASQUERADE

By HERMAN MELVILLE

——

EDITED, WITH AN INTRODUCTION
AND ANNOTATION, BY
H. BRUCE FRANKLIN
STANFORD UNIVERSITY

THE BOBBS–MERRILL COMPANY, INC.
INDIANAPOLIS • NEW YORK

Herman Melville, 1819–1891

The Confidence-Man was first published in 1857

ACKNOWLEDGMENTS

Serious study of *The Confidence-Man* began in the mid 1940's, and the first decade of scholarship was incorporated in Elizabeth Foster's 1954 edition, which in turn has given inestimable help to all subsequent study. In the present edition I have tried to incorporate all this work—that of the first decade, Miss Foster's, and that of the following thirteen years. Since in my footnotes I have acknowledged specific debts to Miss Foster only where her scholarship seemed original or speculative, I here wish to express my profound gratitude to her for performing the many tasks that only a first editor has to face all alone.

This edition profits also from the help of many friends, colleagues, and students. I should like particularly to mention Professor Ian Watt, who read the whole manuscript and made many valuable suggestions; Professor John Seelye, whose contribution is only barely suggested by his frequent appearances in footnotes; Professor Robert Polhemus, who pointed out the extensive relevance of *Martin Chuzzlewit;* Mrs. Carolyn Lury Karcher; Mrs. Helen Trimpi; David Heskett; and Professors Yvor Winters, David Levin, Claude Simpson, and Edgar Dryden. Thanks also are due to the Harvard College Library for permission to edit and publish "The River."

But of course the one who has done the most, as usual, is my wife, who contributed many important discoveries of sources and meanings, edited and criticized the manuscript, read proof, and made it all possible.

January 1967   *H. Bruce Franklin*

CONTENTS

THE PLACE OF *The Confidence-Man* IN MELVILLE'S WORKS

At the age of twenty-seven, just back from the South Seas, Herman Melville published his first book, *Typee* (1846), an immensely popular account of some of his adventures. During the next decade, he wrote all the prose fiction known to be published in his lifetime. Then for thirty-five years he lived in deepening obscurity, writing, with no real hope of regaining the audience he had gradually lost, several volumes of poetry and one final tale, *Billy Budd*, more or less finished just before his death.

The story of Melville's great decade reads like one told by some melancholy, embittered romancer. Acclaimed for his slightest works and sometimes mercilessly abused for his greatest, gaining wisdom and powers as he lost readers and money and health, Melville found more and more ways to make readers participate in his fiction, whether they knew it or not.

After *Typee*, Melville wrote a similarly popular autobiographical adventure story, *Omoo* (1847). Then unexpectedly he plunged into a wild philosophical romance, *Mardi* (1849), which was so badly received that he returned, or seemed to return, to the earlier mode in *Redburn* (1849) and *White-Jacket* (1850), fictionalized accounts of his service on a merchant ship and a man-of-war. In retrospect we can see that these two works are much more subtle, complicated, and original than the first two books and that they point to what was about to happen. But no one besides Melville was prepared for his next book, *Moby-Dick, or, The Whale* (1851). Although a few greeted it with enthusiastic generalizations, the most typical (and practical) critical response was a warning to Melville not to "waste his strength on such purposeless and unequal doings." *Moby-Dick* never made expenses; the much more desperate book that followed, *Pierre, or, The Ambiguities* (1852), met with an almost unanimous response summed up by the opening words of one review: "A bad book!" Melville then turned to the magazines, for which in the next three years he wrote a serialized historical romance, *Israel Potter* (1854), and a score of stories and sketches, including *Bartleby* (1853), *The Encantadas* (1854), and *Benito Cereno* (1855).

In the fiction after *Moby-Dick*, Melville developed many new techniques and new visions. Largely abandoning the relatively simple first-person narrative of *Typee, Omoo, Redburn, White-Jacket*, most of *Mardi*, and much of *Moby-Dick*, he began experimenting with all kinds of masquerade. His language became rich with "Joycean" puns, multiple syntax, and rhythmic verbal reverberations. His art of characterization, often becoming an art of caricature, produced such memorable figures as Reverend Falsgrave and Mrs. Glendinning in *Pierre*, John Paul Jones and Benjamin Franklin in *Israel Potter*, and Hunilla, Bartleby, Turkey, Amasa Delano, and Babo in the short fiction. Working mainly in shorter forms, he attained an astonishing compression and control (witness *Bartleby*). He invented many tricks to make his reader both his subject and victim, ranging from *The Paradise of Bachelors and The Tartarus of Maids*, which takes the reader unwittingly on a tour of the male and female sexual and excretory organs in order to demonstrate the perversions of his society and himself, to *Benito Cereno*, which makes him play the role of a myopic Yankee clown. By 1856 Melville was ready to complete the work which an ever-growing number of readers now considers his masterpiece, the conclusion and culmination of his career as professional author, *The Confidence-Man: His Masquerade*, published, appropriately, on April 1st, 1857.

When first published, *The Confidence-Man* was mildly praised (particularly in England) as a satire on America, and then, along with the rest of Melville's works, it was forgotten. In the 1920's and 1930's, the early days of the Melville revival, when the general view saw *Moby-Dick* as his culmination and everything thereafter as a collapse, *The Confidence-Man* was often cited as proof of Melville's spiritual, moral, and artistic exhaustion. It was called misanthropic, bitter, despairing, desperate, hopeless, sterile, mechanical, and, of all things, incomplete (the 1965 revised edition of *The Oxford Companion to American Literature* still calls it "unfinished"!). Not until after the Second World War did the form or achievement of *The Confidence-Man* begin to emerge publicly, just as it was not until after the First World War that any of Melville's works began to emerge. It is no coincidence that *The Confidence-Man* has been discovered simultaneously with Nabokov and Borges, at the height of the Theatre of the Absurd, in the days of *Invisible Man* and *Catch-22*, while history has been taking the shape of a paranoiac hallucination. *The Confidence-Man*, which appeared stillborn or freakish to earlier critics, comes to full life in the present world, when the freakishness of its form, like that of the ugly duckling, appears to have been in the eye of its beholders.

THE SETTING

America in the 1850's was a jungle in which all kinds of hunters pursued their quarry: slaves, factory workers, buffalo, Indians, Mexicans, Mormons, Catholics, Protestants, gold, land, and suckers. American troops had just seized almost half of Mexico, were now busy exterminating Indians from Florida to Oregon, and were preparing to attack the Mormons in Utah. Slavery had already caused much blood to flow, and the nation was on the brink of civil war. Bands of killers roamed almost at will on both sides of the Mississippi and far to the west, undaunted by meeting the heads of other killers stuck on poles. Violence came from the Gold Rush, land claims, competing settlements, economic catastrophes, obscure feuds, racism, and plain blood lusts. This is the immediate world of *The Confidence-Man*, which refers again and again to the violent events of this world and presents many kinds of men who had their being in these events.

But, though the scene is the central Mississippi, the symbolic center of America, the story contains the violence of many human places and times, from primitive tribes to the ancient Greek and Roman conquerors, from Phalaris and Nero to Torquemada, Cesare Borgia, and Pizarro, from the French Revolution to the revolutions of 1848-1849 and the Crimean War, which had just ended. Only one physical blow is struck on board the riverboat Fidèle, but its decks are slippery with the blood of history.

All the varieties of fraud and swindling are also here. On board the Fidèle are American representatives of herbdoctors, land agents, counterfeiters, impostors, charity agents, card sharps, divines, transcendental philosophers, con men of all kinds. They and their victims discuss, quote, and reenact the roles of the other con men of history, such as Plato, Pontius Pilate, Seneca, Augustine, Machiavelli, Bacon, Rochefoucauld, Chesterfield, and P. T. Barnum.

Many American types and American figures are passengers on the Fidèle. While we are on this ornate riverboat we are floating down the Mississippi River in the middle of nine-teenth-century America, surrounded by local forms, local customs, local language, local characters. But just as black turns out to be an appearance of white, this West is also the East, and this time conjoins past with future.

FICTION, READERS, CHARACTERS, AUTHOR

The Confidence-Man makes many extraordinary demands on the reader. By reference, allusion, parody, and quotation, it appropriates and incorporates whole works into itself: many of Shakespeare's plays, many books of the Bible, Ovid's *Metamorphoses*, the *Aeneid*, *Paradise Lost*, and numerous other works are as integral to *The Confidence-Man* as the little stories told by its own characters. Furthermore, some of these characters are caricatures of historical personages (such as Diogenes, Cooper, Socrates, Emerson, Timon, Thoreau, Poe) and others represent mythic figures (such as Manco Capac, Christ, Orpheus, Satan, Vishnu, Buddha). This edition is intended to help modern readers recognize the players and the acts; but although I have annotated far more extensively than most books require, I caution the reader that in most cases my notes merely introduce the contexts Melville asks him to know.

Nothing in *The Confidence-Man* is wasted, misplaced, or merely decorative. The difficulties of syntax are not mere rhetorical flourishes or meaningless obscurities but constant invitations to the reader both to see all the multiple possibilities they create and to feel the sinuous rhythms and sinister weavings that are entrapping him in a dialectical web. Only a few of the ever present syntactical snares are annotated. Many, many of the words of *The Confidence-Man*, including its title, are significant puns; only a few of these are annotated. And nothing in the book, from the most physical of objects to the most metaphysical of arguments, can, in the last analysis, be separated from every other thing in the book; so the cross-references in the footnotes only hint of the intricacy of the book's design.

Perhaps the most perplexing thing about the book is its diabolical suggestiveness. Elaborate solutions for all problems and mysteries are suggested; but they turn out to be incomplete or ambiguous. Hints are dropped about financial chicanery, religious imposture, physical disease, and sexual perversion; but they usually remain only hints. Darkness obscures all lights. The book ends by asserting that "something further *may* follow of this Masquerade." Behind and through all appearances peeps an author who suggests that he knows all. He asks the reader for his confidence while making it impossible to hear that word again without a most suggestively knowing smile.

The Confidence-Man at first may seem to be a debate about the question, Should one have confidence in Man? One should resist the temptation to read the book as an argument for or against this position. One must also resist the temptation to read it as an unresolved debate; the debate serves to establish a dialectic, and the dialectic serves not to analyze the world that is but to create a new cosmos out of the materials of an old chaos. The principal materials of that old chaos exist within each reader, and it is he who is asked to re-form Man by entering a world in which an author and he define each other in terms of objects and characters they join in creating.

A reader begins, innocently perhaps, trying to read this book as though it were a novel. If he is a good novel-reader, he pays careful attention to the words and the physical objects and actions created out of these words. In the very first words of the book the reader discovers that the actions about to be described take place on April Fools' Day. At this point, he may suspect that the title character is going to be playing tricks on other characters; he may even suspect that the author is going to be playing tricks on him. But will he suspect the possibility that each physical object and action may be an All-Fools' joke because he will either see that it is not physical or else become its victim? Everything he is to see will be like a left-handed monkey wrench, a skyhook, or a can of striped paint, that is, a verbal thing, a tricky fiction created by the interaction of at least two minds. The first action of the book consists of a mysterious stranger coming upon a placard that presents "what purported to be a careful description" of "a mysterious impostor"; the stranger may read this description, but the reader may not. All he can read is the author's description of the stranger, who is a "lamb-like" mute on a riverboat named the Fidèle.

Soon, however, the reader finds himself, together with the passengers on the Fidèle, receiving descriptions of all the subsequent avatars of the Confidence Man in the form of a list of "ge'mmen" reeled off by Black Guinea, a crippled Negro beggar, himself apparently a principal avatar. One by one these avatars appear in person, that is to say, in the author's words rather than in the words of Black Guinea, who is one of his characters. In this world a character creates his author by creating other characters who speak words formed by both of them.

This only begins the involutions of fictive realities. Many subsequent characters at times become authors who create characters, some of whom then create other characters. Melville interpolates three chapters (14, 33, 44) addressed by the author to his readers about the relations among fiction, authors, characters, readers, and the rest of reality. Two characters try to get each other dizzy and confused with bad wine, cheap cigars, and a discussion of what authors mean by the words they put in the mouths of characters (Chapter 30). One of these characters later victimizes the other by telling him a story which he claims to have "told with the purpose of every storyteller—to amuse"; "Hence, if it seem strange to you, that strangeness is the romance; it is what contrasts it with real life; it is the invention, in brief, the fiction as opposed to the fact" (Chapter 35). One character hears a "true" story from two other characters who are evidently the same character in two different forms, and then repeats it, in a somewhat different version, to someone evidently a third form of the same character; we are not permitted to hear any of these versions because, as the authorial "we" tells us: "But as the good merchant could, perhaps, do better justice to the man than the story, we shall venture to tell it in other words than his, though not to any other effect" (Chapter 11). Now what in the world does it mean to do better justice to a man than to a story told about that man? And what then can "not to any other effect" possibly mean? And what is all this hazy shadow play about? Part of the answer lies in the relations between man's imaginative reality, what he thinks, and man's identity, what he is.

Most of us wander through life identifying people in terms of such things as external characteristics (tall, fat, brown, bowlegged, eagle-beaked) or easily labeled groups (Negro, Methodist, Communist, worker, Indian) or more-or-less temporary states (rich, well-dressed, gloomy, angry, young, on a battlefield, in the cabin of the boat) and so forth. When we read most fictions, we are asked to behave in this usual way—only more so. If we are presented with a character described as a crippled Negro beggar on a Mississippi riverboat, we expect that character to remain the same except as he is changed by circumstances we are told about or may infer. He may get off the boat, stop begging, become healed, or, even more miraculously, lose his identity as a Negro; but he changes only as we accept the author's manipulations. If, in the next chapter, there appears a character who does not *appear* to be the same character, he *is* not the same character unless and until we are convinced that he is. Black Guinea's list exposes some of the consequences of these ordinary assumptions about fiction and other forms of existence.

BLACK GUINEA'S LIST

Black Guinea's list of the avatars of the Confidence Man is a list of only the most external characteristics:

"Oh yes, oh yes, dar is aboard here a werry nice, good ge'mman wid a weed, and a ge'mman in a gray coat and white tie, what knows all about me; and a ge'mman wid a big book, too; and a yarb-doctor; and a ge'mman in a yaller west; and a ge'mman wid a brass plate; and a ge'mman in a wiolet robe; and a ge'mman as is a sodjer; and ever so many good, kind, honest ge'mmen more aboard what knows me and will speak for me, God bress 'em; yes, and what knows me as well as dis poor old darkie knows hisself, God bress him! Oh, find 'em, find 'em . . . ."

We share the plight of the bystander who immediately wants to know, "But how are we to find all these people in this great crowd?" Apparently we are supposed to find out who people *are*—and who the Confidence Man *is*—by examining the colors each man wears, the objects he carries, and the role he plays. This is precisely what we see the people on the Fidèle doing and what we customarily do in our daily lives. This is precisely what Black Guinea—almost certainly an avatar of the Confidence Man—wants us to do, and what we have to do in order to read the book with any coherence.

At the same time, Guinea's list, like everything else in *The Confidence-Man*, contains its opposite. We do meet, in order, characters explicitly described as a man with a weed, a man in a gray coat and white tie, a man with a big book, and an herb doctor, all of whom seem to be forms of the Confidence Man. These are precisely half, the first half, of the particularized characters in the list. Of the four who comprise the second half, we meet only one described by the author as described by Guinea (this one is the second of the four). After these eight particular characters, Guinea ends his list with "ever so many good, kind, honest ge'mmen," an indication that there are far more than ten (eight plus Guinea and the lamb-like man) shapes of the Confidence Man in this world and that all shapes may be ambiguous. Furthermore, Guinea speaks in a dialect, making any of his words possibly puns (as he hints by concluding "dis poor ole darkie is werry well *wordy* of all you kind ge'mmen's kind confidence").

Guinea's wordiness, like the muteness of the lamb-like man, expands until it fills the universe of *The Confidence-Man*; his list ultimately includes everybody. To perceive what is involved, one must read his list artfully, always following its movement through precision into ambiguity, through the particular to the universal—or apparently chaotic.

Number 1. "A werry nice, good ge'mman wid a weed." The first listed avatar seems the easiest to find. John Ringman appears with "a long weed on his hat" in Chapter 4 and then is referred to in the title of Chapter 5 as "The man with the weed." But to establish this identity we must assume that the author sticks to Guinea's terms, something later to be made dubious. We might, as one alternative, take Guinea's "weed" to mean tobacco, making each of the two confidence men who force cigars on the other in Chapter 30 a man with a weed; one of them, Frank Goodman, is certainly a "good man wid de weed," to use Guinea's very last words. Or we could take another common meaning of weed, "A covering; that which covers, spreads over vest or vestment, clothing or garment" (Richardson's *Dictionary*, 1844), and see the first of Guinea's listings to be as equivocal and far-reaching as the last. We may create this form of the Confidence Man wherever we see him.

Number 2. "A ge'mman in a gray coat and white tie." In Chapter 6 there appears "a man in a gray coat and white tie." But note that in Chapter 3, when a suspect Methodist minister attacks a cynical cripple, a voice cries out, "The white cravat against the world!"

Number 3. "A ge'mman wid a big book, too." In Chapter 9 there appears a man carrying a ledger-like transfer book; he is the president and transfer agent of the Black Rapids Coal Company. Several characters have small books, so we are asked to distinguish them from the Confidence Man by the size of their books. Then the last character mentioned in *The Confidence-Man* is discovered in possession of the big book of the gentlemen's cabin, the Bible. And both the reader and the author have a book, which may or may not be big.

Number 4. "A yarb-doctor." The relatively unambiguous first half of Guinea's list ends with one of the two unambiguous identifications; the only herb doctor appears just as the sun comes out from behind the clouds in Chapter 16.

Number 6. "A ge'mman wid a brass plate." The relatively unambiguous first half of the book ends with the other unambiguous identification; a man who wears a small brass plate around his neck, having just sold a hypothetical boy, gets ready to disembark as he passes a bluff called the Devil's Joke. As soon as he leaves, Chapter 23, the exact center of the book, describes the ambiguous twilight. After this, not one of Guinea's listings appears as Guinea had described.

Number 5. "A ge'mman in a yaller west" and Number 7. "A ge'mman in a wiolet robe." Neither of these two brightly colored forms is described by the author as described by Guinea. Either or both may be the sun, around which *The Confidence-Man*, like the world it images, revolves. The "man in cream-colors" who appears "at sunrise on a first of April" in the first sentence of the book might be viewed as a *gentle*man in a yellow vest ("vest," from the Latin *vestis*, meant any garment, particularly an outer garment, a robe or coat). Or the last character introduced in the book, a peddler-boy wearing a "fragment of an old linen coat, bedraggled and yellow," may be viewed as a *gamin* in a yellow vest. The herb doctor also wears a yellowish garment; several times he is pointedly identified as the man in the snuff-colored surtout. The sun, which comes out when he does, is then called "a golden huzzar." The Cosmopolitan calls all "moderns" "we golden boys," sees about Shakespeare a "hidden sun . . . at once enlightening and mystifying," and refers to the printing press as the sun, "god Apollo" who "dispenses the day."

As yellow is to the sunrise, violet is to the sunset. The two confidence men who confront each other in Chapters 25 through 35, the extraordinary Cosmopolitan and the ordinary riverboat con man, Charlie Noble, each wear something that resembles a violet robe. The Cosmopolitan "sported a *vest*ure barred with various hues, that of the cochineal predominating"; Charlie wears a "violet vest." A character who flits by in Chapter 6, a "gentleman in a ruby-colored velvet vest," would seem to be merely a red herring. But not to be dismissed is the intensely symbolic "robed man" on the ground-glass shade of the solar lamp in the final chapter; whether or not his robe is violet, the extinction of the solar lamp that illuminates him is much like the setting of the sun. And, after all, what makes colors?

Number 8. "A ge'mman as is a sodjer." Four of the Fidèle's passengers play the role of playing the role of soldier. The lamb-like man, though "apparently a non-resistant," moves through the crowd "shield-like bearing his slate before him." Likewise, the Methodist minister, though he says he was thought "a non-combatant," is a "soldier-like," "martial-look-ing man . . . who in the Mexican War had been volunteer chaplain to a volunteer rifle-regiment." The man with the bandaged nose of Chapter 18, who walks "with a pace that seemed the lingering memento of the lock-step of convicts," is called a "poor wounded huzzar" by the herb doctor. The cripple of the following chapter, entitled "A Soldier of For-tune," claims to the herb doctor to have been crippled in prison but passes himself off to the other passengers as a wounded veteran of the Mexican War. He is both accused of belonging to "the Devil's regiment" (in *White-Jacket* Melville himself had said that any soldier "is but a fiend" who serves the Devil) and acclaimed as a fighter against "Fortune." He illustrates the art of "coming the old soldier," i.e., tricking like "a rogue who pretends to be an old soldier" (Barrère and Leland).

Besides these four passengers, there are other gentlemen who appear "as is a sodjer." There is the sun itself, likened to a "golden huzzar." There is a real soldier, Colonel John More-dock, one of the most important metaphysical (though not physical) passengers. The very word soldier—derived from *soldus* and literally meaning one who receives pay—suggests a fundamental ambiguity. And "sodjer" does not even neces-sarily mean "soldier." "Sodjer" (also spelled "sodger," "sojer," and "soger") in nautical usage meant, as Melville knew, "a red herring." Finally, all these possibilities combine in the possibili-ties foreshadowed by the final sentence of the book: "Some-thing further may follow of this Masquerade." In apocalyptic visions of both the East and the West, the Savior in his last avatar will return as a destroying soldier.

The Confidence-Man AS MYTH

A reader familiar with no other myths than the Judeo-Chris-tian ones may read through *The Confidence-Man* with a good partial understanding. He may see that the lamb-like man

represents either Christ or Satan masquerading as Christ, that
Guinea and the later avatars of the Confidence Man represent
Satan, that the vision of the final chapter is filled with images
from Revelation, and that the sequel hinted in the last sentence
may be a fulfillment of that apocalypse. He may describe the
Confidence Man's assumption of Christianity in familiar Western terms, such as diabolic, wicked, fiendish; and he may see
this role as that of Satan or Anti-Christ.

However, this is not even half the mythic structure. One of
the great achievements of *The Confidence-Man* is its way of
relating the principal Western myths to the principal Eastern
myths and all myth to all other kinds of fiction. In *The Wake
of the Gods: Melville's Mythology*, I discuss these relations in
some detail; here I shall just summarize.

The Confidence-Man begins at sunrise on April 1st and ends
shortly after midnight. All Fools' Day was generally assumed
to be a remnant of the ancient great vernal festival, com-
memorating the rebirth of the sun, celebrated all around the
Northern Hemisphere at the time of the vernal equinox, when
the sun returns from "beneath" the equator. (The date of
course shifts with the precession of the equinoxes.) Most authorities traced the rituals of All Fools' Day to the most ancient known vernal celebration, a Hindu masquerade called the
Huli. These vernal rituals, held on the one day when the duration of light exactly equals and is about to exceed the duration of
darkness (a division precisely reflected in the structure of *The
Confidence-Man*), greeted the sun as the great savior-god returning from the realms of night, i.e., the Southern Hemisphere (whose best-known incarnation of the sun, Manco
Capac, is likened to the lamb-like man in the first sentence of
the book).

The Confidence Man is this sun, this god, this savior. But at
the same time he is the darkness that obscures this sun (as
Black Guinea when he holds up his "old coal-sifter of a tamborine" to indicate the sun, as the President of the Black
Rapids Coal Company, as the Cosmopolitan when he extin-

guishes the last light in the book, a solar lamp); he is the god
who struggles against this god; he is the destroyer. This identity of light and darkness, salvation and destruction, inherently
alien to Christianity, lies at the heart of both Hinduism and
Buddhism.

The avatars of the Confidence Man are quite literally *ava-
tara*, that is, successive incarnations of the great Hindu god of
salvation, Vishnu. The first major avatar of Vishnu is as a fish
who recovers the lost sacred books; the first avatar of the
Confidence Man is, among other things, an "Odd fish!" who
brings to the world injunctions from the Bible. The second
avatar is as a tortoise who upholds the world; the second avatar
of the Confidence Man is as a "grotesque" figure who shuffles
around on leather stumps, who lives "all 'long shore," and who
holds his symbolic "coal-sifter of a tamborine" "high over his
head." After this come eight other major avatars and innumerable minor ones; Black Guinea lists eight other major avatars
and innumerable minor ones ("ever so many good, kind, honest ge'mmen"). For Hinduism and for *The Confidence-Man*
the two most important are the last avatar which has come,
Buddha, and the last avatar, which is to come, Kalki.

The teachings of Buddha ("the enlightened"), who had also
the name of Gotamâ (*go*, senses, and *tamá*, darkness: i.e., "he
who brings darkness to the senses"), aimed toward the achievement of *nirvana*, which means literally the extinguishing of a
flame or lamp. According to Hindus (as opposed to Buddhists),
Buddha was Vishnu incarnate as a deceiver, leading his enemies
into spiritual darkness. The last avatar of the Confidence Man is
the Cosmopolitan, who finally extinguishes the last light, the
solar lamp, and leads man into the ensuing darkness.

In Hinduism, Vishnu the Preserver is one face of a three-
headed godhood, the Trimurti, whose other two faces are
Brahma the Creator and Siva the Destroyer. Brahma has no
role in the created world; but Siva, like Vishnu, has periodic
avatars. The world of *The Confidence-Man: His Masquerade*,

like the world of the Hindus, can be seen as a dialectic masquerade of the two conflicting forms—preservation and destruction, love and hate, confidence and delusion, white and
black, Vishnu and Siva. In both Hinduism and *The Confidence-Man* these two forms are shapes of the same being, in
fact all forms are shapes of the same being, and all men partake
of the unity imaged visually in the god that seems many but is
one.

In Vishnu's last avatar, which is to come, he will appear with
the attributes of Siva the Destroyer as Kalki, an armed warrior, to end the final age of man, the present age, the Age of
Time, by destroying man. This may be both Guinea's
"ge'mman as is a sodjer" and what is hinted in the final sentence: "Something further may follow of this Masquerade."
And it may also explain why the last character introduced into
the book, in the final chapter, is a boy with "leopard-like
teeth," with a face that "wore such a polish of seasoned grime,
that his sloe-eyes sparkled from out it like lustrous sparks in
fresh coal," and clothed in a "red-flannel shirt." For Siva often
appears as "a smoke-coloured boy" whose "teeth are as large as
an ogre's," who appears "clothed in red raiment," and who
"destroys all, or . . . absorbs all essences into himself at last."
When the boy winks at the Cosmopolitan and asks, "is the
wind East, d'ye think?", one may sense their final apocalyptic
union.

Melville makes the Hindu vision of the apocalypse over-
shadow the Christian vision, in which the armed Word of God
vanquishes Satan. Christ in *The Confidence-Man* merges into
Satan as the shape-shifting struggles and ultimate identity of
Vishnu and Siva generate a world in which all objects and
events become fictions, all men become indistinguishable, all
gods become the Confidence Man, salvation means destruction,
and black is only another appearance of white. This vision, at
first appearance so destructive, is in reality most creative. To
experience and survive it is to be re-created.

1819   Herman Melville, third of eight children, born to Allan and Maria Gansevoort Melville on August 1 in New York City.

1830   Family moves to Albany, where Allan Melville sets up a fur business.

1832   Allan Melville dies, leaving family with great business debts. Melville clerks in a bank.

1835   Melville clerks in his brother Allan's store until the business fails, then teaches school near Pittsfield, Massachusetts.

1838   Family moves to Lansingburgh, New York, where Melville studies engineering in an unsuccessful attempt to get a job on the Erie Canal.

1839   Sails to Liverpool and back on the crew of the merchant ship *St. Lawrence*. Teaches school at Greenbush, New York.

1840   Visits his Uncle Thomas Melville in Galena, Illinois.

1841   Ships out in January on the whaler *Acushnet*, which stops at Rio de Janeiro, rounds Cape Horn, and cruises among the Galapagos Islands.

1842   Melville and a shipmate jump ship at Nuka Hiva in the Marquesas Islands, flee into the interior, and live with the notorious Typee tribe for a few weeks. Escapes and signs on the *Lucy Ann*, an Australian whaler. At Tahiti the crew rebels and is arrested by the British consul. Melville escapes to Eimo and ships out on the *Charles and Henry*, a Nantucket whaler.

1843   Does odd jobs in Honolulu. Enlists as ordinary seaman on the frigate *United States*, which visits the Marquesas, Tahiti, and various South American ports.

1844   Melville discharged in Boston; returns home to his family in Lansingburgh.

1845   Writes an account of his adventures in the Marquesas.

1846   This account, later known as *Typee*, published in London and New York.

1847 *Omoo*, an account of his adventures on the *Lucy Ann*, in Tahiti, and on Eimo. Marries Elizabeth Shaw, daughter of Chief Justice of Massachusetts, Lemuel Shaw. Settles in New York City.

1849 *Mardi*, an allegorical and philosophical romance. *Redburn*, based on his first voyage. Sails for England; visits the continent. Son Malcolm born.

1850 *White-Jacket*, based on experiences on the *United States*. Moves to Pittsfield and forms friendship with Hawthorne.

1851 *Moby-Dick, or, The Whale.* Son Stanwix born.

1852 *Pierre, or, The Ambiguities.*

1853 Fire at Harper and Brothers destroys many unsold copies of his seven books. Begins publishing in the magazines. Daughter Elizabeth born.

1855 *Israel Potter* published in book form. Daughter Frances born.

1856 *The Piazza Tales*, a collection of his magazine stories. Finishes *The Confidence-Man*. Sails for Europe and the Holy Land.

1857 *The Confidence-Man* published in New York and London.

1858–60 Public lecturing trips, mostly in the Middle West.

1860 Finishes a volume of poetry. Visits San Francisco on ship commanded by his brother Thomas.

1863 Settles in New York City.

1866 *Battle-Pieces*, a collection of Civil War poems. Becomes an inspector of customs in the port of New York, a position held until 1886.

1867 Eldest son Malcolm dies from self-inflicted pistol wound.

1869 Second son Stanwix goes to sea.

1876 *Clarel: A Poem and Pilgrimage in the Holy Land.*

1886 Stanwix dies in a San Francisco hospital.

1888 *John Marr and Other Sailors*, a collection of poems.

1891 *Timoleon*, a collection of poems. *Billy Budd* almost finished. Dies, September 28.

1924 *Billy Budd* published.

Oliver, Egbert S. "Melville's Goneril and Fanny Kemble," *New England Quarterly*, XVIII (1945), 489–500.

———. "Melville's Picture of Emerson and Thoreau in *The Confidence-Man*," *College English*, VIII (1946), 61–72.

Parker, Hershel. "The Metaphysics of Indian-Hating," *Nineteenth-Century Fiction*, XVIII (1963), 165–173.

Pearce, Roy Harvey. "Melville's Indian-Hater: A Note on the Meaning of *The Confidence-Man*," *PMLA*, LXVII (1952), 942–948.

Pommer, Henry F. *Milton and Melville*. Pittsburgh: University of Pittsburgh Press, 1950.

Reeves, Paschal. "The 'Deaf Mute' Confidence Man: Melville's Imposter in Action," *Modern Language Notes*, LXXV (1960), 18–20.

Rosenberry, Edward Hoffman. *Melville and the Comic Spirit*. Cambridge: Harvard University Press, 1955.

———. "Melville's Ship of Fools," *PMLA*, LXXV (1960), 604–608.

Sedgwick, William Ellery. *Herman Melville: The Tragedy of Mind*. Cambridge: Harvard University Press, 1944.

Seelye, John Douglas. "The Iridescent Scabbard: Melville's Ironic Mode." Unpublished Ph.D. dissertation. Claremont, 1962.

———. "Timothy Flint's 'Wicked River' and *The Confidence-Man*," *PMLA*, LXXVIII (1963), 75–79.

Shroeder, J. W. "Sources and Symbols for Melville's *The Confidence-Man*," *PMLA*, LXVI (1951), 363–380.

Smith, Paul. "*The Confidence-Man* and the Literary World of New York," *Nineteenth-Century Fiction*, XVI (1962), 329–337.

Thompson, Lawrance. *Melville's Quarrel with God*. Princeton: Princeton University Press, 1952.

Tuveson, Ernest. "The Creed of The Confidence-Man," *ELH*, XXXIII (1966), 247–270.

Weissbuch, Ted N. "A Note on the Confidence-Man's Counterfeit Detector," *Emerson Society Quarterly*, No. 19 (1960), 16–18.

Wright, Nathalia. "The Confidence Men in Melville and Cooper: An American Indictment," *American Quarterly*, IV (1952), 266–268.

———. *Melville's Use of the Bible*. Durham: Duke University Press, 1949.

A NOTE ON THE TEXT

The text used is that of the first American edition, April 1st, 1857. No attempt has been made to regularize or modernize either spelling or punctuation. Some minor typographical errors have been silently corrected; a few more serious errors have been corrected with due annotation.

The Confidence-Man:

HIS MASQUERADE

CHAPTER 1

A mute goes aboard a boat on the Mississippi.

At sunrise on a first of April,[1] there appeared, suddenly as
Manco Capac at the lake Titicaca,[2] a man in cream-colors,[3] at
the water-side in the city of St. Louis.[4]

His cheek was fair, his chin downy, his hair flaxen, his hat a
white fur one, with a long fleecy nap.[5] He had neither trunk,
valise, carpet-bag, nor parcel. No porter followed him. He was
unaccompanied by friends. From the shrugged shoulders, tit-
ters, whispers, wonderings of the crowd, it was plain that he
was, in the extremest sense of the word, a stranger.[6]

In the same moment with his advent,[7] he stepped aboard the

[1] All Fools' Day. See Introduction, pages xviii and xxv.

[2] Manco Capac, the first Inca, an incarnation of the sun, appeared first
in the form of a mysterious stranger at Lake Titicaca, between what are
now Peru and Bolivia.

[3] See Introduction, pages xix–xxiii, on the use of colors to identify
characters.

[4] The largest city in the Mississippi valley and situated just below the
confluence of the Missouri with the Mississippi, St. Louis was commonly
viewed as the symbolic crossroads of the West.

[5] Note the combination of bird (down), vegetable (flax), wild animal
(fur), and tame animal (fleece). This description also hints that what
is to take place on the Fidèle is an apocalypse; in Revelation (1:14)
Christ first appears to John as one whose "head and his hairs were white
like wool, as white as snow."

[6] Various characters later in the book are designated simply as "the
stranger." "The extremest sense of the word" points to its etymology
from *extra*, "on the outside." As a central motif, the mysterious stranger
embodies one fusion of man, his gods, and the mystery and strangeness
outside each viewer.

[7] "Advent" first came into English as a strictly religious term to
designate the coming of the Savior and hence the period preceding
His appearance. Since 1843, when William Miller's Adventist prophecies
gained widespread credence, various Adventist sects had been predicting

3

favorite steamer Fidèle,[8] on the point of starting for New Orleans. Stared at, but unsaluted, with the air of one neither courting nor shunning regard, but evenly pursuing the path of duty, lead it through solitudes or cities, he held on his way along the lower deck until he chanced to come to a placard nigh the captain's office, offering a reward for the capture of a mysterious impostor, supposed to have recently arrived from the East;[9] quite an original genius[10] in his vocation, as would appear, though wherein his originality consisted was not clearly given; but what purported to be a careful description of his person followed.[11]

As if it had been a theatre-bill, crowds were gathered about the announcement, and among them certain chevaliers,[12] whose eyes, it was plain, were on the capitals,[13] or, at least, earnestly seeking sight of them from behind intervening coats; but as for their fingers, they were enveloped in some myth;[14]

---

that the Second Advent (and the destruction of the world) would come in a few weeks or months.

[8] The name of the boat ("Faithful"), like confidence, comes from the Latin *fides*, "faith." It may also hint of a tradition of disguise: in Shakespeare's *Cymbeline*, Imogen, disguised as a boy, assumes the name Fidele; Fidelio is the assumed name of women in the same guise in Wycherley's *The Plain Dealer* and Beethoven's opera *Fidelio*.

[9] Either the American East or the Far East.

[10] "Original," a key word in the book, derives from *oriri*, "to rise," the root word of Orient. Here it joins the sunrise now taking place with the mysterious impostor from the East; in Chapter 19 the herb doctor is referred to as "an original genius"; in Chapter 36 "oriental" and "origin" are joined together; all of Chapter 44 is a discussion of the phrase "Quite an Original."

[11] Note the sinister syntax of this sentence, which begins by describing the mysterious stranger and ends by pointedly not repeating the "careful description" of "a mysterious impostor."

[12] A *chevalier d'industrie* (Fr., "knight of industry") is a man who lives by his wits, i.e., a sharper or swindler.

[13] The capital letters on the placard and perhaps also, in the root sense, the capitals (heads) of the crowd as well as their capital (money).

[14] The use of the word "myth" here suggests that any physical object may be a protective fiction or vice versa. This unusual usage implies that

though, during a chance interval, one of these chevaliers somewhat showed his hand in purchasing from another chevalier, ex-officio a peddler of money-belts, one of his popular safeguards, while another peddler, who was still another versatile chevalier, hawked, in the thick of the throng, the lives of Measan,[15] the bandit of Ohio, Murrel,[16] the pirate of the Mississippi, and the brothers Harpe,[17] the Thugs[18] of the

---

in this fictional world all objects may be mythic, that is, fictional, and all myths may be represented by objects.

The hidden hands of these sharpers relate to: the passengers in Chapter 10, most of whom have their "hands in the games" while a few "for the most part keep their hands in their pockets"; the personification of Yellow Fever in Chapter 23 as one whose "hand . . . has not lost its cunning"; and two cries from the dark in the final chapter—". . . if you want to know what wisdom is, go find it under your blankets"; "To bed with ye, ye divils, and don't be after burning your fingers with the likes of wisdom."

[15] Samuel Measan (or Mason) (*c.* 1750–1803), leader of a gang of bloodthirsty bandits.

[16] John A. Murrell (*fl.* 1804–1844), one of the bloodiest and most charming of all outlaws, eventually became head of Murrell's Mystic Clan. The Clan, reputed to have over a thousand members, including some who were respected citizens by day, terrorized most of the Mississippi valley. Murrell and his men would ingratiate themselves with travelers, then murder them and throw their disemboweled bodies, filled with stones, into the river. One of Murrell's favorite gambits was to steal a slave, then resell, resteal, and finally murder him. See Chapter 3, note 9.

[17] James Hall, the source for Chapters 26–28, describes the two fiendish Harpe brothers in these terms: "Neither avarice, want, nor any of the usual inducements to the commission of crime, seemed to govern their conduct. A savage thirst for blood—a deep rooted malignity against human nature, could alone be discovered in their actions. They murdered every defenceless being who fell in their way. . . ." Like Murrell, they were masters of disguise. After Big Harpe was beheaded by a posse, Little Harpe joined Measan's gang and eventually beheaded its leader. He was seized while trying to sell Measan's head, and his own head, like his brother's, ended on a public stake.

[18] Thugs were devotees of Kali, Hindu goddess of destruction, consort of Siva the Destroyer. The term *Thug* means impostor or cheat. Bands of Thugs used to roam throughout India, posing as pilgrims, peddlers,

Green River country, in Kentucky—creatures, with others of
the sort, one and all exterminated at the time, and for the most
part, like the hunted generations of wolves in the same regions,
leaving comparatively few successors; which would seem
cause for unalloyed gratulation, and is such to all except those
who think that in new countries, where the wolves are killed
off, the foxes increase.[19]

Pausing at this spot, the stranger so far succeeded in thread-
ing his way, as at last to plant himself just beside the placard,
when, producing a small slate and tracing some words upon it,
he held it up before him on a level with the placard, so that
they who read the one might read the other. The words were
these:—

"Charity thinketh no evil." [20]

As, in gaining his place, some little perseverance, not to say
persistence, of a mildly inoffensive sort, had been unavoidable,
it was not with the best relish that the crowd regarded his
apparent intrusion; and upon a more attentive survey, perceiv-

---

or ordinary travelers, striking up acquaintances with authentic pilgrims
or travelers and then ritually murdering them. The standard work,
Edward Thornton's *Illustrations and Practices of the Thugs* (London,
1837), relates, pertinently, that "skilled in the arts of deception, they
enter into the conversation, and insinuate themselves by obsequious
attentions into the confidence of travelers of all descriptions," that they
were often aided by children who were becoming initiated into Thuggee,
that they ran their own "clean and inviting" riverboats, and that they
deemed it "a bad omen to meet . . . any person who has lost a limb."

[19] Edwin Fussell suggests as a source Edmund Spenser's *The Shep-
hearde's Calendar* (1579), "September," which has this dialogue about
the results of the royal order to destroy the wolves:

HOBBINOL: But the fewer wolves (the soth to sayne,)
                       The more bene the foxes that here remain.
DIGGON DANE: Yes, but they gang in more secrete wise,
                       And with sheepes clothing doen hem disguise.

Immediately Melville refocuses on the "lamblike" stranger.

[20] This and the following inscriptions on the slate come from I
Corinthians 13.

ing no badge of authority about him, but rather something quite the contrary—he being of an aspect so singularly inno- cent; an aspect, too, which they took to be somehow inappro- priate to the time and place, and inclining to the notion that his writing was of much the same sort: in short, taking him for some strange kind of simpleton, harmless enough, would he keep to himself, but not wholly unobnoxious as an intruder— they made no scruple to jostle him aside; while one, less kind than the rest, or more of a wag, by an unobserved stroke, dexterously flattened down his fleecy hat upon his head.[21] Without readjusting it, the stranger quietly turned, and writ- ing anew upon the slate, again held it up:—

"Charity suffereth long, and is kind."

Illy pleased with his pertinacity, as they thought it, the crowd a second time thrust him aside, and not without epithets and some buffets, all of which were unresented. But, as if at last despairing of so difficult an adventure, wherein one, appar- ently a non-resistant, sought to impose his presence upon fight- ing characters, the stranger now moved slowly away, yet not before altering his writing to this:—

"Charity endureth all things."

Shield-like bearing his slate before him, amid stares and jeers he moved slowly up and down, at his turning points again changing his inscription to—

"Charity believeth all things."

and then—

"Charity never faileth."

[21] It has been suggested that the crowd's treatment of the lamb-like man constitutes a kind of crucifixion, and that this cruel joke has an analogue in the crown of thorns and sop of vinegar placed on Christ's head. Brand's *Popular Antiquities* quotes a conjecture that "the custom of imposing upon and ridiculing people on the first of April may have an allusion to the mockery of the Saviour of the world by the Jews."

The word charity, as originally traced, remained throughout uneffaced, not unlike the left-hand numeral of a printed date, otherwise left for convenience in blank.

To some observers, the singularity, if not lunacy, of the stranger was heightened by his muteness, and, perhaps also, by the contrast to his proceedings afforded in the actions—quite in the wonted and sensible order of things—of the barber of the boat, whose quarters, under a smoking-saloon, and over against a bar-room, was next door but two to the captain's office. As if the long, wide, covered deck, hereabouts built up on both sides with shop-like windowed spaces, were some Constantinople arcade or bazaar, where more than one trade is plied, this river barber, aproned and slippered, but rather crusty-looking for the moment, it may be from being newly out of bed, was throwing open his premises for the day, and suitably arranging the exterior. With business-like dispatch, having rattled down his shutters, and at a palm-tree angle set out in the iron fixture his little ornamental pole, and this without overmuch tenderness for the elbows and toes of the crowd, he concluded his operations by bidding people stand still more aside, when, jumping on a stool, he hung over his door, on the customary nail, a gaudy sort of illuminated pasteboard sign, skillfully executed by himself, gilt with the likeness of a razor elbowed in readiness to shave, and also, for the public benefit, with two words not unfrequently seen ashore gracing other shops besides barbers':—

"No trust."

An inscription which, though in a sense not less intrusive than the contrasted ones of the stranger, did not, as it seemed, provoke any corresponding derision or surprise, much less indignation; and still less, to all appearances, did it gain for the inscriber the repute of being a simpleton.

Meanwhile, he with the slate continued moving slowly up and down, not without causing some stares to change into jeers, and some jeers into pushes, and some pushes into punches; when suddenly, in one of his turns, he was hailed from behind by two porters carrying a large trunk; but as the summons, though loud, was without effect, they accidentally or otherwise swung their burden against him, nearly over-throwing him; when, by a quick start, a peculiar inarticulate moan, and a pathetic telegraphing of his fingers, he involuntarily betrayed that he was not alone dumb, but also deaf.

Presently, as if not wholly unaffected by his reception thus far, he went forward, seating himself in a retired spot on the forecastle, nigh the foot of a ladder there leading to a deck above, up and down which ladder some of the boatmen, in discharge of their duties, were occasionally going.[22]

From his betaking himself to this humble quarter, it was evident that, as a deck-passenger, the stranger, simple though he seemed, was not entirely ignorant of his place, though his taking a deck-passage might have been partly for convenience; as, from his having no luggage, it was probable that his destination was one of the small wayside landings within a few hours' sail. But, though he might not have a long way to go, yet he seemed already to have come from a very long distance.

Though neither soiled nor slovenly, his cream-colored suit had a tossed look, almost linty, as if, traveling night and day from some far country beyond the prairies, he had long been without the solace of a bed. His aspect was at once gentle and jaded, and, from the moment of seating himself, increasing in tired abstraction and dreaminess. Gradually overtaken by slumber, his flaxen head drooped, his whole lamb-like figure relaxed, and, half reclining against the ladder's foot, lay motionless, as some sugar-snow in March, which, softly stealing down over night, with its white placidity startles the brown farmer peering out from his threshold at daybreak.

---

[22] This image subtly suggests Jacob's ladder to heaven, a suggestion which becomes explicit in the beginning of the next chapter. If the boatmen are like the angels of Jacob's vision, then the captain, who is often mentioned but never glimpsed, may be like God.

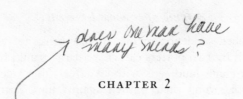
does one man have many minds?

CHAPTER 2

Showing that many men have many minds.

"Odd fish!" [1]
  "Poor fellow!"
  "Who can he be?"
  "Casper Hauser." [2]
  "Bless my soul!"
  "Uncommon countenance."
  "Green prophet from Utah." [3]
  "Humbug!"
  "Singular innocence."
  "Means something."
  "Spirit-rapper." [4]

[1] The first avatar of Vishnu was as a fish (see Introduction, page xxvi). The fish is also, of course, a symbol of Christ. And the French cry *poisson d'avril* ("April fish") at the victims of All Fools' Day jokes.

[2] A mysterious foundling who turned up in Nuremberg in 1828 with a letter giving his birth date as 1812. He said that he had been confined in a dark room all his life. His origin and the philosophical implications of his knowledge or lack of it became matters of great international interest. In 1833 he was stabbed to death by an unknown person who supposedly had lured him with a promise of information as to his origin.

[3] "Green": unseasoned; Utah implies Mormons. Joseph Smith, the first Mormon Prophet, and Brigham Young, his successor as Prophet, were subjects of raging controversy. Smith was attacked as a vicious impostor or a witless enthusiast, Young as his worldly and ambitious Saint Paul. The Mormon "blood atonement" doctrine of 1856, which demanded— and apparently produced—much ritual spilling of blood, the Mormon bands of secret assassins known as Danites, and the territorial aspirations of the Mormons had all induced a violent reaction. While *The Confidence-Man* was going to press, an expedition of U.S. troops was assembling to march against the Mormons.

[4] Someone who professes to communicate with the spirits of deceased persons by eliciting from them raps on a table (cf. Melville's story "The Apple-Tree Table or Original Spiritual Manifestations"). See Chapter

"Moon-calf." [5]

"Piteous."

"Trying to enlist interest."

"Beware of him."

"Fast asleep here, and, doubtless, pick-pockets on board."

"Kind of daylight Endymion." [6]

"Escaped convict, worn out with dodging."

"Jacob dreaming at Luz." [7]

Such the epitaphic comments, conflictingly spoken or thought, of a miscellaneous company, who, assembled on the overlooking, cross-wise balcony at the forward end of the upper deck near by, had not witnessed preceding occurrences.

Meantime, like some enchanted man in his grave, happily oblivious of all gossip, whether chiseled or chatted, the deaf and dumb stranger still tranquilly slept, while now the boat started on her voyage.

The great ship-canal of Ving-King-Ching, in the Flowery Kingdom,[8] seems the Mississippi in parts, where, amply flow-

---

17, note 2. Edwin Fussell notes here a hint for a major source, Orestes Brownson's *The Spirit-Rapper* (1854).

[5] A person or conception influenced by the moon; a monster; a dolt; a deformed foetus. Puns on moon, moon-struck, moonshine, lunar, lunacy, and lunatic appear throughout the book in an elaborate counterpoint with the sun in all its varying forms.

[6] All sources agree that Endymion made love with the goddess Selene, the Moon, but some say that he was made immortal, others that he was hurled to Erebus, still others that he was blessed with eternal sleep. One allegorical interpretation sees Endymion as the setting sun, who sinks into the sea or a cavern to meet the moon.

[7] Genesis 28:12–15 describes Jacob's dream of a ladder reaching from earth to heaven with "the angels of God ascending and descending on it." Above the ladder stands God, who tells Jacob that He will give to him and his seed "the land whereon thou liest." In John 1:51, Christ places Himself in the same image: "Verily, verily, I say unto you, Hereafter ye shall see heaven open, and the angels of God ascending and descending upon the Son of man."

[8] The Grand or Imperial Canal of China; "Ving-King-Ching" remains a mystery.

ing between low, vine-tangled banks, flat as tow-paths, it bears the huge toppling steamers, bedizened and lacquered within like imperial junks.

Pierced along its great white bulk with two tiers of small embrasure-like windows, well above the waterline, the Fidèle, though, might at distance have been taken by strangers for some whitewashed fort on a floating isle.

Merchants on 'change seem the passengers that buzz on her decks, while, from quarters unseen, comes a murmur as of bees in the comb. Fine promenades, domed saloons, long galleries, sunny balconies, confidential passages, bridal chambers, state-rooms plenty as pigeon-holes, and out-of-the-way retreats like secret drawers in an escritoire, present like facilities for publicity or privacy. Auctioneer or coiner,[9] with equal ease, might somewhere here drive his trade.

Though her voyage of twelve hundred miles extends from apple to orange, from clime to clime, yet, like any small ferry-boat, to right and left, at every landing, the huge Fidèle still receives additional passengers in exchange for those that disembark; so that, though always full of strangers, she continually, in some degree, adds to, or replaces them with strangers still more strange; like Rio Janeiro fountain, fed from the Cocovarde ˉmountains,[10] which is ever overflowing with strange waters, but never with the same strange particles in every part.

Though hitherto, as has been seen, the man in cream-colors had by no means passed unobserved, yet by stealing into retirement, and there going asleep and continuing so, he seemed to have courted oblivion, a boon not often withheld from so humble an applicant as he. Those staring crowds on the shore were now left far behind, seen dimly clustering like swallows on eaves; while the passengers' attention was soon drawn away

[9] Counterfeiter; perhaps also an inventor of words and phrases.
[10] The fountains of Rio de Janiero were fed by aqueducts from the Corcovado mountains.

Philosphers —

to the rapidly shooting high bluffs and shot-towers on the
Missouri shore, or the bluff-looking Missourians and towering
Kentuckians among the throngs on the decks.

By-and-by—two or three random stoppages having been
made, and the last transient memory of the slumberer vanished, and he himself, not unlikely, waked up and landed ere
now—the crowd, as is usual, began in all parts to break up
from a concourse into various clusters or squads, which in
some cases disintegrated again into quartettes, trios, and couples, or even solitaires; involuntarily submitting to that natural
law which ordains dissolution equally to the mass, as in time to
the member.

As among Chaucer's Canterbury pilgrims, or those oriental
ones crossing the Red Sea towards Mecca in the festival
month,[11] there was no lack of variety. Natives of all sorts, and
foreigners; men of business and men of pleasure; parlor men
and backwoodsmen; farm-hunters and fame-hunters; heiress-
hunters, gold-hunters, buffalo-hunters, bee-hunters,[12] happi-
ness-hunters, truth-hunters, and still keener hunters after all
these hunters. Fine ladies in slippers, and moccasined squaws;
Northern speculators and Eastern philosophers;[13] English,
Irish, German, Scotch, Danes; Santa Fé traders in striped blankets, and Broadway bucks in cravats of cloth of gold; fine-
looking Kentucky boat-men, and Japanese-looking Mississippi
cotton-planters; Quakers in full drab, and United States sol-

[11] The pilgrimage in *The Canterbury Tales* takes place, like the
present one, in April. The great Moslem pilgrimage takes place in the
twelfth month of the Mohammedan calendar; since this is a strictly
lunar calendar, that month may occur in any season.

[12] Men who hunted wild bees for their honey; common on the
frontier. T. B. Thorpe, *The Mysteries of the Backwoods* (Philadelphia,
1846): "As a country becomes cleared up and settled bee-hunters
disappear." Note that earlier in the chapter the passengers are compared
to bees.

[13] A number of passengers later introduced qualify as Eastern philosophers: they include caricatures of Cooper, Poe, Emerson, Thoreau,
Socrates, and Krishna.

diers in full regimentals; slaves, black, mulatto, quadroon; modish young Spanish Creoles, and old-fashioned French Jews; Mormons and Papists; Dives and Lazarus; [14] jesters and mourners, teetotalers and convivialists, deacons and blacklegs; hard-shell Baptists and clay-eaters; [15] grinning negroes, and Sioux chiefs solemn as high-priests. In short, a piebald parliament, an Anacharsis Cloots congress [16] of all kinds of that multiform pilgrim species, man.

As pine, beech, birch, ash, hackmatack, hemlock, spruce, bass-wood, maple, interweave their foliage in the natural wood, so these varieties of mortals blended their varieties of visage and garb. A Tartar-like picturesquesness; [17] a sort of pagan abandonment and assurance. Here reigned the dashing and all-fusing spirit of the West, whose type is the Mississippi itself, which, uniting the streams of the most distant and opposite zones, pours them along, helter-skelter, in one cosmopolitan and confident tide.

[14] See Chapter 9, note 5 and Chapter 15, note 6.

[15] "Clay eater. One who eats clay; spec. a low-class white person of the South." *Dictionary of American English.* Goneril (in Chapter 12) is literally a clay-eater.

[16] Baron Jean Baptiste Cloots (or Clootz), a Prussian enthusiast of the French Revolution, changed his name to Anacharsis, came to Paris, gathered from the coffee-houses representatives of the nations and races of the world, and was admitted with his congress of "ambassadors of the human race" into the Convention of 1792. Variously called "the Speaker of Mankind" and "World-Citizen," Cloots produced his "mute representatives" of the "tongue-tied" nations of the world as witnesses for a universal republic. He was guillotined in 1794. See the famous account in Carlyle's *The French Revolution.* Melville uses Cloots in both *Moby-Dick* and *Billy Budd.*

[17] "Tartar" is both a short form of Tartarus (Hell) and an alternate form of Tartar (the great tribe of Mongolia and Manchuria). Melville's pun here (as in the chapter "The Try-Works" in *Moby-Dick*) seems to reflect the apocryphal pun of the French king St. Louis, "Well may they be called *Tartars*, for their deeds are those of fiends from *Tartarus*." The pun fits these passengers who begin their voyage at sunrise in St. Louis and end in darkness.

CHAPTER 3

In which a variety of characters appear.

In the forward part of the boat, not the least attractive object, for a time, was a grotesque negro cripple, in tow-cloth attire and an old coal-sifter of a tamborine in his hand, who, owing to something wrong about his legs, was, in effect, cut down to the stature of a Newfoundland dog; his knotted black fleece and good-natured, honest black face rubbing against the upper part of people's thighs as he made shift to shuffle about, making music, such as it was, and raising a smile even from the gravest. It was curious to see him, out of his very deformity, indigence, and houselessness, so cheerily endured, raising mirth in some of that crowd, whose own purses, hearths, hearts, all their possessions, sound limbs included, could not make gay.

"What is your name, old boy?" said a purple-faced drover, putting his large purple hand on the cripple's bushy wool, as if it were the curled forehead of a black steer.

"Der Black Guinea [1] dey calls me, sar."

"And who is your master, Guinea?"

"Oh sar, I am der dog [2] widout massa." [3]

[1] "Guinea" was short for Guinea Negro and guinea pig. As John Seelye has pointed out to me, since a guinea was a gold piece, a black guinea would be a counterfeit, probably of brass.

[2] "Dog" introduces another of the key puns of the book, which will eventually present a number of Cynic (literally "dog-like") and mock-Cynic characters and views.

[3] Guinea's Negro dialect is actually a kind of dialectic made of puns, of which only a few are annotated. With his tambourine and this dialect, he suggests a character from the Negro minstrel shows, then at the height of their popularity. "Massa," the conventional Negro dialect term for master, here suggests Guinea's position in the cosmos: without a master, he may also be without mass.

"A free dog, eh? Well, on your account, I'm sorry for that, Guinea. Dogs without masters fare hard."

"So dey do, sar; so dey do. But you see, sar, dese here legs? What ge'mman want to own dese here legs?"

"But where do you live?"

"All 'long shore, sar; dough [4] now I'se going to see brodder at der landing; but chiefly I libs in der city."

"St. Louis, ah? Where do you sleep there of nights?"

"On der floor of der good baker's oven, sar."

"In an oven? whose, pray? What baker, I should like to know, bakes such black bread in his oven, alongside of his nice white rolls, too. Who is that too charitable baker, pray?"

"Dar he be," with a broad grin lifting his tambourine high over his head.

"The sun is the baker, eh?"

"Yes sar, in der city dat good baker warms der stones for dis ole darkie when he sleeps out on der pabements o' nights."

"But that must be in the summer only, old boy. How about winter, when the cold Cossacks come clattering and jingling? How about winter, old boy?"

"Den dis poor old darkie shakes werry bad, I tell you, sar. Oh sar, oh! don't speak ob [5] der winter," he added, with a reminiscent shiver, shuffling off into the thickest of the crowd, like a half-frozen black sheep nudging itself a cozy berth in the heart of the white flock.

Thus far not very many pennies had been given him, and, used at last to his strange looks, the less polite passengers of those in that part of the boat began to get their fill of him as a curious object; when suddenly the negro more than revived their first interest by an expedient which, whether by chance or design, was a singular temptation at once to *diversion* and

[4] Foreshadowing the elaborate metaphor of the baker.

[5] Everywhere else "of" appears in Guinea's dialect as either "o'" or "of." Apparently Guinea is here responding to the drover's "cold Cossacks" with the masked name of their northernmost site, the great river Ob, which flows into an inlet of the Arctic Ocean.

charity, though, even more than his crippled limbs, it put him
on a canine footing. In short, as in appearance he seemed a dog,
so now, in a merry way, like a dog he began to be treated. Still
shuffling among the crowd, now and then he would pause,
throwing back his head and opening his mouth like an elephant
for tossed apples at a menagerie; when, making a space before
him, people would have a bout at a strange sort of pitch-penny
game, the cripple's mouth being at once target and purse, and
he hailing each expertly-caught copper with a cracked bravura
from his tambourine. To be the subject of alms-giving is trying, and to feel in duty bound to appear cheerfully grateful
under the trial, must be still more so; but whatever his secret
emotions, he swallowed them, while still retaining each copper
this side the oesophagus. And nearly always he grinned, and
only once or twice did he wince, which was when certain coins,
tossed by more playful almoners, came inconveniently nigh to
his teeth, an accident whose unwelcomeness was not unedged
by the circumstance that the pennies thus thrown proved
buttons.

While this game of charity was yet at its height, a limping,
gimlet-eyed, sour-faced person—it may be some discharged
custom-house officer,[6] who, suddenly stripped of convenient
means of support, had concluded to be avenged on government and humanity by making himself miserable for life, either by hating or suspecting everything and everybody—this
shallow unfortunate, after sundry sorry observations of the
negro, began to croak out something about his deformity
being a sham, got up for financial purposes, which immediately
threw a damp upon the frolic benignities of the pitch-penny
players.

But that these suspicions came from one who himself on a
wooden leg went halt, this did not appear to strike anybody
present. That cripples, above all men should be companionable, or, at least, refrain from picking a fellow-limper to pieces,

[6] Hawthorne had been abruptly discharged from the Salem Custom-
house in 1849.

in short, should have a little sympathy in common misfortune, seemed not to occur to the company.

Meantime, the negro's countenance, before marked with even more than patient good-nature, drooped into a heavy-hearted expression, full of the most painful distress. So far abased beneath its proper physical level, that Newfoundland-dog face turned in passively hopeless appeal, as if instinct told it that the right or the wrong might not have overmuch to do with whatever wayward mood superior intelligences might yield to.

But instinct, though knowing, is yet a teacher set below reason, which itself says, in the grave words of Lysander in the comedy, after Puck has made a sage of him with his spell:—

"The will of man is by his reason swayed." [7]

So that, suddenly change as people may, in their dispositions, it is not always waywardness, but improved judgment, which, as in Lysander's case, or the present, operates with them.

Yes, they began to scrutinize the negro curiously enough; when, emboldened by this evidence of the efficacy of his words, the wooden-legged man hobbled up to the negro, and, with the air of a beadle, would, to prove his alleged imposture on the spot, have stripped him and then driven him away, but was prevented by the crowd's clamor, now taking part with

[7] In *A Midsummer Night's Dream*, Puck, trying to follow the orders of Oberon, King of the Fairies, who wishes to restore Demetrius to Helena, mistakes Lysander for Demetrius and therefore throws on his sleeping eyelids the magic juice that will make him "madly dote upon the next live creature" he sees. Helena arrives, and Lysander wakes and switches his loves in a twinkling because, he claims, "The will of man is by his reason swayed" (II, *ii.* 115). Thus Oberon, in attempting to free Hermia for her true lover Lysander, makes Lysander love Helena, thereby reducing the human relationships touched by the immortals to absurdity. Mortals, both in Shakespeare's play and this chapter, "In Which a Variety of Characters Appear," shift their characters neither through instinct nor through reason, but through the wayward touches of unknown powers—be they spirits, gods, or authors.

the poor fellow, against one who had just before turned nearly all minds the other way. So he with the wooden leg was forced to retire; when the rest, finding themselves left sole judges in the case, could not resist the opportunity of acting the part: not because it is a human weakness to take pleasure in sitting in judgment upon one in a box, as surely this unfortunate negro now was, but that it strangely sharpens human perceptions, when, instead of standing by and having their fellow-feelings touched by the sight of an alleged culprit severely handled by some one justiciary, a crowd suddenly come to be all justi-ciaries in the same case themselves; as in Arkansas once, a man proved guilty, by law, of murder, but whose condemnation was deemed unjust by the people, so that they rescued him to try him themselves; whereupon, they, as it turned out, found him even guiltier than the court had done, and forthwith pro-ceeded to execution; so that the gallows presented the truly warning spectacle of a man hanged by his friends.

But not to such extremities, or anything like them, did the present crowd come; they, for the time, being content with putting the negro fairly and discreetly to the question; among other things, asking him, had he any documentary proof, any plain paper about him, attesting that his case was not a spurious one.

"No, no, dis poor ole darkie haint none o' dem waloable papers," he wailed.

"But is there not some one who can speak a good word for you?" here said a person newly arrived from another part of the boat, a young Episcopal clergyman, in a long, straight-bodied black coat; small in stature, but manly; with a clear face and blue eye; innocence, tenderness, and good sense tri-umvirate in his air.

"Oh yes, oh yes, ge'mmen," he eagerly answered, as if his memory, before suddenly frozen up by cold charity, as sud-denly thawed back into fluidity at the first kindly word. "Oh yes, oh yes, dar is aboard here a werry nice, good ge'mman

wid a weed,[8] and a ge'mman in a gray coat and white tie, what
knows all about me; and a ge'mman wid a big book, too; and a
yarb-doctor; and a ge'mman in a yaller west; and a ge'mman
wid a brass plate; and a ge'mman in a wiolet robe; and a
ge'mman as is a sodjer; and ever so many good, kind, honest
ge'mmen more aboard what knows me and will speak for me,
God bress 'em; yes, and what knows me as well as dis poor old
darkie knows hisself, God bress him! Oh, find 'em, find 'em,"
he earnestly added, "and let 'em come quick, and show you all,
ge'mmem, dat dis poor ole darkie is werry well wordy of all
you kind ge'mmen's kind confidence."

"But how are we to find all these people in this great
crowd?" was the question of a bystander, umbrella in hand; a
middle-aged person, a country merchant apparently, whose
natural good-feeling had been made at least cautious by the
unnatural ill-feeling of the discharged custom-house officer.

"Where are we to find them?" half-rebukefully echoed the
young Episcopal clergymen. "I will go find one to begin
with," he quickly added, and, with kind haste suiting the
action to the word, away he went.

"Wild goose chase!" croaked he with the wooden leg, now
again drawing nigh. "Don't believe there's a soul of them
aboard. Did ever beggar have such heaps of fine friends? He
can walk fast enough when he tries, a good deal faster than I;
but he can lie yet faster. He's some white operator, betwisted
and painted up for a decoy. He and his friends are all humbugs."

"Have you no charity, friend?" here in self-subdued tones,
singularly contrasted with his unsubdued person, said a
Methodist minister,[9] advancing; a tall, muscular, martial-

[8] Guinea's list is an ambiguous list of the principal avatars of the
Confidence Man (see Introduction, pages xx–xxiv).

[9] The Methodist minister chronologically follows the Episcopalian just
as Methodism chronologically followed the Episcopal establishment; the
Episcopal searches for higher authority, whereas the Methodist tries to
settle the issue personally.

One of the most famous disguises of Murrell was as a Methodist looking man, a Tennessean by birth,[10] who in the Mexican war had been volunteer chaplain to a volunteer rifle-regiment.

"Charity is one thing, and truth is another," rejoined he with the wooden leg: "he's a rascal, I say."

"But why not, friend, put as charitable a construction as one can upon the poor fellow?" said the soldier-like Methodist, with increased difficulty maintaining a pacific demeanor towards one whose own asperity seemed so little to entitle him to it: "he looks honest, don't he?"

"Looks are one thing, and facts are another," snapped out the other perversely; "and as to your constructions, what construction can you put upon a rascal, but that a rascal he is?"

"Be not such a Canada thistle," [11] urged the Methodist, with something less of patience than before. "Charity, man, charity."

"To where it belongs with your charity! to heaven with it!" again snapped out the other, diabolically; "here on earth, true charity dotes, and false charity plots. Who betrays a fool with a kiss,[12] the charitable fool has the charity to believe is in love with him, and the charitable knave on the stand gives charitable testimony for his comrade in the box."

"Surely, friend," returned the noble Methodist, with much ado restraining his still waxing indignation—"surely, to say the least, you forget yourself. Apply it home," he continued, with exterior calmness tremulous with inkept emotion. "Suppose, now, I should exercise no charity in judging your own character by the words which have fallen from you; what sort of vile, pitiless man do you think I would take you for?"

"No doubt"—with a grin—"some such pitiless man as has

---

minister and the last disguise of the brothers Harpe was as a pair of Methodist ministers (see Chapter 1, notes 16 and 17). See Chapter 6, note 3, for evidence that the Methodist minister is in disguise.

[10] Murrell was also a tall, muscular, martial-looking man, a Tennessean by birth.

[11] In the language of flowers the Canada thistle meant misanthropy (Seelye).

[12] Perhaps an allusion to Judas.

lost his piety in much the same way that the jockey [13] loses his honesty."

"And how is that, friend?" still conscientiously holding back the old Adam [14] in him, as if it were a mastiff he had by the neck.

"Never you mind how it is"—with a sneer; "but all horses aint virtuous, no more than all men kind; and come close to, and much dealt with, some things are catching. When you find me a virtuous jockey, I will find you a benevolent wise man."

"Some insinuation there."

"More fool you that are puzzled by it."

"Reprobate!" cried the other, his indignation now at last almost boiling over; "godless reprobate! if charity did not restrain me, I could call you by names you deserve."

"Could you, indeed?" with an insolent sneer.

"Yea, and teach you charity on the spot," cried the goaded Methodist, suddenly catching this exasperating opponent by his shabby coat-collar, and shaking him till his timber-toe clattered on the deck like a nine-pin. "You took me for a non-combatant did you?—thought, seedy coward that you are, that you could abuse a Christian with impunity. You find your mistake"—with another hearty shake.

"Well said and better done, church militant!" cried a voice.

"The white cravat against the world!" cried another.

"Bravo, bravo!" chorused many voices, with like enthusiasm taking sides with the resolute champion.

"You fools!" cried he with the wooden leg, writhing himself loose and inflamedly turning upon the throng; "you flock of fools, under this captain of fools, in this ship of fools!" [15]

[13] A man who works with horses; specifically a horse-trader, and hence, a cheat.

[14] The evil inherent in human nature consequent upon the Fall of Adam.

[15] The English literary tradition of viewing the world as a microcosmic shipload of fools goes back to *The Ship of Fools*, Alexander Barclay's 1508 version of Sebastian Brant's *Das Narrenschiff*.

With which exclamations, followed by idle threats against his admonisher, this condign victim to justice hobbled away, as disdaining to hold further argument with such a rabble. But his scorn was more than repaid by the hisses that chased him, in which the brave Methodist, satisfied with the rebuke already administered, was, to omit still better reasons, too magnanimous to join. All he said was, pointing towards the departing recusant, "There he shambles off on his one lone leg, emblematic of his one-sided view of humanity." — → *implying that the Methodist talks from this — sides are two faced an impostic' a Confidence man.*

"But trust your painted decoy," retorted the other from a distance, pointing back to the black cripple, "and I have my revenge."

"But we aint agoing to trust him!" shouted back a voice.

"So much the better," he jeered back. "Look you," he added, coming to a dead halt where he was; "look you, I have been called a Canada thistle. Very good. And a seedy one: still better. And the seedy Canada thistle has been pretty well shaken among ye: best of all. Dare say some seed has been shaken out; and won't it spring though? And when it does spring, do you cut down the young thistles, and won't they spring the more? It's encouraging and coaxing 'em. Now, when with my thistles your farms shall be well stocked, why then—you may abandon 'em!"

"What does all that mean, now?" asked the country merchant, staring.

"Nothing; the foiled wolf's parting howl," said the Methodist. "Spleen, much spleen, which is the rickety child of his evil heart of unbelief: it has made him mad. I suspect him for one naturally reprobate. Oh, friends," raising his arms as in the pulpit, "oh beloved, how are we admonished by the melancholy spectacle of this raver. Let us profit by the lesson; and is it not this: that if, next to mistrusting Providence, there be aught that man should pray against, it is against mistrusting his fellow-man. I have been in mad-houses full of tragic mopers, and seen there the end of suspicion: the cynic, in the moody madness muttering in the corner; for years a barren fixture there; head lopped over, gnawing his own lip, vulture of himself; while, by fits and starts, from the corner opposite came the grimace of the idiot at him."

"What an example," whispered one.

"Might deter Timon," [16] was the response.

"Oh, oh, good ge'mmen, have you no confidence in dis poor ole darkie?" now wailed the returning negro, who, during the late scene, had stumped apart in alarm.

"Confidence in you?" echoed he who had whispered, with abruptly changed air turning short round; "that remains to be seen."

"I tell you what it is, Ebony," in similarly changed tones said he who had responded to the whisperer, "yonder churl," pointing toward the wooden leg in the distance, "is, no doubt, a churlish fellow enough, and I would not wish to be like him; but that is no reason why you may not be some sort of black Jeremy Diddler." [17] — *shades of Poe*

"No confidence in dis poor ole darkie, den?"

"Before giving you our confidence," said a third, "we will wait the report of the kind gentleman who went in search of one of your friends who was to speak for you."

"Very likely, in that case," said a fourth, "we shall wait here till Christmas. Shouldn't wonder, did we not see that kind gentleman again. After seeking awhile in vain, he will conclude

16 Timon the Misanthrope of Athens hated all men because he was spurned by his friends after using up all his money on them. According to the main sources (Plutarch's *Life of Antony*, Diogenes Laertius' *Lives of the Philosophers*, Lucian's *Timon*, and Shakespeare's *Timon of Athens*), he went to live by himself in a cave. Timon turns up again in Chapters 23, 24, 30, 42, and 43.

17 Originally the hero of James Kenney's popular *Raising the Wind, A Farce* (1803), in which he is a charming gentleman who lives by his wits, i.e., a swindler. He became a stock farce character, and the verb "diddle" may derive from his name.

The speaker who here uses Jeremy Diddler's name (and who has just used Timon's) is ambiguously identified. In Chapter 24, when Pitch, in a similar tone, belligerently asks the Cosmopolitan whether he is "Jeremy Diddler No. 3," the Cosmopolitan tries to deter him from imitating that "injudicious gentleman, Lord Timon."

he has been made a fool of, and so not return to us for pure
shame. Fact is, I begin to feel a little qualmish about the darkie
myself. Something queer about this darkie, depend upon it."

Once more the negro wailed, and turning in despair from
the last speaker, imploringly caught the Methodist by the skirt
of his coat. But a change had come over that before impas-
sioned intercessor. With an irresolute and troubled air, he
mutely eyed the suppliant; against whom, somehow, by what
seemed instinctive influences, the distrusts first set on foot
were now generally reviving, and, if anything, with added
severity.

"No confidence in dis poor ole darkie," yet again wailed the
negro, letting go the coat-skirts and turning appealingly all
round him.

"Yes, my poor fellow, *I* have confidence in you," now exclaimed the country merchant before named, whom the negro's appeal, coming so piteously on the heel of pitilessness,
seemed at last humanely to have decided in his favor. "And
here, here is some proof of my trust," with which, tucking his
umbrella under his arm, and diving down his hand into his
pocket, he fished forth a purse, and, accidentally, along with it,
his business card, which, unobserved, dropped to the deck.
"Here, here, my poor fellow," he continued, extending a half
dollar.

Not more grateful for the coin than the kindness, the cripple's face glowed like a polished copper saucepan, and shuffling
a pace nigher, with one upstretched hand he received the alms,
while, as unconsciously, his one advanced leather stump covered the card.

Done in despite of the general sentiment, the good deed of
the merchant was not, perhaps, without its unwelcome return
from the crowd, since that good deed seemed somehow to
convey to them a sort of reproach. Still again, and more perti-
naciously than ever, the cry arose against the negro, and still
again he wailed forth his lament and appeal; among other
things, repeating that the friends, of whom already he had

partially run off the list, would freely speak for him, would anybody go find them.

"Why don't you go find 'em yourself?" demanded a gruff boatman.

"How can I go find 'em myself? Dis poor ole game-legged darkie's friends must come to him. Oh, whar, whar is dat good friend of dis darkie's, dat good man wid de weed?"

At this point, a steward ringing a bell came along, summoning all persons who had not got their tickets to step to the captain's office; an announcement which speedily thinned the throng about the black cripple, who himself soon forlornly stumped out of sight, probably on much the same errand as the rest.

CHAPTER 4

Renewal of old acquaintance.

"How do you do, Mr. Roberts?"

"Eh?"

"Don't you know me?"

"No, certainly."

The crowd about the captain's office, having in good time melted away, the above encounter took place in one of the side balconies astern, between a man in mourning clean and respectable, but none of the glossiest, a long weed on his hat, and the country-merchant before-mentioned, whom, with the familiarity of an old acquaintance, the former had accosted.

"Is it possible, my dear sir," resumed he with the weed, "that you do not recall my countenance? why yours I recall distinctly as if but half an hour, instead of half an age, had passed since I saw you. Don't you recall me, now? Look harder."

"In my conscience—truly—I protest," honestly bewildered, "bless my soul, sir, I don't know you—really, really. But stay, stay," he hurriedly added, not without gratification, glancing up at the crape on the stranger's hat, "stay—yes—seems to me, though I have not the pleasure of personally knowing you, yet I am pretty sure I have at least *heard* of you, and recently too, quite recently. A poor negro aboard here referred to you, among others, for a character, I think."

"Oh, the cripple. Poor fellow, I know him well. They found me. I have said all I could for him. I think I abated their distrust. Would I could have been of more substantial service. And apropos, sir," he added, "now that it strikes me, allow me to ask, whether the circumstance of one man, however humble, referring for a character to another man, however

27

afflicted, does not argue more or less of moral worth in the latter?"

The good merchant looked puzzled.

"Still you don't recall my countenance?"

"Still does truth compel me to say that I cannot, despite my best efforts," was the reluctantly-candid reply.

"Can I be so changed? Look at me. Or is it I who am mistaken?—Are you not, sir, Henry Roberts, forwarding merchant, of Wheeling, Pennsylvania? [1] Pray, now, if you use the advertisement of business cards, and happen to have one with you, just look at it, and see whether you are not the man I take you for."

"Why," a bit chafed, perhaps, "I hope I know myself."

"And yet self-knowledge is thought by some not so easy. Who knows, my dear sir, but for a time you may have taken yourself for somebody else? Stranger things have happened."

The good merchant stared.

"To come to particulars, my dear sir, I met you, now some six years back, at Brade Brothers & Co.'s office, I think. I was traveling for a Philadelphia house. The senior Brade introduced us, you remember; some business-chat followed, then you forced me home with you to a family tea, and a family time we had. Have you forgotten about the urn, and what I said about Werter's Charlotte, and the bread and butter,[2] and

---

[1] The principal city of the Virginia panhandle, territory once claimed by Pennsylvania, Wheeling was the seat of periodic agitation for dismemberment of the Trans-Alleghany counties from Virginia and their attachment to Pennsylvania or Maryland. (West Virginia was to be created at Wheeling in 1861.)

[2] In Goethe's *The Sorrows of Young Werther* (1744), Book I, June 16, Werther ascribes the beginning of his tragic love for Charlotte to the moment when he sees her serving bread to her little brothers and sisters. Thackery parodied this in his ballad, "Sorrows of Werther," which begins and ends like this:

> Werther had a love for Charlotte.
> Such as words could never utter;
> Would you know how first he met her?

that capital story you told of the large loaf.[3] A hundred times
since, I have laughed over it. At least you must recall my
name. Ringman, John Ringman." [4]

"Large loaf? Invited you to tea? Ringman? Ringman? Ring?
Ring?"

"Ah sir," sadly smiling, "don't ring the changes [5] that way. I
see you have a faithless memory, Mr. Roberts. But trust in the
faithfulness of mine."

"Well, to tell the truth, in some things my memory aint of
the very best," was the honest rejoinder. "But still," he perplexedly added, "still I—"

"Oh sir, suffice it that it is as I say. Doubt not that we are all
well acquainted."

"But—but I don't like this going dead against my own
memory; I—"

"But didn't you admit, my dear sir, that in some things this
memory of yours is a little faithless? Now, those who have
faithless memories, should they not have some little confidence
in the less faithless memories of others?"

"But, of this friendly chat and tea, I have not the slightest—"

"I see, I see; quite erased from the tablet.[6] Pray, sir," with a
sudden illumination, "about six years back, did it happen to

She was cutting bread and butter.

. . . .

Charlotte, having seen his body
Borne before her on a shutter,
Like a well-conducted person,
Went on cutting bread and butter.

[3] Possibly a joking explanation of Christ's feeding of the multitude
with five loaves of bread and two small fishes.

[4] "Ring-man" was old slang for the ring (middle) finger and for "a
sporting man" (*Oxford English Dictionary*); Mr. Ringman seems an
aptly-named "*ge'm*man."

[5] Underworld cant for "replace good money with bad."

[6] An allusion to the notion that the mind is originally a *tabula rasa*
(erased tablet) upon which is written all that is learned; perhaps also
an allusion to the slate tablet of the lamb-like man.

you to receive any injury on the head? Surprising effects have
arisen from such a cause. Not alone unconsciousness as to
events for a greater or less time immediately subsequent to the
injury, but likewise—strange to add—oblivion, entire and
incurable, as to events embracing a longer or shorter period
immediately preceding it; that is, when the mind at the time
was perfectly sensible of them, and fully competent also to
register them in the memory, and did in fact so do; but all in
vain, for all was afterwards bruised out by the injury."

After the first start, the merchant listened with what appeared more than ordinary interest. The other proceeded:

"In my boyhood I was kicked by a horse, and lay insensible
for a long time. Upon recovering, what a blank! No faintest
trace in regard to how I had come near the horse, or what
horse it was, or where it was, or that it was a horse at all that
had brought me to that pass. For the knowledge of those particulars I am indebted solely to my friends, in whose statements, I need not say, I place implicit reliance, since particulars of some sort there must have been, and why should they
deceive me? You see, sir, the mind is ductile, very much so:
but images, ductilely received into it, need a certain time to
harden and bake in their impressions, otherwise such a casualty
as I speak of will in an instant obliterate them, as though they
had never been. We are but clay, sir, potter's clay,[7] as the
good book says, clay, feeble, and too-yielding clay. But I will
not philosophize. Tell me, was it your misfortune to receive
any concussion upon the brain about the period I speak of?
If so, I will with pleasure supply the void in your memory
by more minutely rehearsing the circumstances of our
acquaintance."

The growing interest betrayed by the merchant had not
relaxed as the other proceeded. After some hesitation, indeed,
something more than hesitation, he confessed that, though he

[7] Isaiah 64:8: "But now, O Lord, thou art our father; we are the clay,
and thou our potter; and we all are the work of thy hand." The man
with the weed here subtly shifts his image of the tablet.

had never received any injury of the sort named, yet, about the time in question, he had in fact been taken with a brain fever, losing his mind completely for a considerable interval. He was continuing, when the stranger with much animation exclaimed:

"There now, you see, I was not wholly mistaken. That brain fever accounts for it all."

"Nay; but—"

"Pardon me, Mr. Roberts," respectfully interrupting him, "but time is short, and I have something private and particular to say to you. Allow me."

Mr. Roberts, good man, could but acquiesce, and the two having silently walked to a less public spot, the manner of the man with the weed suddenly assumed a seriousness almost painful. What might be called a writhing expression stole over him. He seemed struggling with some disastrous necessity inkept. He made one or two attempts to speak, but words seemed to choke him. His companion stood in humane surprise, wondering what was to come. At length, with an effort mastering his feelings, in a tolerably composed tone he spoke:

"If I remember, you are a mason,[8] Mr. Roberts?"

"Yes, yes."

Averting himself a moment, as to recover from a return of agitation, the stranger grasped the other's hand; "and would you not loan a brother a shilling if he needed it?"

The merchant started, apparently, almost as if to retreat.

"Ah, Mr. Roberts, I trust you are not one of those business men, who make a business of never having to do with unfortunates. For God's sake don't leave me. I have something on my heart—on my heart. Under deplorable circumstances thrown among strangers, utter strangers. I want a friend in whom I may confide. Yours, Mr. Roberts, is almost the first known face I've seen for many weeks."

[8] The secret identifications of the freemasons, intended to screen out imposters, supposedly derive from the need of medieval stonemasons in strange places to prove themselves authentic. See Chapter 9, note 6.

It was so sudden an outburst; the interview offered such a contrast to the scene around, that the merchant, though not used to be very indiscreet, yet, being not entirely inhumane, remained not entirely unmoved.

The other, still tremulous, resumed:

"I need not say, sir, how it cuts me to the soul, to follow up a social salutation with such words as have just been mine. I know that I jeopardize your good opinion. But I can't help it: necessity knows no law, and heeds no risk. Sir, we are masons, one more step aside; I will tell you my story."

In a low, half-suppressed tone, he began it. Judging from his auditor's expression, it seemed to be a tale of singular interest, involving calamities against which no integrity, no forethought, no energy, no genius, no piety, could guard.

At every disclosure, the hearer's commiseration increased. No sentimental pity. As the story went on, he drew from his wallet a bank note, but after a while, at some still more unhappy revelation, changed it for another, probably of a somewhat larger amount; which, when the story was concluded, with an air studiously disclamatory of alms-giving, he put into the stranger's hands; who, on his side, with an air studiously disclamatory of alms-taking, put it into his pocket.

Assistance being received, the stranger's manner assumed a kind and degree of decorum which, under the circumstances, seemed almost coldness. After some words, not over ardent, and yet not exactly inappropriate, he took leave, making a bow which had one knows not what of a certain chastened independence about it; as if misery, however burdensome, could not break down self-respect, nor gratitude, however deep, humiliate a gentleman.

He was hardly yet out of sight, when he paused as if thinking; then with hastened steps returning to the merchant, "I am just reminded that the president, who is also transfer-agent, of the Black Rapids Coal Company, happens to be on board here, and, having been subpoenaed as witness in a stock case on the docket in Kentucky, has his transfer-book with him. A month since, in a panic contrived by artful alarmists, some credulous stock-holders sold out; but, to frustrate the aim of the alarmists, the Company, previously advised of their scheme, so managed it as to get into its own hands those sacrificed shares, resolved that, since a spurious panic must be, the panic-makers should be no gainers by it. The Company, I hear, is now ready, but not anxious, to redispose of those shares; and having obtained them at their depressed value, will now sell them at par, though, prior to the panic, they were held at a handsome figure above. That the readiness of the Company to do this is not generally known, is shown by the fact that the stock still stands on the transfer-book in the Company's name, offering to one in funds a rare chance for investment. For, the panic subsiding more and more every day, it will daily be seen how it originated; confidence will be more than restored; there will be a reaction; from the stock's descent its rise will be higher than from no fall, the holders trusting themselves to fear no second fate." [9]

Having listened at first with curiosity, at last with interest, the merchant replied to the effect, that some time since, through friends concerned with it, he had heard of the company, and heard well of it, but was ignorant that there had latterly been fluctuations. He added that he was no speculator; that hitherto he had avoided having to do with stocks of any sort, but in the present case he really felt something like being tempted. "Pray," in conclusion, "do you think that upon a pinch anything could be transacted on board here with the transfer-agent? Are you acquainted with him?"

"Not personally. I but happened to hear that he was a passenger. For the rest, though it might be somewhat informal,

[9] Henry Pommer points out in *Milton and Melville*, page 31, that this passage echoes Satan's speech to the fallen angels in *Paradise Lost*, II, 14–17:

> From this *descent*
> Celestial Virtues *rising*, will appear
> More glorious and more dread than from no fall,
> And trust themselves to fear no second fate.

the gentleman might not object to doing a little business on board. Along the Mississippi, you know, business is not so ceremonious as at the East." [10]

"True," returned the merchant, and looked down a moment in thought, then, raising his head quickly, said, in a tone not so benign as his wonted one, "This would seem a rare chance, indeed; why, upon first hearing it, did you not snatch at it? I mean for yourself!"

"I?—would it had been possible!"

Not without some emotion was this said, and not without some embarrassment was the reply. "Ah, yes, I had forgotten."

Upon this, the stranger regarded him with mild gravity, not a little disconcerting; the more so, as there was in it what seemed the aspect not alone of the superior, but, as it were, the rebuker; which sort of bearing, in a beneficiary towards his benefactor, looked strangely enough; none the less, that, somehow, it sat not altogether unbecomingly upon the beneficiary, being free from anything like the appearance of assumption, and mixed with a kind of painful conscientiousness, as though nothing but a proper sense of what he owed to himself swayed him. At length he spoke:

"To reproach a penniless man with remissness in not availing himself of an opportunity for pecuniary investment—but, no, no; it was forgetfulness; and this, charity will impute to some lingering effect of that unfortunate brain-fever, which, as to occurrences dating yet further back, disturbed Mr. Roberts's memory still more seriously."

"As to that," said the merchant, rallying, "I am not—"

"Pardon me, but you must admit, that just now, an unpleasant distrust, however vague, was yours. Ah, shallow as it is, yet, how subtle a thing is suspicion, which at times can invade the humanest of hearts and wisest of heads. But, enough. My object, sir, in calling your attention to this stock, is by way of acknowledgment of your goodness. I but seek to

[10] Referring to either the American East, the Orient, or both.

be grateful; if my information leads to nothing, you must remember the motive."

He bowed, and finally retired, leaving Mr. Roberts not wholly without self-reproach, for having momentarily indulged injurious thoughts against one who, it was evident, was possessed of a self-respect which forbade his indulging them himself.

CHAPTER 5

The man with the weed makes it an even
question whether he be a great sage or a
great simpleton.

"Well, there is sorrow in the world, but goodness too; and goodness that is not greenness, either, no more than sorrow is. Dear good man. Poor beating heart!"

It was the man with the weed, not very long after quitting the merchant, murmuring to himself with his hand to his side like one with the heart-disease.

Meditation over kindness received seemed to have softened him something, too, it may be, beyond what might, perhaps, have been looked for from one whose unwonted self-respect in the hour of need, and in the act of being aided, might have appeared to some not wholly unlike pride out of place; and pride, in any place, is seldom very feeling. But the truth, perhaps, is, that those who are least touched with that vice, besides being not unsusceptible to goodness, are sometimes the ones whom a ruling sense of propriety makes appear cold, if not thankless, under a favor. For, at such a time, to be full of warm, earnest words, and heart-felt protestations, is to create a scene; and well-bred people dislike few things more than that; which would seem to look as if the world did not relish earnestness; but, not so; because the world, being earnest itself, likes an earnest scene, and an earnest man, very well, but only in their place—the stage. See what sad work they make of it, who, ignorant of this, flame out in Irish enthusiasm and with Irish sincerity, to a benefactor, who, if a man of sense and respectability, as well as kindliness, can but be more or less annoyed by it; and, if of a nervously fastidious nature, as some are, may be led to think almost as much less favorably of the beneficiary paining him by his gratitude, as if he had been guilty of its contrary, instead only of an indiscretion. But, beneficiaries who know better, though they may feel as much, if not more, neither inflict such pain, nor are inclined to run any risk of so doing. And these, being wise, are the majority. By which one sees how inconsiderate those persons are, who, from the absence of its officious manifestations in the world, complain that there is not much gratitude extant; when the truth is, that there is as much of it as there is of modesty; but, both being for the most part votarists of the shade, for the most part keep out of sight.

What started this was, to account, if necessary, for the changed air of the man with the weed, who, throwing off in private the cold garb of decorum, and so giving warmly loose to his genuine heart, seemed almost transformed into another being. This subdued air of softness, too, was toned with melancholy, melancholy unreserved; a thing which, however at variance with propriety, still the more attested his earnestness; for one knows not how it is, but it sometimes happens that, where earnestness is, there, also, is melancholy.

At the time, he was leaning over the rail at the boat's side, in his pensiveness, unmindful of another pensive figure near—a young gentleman with a swan-neck, wearing a lady-like open shirt collar, thrown back, and tied with a black ribbon. From a square, tableted broach, curiously engraved with Greek characters,[1] he seemed a collegian—not improbably, a sophomore —on his travels; possibly, his first. A small book bound in Roman vellum was in his hand.

Overhearing his murmuring neighbor, the youth regarded him with some surprise, not to say interest. But, singularly for a collegian, being apparently of a retiring nature, he did not speak; when the other still more increased his diffidence by changing from soliloquy to colloquy, in a manner strangely mixed of familiarity and pathos.

[1] Probably a fraternity pin.

"Ah, who is this? You did not hear me, my young friend, did you? Why, you, too, look sad. My melancholy is not catching!"

"Sir, sir," stammered the other.

"Pray, now," with a sort of sociable sorrowfulness, slowly sliding along the rail, "Pray, now, my young friend, what volume have you there? Give me leave," gently drawing it from him. "Tacitus!" Then opening it at random, read: "In general a black and shameful period lies before me." [2] "Dear young sir," touching his arm alarmedly, "don't read this book. It is poison, moral poison. Even were there truth in Tacitus, such truth would have the operation of falsity, and so still be poison, moral poison. Too well I know this Tacitus. In my college-days he came near souring me into cynicism. Yes, I began to turn down my collar, and go about with a disdainfully joyless expression."

"Sir, sir, I—I—"

"Trust me. Now, young friend, perhaps you think that Tacitus, like me, is only melancholy; but he's more—he's ugly. A vast difference, young sir, between the melancholy view and the ugly. The one may show the world still beautiful, not so the other. The one may be compatible with benevolence, the other not. The one may deepen insight, the other shallows it. Drop Tacitus. Phrenologically, my young friend, you would seem to have a well-developed head, and large; but cribbed within the ugly view, the Tacitus view, your large brain, like your large ox in the contracted field, will but starve the more. And don't dream, as some of you students may, that, by taking this same ugly view, the deeper meanings of the deeper books will so alone become revealed to you. Drop Tacitus. His subtlety is falsity. To him, in his double-refined anatomy of

[2] No passage precisely like this occurs in either the *Histories* or *Annals* of Tacitus (*c*. 55–after 117), the Roman historian. The joke is that such a passage could occur "at random," for it aptly describes Tacitus' view of all the history he narrates and he often makes such statements (with due apologies to the reader). See Chapter 12 note 1.

human nature, is well applied the Scripture saying—'There is a subtle man, and the same is deceived.' [3] Drop Tacitus. Come, now, let me throw the book overboard."

"Sir, I—I—"

"Not a word; I know just what is in your mind, and that is just what I am speaking to. Yes, learn from me that, though the sorrows of the world are great, its wickedness—that is, its ugliness [4]—is small. Much cause to pity man, little to distrust him. I myself have known adversity, and know it still. But for that, do I turn cynic? No, no: it is small beer that sours. To my fellow-creatures I owe alleviations. So, whatever I may have undergone, it but deepens my confidence in my kind. Now, then" (winningly), "this book—will you let me drown it for you?" [5]

"Really, sir—I—"

"I see, I see. But of course you read Tacitus in order to aid you in understanding human nature—as if truth was ever got at by libel. [6] My young friend, if to know human nature is your object, drop Tacitus and go north to the cemeteries of Auburn and Greenwood." [7]

"Upon my word, I—I—"

"Nay, I foresee all that. But you carry Tacitus, that shallow Tacitus. What do *I* carry? See"—producing a pocket-volume —"Akenside—his 'Pleasures of Imagination.' [8] One of these

---

[3] A summary of several verses from Chapters 19 and 20 of the apocryphal The Wisdom of Jesus, the Son of Sirach, or Ecclesiasticus, a book which serves as a text for the final chapter of *The Confidence-Man*.

[4] The man with the weed sees moral evil as merely aesthetic evil.

[5] When Prospero in *The Tempest* (V, *i*, 56–57) says, "I'll drown my book," he thereby indicates that he will give up his greatest earthly powers.

[6] Cf. the argument about libel at the end of the man with the weed's story (Chapter 12).

[7] Mount Auburn Cemetery in Cambridge and Watertown, Massachusetts, and Greenwood Cemetery in Brooklyn, New York.

[8] Mark Akenside's "The Pleasures of Imagination" (1744), a long

days you will know it. Whatever our lot, we should read serene and cheery books, fitted to inspire love and trust. But Tacitus! I have long been of opinion that these classics are the bane of colleges; for—not to hint of the immorality of Ovid, Horace, Anacreon, and the rest, and the dangerous theology of Eschylus and others—where will one find views so injurious to human nature as in Thucydides, Juvenal, Lucian, but more particularly Tacitus? When I consider that, ever since the revival of learning, these classics have been the favorites of successive generations of students and studious men, I tremble to think of that mass of unsuspected heresy on every vital topic which for centuries must have simmered unsurmised in the heart of Christendom. But Tacitus—he is the most extraordinary example of a heretic; not one iota of confidence in his kind. What a mockery that such an one should be reputed wise, and Thucydides be esteemed the statesman's manual! But Tacitus—I hate Tacitus; not, though, I trust, with the hate that sins, but a righteous hate. Without confidence himself, Tacitus destroys it in all his readers. Destroys confidence, paternal confidence, of which God knows that there is in this world none to spare. For, comparatively inexperienced as you are, my dear young friend, did you never observe how little, very little, confidence, there is? I mean between man and man— more particularly between stranger and stranger. In a sad world it is the saddest fact. Confidence! I have sometimes almost thought that confidence is fled; that confidence is the New Astrea [9]—emigrated—vanished—gone." Then softly sliding nearer, with the softest air, quivering down and looking up, "could you now, my dear young sir, under such circum-

---

didactic blank verse poem. The second of its three books concludes by arguing that "heart-ennobling sorrows" constitute one of the greatest human pleasures.

[9] Cf. the New Jerusalem of Chapter 9. Astraea, goddess of justice, daughter of Zeus and Themis, was the last of the gods to leave men. Her departure from earth marked the transition from the brazen age to the iron age. She became a symbol of all the divine grace missing from human society.

stances, by way of experiment, simply have confidence in *me?*"

From the outset, the sophomore, as has been seen, had struggled with an ever-increasing embarrassment, arising, perhaps, from such strange remarks coming from a stranger—such persistent and prolonged remarks, too. In vain had he more than once sought to break the spell by venturing a deprecatory or leave-taking word. In vain. Somehow, the stranger fascinated him. Little wonder, then, that, when the appeal came, he could hardly speak, but, as before intimated, being apparently of a retiring nature, abruptly retired from the spot, leaving the chagrined stranger to wander away in the opposite direction.

CHAPTER 6

At the outset of which certain passengers
prove deaf to the call of charity.

—"You—pish! Why will the captain suffer these begging fellows on board?"

These pettish words were breathed by a well-to-do gentleman in a ruby-colored velvet vest, and with a ruby-colored cheek, a ruby-headed cane in his hand, to a man in a gray coat and a white tie, who, shortly after the interview last described, had accosted him for contributions to a Widow and Orphan Asylum recently founded among the Seminoles.[1] Upon a cursory view, this last person might have seemed, like the man with the weed, one of the less unrefined children of misfortune; but, on a closer observation, his countenance revealed little of sorrow, though much of sanctity.

With added words of touchy disgust, the well-to-do gentleman hurried away. But, though repulsed, and rudely, the man in gray did not reproach, for a time patiently remaining in the chilly loneliness to which he had been left, his countenance, however, not without token of latent though chastened reliance.

At length an old gentleman, somewhat bulky, drew nigh, and from him also a contribution was sought.

"Look, you," coming to a dead halt, and scowling upon him. "Look, you,"[2] swelling his bulk out before him like a swaying

[1] The Seminole Indians, a Florida tribe, had revolted against the attempt to cart them beyond the Mississippi, resulting in the bloody Seminole War of 1835–1842.

[2] An echo of the man with the wooden leg in Chapter 3: "'Look you,' he added, coming to a dead halt where he was; 'look you . . .'" When he reappears in the present chapter and argues that a man may pretend

balloon, "look, you, you on others' behalf ask for money; you, a fellow with a face as long as my arm. Hark ye, now: there is such a thing as gravity, and in condemned felons it may be genuine; but of long faces there are three sorts; that of grief's drudge, that of the lantern-jawed man, and that of the impostor. You know best which yours is."

"Heaven give you more charity, sir."

"And you less hypocrisy, sir."

With which words, the hard-hearted old gentleman marched off.

While the other still stood forlorn, the young clergyman, before introduced, passing that way, catching a chance sight of him, seemed suddenly struck by some recollection; and, after a moment's pause, hurried up with: "Your pardon, but shortly since I was all over looking for you."

"For me?" as marveling that one of so little account should be sought for.

"Yes, for you; do you know anything about the negro, apparently a cripple, aboard here? Is he, or is he not, what he seems to be?"

"Ah, poor Guinea! have you, too, been distrusted? you, upon whom nature has placarded the evidence of your claims?"

"Then you do really know him, and he is quite worthy? It relieves me to hear it—much relieves me. Come, let us go find him, and see what can be done."

"Another instance that confidence may come too late. I am sorry to say that at the last landing I myself—just happening to catch sight of him on the gangway-plank—assisted the cripple ashore. No time to talk, only to help. He may not have told you, but he has a brother in that vicinity."

"Really, I regret his going without my seeing him again; regret it, more, perhaps, than you can readily think. You see,

to be a cripple, there is a suggestion that he may be this "old gentleman, somewhat bulky." This is one of many hints that the Confidence Man's opponents may also be roles in a masquerade.

shortly after leaving St. Louis, he was on the forecastle, and there, with many others, I saw him, and put trust in him; so much so, that, to convince those who did not, I, at his entreaty, went in search of you, you being one of several individuals he mentioned, and whose personal appearance he more or less described, individuals who he said would willingly speak for him. But, after diligent search, not finding you, and catching no glimpse of any of the others he had enumerated, doubts were at last suggested; but doubts indirectly originating, as I can but think, from prior distrust unfeelingly proclaimed by another. Still, certain it is, I began to suspect."

"Ha, ha, ha!"

A sort of laugh more like a groan than a laugh; and yet, somehow, it seemed intended for a laugh.

Both turned, and the young clergyman started at seeing the wooden-legged man close behind him, morosely grave as a criminal judge with a mustard-plaster on his back. In the present case the mustard-plaster might have been the memory of certain recent biting rebuffs and mortifications.

"Wouldn't think it was I who laughed, would you?"

"But who was it you laughed at? or rather, tried to laugh at?" demanded the young clergyman, flushing, "me?"

"Neither you nor any one within a thousand miles of you. But perhaps you don't believe it."

"If he were of a suspicious temper, he might not," interposed the man in gray calmly, "it is one of the imbecilites of the suspicious person to fancy that every stranger, however absent-minded, he sees so much as smiling or gesturing to himself in any odd sort of way, is secretly making him his butt. In some moods, the movements of an entire street, as the suspicious man walks down it, will seem an express pantomimic jeer at him. In short, the suspicious man kicks himself with his own foot."

"Whoever can do that, ten to one he saves other folks' sole-leather," said the wooden-legged man with a crusty attempt at humor. But with augmented grin and squirm, turning directly upon the young clergyman, "you still think it was *you* I was laughing at, just now. To prove your mistake, I will tell you what I *was* laughing at; a story I happened to call to mind just then."

Whereupon, in his porcupine way, and with sarcastic details, unpleasant to repeat, he related a story, which might, perhaps, in a good-natured version, be rendered as follows:

A certain Frenchman of New Orleans, an old man, less slender in purse than limb, happening to attend the theatre one evening, was so charmed with the character of a faithful wife, as there represented to the life, that nothing would do but he must marry upon it. So, marry he did, a beautiful girl from Tennessee, who had first attracted his attention by her liberal mould, and was subsequently recommended to him through her kin, for her equally liberal education and disposition. Though large, the praise proved not too much. For, ere long, rumor more than corroborated it, by whispering that the lady was liberal to a fault. But though various circumstances, which by most Benedicts would have been deemed all but conclusive, were duly recited to the old Frenchman by his friends, yet such was his confidence that not a syllable would he credit, till, chancing one night to return unexpectedly from a journey, upon entering his apartment, a stranger burst from the alcove: "Begar!" cried he, "now I *begin* to suspec."

His story told, the wooden-legged man threw back his head, and gave vent to a long, gasping, rasping sort of taunting cry, intolerable as that of a high-pressure engine jeering off steam; and that done, with apparent satisfaction hobbled away.

"Who is that scoffer," said the man in gray, not without warmth. "Who is he, who even were truth on his tongue, his way of speaking it would make truth almost offensive as falsehood. Who is he?"

"He who I mentioned to you as having boasted his suspicion of the negro," replied the young clergyman, recovering from disturbance, "in short, the person to whom I ascribe the origin of my own distrust; he maintained that Guinea was some white scoundrel, betwisted and painted up for a decoy. Yes, these were his very words, I think."

"Impossible! [3] he could not be so wrong-headed. Pray, will you call him back, and let me ask him if he were really in earnest?"

The other complied; and, at length, after no few surly objections, prevailed upon the one-legged individual to return for a moment. Upon which, the man in gray thus addressed him: "This reverend gentleman tells me, sir, that a certain cripple, a poor negro, is by you considered an ingenious impostor. Now, I am not unaware that there are some persons in this world, who, unable to give better proof of being wise, take a strange delight in showing what they think they have sagaciously read in mankind by uncharitable suspicions of them. I hope you are not one of these. In short, would you tell me now, whether you were not merely joking in the notion you threw out about the negro. Would you be so kind?"

"No, I won't be so kind, I'll be so cruel."

"As you please about that."

"Well, he's just what I said he was."

"A white masquerading as a black?"

"Exactly."

The man in gray glanced at the young clergyman a moment, then quietly whispered to him, "I thought you represented your friend here as a very distrustful sort of person, but he appears endued with a singular credulity. —Tell me, sir, do

[3] What is impossible is that the clergyman could know the cripple's very words—unless this "young clergyman, before introduced," is both the Episcopal and Methodist ministers united in one shape-shifting being. In Chapter 3 the Episcopal minister had come, "as a person newly arrived from another part of the boat," only after the cripple had been "forced to retire." He arrived with no trust, but a suspicion which evoked Black Guinea's list; and then "away he went." Only then did the cripple return and speak the very words upon which the present clergyman blames his distrust. And it was the Methodist minister who then strode forward to challenge these words. Perhaps it is no error that the first minister was described as "the young Episcopal clergymen" (page 20).

you really think that a white could look the negro so? For one,
I should call it pretty good acting."

"Not much better than any other man acts."

"How? Does all the world act? Am *I*, for instance, an actor?
Is my reverend friend here, too, a performer?"

"Yes, don't you both perform acts? To do, is to act; so all
doers are actors."

"You trifle.—I ask again, if a white, how could he look the
negro so?"

"Never saw the negro-minstrels, I suppose?"

"Yes, but they are apt to overdo the ebony; exemplifying
the old saying, not more just than charitable, that 'the devil is
never so black as he is painted.' [4] But his limbs, if not a cripple,
how could he twist his limbs so?"

"How do other hypocritical beggars twist theirs? Easy
enough to see how they are hoisted up."

"The sham is evident, then?"

"To the discerning eye," with a horrible screw of his gimlet
one.

"Well, where is Guinea?" said the man in gray; "where is
he? Let us at once find him, and refute beyond cavil this
injurious hypothesis."

"Do so," cried the one-eyed man, "I'm just in the humor
now for having him found, and leaving the streaks of these
fingers on his paint, as the lion leaves the streaks of his nails on
a caffre.[5] They wouldn't let me touch him before. Yes, find
him, I'll make wool fly, and him after."

"You forget," here said the young clergyman to the man in
gray, "that yourself helped poor Guinea ashore."

"So I did, so I did; how unfortunate. But look now," to the

[4] Thus the man in *gray* appropriately questions the possibility of "A
white masquerading as a black."

[5] *Caffre* (or *Kafir*): Arabic for infidel. The term was applied by
Mohammedans to Christian and pagan Negroes, and thereby came to
designate a particular group of the Bantus, including the Zulus, who
resisted all efforts of conversion and resolutely maintained their
cultural independence.

other, "I think that without personal proof I can convince you of your mistake. For I put it to you, is it reasonable to suppose that a man with brains, sufficient to act such a part as you say, would take all that trouble, and run all that hazard, for the mere sake of those few paltry coppers, which, I hear, was all he got for his pains, if pains they were?"

"That puts the case irrefutably," said the young clergyman, with a challenging glance towards the one-legged man.

"You two green-horns! Money, you think, is the sole motive to pains and hazard, deception and deviltry, in this world. How much money did the devil make by gulling Eve?"

Whereupon he hobbled off again with a repetition of his intolerable jeer.

The man in gray stood silently eyeing his retreat a while, and then, turning to his companion, said: "A bad man, a dangerous man; a man to be put down in any Christian community.—And this was he who was the means of begetting your distrust? Ah, we should shut our ears to distrust, and keep them open only for its opposite."

"You advance a principle, which, if I had acted upon it this morning, I should have spared myself what I now feel.—That but one man, and he with one leg, should have such ill power given him; his one sour word leavening into congenial sourness (as, to my knowledge, it did) the dispositions, before sweet enough, of a numerous company. But, as I hinted, with me at the time his ill words went for nothing; the same as now; only afterwards they had effect; and I confess, this puzzles me."

"It should not. With humane minds, the spirit of distrust works something as certain potions do; it is a spirit which may enter such minds, and yet, for a time, longer or shorter, lie in them quiescent; but only the more deplorable its ultimate activity."

"An uncomfortable solution; for, since that baneful man did but just now anew drop on me his bane, how shall I be sure that my present exemption from its effects will be lasting."

"You cannot be sure, but you can strive against it."

"How?"

"By strangling the least symptom of distrust, of any sort, which hereafter, upon whatever provocation, may arise in you."

"I will do so." Then added as in soliloquy, "Indeed, indeed, I was to blame in standing passive under such influences as that one-legged man's. My conscience upbraids me.—The poor negro: You see him occasionally, perhaps?"

"No, not often; though in a few days, as it happens, my engagements will call me to the neighborhood of his present retreat; and, no doubt, honest Guinea, who is a grateful soul, will come to see me there."

"Then you have been his benefactor?"

"His benefactor? I did not say that. I have known him."

"Take this mite. Hand it to Guinea when you see him; say it comes from one who has full belief in his honesty, and is sincerely sorry for having indulged, however transiently, in a contrary thought."

"I accept the trust. And, by-the-way, since you are of this truly charitable nature, you will not turn away an appeal in behalf of the Seminole Widow and Orphan Asylum?"

"I have not heard of that charity."

"But recently founded."

After a pause, the clergyman was irresolutely putting his hand in his pocket, when, caught by something in his companion's expression, he eyed him inquisitively, almost uneasily.

"Ah, well," smiled the other wanly, "if that subtle bane, we were speaking of but just now, is so soon beginning to work, in vain my appeal to you. Good-by."

"Nay," not untouched, "you do me injustice; instead of indulging present suspicions, I had rather make amends for previous ones. Here is something for your asylum. Not much; but every drop helps. Of course you have papers?"

"Of course," producing a memorandum book and pencil. "Let me take down name and amount. We publish these names. And now let me give you a little history of our asylum, and the providential way in which it was started."

CHAPTER 7

A gentleman with gold sleeve-buttons.

At an interesting point of the narration, and at the moment when, with much curiosity, indeed, urgency, the narrator was being particularly questioned upon that point, he was, as it happened, altogether diverted both from it and his story, by just then catching sight of a gentleman who had been standing in sight from the beginning, but, until now, as it seemed, without being observed by him.

"Pardon me," said he, rising, "but yonder is one who I know will contribute, and largely. Don't take it amiss if I quit you."

"Go: duty before all things," was the conscientious reply.

The stranger was a man of more than winsome aspect.[1] There he stood apart and in repose, and yet, by his mere look, lured the man in gray from his story, much as, by its graciousness of bearing, some full-leaved elm, alone in a meadow, lures the noon sickleman to throw down his sheaves, and come and apply for the alms of its shade.

But, considering that goodness is no such rare thing among men—the world familiarly know the noun; a common one in every language—it was curious that what so signalized the stranger, and made him look like a kind of foreigner, among the crowd (as to some it may make him appear more or less unreal in this portraiture), was but the expression of so prevailent a quality. Such goodness seemed his, allied with such fortune, that, so far as his own personal experience could have

[1] Compare this "stranger" of "more than winsome aspect" to Mark Winsome (Chapter 36), who in the dialogue is identified as "the stranger."

gone, scarcely could he have known ill, physical or moral; and as for knowing or suspecting the latter in any serious degree (supposing such degree of it to be), by observation or philosophy; for that, probably, his nature, by its opposition, was imperfectly qualified, or from it wholly exempted. For the rest, he might have been five and fifty, perhaps sixty, but tall, rosy, between plump and portly, with a primy, palmy air, and for the time and place, not to hint of his years, dressed with a strangely festive finish and elegance. The inner-side of his coatskirts was of white satin, which might have looked especially inappropriate, had it not seemed less a bit of mere tailoring than something of an emblem, as it were; an involuntary emblem, let us say, that what seemed so good about him was not all outside; no, the fine covering had a still finer lining. Upon one hand he wore a white kid glove, but the other hand, which was ungloved, looked hardly less white. Now, as the Fidèle, like most steamboats, was upon deck a little soot-streaked here and there, especially about the railings, it was a marvel how, under such circumstances, these hands retained their spotlessness. But, if you watched them a while, you noticed that they avoided touching anything; you noticed, in short, that a certain negro body-servant, whose hands nature had dyed black, perhaps with the same purpose that millers wear white, this negro servant's hands did most of his master's handling for him; having to do with dirt on his account, but not to his prejudices. But if, with the same undefiledness of consequences to himself, a gentleman could also sin by deputy, how shocking would that be! But it is not permitted to be; and even if it were, no judicious moralist would make proclamation of it.[2]

This gentleman, therefore, there is reason to affirm, was one who, like the Hebrew governor, knew how to keep his hands

[2] This stranger, who replaces the Christian clergyman, has two kinds of scapegoat: a black servant and a white *kid* glove. See Chapter 34 for the story of a "gentleman" who tries to save the world from a sin by taking it on his own back.

clean,[3] and who never in his life happened to be run suddenly against by hurrying house-painter, or sweep; in a word, one whose very good luck it was to be a very good man.

Not that he looked as if he were a kind of Wilberforce [4] at all; that superior merit, probably, was not his; nothing in his manner bespoke him righteous, but only good, and though to be good is much below being righteous, and though there is a difference between the two, yet not, it is to be hoped, so incompatible as that a righteous man can not be a good man; though, conversely, in the pulpit it has been with much cogency urged, that a merely good man, that is, one good merely by his nature, is so far from there by being righteous, that nothing short of a total change and conversion can make him so; which is something which no honest mind, well read in the history of righteousness, will care to deny; nevertheless, since St. Paul himself, agreeing in a sense with the pulpit distinction, though not altogether in the pulpit deduction, and also pretty plainly intimating which of the two qualities in question enjoys his apostolic preference; I say, since St. Paul has so meaningly said, that, "scarcely for a righteous man will one die, yet peradventure for a good man some would even dare to die;" [5] therefore, when we repeat of this gentleman, that he was only a good man, whatever else by severe censors may be objected to him, it is still to be hoped that his goodness will not at least be considered criminal in him. At all events, no man, not even a righteous man, would think it quite right to commit this gentleman to prison for the crime, extraordinary as he might deem it; more especially, as, until everything could be known, there would be some chance that the gentleman might after all be quite as innocent of it as he himself.

It was pleasant to mark the good man's reception of the

[3] An allusion to Pontius Pilate's symbolic handwashing (Matthew 27:24).

[4] William Wilberforce (1759–1833), English philanthropist and politician, noted for his struggle for abolition of Negro slavery.

[5] Romans 5:7.

salute of the righteous man, that is, the man in gray; his inferior, apparently, not more in the social scale than in stature.
Like the benign elm again, the good man seemed to wave the
canopy of his goodness over that suitor, not in conceited condescension, but with that even amenity of true majesty, which
can be kind to any one without stooping to it.

To the plea in behalf of the Seminole widows and orphans,
the gentleman, after a question or two duly answered, responded by producing an ample pocketbook in the good old
capacious style, of fine green French morocco and workman-
ship, bound with silk of the same color, not to omit bills crisp
with newness, fresh from the bank, no muckworms' grime
upon them. Lucre those bills might be, but as yet having been
kept unspotted from the world, not of the filthy sort. Placing
now three of those virgin bills in the applicant's hands, he
hoped that the smallness of the contribution would be pardoned; to tell the truth, and this at last accounted for his toilet,
he was bound but a short run down the river, to attend, in a
festive grove, the afternoon wedding of his niece: so did not
carry much money with him.

The other was about expressing his thanks when the gentleman in his pleasant way checked him: the gratitude was on the
other side. To him, he said, charity was in one sense not an
effort, but a luxury; against too great indulgence in which his
steward, a humorist, had sometimes admonished him.

In some general talk which followed, relative to organized
modes of doing good, the gentleman expressed his regrets that
so many benevolent societies as there were, here and there
isolated in the land, should not act in concert by coming together, in the way that already in each society the individuals
composing it had done, which would result, he thought, in like
advantages upon a larger scale. Indeed, such a confederation
might, perhaps, be attended with as happy results as politically
attended that of the states.

Upon his hitherto moderate enough companion, this suggestion had an effect illustrative in a sort of that notion of Socra-

tes, that the soul is a harmony; [6] for as the sound of a flute, in any particular key, will, it is said, audibly affect the corresponding chord of any harp in good tune, within hearing, just so now did some string in him respond, and with animation.

Which animation, by the way, might seem more or less out of character in the man in gray, considering his unsprightly manner when first introduced, had he not already, in certain after colloquies, given proof, in some degree, of the fact, that, with certain natures, a soberly continent air at times, so far from arguing emptiness of stuff, is good proof it is there, and plenty of it, because unwasted, and may be used the more effectively, too, when opportunity offers. What now follows on the part of the man in gray will still further exemplify, perhaps somewhat strikingly, the truth, or what appears to be such, of this remark.

"Sir," said he eagerly, "I am before you. A project, not dissimilar to yours, was by me thrown out at the World's Fair in London." [7]

"World's Fair? You there? Pray how was that?"

"First, let me—"

"Nay, but first tell me what took you to the Fair?"

"I went to exhibit an invalid's easy-chair I had invented."

"Then you have not always been in the charity business?"

"Is it not charity to ease human suffering? I am, and always have been, as I always will be, I trust, in the charity business, as you call it; but charity is not like a pin, one to make the head, and the other the point; [8] charity is a work to which a good workman may be competent in all its branches. I in-

[6] A basic Socratic notion expounded at length in the *Republic, Phaedo, Protagoras,* and elsewhere.

[7] The London Great Exhibition, held in the Crystal Palace, Hyde Park, in 1851, became a widely used nineteenth-century symbol of the utopian future toward which the world was progressing.

[8] Elizabeth Foster suggests that this is an allusion to the passage in Adam Smith's *Wealth of Nations* (1776; 11th ed., 3 vols., London, 1805, I, 3) about the division of labor in pin-making.

vented my Protean easy-chair [9] in odd intervals stolen from meals and sleep."

"You call it the Protean easy-chair; pray describe it."

"My Protean easy-chair is a chair so all over bejointed, behinged, and bepadded, everyway so elastic, springy, and docile to the airiest touch, that in some one of its endlessly-changeable accommodations of back, seat, footboard, and arms, the most restless body, the body most racked, nay, I had almost added the most tormented conscience must, somehow and somewhere, find rest. Believing that I owed it to suffering humanity to make known such a chair to the utmost, I scraped together my little means and off to the World's Fair with it."

"You did right. But your scheme; how did you come to hit upon that?"

"I was going to tell you. After seeing my invention duly catalogued and placed, I gave myself up to pondering the scene about me. As I dwelt upon that shining pageant of arts, and moving concourse of nations, and reflected that here was the pride of the world glorying in a glass house, a sense of the fragility of worldly grandeur profoundly impressed me. And I said to myself, I will see if this occasion of vanity cannot supply a hint toward a better profit than was designed. Let some world-wide good to the world-wide cause be now done. In short, inspired by the scene, on the fourth day I issued at the World's Fair my prospectus of the World's Charity."

"Quite a thought. But, pray explain it."

"The World's Charity is to be a society whose members shall comprise deputies from every charity and mission extant; the one object of the society to be the methodization of the world's benevolence; to which end, the present system of voluntary and promiscuous contribution to be done away, and

---

[9] Several reclining chairs for invalids were in fact exhibited at the Great Exhibition in London (Foster). The man in gray aptly names his invention for the Greek sea-god Proteus, who could change his shape at will.

the Society to be empowered by the various governments to levy, annually, one grand benevolence tax upon all mankind; as in Augustus Caesar's time, the whole world to come up to be taxed; a tax which, for the scheme of it, should be something like the income-tax in England, a tax, also, as before hinted, to be a consolidation-tax of all possible benevolence taxes; as in America here, the state-tax, and the county-tax, and the town-tax, and the poll-tax, are by the assessors rolled into one. This tax, according to my tables, calculated with care, would result in the yearly raising of a fund little short of eight hundred millions; this fund to be annually applied to such objects, and in such modes, as the various charities and missions, in general congress represented, might decree; whereby, in fourteen years, as I estimate, there would have been devoted to good works the sum of eleven thousad two hundred millions; which would warrant the dissolution of the society, as that fund judiciously expended, not a pauper or heathen could remain the round world over."

"Eleven thousand two hundred millions! And all by passing round a *hat*, as it were."

"Yes, I am no Fourier,[10] the projector of an impossible scheme, but a philanthropist and a financier setting forth a philanthropy and a finance which are practicable."

"Practicable?"

"Yes. Eleven thousand two hundred millions; it will frighten none but a retail philanthropist. What is it but eight hundred millions for each of fourteen years? Now eight hundred millions—what is that, to average it, but one little dollar a head for the population of the planet? And who will refuse, what Turk or Dyak even, his own little dollar for sweet charity's sake? Eight hundred millions! More than that sum is yearly expended by mankind, not only in vanities, but miseries. Con-

10 François Marie Charles Fourier (1772–1837), French utopist. His system, Fourierism, saw all society organized into phalanxes, communities large enough only for all economic and social requirements. Brook Farm was influenced by this concept.

sider that bloody spendthrift, War. And are mankind so
stupid, so wicked, that, upon the demonstration of these things
they will not, amending their ways, devote their superfluities
to blessing the world instead of cursing it? Eight hundred
millions! They have not to make it, it is theirs already; they
have but to direct it from ill to good. And to this, scarce a self-
denial is demanded. Actually, they would not in the mass be
one farthing the poorer for it; as certainly would they be all
the better and happier. Don't you see? But admit, as you must,
that mankind is not mad, and my project is practicable. For,
what creature but a madman would not rather do good than
ill, when it is plain that, good or ill, it must return upon
himself?"

"Your sort of reasoning," said the good gentleman, adjusting
his gold sleeve-buttons, "seems all reasonable enough, but with
mankind it won't do."

"Then mankind are not reasoning beings, if reason won't do
with them."

"That is not to the purpose. By-the-way, from the manner
in which you alluded to the world's census, it would appear
that, according to your world-wide scheme, the pauper not
less than the nabob is to contribute to the relief of pauperism,
and the heathen not less than the Christian to the conversion of
heathenism. How is that?"

"Why, that—pardon me—is quibbling. Now, no philanthropist likes to be opposed with quibbling."

"Well, I won't quibble any more. But, after all, if I understand your project, there is little specially new in it, further
than the magnifying of means now in operation."

"Magnifying and energizing. For one thing, missions I
would thoroughly reform. Missions I would quicken with the
Wall street spirit."

"The Wall street spirit?"

"Yes; for if, confessedly, certain spiritual ends are to be
gained but through the auxiliary agency of worldly means,
then, to the surer gaining of such spiritual ends, the example of

worldly policy in worldly projects should not by spiritual projectors be slighted. In brief, the conversion of the heathen, so far, at least, as depending on human effort, would, by the world's charity, be let out on contract. So much by bid for converting India, so much for Borneo, so much for Africa. Competition allowed, stimulus would be given. There would be no lethargy of monopoly. We should have no mission-house or tract-house of which slanderers could, with any plausibility, say that it had degenerated in its clerkships into a sort of custom-house. But the main point is the Archimedean money-power that would be brought to bear." [11]

"You mean the eight hundred million power?"

"Yes. You see, this doing good to the world by driblets amounts to just nothing. I am for doing good to the world with a will. I am for doing good to the world once for all and having done with it. Do but think, my dear sir, of the eddies and maëlstroms of pagans in China. People here have no conception of it. Of a frosty morning in Hong Kong, pauper pagans are found dead in the streets like so many nipped peas in a bin of peas. To be an immortal being in China is no more distinction than to be a snow-flake in a snow-squall. What are a score or two of missionaries to such a people? A pinch of snuff to the kraken.[12] I am for sending ten thousand missionaries in a body and converting the Chinese *en masse* within six months of the debarkation. The thing is then done, and turn to something else."

"I fear you are too enthusiastic."

"A philanthropist is necessarily an enthusiast; for without enthusiasm what was ever achieved but commonplace? But again: consider the poor in London. To that mob of misery, what is a joint here and a loaf there? I am for voting to them twenty thousand bullocks and one hundred thousand barrels of flour to begin with. They are then comforted, and no more

[11] Archimedes invented the water-screw and discovered the principle of the lever. He is supposed to have said, referring to the lever, "Give me a place to stand, and I will move the world."

[12] A gigantic sea-monster said to appear off the coast of Norway.

hunger for one while among the poor of London. And so all round."

"Sharing the character of your general project, these things, I take it, are rather examples of wonders that were to be wished, than wonders that will happen."

"And is the age of wonders passed? Is the world too old? Is it barren? Think of Sarah."

"Then I am Abraham reviling the angel [13] (with a smile). But still, as to your design at large, there seems a certain audacity."

"But if to the audacity of the design there be brought a commensurate circumspectness of execution, how then?"

"Why, do you really believe that your world's charity will ever go into operation?"

"I have confidence that it will."

"But may you not be over-confident?"

"For a Christian to talk so!"

"But think of the obstacles!"

"Obstacles? I have confidence to remove obstacles, though mountains.[14] Yes, confidence in the world's charity to that degree, that, as no better person offers to supply the place, I have nominated myself provisional treasurer, and will be happy to receive subscriptions, for the present to be devoted to striking off a million more of my prospectuses."

The talk went on; the man in gray revealed a spirit of benevolence which, mindful of the millennial promise,[15] had

[13] When God told Abraham that Sarah will finally bear a son, "Abraham fell upon his face, and laughed, and said in his heart, Shall a child be born unto him that is an hundred years old? and shall Sarah, that is ninety years old, bear?" (Genesis 17:17).

[14] I Corinthians 13:2: " . . . though I have all faith, so that I could remove mountains, and have not charity, I am nothing." The lamb-like man's inscriptions begin two verses later.

[15] Revelation 20 prophesies a millennium during which, among other things, Satan will be bound and unable to "deceive the nations." In his next avatar, the Confidence Man will try to sell stock in the New Jerusalem of Revelation 21-22.

gone abroad over all the countries of the globe, much as the diligent spirit of the husbandman, stirred by forethought of the coming seed-time, leads him, in March reveries at his fireside, over every field of his farm. The master chord of the man in gray had been touched, and it seemed as if it would never cease vibrating. A not unsilvery tongue,[16] too, was his, with gestures that were a Pentecost of added ones [17] and persuasiveness before which granite hearts might crumble into gravel.

Strange, therefore, how his auditor, so singularly good-hearted as he seemed, remained proof to such eloquence; though not, as it turned out, to such pleadings. For, after listening a while longer with pleasant incredulity, presently, as the boat touched his place of destination, the gentleman, with a look half humor, half pity, put another bank-note into his hands; charitable to the last, if only to the dreams of enthusiasm.

[16] Baruch 6 (Apocrypha): "4. Now shall ye see in Babylon gods of silver, and of gold, and of wood, borne upon shoulders, which cause the nations to fear." "8. As for their tongue, it is polished by the workmen, and they themselves are gilded and laid over with gold; Yet they are false, and cannot speak."

[17] Acts 2:1–11 describes how the apostles on the day of Pentecost "began to speak with other tongues, as the Spirit gave them utterance."

CHAPTER 8

A charitable lady.

If a drunkard in a sober fit is the dullest of mortals, an enthusiast in a reason-fit is not the most lively. And this, without
prejudice to his greatly improved understanding; for, if his
elation was the height of his madness, his despondency is but
the extreme of his sanity. Something thus now, to all appearance, with the man in gray. Society his stimulus, loneliness was
his lethargy. Loneliness, like the sea-breeze, blowing off from a
thousand leagues of blankness, he did not find, as veteran solitaires do, if anything, too bracing. In short, left to himself,
with none to charm forth his latent lymphatic, he insensibly
resumes his original air, a quiescent one, blended of sad humility and demureness.

Ere long he goes laggingly into the ladies' saloon, as in spirit-
less quest of somebody; but, after some disappointed glances
about him, seats himself upon a sofa with an air of melancholy
exhaustion and depression.

At the sofa's further end sits a plump and pleasant person,
whose aspect seems to hint that, if she have any weak point, it
must be anything rather than her excellent heart. From her
twilight dress, neither dawn nor dark, apparently she is a
widow just breaking the chrysalis of her mourning.[1] A small

[1] The last victim of the man in gray here unites the book's most
essential images—the rising and setting of the sun and the metamorphoses
of the butterfly. She, in her "twilight dress," and he, in gray, are both
between day and night; "mourning" is a pun. The chrysalis, from the
Greek *chrysos* ("gold"), is the pupa stage from which the resplendent
butterfly, classic symbol of the soul and later identified with the
metamorphosing Confidence Man, will arise. Note the "small *gilt*
testament" which has been illuminated by the rising-sun figure of
Chapter 1.

gilt testament is in her hand, which she has just been reading. Half-relinquished, she holds the book in reverie, her finger inserted at the xiii. of 1st Corinthians, to which chapter possibly her attention might have recently been turned, by witnessing the scene of the monitory mute and his slate.[2]

The sacred page no longer meets her eye; but, as at evening, when for a time the western hills shine on though the sun be set, her thoughtful face retains its tenderness though the teacher is forgotten.

Meantime, the expression of the stranger is such as ere long to attract her glance. But no responsive one. Presently, in her somewhat inquisitive survey, her volume drops. It is restored. No encroaching politeness in the act, but kindness, unadorned. The eyes of the lady sparkle. Evidently, she is not now unprepossessed. Soon, bending over, in a low, sad tone, full of deference, the stranger breathes, "Madam, pardon my freedom, but there is something in that face which strangely draws me. May I ask, are you a sister of the Church?"

"Why—really—you—"

In concern for her embarrassment, he hastens to relieve it, but, without seeming so to do. "It is very solitary for a brother here," eying the showy ladies brocaded in the background, "I find none to mingle souls with. It may be wrong—I *know* it is—but I cannot force myself to be easy with the people of the world. I prefer the company, however silent, of a brother or sister in good standing. By the way, madam, may I ask if you have confidence?"

"Really, sir—why sir—really—I—"

"Could you put confidence in *me* for instance?"

"Really, sir—as much—I mean, as one may wisely put in a—a—stranger, an entire stranger, I had almost said," rejoined the lady, hardly yet at ease in her affability, drawing aside a little in body, while at the same time her heart might have

[2] The man in gray has also just been quoting I Corinthians 13 (Chapter 7, note 14).

been drawn as far the other way. A natural struggle between charity and prudence.

"Entire stranger!" with a sigh. "Ah, who would be a stranger? In vain, I wander; no one will have confidence in me."

"You interest me," said the good lady, in mild surprise.
"Can I any way befriend you?"

"No one can befriend me, who has not confidence."

"But I—I have—at least to that degree—I mean that—"

"Nay, nay, you have none—none at all. Pardon, I see it. No
confidence. Fool, fond fool that I am to seek it!"

"You are unjust, sir," rejoins the good lady with heightened
interest; "but it may be that something untoward in your experiences has unduly biased you. Not that I would cast reflections. Believe me, I—yes, yes—I may say—that—that—"

"That you have confidence? Prove it. Let me have twenty
dollars."

"Twenty dollars!"

"There, I told you, madam, you had no confidence."

The lady was, in an extraordinary way, touched. She sat in a
sort of restless torment, knowing not which way to turn. She
began twenty different sentences, and left off at the first syllable of each. At last, in desperation, she hurried out, "Tell me,
sir, for what you want the twenty dollars?"

"And did I not—" then glancing at her half-mourning, "for
the widow and the fatherless. I am traveling agent of the
Widow and Orphan Asylum, recently founded among the
Seminoles."

"And why did you not tell me your object before?" As not
a little relieved. "Poor souls—Indians, too—those cruelly-used
Indians. Here, here; how could I hesitate. I am so sorry it is no
more."

"Grieve not for that, madam," rising and folding up the
bank-notes. "This is an inconsiderable sum, I admit,[3] but," tak-

[3] The modern reader should remember throughout the book that the
value of currency has changed drastically. In *Walden* (1854) Thoreau

ing out his pencil and book, "though I here but register the amount, there is another register, where is set down the motive. Good-bye; you have confidence. Yea, you can say to me as the apostle said to the Corinthians, 'I rejoice that I have confidence in you in all things.' "[4]

lists the total cost of all the materials required to build his house and woodshed at Walden pond as $28.12½.

With this in mind, compare the parable of the story of the poor widow who donates her two mites (Mark 12:41–44). Christ says that she has given more than the rich, "For all they did cast in of their abundance: but she of her want did cast in all that she had, even all her living."

[4] II Corinthians 7:16. The apostle is Paul.

CHAPTER 9

Two business men transact a little business.

—"Pray, sir, have you seen a gentleman with a weed here-abouts, rather a saddish gentleman? Strange where he can have gone to. I was talking with him not twenty minutes since."

By a brisk, ruddy-cheeked man in a tasseled traveling-cap, carrying under his arm a ledger-like volume, the above words were addressed to the collegian before introduced, suddenly accosted by the rail to which not long after his retreat, as in a previous chapter recounted, he had returned, and there remained.

"Have you seen him, sir?"

Rallied from his apparent diffidence by the genial jauntiness of the stranger, the youth answered with unwonted promptitude: "Yes, a person with a weed was here not very long ago."

"Saddish?"

"Yes, and a little cracked, too, I should say."

"It was he. Misfortune, I fear, has disturbed his brain. Now quick, which way did he go?"

"Why just in the direction from which you came, the gangway yonder."

"Did he? Then the man in the gray coat, whom I just met, said right: he must have gone ashore. How unlucky!"

He stood vexedly twitching at his cap-tassel, which fell over by his whisker, and continued: "Well, I am very sorry. In fact, I had something for him here."—Then drawing nearer, "you see, he applied to me for relief, no, I do him injustice, not that, but he began to intimate, you understand. Well, being very busy just then, I declined; quite rudely, too, in a cold, morose, unfeeling way, I fear. At all events, not three minutes afterwards I felt self-reproach, with a kind of prompting, very peremptory, to deliver over into that unfortunate man's hands a ten-dollar bill. You smile. Yes, it may be superstition, but I can't help it; I have my weak side, thank God. Then again," he rapidly went on, "we have been so very prosperous lately in our affairs—by we, I mean the Black Rapids Coal Company—that, really, out of my abundance, associative and individual, it is but fair that a charitable investment or two should be made, don't you think so?"

"Sir," said the collegian without the least embarrassment, "do I understand that you are officially connected with the Black Rapids Coal Company?"

"Yes, I happen to be president and transfer-agent."

"You are?"

"Yes, but what is it to you? You don't want to invest?"

"Why, do you sell the stock?"

"Some might be bought, perhaps; but why do you ask? you don't want to invest?"

"But supposing I did," with cool self-collectedness, "could you do up the thing for me, and here?"

"Bless my soul," gazing at him in amaze, "really, you are quite a business man. Positively, I feel afraid of you."

"Oh, no need of that.—You could sell me some of that stock, then?"

"I don't know, I don't know. To be sure, there are a few shares under peculiar circumstances bought in by the Company; but it would hardly be the thing to convert this boat into the Company's office. I think you had better defer investing. So," with an indifferent air, "you have seen the unfortunate man I spoke of?"

"Let the unfortunate man go his ways.—What is that large book you have with you?"

"My transfer-book. I am subpoenaed with it to court."

"Black Rapids Coal Company," obliquely reading the gilt inscription on the back; "I have heard much of it. Pray do you happen to have with you any statement of the condition of your company."

"A statement has lately been printed."

"Pardon me, but I am naturally inquisitive. Have you a copy with you?"

"I tell you again, I do not think that it would be suitable to convert this boat into the Company's office.—That unfortunate man, did you relieve him at all?"

"Let the unfortunate man relieve himself.[1]—Hand me the statement."

"Well, you are such a business-man, I can hardly deny you. Here," handing a small, printed pamphlet.

The youth turned it over sagely.

"I hate a suspicious man," said the other, observing him; "but I must say I like to see a cautious one."

"I can gratify you there," languidly returning the pamphlet; "for, as I said before, I am naturally inquisitive; I am also circumspect. No appearances can deceive me. Your statement," he added "tells a very fine story; but pray, was not your stock a little heavy a while ago? downward tendency? Sort of low spirits among holders on the subject of that stock?"

"Yes, there was a depression. But how came it? who devised it? The 'bears,' sir. The depression of our stock was solely owing to the growling, the hypocritical growling, of the bears."

"How, hypocritical?"

"Why, the most monstrous of all hypocrites are these bears: hypocrites by inversion; hypocrites in the simulation of things dark instead of bright; souls that thrive, less upon depression, than the fiction of depression;[2] professors of the wicked art of manufacturing depressions; spurious Jeremiahs;[3] sham

[1] A sexual joke.

[2] Note that the bears (those who sell securities short) are here labeled as fiction makers and bringers of darkness.

[3] The biblical Book of the Prophet Jeremiah consists largely of denunciations of present sins and warnings of doom to come. 10:8 asserts that "the stock is a doctrine of vanities." The authenticity of some parts of Jeremiah had been under question during the first half of the century. In Chapter 24 the Cosmopolitan says, "I have heard of Jeremy the prophet."

Heraclituses,[4] who, the lugubrious day done, return, like sham Lazaruses among the beggars,[5] to make merry over the gains got by their pretended sore heads—scoundrelly bears!"

"You are warm against these bears?"

"If I am, it is less from the remembrance of their stratagems as to our stock, than from the persuasion that these same destroyers of confidence, and gloomy philosophers of the stock-market, though false in themselves are yet true types of most destroyers of confidence and gloomy philosophers, the world over. Fellows who, whether in stocks, politics, bread-stuffs, morals, metaphysics, religion—be it what it may—trump up their black panics in the naturally-quiet brightness, solely with a view to some sort of covert advantage. That corpse of calamity which the gloomy philosopher parades, is but his Good-Enough-Morgan." [6]

"I rather like that," knowingly drawled the youth. "I fancy these gloomy souls as little as the next one. Sitting on my sofa after a champagne dinner, smoking my plantation cigar, if a gloomy fellow come to me—what a bore!"

"You tell him it's all stuff, don't you?"

"I tell him it ain't natural. I say to him, you are happy enough, and you know it; and everybody else is as happy as you, and you know that, too; and we shall all be happy after we are no more, and you know that, too; but no, still you must have your sulk."

[4] Heraclitus of Ephesus (c. 540–475 B.C.), called the Dark or Weeping Philosopher; he held that all was eternal flux. Because of his scorn of mankind, he had also the nickname "he who rails at the people."

[5] Lazarus was the beggar in the parable of the rich man and the beggar (Luke 16); his name came to mean any diseased beggar. The parable is referred to in Chapters 2 and 15.

[6] In 1826, a William Morgan, who was about to publish a book revealing the secrets of Freemasonry, was kidnapped. A corpse found in the Niagara River was asserted to be his. When this identification was challenged, Thurlow Weed, a prominent anti-Mason, supposedly said that the corpse was "a good enough Morgan until after the election." Hence a good-enough-Morgan was any device which could be used as a temporary means of influencing voters.

"And do you know whence this sort of fellow gets his sulk? not from life; for he's often too much of a recluse, or else too young to have seen anything of it. No, he gets it from some of those old plays he sees on the stage, or some of those old books he finds up in garrets. Ten to one, he has lugged home from auction a musty old Seneca,[7] and sets about stuffing himself with that stale old hay; and, thereupon, thinks it looks wise and antique to be a croaker, thinks it's taking a stand way above his kind."

"Just so," assented the youth. "I've lived some, and seen a good many such ravens at second hand. By the way, strange how that man with the weed, you were inquiring for, seemed to take me for some soft sentimentalist, only because I kept quiet, and thought, because I had a copy of Tacitus with me, that I was reading him for his gloom, instead of his gossip. But I let him talk. And, indeed, by my manner humored him."

"You shouldn't have done that, now. Unfortunate man, you must have made quite a fool of him."

"His own fault if I did. But I like prosperous fellows, comfortable fellows; fellows that talk comfortably and prosperously, like you. Such fellows are generally honest. And, I say now, I happen to have a superfluity in my pocket, and I'll just—"

"—Act the part of a brother to that unfortunate man?"

"Let the unfortunate man be his own brother. What are you dragging him in for all the time? One would think you didn't care to register any transfers, or dispose of any stock—mind running on something else. I say I will invest."

"Stay, stay, here come some uproarious fellows—this way, this way."

And with off-handed politeness the man with the book escorted his companion into a private little haven removed from the brawling swells without.

Business transacted, the two came forth, and walked the deck.

[7] Lucius Annaeus Seneca (c. 4 B.C.–65 A.D.), Stoic philosopher, wily politician, and writer of bloody tragedies. See Chapter 37, note 6.

"Now tell me, sir," said he with the book, "how comes it that a young gentleman like you, a sedate student at the first appearance, should dabble in stocks and that sort of thing?"

"There are certain sophomorean errors in the world," drawled the sophomore, deliberately adjusting his shirt-collar, "not the least of which is the popular notion touching the nature of the modern scholar, and the nature of the modern scholastic sedateness."

"So it seems, so it seems. Really, this is quite a new leaf in my experience."

"Experience, sir," originally observed the sophomore, "is the only teacher."

"Hence am I your pupil; for it's only when experience speaks, that I can endure to listen to speculation."

"My speculations, sir," dryly drawing himself up, "have been chiefly governed by the maxim of Lord Bacon; I speculate in those philosophies which come home to my business and bosom [8]—pray, do you know of any other good stocks?"

"You wouldn't like to be concerned in the New Jerusalem,[9] would you?"

"New Jerusalem?"

"Yes, the new and thriving city, so called, in northern Minnesota. It was originally founded by certain fugitive Mormons.[10] Hence the name. It stands on the Mississippi. Here, here is the map," producing a roll. "There—there, you see are

[8] Bacon's dedication to the 1625 edition of *Essays, Counsels, Civil and Morall* claims that his essays "come home to men's business and bosoms." Bacon is referred to again in Chapter 24 and Chapter 37, there immediately after a reference to Seneca.

[9] Revelation 21–22 describes the New Jerusalem. The New Jerusalem Church was organized by the Swedenborgians in 1778 (in Chapter 37 Swedenborg is mentioned in the same sentence with Seneca and Bacon). There was an actual New Jerusalem in Ohio.

[10] This suggests a relation to the city of Nauvoo, Illinois, which was founded on the Mississippi in 1840 by the fugitive Mormons driven out of Missouri. The Mormons were expelled in 1846, and Nauvoo became in 1850 the seat of the Icarian community.

the public buildings—here the landing—there the park—yonder the botanic gardens—and this, this little dot here, is a perpetual fountain,[11] you understand. You observe there are twenty asterisks. Those are for the lyceums. They have lignum-vitae [12] rostrums."

"And are all these buildings now standing?"

"All standing—bona fide."

"These marginal squares here, are they the water-lots?"

"Water-lots in the city of New Jerusalem? All terra firma—you don't seem to care about investing, though?" [13]

"Hardly think I should read my title clear, as the law students say," yawned the collegian.

"Prudent—you are prudent. Don't know that you are wholly out, either. At any rate, I would rather have one of your shares of coal stock than two of this other. Still, considering that the first settlement was by two fugitives, who had swum over naked from the opposite shore [14]—it's a surprising place. It is, *bona fide.*—But dear me, I must go. Oh, if by possibility you should come across that unfortunate man—"

"—In that case," with drawling impatience, "I will send for the steward, and have him and his misfortunes consigned overboard."

[11] See Revelation 21:6 and 22:1 for a description of "the fountain of the water of life" in the New Jerusalem.

[12] Wood of the tree *Guaiacum officinale*; this lignum (wood) vitae (of life) represents the tree of life in the New Jerusalem, described in Revelation 22:2.

[13] Selling sites in supposedly thriving communities, actually wastelands, was one of the favorite swindles of the day. The present proposed transaction seems to have reference to the sale of a site in the "city" of Eden to Martin Chuzzlewit in Dickens' novel. On the Eden Land Corporation map "were banks, churches, cathedrals, market-places, factories, hotels, stores, mansions, wharves; an exchange, a theatre; public buildings of all kinds"; but Eden turns out to be a deadly swamp. Chapter 23 of *The Confidence-Man* describes the actual place which was the model for the Eden of *Martin Chuzzlewit*, Cairo, Illinois; see Chapter 22, note 38 on the relations with Dickens' novel.

[14] Probably the first two fugitives, Adam and Eve.

"Ha ha!—now were some gloomy philosopher here, some theological bear, forever taking occasion to growl down the stock of human nature (with ulterior views, d'ye see, to a fat benefice in the gift of the worshipers of Ariamius),[15] he would pronounce that the sign of a hardening heart and a softening brain. Yes, that would be his sinister construction. But it's nothing more than the oddity of a genial humor—genial but dry. Confess it. Good-bye."

[15] An alternative spelling of Arimanius (or Ahriman or Angra Mainyu), the incarnation of darkness and evil in Zoroastrianism. The forces of light, incarnate in Ormazd (or Ormuzd or Ahura Mazda), have been eternally struggling against Arimanius and will eventually succeed in establishing the good kingdom, vohukhshathra.

The ambiguous prepositions in this parenthetical insinuation hint at many relations between Christian and Zoroastrian cosmic history.

CHAPTER 10

In the cabin.

Stools, settees, sofas, divans, ottomans; occupying them are clusters of men, old and young, wise and simple; in their hands are cards spotted with diamonds, spades, clubs, hearts; the favorite games are whist, cribbage, and brag. Lounging in arm-chairs or sauntering among the marble-topped tables, amused with the scene, are the comparatively few, who, instead of having hands in the games, for the most part keep their hands in their pockets. These may be the philosophers.[1] But here and there, with a curious expression, one is reading a small sort of handbill of anonymous poetry, rather wordily entitled:—

"ODE
ON THE INTIMATIONS
OF
DISTRUST IN MAN, [2]
UNWILLINGLY INFERRED FROM REPEATED REPULSES,
IN DISINTERESTED ENDEAVORS
TO PROCURE HIS
CONFIDENCE."

On the floor are many copies, looking as if fluttered down from a balloon. The way they came there was this: A some-what elderly person, in the quaker dress, had quietly passed through the cabin, and, much in the manner of those railway book-peddlers who precede their proffers of sale by a distribu-tion of puffs, direct or indirect, of the volumes to follow, had, without speaking, handed about the odes, which, for the most part, after a cursory glance, had been disrespectfully tossed

[1] See Chapter 1, note 14.
[2] Perhaps a rebuttal to Wordsworth's "Ode: Intimations of Immortality. . . ."

aside, as no doubt, the moonstruck production of some wandering rhapsodist.

In due time, book under arm, in trips the ruddy man with the traveling-cap, who, lightly moving to and fro, looks animatedly about him, with a yearning sort of gratulatory affinity and longing, expressive of the very soul of sociality; as much as to say, "Oh, boys, would that I were personally acquainted with each mother's son of you, since what a sweet world, to make sweet acquaintance in, is ours, my brothers; yea, and what dear, happy dogs are we all!"

And just as if he had really warbled it forth, he makes fraternally up to one lounging stranger or another, exchanging with him some pleasant remark.

"Pray, what have you there?" he asked of one newly accosted, a little, dried-up man, who looked as if he never dined.

"A little ode, rather queer, too," was the reply, "of the same sort you see strewn on the floor here."

"I did not observe them. Let me see;" picking one up and looking it over. "Well now, this is pretty; plaintive, especially the opening:—

> 'Alas for man, he hath small sense
> Of genial trust and confidence.'

—If it be so, alas for him, indeed. Runs off very smoothly, sir. Beautiful pathos. But do you think the sentiment just?"

"As to that," said the little dried-up man, "I think it a kind of queer thing altogether, and yet I am almost ashamed to add, it really has set me to thinking; yes and to feeling. Just now, somehow, I feel as it were trustful and genial. I don't know that ever I felt so much so before. I am naturally numb in my sensibilities; but this ode, in its way, works on my numbness not unlike a sermon, which, by lamenting over my lying dead in trespasses and sins, thereby stirs me up to be all alive in well-doing."

"Glad to hear it, and hope you will do well, as the doctors say. But who snowed the odes about here?"

"I cannot say; I have not been here long."

"Wasn't an angel, was it? Come, you say you feel genial, let us do as the rest, and have cards."

"Thank you, I never play cards."

"A bottle of wine?"

"Thank you, I never drink wine."

"Cigars?"

"Thank you, I never smoke cigars."

"Tell stories?"

"To speak truly, I hardly think I know one worth telling."

"Seems to me, then, this geniality you say you feel waked in you, is as water-power in a land without mills. Come, you had better take a genial hand at the cards. To begin, we will play for as small a sum as you please; just enough to make it interesting."

"Indeed, you must excuse me. Somehow I distrust cards."

"What, distrust cards? Genial cards? Then for once I join with our sad Philomel here:—

'Alas for man, he hath small sense
Of genial trust and confidence.'

Good-bye!"

Sauntering and chatting here and there, again, he with the book at length seems fatigued, looks round for a seat, and spying a partly-vacant settee drawn up against the side, drops down there; soon, like his chance neighbor, who happens to be the good merchant, becoming not a little interested in the scene more immediately before him; a party at whist; two cream-faced, giddy, unpolished youths, the one in a red cravat, the other in a green, opposed to two bland, grave, handsome, self-possessed men of middle age, decorously dressed in a sort of professional black, and apparently doctors of some eminence in the civil law.

By-and-by, after a preliminary scanning of the new comer next him the good merchant, sideways leaning over, whispers behind a crumpled copy of the Ode which he holds: "Sir, I don't like the looks of those two, do you?"

"Hardly," was the whispered reply; "those colored cravats are not in the best taste, at least not to mine; but my taste is no rule for all."

"You mistake; I mean the other two, and I don't refer to dress, but countenance. I confess I am not familiar with such gentry any further than reading about them in the papers—but those two are—are sharpers, aint they?"

"Far be from us the captious and fault-finding spirit, my dear sir."

"Indeed, sir, I would not find fault; I am little given that way; but certainly, to say the least, these two youths can hardly be adepts, while the opposed couple may be even more."

"You would not hint that the colored cravats would be so bungling as to lose, and the dark cravats so dextrous as to cheat?—Sour imaginations, my dear sir. Dismiss them. To little purpose have you read the Ode you have there. Years and experience, I trust, have not sophisticated you. A fresh and liberal construction would teach us to regard those four players—indeed, this whole cabin-full of players—as playing at games in which every player plays fair, and not a player but shall win."

"Now, you hardly mean that; because games in which all may win, such games remain as yet in this world uninvented, I think."

"Come, come," luxuriously laying himself back, and casting a free glance upon the players, "fares all paid; digestion sound; care, toil, penury, grief, unknown; lounging on this sofa, with waistband relaxed, why not be cheerfully resigned to one's fate, nor peevishly pick holes in the blessed fate of the world?"

Upon this, the good merchant, after staring long and hard, and then rubbing his forehead, fell into meditation, at first uneasy, but at last composed, and in the end, once more addressed his companion: "Well, I see it's good to out with one's private thoughts now and then. Somehow, I don't know why, a certain misty suspiciousness seems inseparable from most of one's private notions about some men and some things; but once out with these misty notions, and their mere contact with other men's soon dissipates, or, at least, modifies them."

"You think I have done you good, then? may be, I have. But don't thank me, don't thank me. If by words, casually delivered in the social hour, I do any good to right or left, it is but involuntary influence—locust-tree sweetening the herbage under it; [3] no merit at all; mere wholesome accident, of a wholesome nature.—Don't you see?"

Another stare from the good merchant, and both were silent again.

Finding his book, hitherto resting on his lap, rather irksome there, the owner now places it edgewise on the settee, between himself and neighbor; in so doing, chancing to expose the lettering on the back—"*Black Rapids Coal Company*"—which the good merchant, scrupulously honorable, had much ado to avoid reading, so directly would it have fallen under his eye, had he not conscientiously averted it. On a sudden, as if just reminded of something, the stranger starts up, and moves away, in his haste leaving his book; which the merchant observing, without delay takes it up, and, hurrying after, civilly returns it; in which act he could not avoid catching sight by an involuntary glance of part of the lettering.

"Thank you, thank you, my good sir," said the other, receiving the volume, and was resuming his retreat, when the merchant spoke: "Excuse me, but are you not in some way connected with the—the Coal Company I have heard of?"

"There is more than one Coal Company that may be heard of, my good sir," smiled the other, pausing with an expression of painful impatience, disinterestedly mastered.

"But you are connected with one in particular.—The 'Black Rapids,' are you not?"

"How did you find that out?"

[3] Cf. the tall gentleman of Chapter 7 who waves "the canopy of his goodness" like a "benign elm" over the man in gray, and the comparison of men and trees in the last paragraph of Chapter 2.

"Well, sir, I have heard rather tempting information of your Company."

"Who is your informant, pray," somewhat coldly.

"A—a person by the name of Ringman."

"Don't know him. But, doubtless, there are plenty who know our Company, whom our Company does not know; in the same way that one may know an individual, yet be unknown to him.—Known this Ringman long? Old friend, I suppose.—But pardon, I must leave you."

"Stay, sir, that—that stock."

"Stock?"

"Yes, it's a little irregular, perhaps, but—"

"Dear me, you don't think of doing any business with me, do you? In my official capacity I have not been authenticated to you. This transfer-book, now," holding it up so as to bring the lettering in sight, "how do you know that it may not be a bogus one? And I, being personally a stranger to you, how can you have confidence in me?"

"Because," knowingly smiled the good merchant, "if you were other than I have confidence that you are, hardly would you challenge distrust that way."

"But you have not examined my book."

"What need to, if already I believe that it is what it is lettered to be?"

"But you had better. It might suggest doubts."

"Doubts, may be, it might suggest, but not knowledge; for how, by examining the book, should I think I knew any more than I now think I do; since, if it be the true book, I think it so already; and since if it be otherwise, then I have never seen the true one, and don't know what that ought to look like."

"Your logic I will not criticize, but your confidence I admire, and earnestly, too, jocose as was the method I took to draw it out. Enough, we will go to yonder table, and if there be any business which, either in my private or official capacity, I can help you do, pray command me."

CHAPTER 11

Only a page or so.

The transaction concluded, the two still remained seated, falling into familiar conversation, by degrees verging into that confidential sort of sympathetic silence, the last refinement and luxury of unaffected good feeling. A kind of social superstition, to suppose that to be truly friendly one must be saying friendly words all the time, any more than be doing friendly deeds continually. True friendliness, like true religion, being in a sort independent of works.

At length, the good merchant, whose eyes were pensively resting upon the gay tables in the distance, broke the spell by saying that, from the spectacle before them, one would little divine what other quarters of the boat might reveal. He cited the case, accidentally encountered but an hour or two previous, of a shrunken old miser, clad in shrunken old moleskin, stretched out, an invalid, on a bare plank in the emigrants' quarters, eagerly clinging to life and lucre, though the one was gasping for outlet, and about the other he was in torment lest death, or some other unprincipled cut-purse should be the means of his losing it; by like feeble tenure holding lungs and pouch, and yet knowing and desiring nothing beyond them; for his mind, never raised above mould, was now all but mouldered away. To such a degree, indeed, that he had no trust in anything, not even in his parchment bonds, which, the better to preserve from the tooth of time, he had packed down and sealed up, like brandy peaches, in a tin case of spirits.

The worthy man proceeded at some length with these dispiriting particulars. Nor would his cheery companion wholly deny that there might be a point of view from which such a case of extreme want of confidence might, to the humane mind, present features not altogether welcome as wine and olives after dinner. Still, he was not without compensatory considerations, and, upon the whole, took his companion to task for evincing what, in a good-natured, round-about way, he hinted to be a somewhat jaundiced sentimentality. Nature, he added, in Shakespeare's words, had meal and bran;[1] and, rightly regarded, the bran in its way was not to be condemned.

The other was not disposed to question the justice of Shakespeare's thought, but would hardly admit the propriety of the application in this instance, much less of the comment. So, after some further temperate discussion of the pitiable miser, finding that they could not entirely harmonize, the merchant cited another case, that of the negro cripple. But his companion suggested whether the alleged hardships of that alleged unfortunate might not exist more in the pity of the observer than the experience of the observed. He knew nothing about the cripple, nor had seen him, but ventured to surmise that, could one but get at the real state of his heart, he would be found about as happy as most men, if not, in fact, full as happy as the speaker himself. He added that negroes were by nature a singularly cheerful race;[2] no one ever heard of a native-born

---

[1] In the midst of the many disguises of *Cymbeline*, shortly after Imogen has declared herself to be the boy "Fidele," Belarius, in a moment of insight, says:

> Cowards father cowards and base things sire base.
> Nature hath meal and bran, contempt and grace.   (IV,*ii*,26–27)

Because the good merchant knows not the full couplet, its speaker, nor its context, he immediately falls into confusion about the quotation. Chapter 30 explores the problems of finding Shakespeare's meanings in the words of his characters.

[2] Immediately after hinting that he himself may be Black Guinea, the President of the Black Rapids Coal Company makes the kind of racial generalization that blinds the naive American Captain Delano in *Benito Cereno* (Delano mistakes part of the Negroes' cruel restaging of the Spanish Inquisition for a display of their amusing love of bright colors). Compare this entire passage to the racial generalizations of Chapter 26.

African Zimmermann [3] or Torquemada; [4] that even from religion they dismissed all gloom; in their hilarious rituals they danced, so to speak, and, as it were, cut pigeon-wings. It was improbable, therefore, that a negro, however reduced to his stumps by fortune, could be ever thrown off the legs of a laughing philosophy. [5]

Foiled again, the good merchant would not desist, but ventured still a third case, that of the man with the weed, whose story, as narrated by himself, and confirmed and filled out by the testimony of a certain man in a gray coat, whom the merchant had afterwards met, he now proceeded to give; and that, without holding back those particulars disclosed by the second informant, but which delicacy had prevented the unfortunate man himself from touching upon.

But as the good merchant could, perhaps, do better justice to the man than the story, we shall venture to tell it in other words than his, though not to any other effect.

[3] Johann Georg, Ritter von Zimmermann (1728–1795), Swiss physician and ethical writer; his most famous work was *Über die Einsamkeit* (*On Solitude*), an exaltation of solitude. See Chapter 24, note 14.

[4] Tomas de Torquemada (1420–1498), inquisitor-general, organizer of the Spanish Inquisition, mass torturer, mass murderer.

[5] Democritus was called the Laughing Philosopher, in contrast to Heraclitus, the Weeping Philosopher (mentioned in Chapter 9).

CHAPTER 12

*Story of the unfortunate man, from which
may be gathered whether or no he has
been justly so entitled.*

It appeared that the unfortunate man had had for a wife one of
those natures, anomalously vicious, which would almost tempt
a metaphysical lover of our species to doubt whether the
human form be, in all cases, conclusive evidence of humanity,
whether, sometimes, it may not be a kind of unpledged and
indifferent tabernacle, and whether, once for all to crush the
saying of Thrasea, (an unaccountable one, considering that he
himself was so good a man) that "he who hates vice, hates
humanity," [1] it should not, in self-defense, be held for a reasonable maxim, that none but the good are human.

Goneril [2] was young, in person lithe and straight, too

[1] Publius Clodius Paetus Thrasea (d. A.D. 66), Roman senator and Stoic,
courageously stood up against Nero, who therefore had him slain. The
Annals of Tacitus ends abruptly in the description of his death, which
is prefaced by the famous: "After slaughtering so many distinguished
men, Nero at last sought to destroy Virtue herself by murdering
Thrasea Paetus . . . ." (See Chapter 5, note 2.) The source of Thrasea's
epigram is Pliny, Book VIII, Epistle 22: ". . . the great Thrasea used
frequently to say: 'He who hates vice, hates humanity' (*Qui vitia odit,
homines odit*)."

[2] Goneril is one of Lear's two perfidious and malevolent daughters in
Shakespeare's *King Lear*.

In "Melville's Goneril and Fanny Kemble" (*NEQ*, XVIII [December,
1945], 489–500), Egbert S. Oliver argues that Goneril is a caricature of
the famous actress Fanny Kemble, "the most widely discussed inter-
preter of Shakespeare's women of that generation" and participant in
one of the most widely discussed divorce cases of the century. Elizabeth

straight, indeed, for a woman, a complexion naturally rosy, and which would have been charmingly so, but for a certain hardness and bakedness, like that of the glazed colors on stoneware. Her hair was of a deep, rich chestnut, but worn in close, short curls all round her head. Her Indian figure was not without its impairing effect on her bust, while her mouth would have been pretty but for a trace of moustache. Upon the whole, aided by the resources of the toilet, her appearance at distance was such, that some might have thought her, if anything, rather beautiful, though of a style of beauty rather peculiar and cactus-like.

It was happy for Goneril that her more striking peculiarities were less of the person than of temper and taste. One hardly knows how to reveal, that, while having a natural antipathy to such things as the breast of chicken, or custard, or peach, or grape, Goneril could yet in private make a satisfactory lunch on hard crackers and brawn of ham. She liked lemons, and the only kind of candy she loved were little dried sticks of blue clay,[3] secretly carried in her pocket. Withal she had hard, steady health like a squaw's, with as firm a spirit and resolu-

---

Foster offers a rebuttal (pages 311–314). Whether or not Melville had Fanny Kemble in mind, one should recognize that Goneril, presented by a most ambiguous mixture of narrators, cannot simply be taken as Melville's view of the historical woman, nor, for that matter, the fictional woman.

[3] The list of passengers in Chapter 2 included "clay-eaters" (see note 15). Goneril may be a clay-eater in another sense, as explained in the article "Dirt-Eating" in *The American Magazine of Useful and Entertaining Knowledge*, II (May, 1836), 372: "Those affected with it [this singular disease] are listless and stupid, almost to idiocy, in reference to things in general, yet evince a very remarkable cunning, in satisfying their depraved appetites . . . the devouring of charcoal, chalk, dried mortar, mud, clay, sand, shells, . . . is merely a symptom of disease, and is just as involuntary as the shivering-fit of a fever. . . . The disease, when once seated, is incurable: The bodies of the patients become ulcerated; and death ensues. The only possible method of restraining a dirt-eater from his pernicious habit, is to confine his mouth in a metallic mask, secured by a lock."

tion. Some other points about her were likewise such as pertain
to the women of savage life. Lithe though she was, she loved
supineness, but upon occasion could endure like a stoic. She
was taciturn,[4] too. From early morning till about three o'clock
in the afternoon she would seldom speak—it taking that time to
thaw her, by all accounts, into but talking terms with humanity. During the interval she did little but look, and keep looking out of her large, metallic eyes, which her enemies called
cold as a cuttle-fish's, but which by her were esteemed gazelle-
like; for Goneril was not without vanity. Those who thought
they best knew her, often wondered what happiness such a
being could take in life, not considering the happiness which is
to be had by some natures in the very easy way of simply
causing pain to those around them. Those who suffered from
Goneril's strange nature, might, with one of those hyberboles
to which the resentful incline, have pronounced her some kind
of toad; but her worst slanderers could never, with any show
of justice, have accused her of being a toady. In a large sense
she possessed the virtue of independence of mind. Goneril held
it flattery to hint praise even of the absent, and even if mer-
ited; but honesty, to fling people's imputed faults into their
faces. This was thought malice, but it certainly was not passion. Passion is human. Like an icicle-dagger, Goneril at once
stabbed and froze; so at least they said; and when she saw
frankness and innocence tyrannized into sad nervousness under
her spell, according to the same authority, inly she chewed her
blue clay, and you could mark that she chuckled. These peculiarities were strange and unpleasing; but another was alleged,
one really incomprehensible. In company she had a strange
way of touching, as by accident, the arm or hand of comely
young men, and seemed to reap a secret delight from it, but
whether from the humane satisfaction of having given the evil-
touch,[5] as it is called, or whether it was something else in her,

[4] Note the relation between "stoic" and "taciturn." In Chapter 5 the
unfortunate man, allegedly Goneril's husband, had expressed his aversion
to Tacitus.

[5] An especially powerful form of the Evil Eye.

not equally wonderful, but quite as deplorable, remained an enigma.

Needless to say what distress was the unfortunate man's, when, engaged in conversation with company, he would suddenly perceive his Goneril bestowing her mysterious touches, especially in such cases where the strangeness of the thing seemed to strike upon the touched person, notwithstanding good-breeding forbade his proposing the mystery, on the spot, as a subject of discussion for the company. In these cases, too, the unfortunate man could never endure so much as to look upon the touched young gentleman afterwards, fearful of the mortification of meeting in his countenance some kind of more or less quizzingly-knowing expression. He would shudderingly shun the young gentleman. So that here, to the husband, Goneril's touch had the dread operation of the heathen taboo. Now Goneril brooked no chiding. So, at favorable times, he, in a wary manner, and not indelicately, would venture in private interviews gently to make distant allusions to this questionable propensity. She divined him. But, in her cold loveless way, said it was witless to be telling one's dreams, especially foolish ones; but if the unfortunate man liked connubially to rejoice his soul with such chimeras, much connubial joy might they give him. All this was sad—a touching case—but all might, perhaps, have been borne by the unfortunate man— conscientiously mindful of his vow—for better or for worse— to love and cherish his dear Goneril so long as kind heaven might spare her to him—but when, after all that had happened, the devil of jealousy entered her, a calm, clayey, cakey devil, for none other could possess her, and the object of that deranged jealousy, her own child, a little girl of seven, her father's consolation and pet; when he saw Goneril artfully torment the little innocent, and then play the maternal hypocrite with it, the unfortunate man's patient long-suffering gave way. Knowing that she would neither confess nor amend, and might, possibly, become even worse than she was, he thought it but duty as a father, to withdraw the child from her; but, loving it as he did, he could not do so without accompanying it into domestic exile himself.[6] Which, hard though it was, he did. Whereupon the whole female neighborhood, who till now had little enough admired dame Goneril, broke out in indignation against a husband, who, without assigning a cause, could deliberately abandon the wife of his bosom, and sharpen the sting to her, too, by depriving her of the solace of retaining her offspring. To all this, self-respect, with Christian charity towards Goneril, long kept the unfortunate man dumb. And well had it been had he continued so; for when, driven to desperation, he hinted something of the truth of the case, not a soul would credit it; while for Goneril, she pronounced all he said to be a malicious invention. Ere long, at the suggestion of some woman's-rights women, the injured wife began a suit, and, thanks to able counsel and accommodating testimony, succeeded in such a way, as not only to recover custody of the child, but to get such a settlement awarded upon a separation, as to make penniless the unfortunate man (so he averred), besides, through the legal sympathy she enlisted, effecting a judicial blasting of his private reputation. What made it yet more lamentable was, that the unfortunate man, thinking that, before the court, his wisest plan, as well as the most Christian besides, being, as he deemed, not at variance with the truth of the matter, would be to put forth the plea of the mental derangement of Goneril, which done, he could, with less of mortification to himself, and odium to her, reveal in self-defense those eccentricities which had led to his retirement from the joys of wedlock, had much ado in the end to prevent this charge of derangement from fatally recoiling upon himself —especially, when, among other things, he alleged her mysterious touchings. In vain did his counsel, striving to make out

[6] Coming as a result of Goneril's sexual jealousy, this exile with his daughter is certainly ambiguous. It also suggests King Lear's final moments with his faithful daughter Cordelia; like Lear, the unfortunate man is persecuted by Goneril and attracted only to a daughter who is "her father's consolation and pet." Another gloomy father traveling with his young daughter appears in Chapter 17.

the derangement to be where, in fact, if anywhere, it was, urge that, to hold otherwise, to hold that such a being as Goneril was sane, this was constructively a libel upon womankind. Libel be it.[7] And all ended by the unfortunate man's subsequently getting wind of Goneril's intention to procure him to be permanently committed for a lunatic. Upon which he fled, and was now an innocent outcast, wandering forlorn in the great valley of the Mississippi, with a weed on his hat for the loss of his Goneril; for he had lately seen by the papers that she was dead, and thought it but proper to comply with the prescribed form of mourning in such cases. For some days past he had been trying to get money enough to return to his child, and was but now started with inadequate funds.

Now all of this, from the beginning, the good merchant could not but consider rather hard for the unfortunate man.

[7] Compare these two sentences with the last sentence of the first paragraph of this chapter and with the unfortunate man's comment on Tacitus in Chapter 5: "But of course you read Tacitus in order to aid you in understanding human nature—as if truth was ever got at by libel." As a tale allegedly told by the unfortunate man and the man in gray, both evidently avatars of the Confidence Man, and repeated to a third avatar by the good merchant, who would "perhaps, do better justice to the man than the story," but narrated to us "in other words than his, though not to any other effect," the story of the unfortunate man poses the question: What kinds of truth does fiction present?

CHAPTER 13

*The man with the traveling-cap evinces much
humanity, and in a way which would seem
to show him to be one of the most
logical of optimists.*

Years ago, a grave American savan, being in London, observed
at an evening party there, a certain coxcombical fellow, as he
thought, an absurd ribbon in his lapel, and full of smart persi-
flage, whisking about to the admiration of as many as were
disposed to admire. Great was the savan's disdain; but, chancing ere long to find himself in a corner with the jackanapes,
got into conversation with him, when he was somewhat ill-
prepared for the good sense of the jackanapes, but was altogether thrown aback, upon subsequently being whispered by a
friend that the jackanapes was almost as great a savan as himself, being no less a personage than Sir Humphrey Davy.[1]

The above anecdote is given just here by way of an antici-
pative reminder to such readers as, from the kind of jaunty
levity, or what may have passed for such, hitherto for the most
part appearing in the man with the traveling-cap, may have
been tempted into a more or less hasty estimate of him; that
such readers, when they find the same person, as they presently will, capable of philosophic and humanitarian discourse
—no mere casual sentence or two as heretofore at times, but
solidly sustained throughout an almost entire sitting; that they
may not, like the American savan, be thereupon betrayed into

[1] Sir Humphry Davy (1778–1829), great English chemist, minor poet,
inventor of the safety lamp, friend of Scott, Southey, and Coleridge.
His deceptively boyish appearance and enthusiastic manner, together
with what Coleridge considered his foppishness, caused many incidents
similar to that described here, but I have been unable to discover one
involving a grave American savan.

any surprise incompatible with their own good opinion of their previous penetration.

The merchant's narration being ended, the other would not deny but that it did in some degree affect him. He hoped he was not without proper feeling for the unfortunate man. But he begged to know in what spirit he bore his alleged calamities. Did he despond or have confidence?

The merchant did not, perhaps, take the exact import of the last member of the question; but answered, that, if whether the unfortunate man was becomingly resigned under his affliction or no, was the point, he could say for him that resigned he was, and to an exemplary degree: for not only, so far as known, did he refrain from any one-sided reflections upon human goodness and human justice, but there was observable in him an air of chastened reliance, and at times tempered cheerfulness.

Upon which the other observed, that since the unfortunate man's alleged experience could not be deemed very conciliatory towards a view of human nature better than human nature was, it largely redounded to his fair-mindedness, as well as piety, that under the alleged dissuasives, apparently so, from philanthropy, he had not, in a moment of excitement, been warped over to the ranks of the misanthropes. He doubted not, also, that with such a man his experience would, in the end, act by a complete and beneficent inversion, and so far from shaking his confidence in his kind, confirm it, and rivet it. Which would the more surely be the case, did he (the unfortunate man) at last become satisfied (as sooner or later he probably would be) that in the distraction of his mind his Goneril had not in all respects had fair play. At all events, the description of the lady, charity could not but regard as more or less exaggerated, and so far unjust. The truth probably was that she was a wife with some blemishes mixed with some beauties. But when the blemishes were displayed, her husband, no adept in the female nature, had tried to use reason with her, instead of something far more persuasive. Hence his failure to convince and convert. The act of withdrawing from her, seemed, under the circumstances, abrupt. In brief, there were probably small faults on both sides, more than balanced by large virtues; and one should not be hasty in judging.

When the merchant, strange to say, opposed views so calm and impartial, and again, with some warmth, deplored the case of the unfortunate man, his companion, not without serious-ness, checked him, saying, that this would never do; that, though but in the most exceptional case, to admit the existence of unmerited misery, more particularly if alleged to have been brought about by unhindered arts of the wicked, such an ad-mission was, to say the least, not prudent; since, with some, it might unfavorably bias their most important persuasions. Not that those persuasions were legitimately servile to such influ-ences. Because, since the common occurrences of life could never, in the nature of things, steadily look one way and tell one story, as flags in the trade-wind; hence, if the conviction of a Providence, for instance, were in any way made depend-ent upon such variabilities as everyday events, the degree of that conviction would, in thinking minds, be subject to fluctu-ations akin to those of the stock-exchange during a long and uncertain war. Here he glanced aside at his transfer-book, and after a moment's pause continued. It was of the essence of a right conviction of the divine nature, as with a right convic-tion of the human, that, based less on experience than intui-tion, it rose above the zones of weather.

When now the merchant, with all his heart, coincided with this (as being a sensible, as well as religious person, he could not but do), his companion expressed satisfaction, that, in an age of some distrust on such subjects, he could yet meet with one who shared with him, almost to the full, so sound and sublime a confidence.

Still, he was far from the illiberality of denying that philos-ophy duly bounded was not permissible. Only he deemed it at least desirable that, when such a case as that alleged of the unfortunate man was made the subject of philosophic discus-sion, it should be so philosophized upon, as not to afford handles to those unblessed with the true light. For, but to grant that there was so much as a mystery about such a case, might by those persons be held for a tacit surrender of the question. And as for the apparent license temporarily permitted sometimes, to the bad over the good (as was by implication alleged with regard to Goneril and the unfortunate man), it might be injudicious there to lay too much polemic stress upon the doctrine of future retribution as the vindication of present impunity. For though, indeed, to the right-minded that doctrine was true, and of sufficient solace, yet with the perverse the polemic mention of it might but provoke the shallow, though mischievous conceit, that such a doctrine was but tantamount to the one which should affirm that Providence was not now, but was going to be. In short, with all sorts of cavilers, it was best, both for them and everybody, that whoever had the true light should stick behind the secure Malakoff [2] of confidence, nor be tempted forth to hazardous skirmishes on the open ground of reason. Therefore, he deemed it unadvisable in the good man, even in the privacy of his own mind, or in communion with a congenial one, to indulge in too much latitude of philosophizing, or, indeed, of compassionating, since this might beget an indiscreet habit of thinking and feeling which might unexpectedly betray him upon unsuitable occasions. Indeed, whether in private or public, there was nothing which a good man was more bound to guard himself against than, on some topics, the emotional unreserve of his natural heart; for, that the natural heart, in certain points, was not what it might be, men had been authoritatively admonished.

But he thought he might be getting dry.

The merchant, in his good-nature, thought otherwise, and said that he would be glad to refresh himself with such fruit all day. It was sitting under a ripe pulpit, and better such a seat than under a ripe peach-tree.[3]

[2] In 1855, during the Crimean War, the so-called impregnable fortress of Malakoff, one of the principal defenses of Sebastopol, had been overrun by the French, thus necessitating the evacuation of the city.

[3] See Chapter 10, note 3.

The other was pleased to find that he had not, as he feared, been prosing; but would rather not be considered in the formal light of a preacher; he preferred being still received in that of the equal and genial companion. To which end, throwing still more of sociability into his manner, he again reverted to the unfortunate man. Take the very worst view of that case; admit that his Goneril was, indeed, a Goneril; how fortunate to be at last rid of this Goneril, both by nature and by law? If he were acquainted with the unfortunate man, instead of condoling with him, he would congratulate him. Great good fortune had this unfortunate man. Lucky dog, he dared say, after all.

To which the merchant replied, that he earnestly hoped it might be so, and at any rate he tried his best to comfort himself with the persuasion that, if the unfortunate man was not happy in this world, he would, at least, be so in another.

His companion made no question of the unfortunate man's happiness in both worlds; and, presently calling for some champagne, invited the merchant to partake, upon the playful plea that, whatever notions other than felicitous ones he might associate with the unfortunate man, a little champagne would readily bubble away.

At intervals they slowly quaffed several glasses in silence and thoughtfulness. At last the merchant's expressive face flushed, his eye moistly beamed, his lips trembled with an imaginative and feminine sensibility. Without sending a single fume to his head, the wine seemed to shoot to his heart, and begin soothsaying there. "Ah," he cried, pushing his glass from him, "Ah, wine is good, and confidence is good; but can wine or confidence percolate down through all the stony strata of hard considerations, and drop warmly and ruddily into the cold cave of truth? Truth will *not* be comforted. Led by dear charity, lured by sweet hope, fond fancy essays this feat; but in vain; mere dreams and ideals, they explode in your hand, leaving naught but the scorching behind!"

"Why, why, why!" in amaze, at the burst; "bless me, if *In*

vino veritas [4] be a true saying, then, for all the fine confidence you professed with me, just now, distrust, deep distrust, underlies it; and ten thousand strong, like the Irish Rebellion,[5] breaks out in you now. That wine, good wine, should do it! Upon my soul," half seriously, half humorously, securing the bottle, "you shall drink no more of it. Wine was meant to gladden the heart, not grieve it; to heighten confidence, not depress it."

Sobered, shamed, all but confounded, by this raillery, the most telling rebuke under such circumstances, the merchant stared about him, and then, with altered mien, stammeringly confessed, that he was almost as much surprised as his companion, at what had escaped him. He did not understand it; was quite at a loss to account for such a rhapsody popping out of him unbidden. It could hardly be the champagne; he felt his brain unaffected; in fact, if anything, the wine had acted upon it something like white of egg in coffee, clarifying and brightening.

"Brightening? brightening it may be, but less like the white of egg in coffee, than like stove-lustre on a stove—black, brightening seriously, I repent calling for the champagne. To a temperament like yours, champagne is not to be recommended. Pray, my dear sir, do you feel quite yourself again? Confidence restored?"

"I hope so; I think I may say it is so. But we have had a long talk, and I think I must retire now."

So saying, the merchant rose, and making his adieus, left the table with the air of one, mortified at having been tempted by his own honest goodness, accidentally stimulated into making mad disclosures—to himself as to another—of the queer, unaccountable caprices of his natural heart.

[4] The kind of truth to be found in wine is one subject of Chapter 30.
[5] Probably the most recent of the many Irish rebellions since the sixteenth century, the "Young Ireland" rebellion of 1848.

CHAPTER 14

*Worth the consideration of those to whom
it may prove worth considering.* [1]

As the last chapter was begun with a reminder looking for-
wards, so the present must consist of one glancing backwards.

To some, it may raise a degree of surprise that one so full of
confidence, as the merchant has throughout shown himself, up
to the moment of his late sudden impulsiveness, should, in that
instance, have betrayed such a depth of discontent. He may be
thought inconsistent, and even so he is. But for this, is the
author to be blamed? True, it may be urged that there is
nothing a writer of fiction should more carefully see to, as
there is nothing a sensible reader will more carefully look for,
than that, in the depiction of any character, its consistency
should be preserved. But this, though at first blush, seeming
reasonable enough, may, upon a closer view, prove not so much
so. For how does it couple with another requirement—equally
insisted upon, perhaps—that while to all fiction is allowed some
play of invention, yet, fiction based on fact should never be
contradictory to it; and is it not a fact, that, in real life, a
consistent character is a *rara avis?* Which being so, the distaste
of readers to the contrary sort in books, can hardly arise from
any sense of their untrueness. It may rather be from perplexity
as to understanding them. But if the acutest sage be often at his
wits' ends to understand living character, shall those who are
not sages expect to run and read [2] character in those mere
phantoms which flit along a page, like shadows along a wall?

[1] The first of three chapters (the others are 33 and 44) in an authorial
voice (but not to be construed as nonfictional or unmasked) about the
nature of fiction.

[2] Habakkuk 2:2: "And the Lord answered me, and said, Write the
vision, and make it plain upon tables, that he may run that readeth it."

That fiction, where every character can, by reason of its consistency, be comprehended at a glance, either exhibits but sections of character, making them appear for wholes, or else is very untrue to reality; while, on the other hand, that author who draws a character, even though to common view incongruous in its parts, as the flying-squirrel, and, at different periods, as much at variance with itself as the butterfly is with the caterpillar from [3] which it changes, may yet, in so doing, be not false but faithful to facts.

If reason be judge, no writer has produced such inconsistent characters as nature herself has. It must call for no small sagacity in a reader unerringly to discriminate in a novel between the inconsistencies of conception and those of life as elsewhere. Experience is the only guide here; [4] but as no one man can be coextensive with *what is*, it may be unwise in every case to rest upon it. When the duck-billed beaver of Australia was first brought stuffed to England, the naturalists, appealing to their classifications, maintained that there was, in reality, no such creature; the bill in the specimen must needs be, in some way, artificially stuck on.[5]

[3] The first editions had "*into* which it changes," clearly an error caused by the heavily revised manuscript.

The metaphor of caterpillar and butterfly, introduced in Chapter 8, becomes essential to the masquerade. In Chapter 22 the man from the Philosophical Intelligence Office argues that one should not "visit upon the butterfly the sins of the caterpillar," but his cynical interlocuter retorts that the butterfly is an impostor, "a caterpillar in a gaudy cloak." The gaudy-colored Cosmopolitan may be the butterfly into which the caterpillar of the first half of the book metamorphoses.

[4] See Chapter 9: " 'Experience, sir,' originally observed the sophomore, 'is the only teacher.' "

[5] The western career of the *Ornithorhyncus Paradoxus* or *Anatinus*, the platypus, began with scientists believing that the specimens were products of the notorious oriental taxidermists who artfully stitched together "mermaids" and other creatures for sale to ignorant mariners. By 1842, P. T. Barnum was advertising the platypus as "the connecting link between the seal and the duck . . . in the great chain of Animated Nature."

But let nature, to the perplexity of the naturalists, produce her duck-billed beavers as she may, lesser authors, some may hold, have no business to be perplexing readers with duck-billed characters. Always, they should represent human nature not in obscurity, but transparency, which, indeed, is the practice with most novelists, and is, perhaps, in certain cases someway felt to be a kind of honor rendered by them to their kind. But whether it involve honor or otherwise might be mooted, considering that, if these waters of human nature can be readily seen through, it may be either that they are very pure or very shallow. Upon the whole, it might rather be thought, that he, who, in view of its inconsistencies, says of human nature the same that, in view of its contrasts, is said of the divine nature, that it is past finding out, thereby evinces a better appreciation of it than he who, by always representing it in a clear light, leaves it to be inferred that he clearly knows all about it.[6]

But though there is a prejudice against inconsistent characters in books, yet the prejudice bears the other way, when what seemed at first their inconsistency, afterwards, by the skill of the writer, turns out to be their good keeping. The great masters excel in nothing so much as in this very particular. They challenge astonishment at the tangled web of some character, and then raise admiration still greater at their satisfactory unraveling of it; in this way throwing open, sometimes to the understanding even of school misses, the last complications of that spirit which is affirmed by its Creator to be fearfully and wonderfully made.[7]

At least, something like this is claimed for certain psycho-

[6] Compare the message of the man with the book in the preceding chapter: "It was of the essence of a right conviction of the divine nature, as with a right conviction of the human, that, based less on experience than intuition, it rose above the zones of weather."

[7] Psalms 139:14: "I will praise thee; for I am fearfully and wonderfully made: marvellous are thy works; and that my soul knoweth right well."

logical novelists; nor will the claim be here disputed. Yet, as touching this point, it may prove suggestive, that all those sallies of ingenuity, having for their end the revelation of human nature on fixed principles, have, by the best judges, been excluded with contempt from the ranks of the sciences—palmistry, physiognomy, phrenology, psychology. Likewise, the fact, that in all ages such conflicting views have, by the most eminent minds, been taken of mankind, would, as with other topics, seem some presumption of a pretty general and pretty thorough ignorance of it. Which may appear the less improbable if it be considered that, after poring over the best novels professing to portray human nature, the studious youth will still run risk of being too often at fault upon actually entering the world; whereas, had he been furnished with a true delineation, it ought to fare with him something as with a stranger entering, map in hand, Boston town; the streets may be very crooked, he may often pause; but, thanks to his true map, he does not hopelessly lose his way. Nor, to this comparison, can it be an adequate objection, that the twistings of the town are always the same, and those of human nature subject to variation. The grand points of human nature are the same to-day they were a thousand years ago. The only variability in them is in expression, not in feature.

But as, in spite of seeming discouragement, some mathematicians are yet in hopes of hitting upon an exact method of determining the longitude, the more earnest psychologists may, in the face of previous failures, still cherish expectations with regard to some mode of infallibly discovering the heart of man.

But enough has been said by way of apology for whatever may have seemed amiss or obscure in the character of the merchant; so nothing remains but to turn to our comedy, or, rather, to pass from the comedy of thought to that of action.

CHAPTER 15

*An old miser, upon suitable representations, is
prevailed upon to venture an investment.*

The merchant having withdrawn, the other remained seated
alone for a time, with the air of one who, after having conversed with some excellent man, carefully ponders what fell
from him, however intellectually inferior it may be, that none
of the profit may be lost; happy if from any honest word he
has heard he can derive some hint, which, besides confirming
him in the theory of virtue, may, likewise, serve for a finger-
post to virtuous action.

Ere long his eye brightened, as if some such hint was now
caught. He rises, book in hand, quits the cabin, and enters upon a
sort of corridor, narrow and dim, a by-way to a retreat less ornate and cheery than the former; in short, the emigrants' quarters; but which, owing to the present trip being a down-river
one, will doubtless be found comparatively tenantless. Owing to
obstructions against the side windows, the whole place is dim
and dusky; very much so, for the most part; yet, by starts,
haggardly lit here and there by narrow, capricious sky-lights
in the cornices. But there would seem no special need for
light, the place being designed more to pass the night in, than
the day; in brief, a pine barrens [1] dormitory, of knotty pine
bunks, without bedding. As with the nests in the geometrical
towns of the associate penguin and pelican,[2] these bunks were

[1] A semi-desert, sparsely covered with pine trees.

[2] Freaks of nature to be compared with the "duck-billed beaver" of
the preceding chapter. In *The Encantadas*, Melville describes these birds
together, calling the penguin "the most ambiguous and least lovely
creature," "truly neither fish, flesh, nor fowl," and the pelican a "strange
fowl."

disposed with Philadelphia regularity,[3] but, like the cradle of the oriole, they were pendulous, and, moreover, were, so to speak, three-story cradles; the description of one of which will suffice for all.

Four ropes, secured to the ceiling, passed downwards through auger-holes bored in the corners of three rough planks, which at equal distances rested on knots vertically tied in the ropes, the lowermost plank but an inch or two from the floor, the whole affair resembling, on a large scale, rope book-shelves; only, instead of hanging firmly against a wall, they swayed to and fro at the least suggestion of motion, but were more especially lively upon the provocation of a green emigrant sprawling into one, and trying to lay himself out there, when the cradling would be such as almost to toss him back whence he came. In consequence, one less inexperienced, essaying repose on the uppermost shelf, was liable to serious disturbance, should a raw beginner select a shelf beneath. Sometimes a throng of poor emigrants, coming at night in a sudden rain to occupy these oriole nests, would—through ignorance of their peculiarity—bring about such a rocking uproar of carpentry, joining to it such an uproar of exclamations, that it seemed as if some luckless ship, with all its crew, was being dashed to pieces among the rocks. They were beds devised by some sardonic foe of poor travelers, to deprive them of that tranquillity which should precede, as well as accompany, slumber.—Procrustean beds,[4] on whose hard grain humble worth and honesty writhed, still invoking

[3] The streets of Philadelphia were noted for their right-angled meetings.

[4] Procrustes ("the stretcher"), a legendary Attic robber slain by Theseus, had a bed upon which he tortured his prisoners: those who were too short were stretched to fit the bed; those who were too long had their legs cut off to fit. Compare these Procrustean beds to the Protean easy-chair of Chapter 7, and note that in Chapter 1 the barber appears "rather crusty-looking for the moment, it may be from being newly out of bed."

repose, while but torment responded. Ah, did any one make such a bunk for himself, instead of having it made for him, it might be just, but how cruel, to say, You must lie on it!

But, purgatory as the place would appear, the stranger advances into it; and, like Orpheus in his gay descent to Tartarus,[5] lightly hums to himself an opera snatch.

Suddenly there is a rustling, then a creaking, one of the cradles swings out from a murky nook, a sort of wasted penguin-flipper is supplicatingly put forth, while a wail like that of Dives [6] is heard:—"Water, water!"

It was the miser of whom the merchant had spoken.

Swift as a sister-of-charity, the stranger hovers over him:—

"My poor, poor sir, what can I do for you?"

"Ugh, ugh [7]—water!"

Darting out, he procures a glass, returns, and, holding it to the sufferer's lips, supports his head while he drinks: "And did they let you lie here, my poor sir, racked with this parching thirst?"

The miser, a lean old man, whose flesh seemed salted codfish, dry as combustibles; head, like one whittled by an idiot

[5] Grief-stricken by the death of his wife Eurydice, Orpheus descended into the underworld to recover or join her. His lyre and love so charmed Pluto and Proserpina that they released Eurydice on the condition that Orpheus not look back upon her until she was back in the world of the living. On the verge of escape, he looked back in devotion and she was lost forever.

Orpheus was considered by some of the ancient authorities to be the son of Apollo and regarded by most as a savior figure who helped to civilize primitive man.

[6] Luke 16:19-31 relates the parable of the beggar Lazarus, who goes to heaven, and "a certain rich man" (Latin *dives*), who cries out from the flames of hell for Lazarus to come and "dip the tip of his finger in water, and cool my tongue." The list of passengers in Chapter 2 had included "Dives and Lazarus," and Lazarus had been mentioned in Chapter 9.

[7] This old man, whose words are interspersed with "ugh, ugh" and "how, how," in Chapter 21 is likened to a savage.

out of a knot; flat, bony mouth, nipped between buzzard nose and chin; expression, flitting between hunks and imbecile—now one, now the other—he made no response. His eyes were closed, his cheek lay upon an old white moleskin coat, rolled under his head like a wizened apple upon a grimy snow-bank.

Revived at last, he inclined towards his ministrant, and, in a voice disastrous with a cough, said:—"I am old and miserable, a poor beggar, not worth a shoe-string—how can I repay you?"

"By giving me your confidence."

"Confidence!" he squeaked, with changed manner, while the pallet swung, "little left at my age, but take the stale remains, and welcome."

"Such as it is, though, you give it. Very good. Now give me a hundred dollars."

Upon this the miser was all panic. His hands groped towards his waist, then suddenly flew upward beneath his moleskin pillow, and there lay clutching something out of sight. Meantime, to himself he incoherently mumbled:—"Confidence? Cant, gammon! Confidence? hum, bubble!—Confidence? fetch, gouge! [8]—Hundred dollars?—hundred devils?"

Half spent, he lay mute awhile, then feebly raising himself, in a voice for the moment made strong by the sarcasm, said, "A hundred dollars? rather high price to put upon confidence. But don't you see I am a poor, old rat here, dying in the wainscot? You have served me; but, wretch that I am, I can but cough you my thanks,—ugh, ugh, ugh!"

This time his cough was so violent that its convulsions were imparted to the plank, which swung him about like a stone in a sling preparatory to its being hurled.

"Ugh, ugh, ugh!"

"What a shocking cough. I wish, my friend, the herb-doctor

[8] The miser uses rogues' cant to accuse the man with the big book of using rogues' cant. In this underworld language, "gammon" means "nonsense," "a ridiculous deceitful story"; "bubble" means "cheat," "swindle"; "fetch" means "steal," "gouge," "swindle."

was here now; a box of his Omni-Balsamic Reinvigorator would do you good."

"Ugh, ugh, ugh!"

"I've a good mind to go find him. He's aboard somewhere. I saw his long, snuff-colored surtout. Trust me, his medicines are the best in the world."

"Ugh, ugh, ugh!"

"Oh, how sorry I am."

"No doubt of it," squeaked the other again, "but go, get your charity out on deck. There parade the pursy peacocks; they don't cough down here in desertion and darkness, like poor old me. Look how scaly a pauper I am, clove with this churchyard cough. Ugh, ugh, ugh!"

"Again, how sorry I feel, not only for your cough, but your poverty. Such a rare chance made unavailable. Did you have but the sum named, how I could invest it for you. Treble profits. But confidence—I fear that, even had you the precious cash, you would not have the more precious confidence I speak of."

"Ugh, ugh, ugh!" flightily raising himself. "What's that? How, how? Then you don't want the money for yourself?"

"My dear, *dear* sir, how could you impute me to such preposterous self-seeking? To solicit out of hand, for my private behoof, an hundred dollars from a perfect stranger? I am not mad, my dear sir."

"How, how?" still more bewildered, "do you, then, go about the world, gratis, seeking to invest people's money for them?"

"My humble profession, sir. I live not for myself; but the world will not have confidence in me, and yet confidence in me were great gain."

"But, but," in a kind of vertigo, "what do—do you do—do with people's money? Ugh, ugh! How is the gain made?"

"To tell that would ruin me. That known, everyone would be going into the business, and it would be overdone. A secret, a mystery—all I have to do with you is to receive your confidence, and all you have to do with me is, in due time, to receive it back, thrice paid in trebling profits."

"What, what?" imbecility in the ascendant once more; "but the vouchers, the vouchers," suddenly hunkish again.

"Honesty's best voucher is honesty's face."

"Can't see yours, though," peering through the obscurity.

From this last alternating flicker of rationality, the miser fell back, sputtering, into his previous gibberish, but it took now an arithmetical turn. Eyes closed, he lay muttering to himself—

"One hundred, one hundred—two hundred, two hundred—three hundred, three hundred."

He opened his eyes, feebly stared, and still more feebly said—

"It's a little dim here, ain't it? Ugh, ugh! But, as well as my poor old eyes can see, you look honest."

"I am glad to hear that."

"If—if, now, I should put"—trying to raise himself, but vainly, excitement having all but exhausted him—"if, if now, I should put, put—"

"No ifs. Downright confidence, or none. So help me heaven, I will have no half-confidences."

He said it with an indifferent and superior air, and seemed moving to go.

"Don't, don't leave me, friend; bear with me; age can't help some distrust; it can't, friend, it can't. Ugh, ugh, ugh! Oh, I am so old and miserable. I ought to have a guardeean. Tell me, if—"

"If? No more!"

"Stay! how soon—ugh, ugh!—would my money be trebled? How soon, friend?"

"You won't confide. Good-bye!"

"Stay, stay," falling back now like an infant, "I confide, I confide; help, friend, my distrust!" [9]

From an old buckskin pouch, tremulously dragged forth,

---

[9] In Mark 9, Christ casts a deaf and dumb spirit out of a child whose father says, "Lord, I believe; help thou mine unbelief."

ten hoarded eagles, tarnished into the appearance of ten old horn-buttons, were taken, and half-eagerly, half-reluctantly, offered.

"I know not whether I should accept this slack confidence," said the other coldly, receiving the gold, "but an eleventh-hour confidence, a sick-bed confidence, a distempered, death-bed confidence, after all. Give me the healthy confidence of healthy men, with their healthy wits about them. But let that pass. All right. Good-bye!"

"Nay, back, back—receipt, my receipt! Ugh, ugh, ugh! Who are you? What have I done? Where go you? My gold, my gold! Ugh, ugh, ugh!"

But, unluckily for this final flicker of reason,[10] the stranger was now beyond ear-shot, nor was any one else within hearing of so feeble a call.

[10] May refer to either "My gold, my gold!" or "Ugh, ugh, ugh!"

CHAPTER 16

*A sick man, after some impatience, is induced
to become a patient.*

The sky slides into blue, the bluffs into bloom; the rapid Mississippi expands; runs sparkling and gurgling, all over in eddies; one magnified wake of a seventy-four.[1] The sun comes out, a golden huzzar,[2] from his tent, flashing his helm on the world. All things, warmed in the landscape, leap. Speeds the daedal[3] boat as a dream.

But, withdrawn in a corner, wrapped about in a shawl, sits an unparticipating man, visited, but not warmed, by the sun— a plant whose hour seems over, while buds are blowing and seeds are astir. On a stool at his left sits a stranger in a snuff-colored surtout,[4] the collar thrown back; his hand waving in

[1] A seventy-four-gun warship.

[2] Here the sun itself fits Black Guinea's listing of "a ge'mman as is a sodjer." Compare the "Poor wounded huzzar!" of Chapter 18.

[3] "Displaying artistic cunning or fertility of invention; maze-like" (*NED*). From Daedalus ("skillful"), the fabulous Athenian artificer who made the Cretan labyrinth and all kinds of ingenious devices; he was regarded as the personification of all handicrafts and art. Melville's boat would seem to be "daedal" in many senses.

[4] A snuff-colored surtout (literally "above-all") is appropriate attire for this stranger who arrives with the sun and claims to represent the revivifying powers of nature. In *Redburn* (1849), Melville had described a strikingly similar person in the character of an English Chartist (a radical populist reformer):

> Addressing this orderly throng was a pale, hollow-eyed young man, in a snuff-colored surtout, who looked worn with much watching, or much toil, or too little food. His features were good, his whole air was respectable, and there was no mistaking the fact, that he was strongly in earnest in what he was saying.
> In his hand was a soiled, inflammatory-looking pamphlet, from

persuasive gesture, his eye beaming with hope. But not easily may hope be awakened in one long tranced into hopelessness by a chronic complaint.

To some remark the sick man, by word or look, seemed to have just made an impatiently querulous answer, when, with a deprecatory air, the other resumed:

"Nay, think not I seek to cry up my treatment by crying down that of others. And yet, when one is confident he has truth on his side, and that it is not on the other, it is no very easy thing to be charitable; not that temper is the bar, but conscience; for charity would beget toleration, you know, which is a kind of implied permitting, and in effect a kind of countenancing; and that which is countenanced is so far furthered. But should untruth be furthered? Still, while for the world's good I refuse to further the cause of these mineral doctors,[5] I would fain regard them, not as willful wrong-doers, but good Samaritans erring.[6] And is this—I put it to you, sir—is this the view of an arrogant rival and pretender?"

His physical power all dribbled and gone, the sick man replied not by voice or by gesture; but, with feeble dumb-show of his face, seemed to be saying "Pray leave me; who was ever cured by talk?"

But the other, as if not unused to make allowances for such despondency, proceeded; and kindly, yet firmly:

"You tell me, that by advice of an eminent physiologist in Louisville, you took tincture of iron. For what? To restore

---

which he frequently read; following up the quotations with nervous appeals to his hearers, a rolling of his eyes, and sometimes the most frantic gestures.

[5] For centuries disputes had raged between those favoring vegetable cures and those favoring mineral cures. In Chapter 21 the argument of a mineral doctor is presented.

[6] Luke 10:30–35 describes the good man from Samaria who succors a man attacked by thieves, left "half-dead," and ignored by passersby. Cf. the reference in Chapter 39 to "the good Samaritan pouring out at need the purse as the vial!"

your lost energy. And how? Why, in healthy subjects iron is
naturally found in the blood, and iron in the bar is strong;
ergo, iron is the source of animal invigoration. But you being
deficient in vigor, it follows that the cause is deficiency of
iron. Iron, then, must be put into you; and so your tincture.
Now as to the theory here, I am mute. But in modesty assuming its truth, and then, as a plain man viewing that theory in
practice, I would respectfully question your eminent physiologist: 'Sir,' I would say, 'though by natural processes, lifeless
natures taken as nutriment become vitalized, yet is a lifeless
nature, under any circumstances, capable of a living transmis-
sion, with all its qualities as a lifeless nature unchanged? If, sir,
nothing can be incorporated with the living body but by as-
similation, and if that implies the conversion of one thing to a
different thing (as, in a lamp, oil is assimilated into flame), is it,
in this view, likely, that by banqueting on fat, Calvin Edson [7]
will fatten? That is, will what is fat on the board prove fat on
the bones? If it will, then, sir, what is iron in the vial will
prove iron in the vein.' Seems that conclusion too confident?"

But the sick man again turned his dumb-show look, as much
as to say, "Pray leave me. Why, with painful words, hint the
vanity of that which the pains of this body have too painfully
proved?"

But the other, as if unobservant of that querulous look, went
on:

"But this notion, that science can play farmer to the flesh,
making there what living soil it pleases, seems not so strange as
that other conceit—that science is now-a-days so expert that,
in consumptive cases, as yours, it can, by prescription of the
inhalation of certain vapors, achieve the sublimest act of omni-
potence, breathing into all but lifeless dust the breath of life.
For did you not tell me, my poor sir, that by order of the
great chemist in Baltimore,[8] for three weeks you were never

[7] A "living skelton" who was displayed (along with the "duck-billed
beaver" of Chapter 14) at P. T. Barnum's American Museum.
[8] Unidentified.

driven out without a respirator, and for a given time of every day sat bolstered up in a sort of gasometer, inspiring vapors generated by the burning of drugs? as if this concocted atmosphere of man were an antidote to the poison of God's natural air. Oh, who can wonder at that old reproach against science, that it is atheistical? And here is my prime reason for opposing these chemical practitioners, who have sought out so many inventions. For what do their inventions indicate, unless it be that kind and degree of pride in human skill, which seems scarce compatible with reverential dependence upon the power above? Try to rid my mind of it as I may, yet still these chemical practitioners with their tinctures, and fumes, and braziers, and occult incantations, seem to me like Pharaoh's vain sorcerers, trying to beat down the will of heaven.[9] Day and night, in all charity, I intercede for them, that heaven may not, in its own language, be provoked to anger with their inventions; may not take vengeance of their inventions.[10] A thousand pities that you should ever have been in the hands of these Egyptians."

But again came nothing but the dumb-show look, as much as to say, "Pray leave me; quacks, and indignation against quacks, both are vain."

But, once more, the other went on: "How different we herb-doctors! who claim nothing, invent nothing; but staff in hand, in glades, and upon hillsides, go about in nature, humbly seeking her cures. True Indian doctors, though not learned in names, we are not unfamiliar with essences—successors of Solomon the Wise, who knew all vegetables, from the cedar of

[9] Exodus 7–9 describes the efforts of Pharaoh's magicians to match the magic of Moses and Aaron, which calls down plague after plague on all of Egypt save for the land of Goshen (see Chapter 24, note 10). When Pharaoh's "magicians could not stand before Moses because of the boils" upon them (Exodus 9:11), they stand defeated by the will of heaven.

[10] Psalm 106:29 describes the consequences of the rebellion in the wilderness: "Thus they provoked him to anger with their inventions: and the plague brake in upon them."

Lebanon, to the hyssop on the wall.[11] Yes, Solomon was the first of herb-doctors. Nor were the virtues of herbs unhonored by yet older ages. Is it not writ, that on a moonlight night,

> "Medea gathered the enchanted herbs
> That did renew old Æson?" [12]

Ah, would you but have confidence, you should be the new Æson, and I your Medea.[13] A few vials of my Omni-Balsamic Reinvigorator would, I am certain, give you some strength."

Upon this, indignation and abhorrence seemed to work by their excess the effect promised of the balsam. Roused from that long apathy of impotence, the cadaverous man started,

[11] I Kings 4:33 tells how Solomon "spake of trees, from the cedar tree that is in Lebanon even unto the hyssop that springeth out of the wall." In Chapter 39 Egbert asserts that he is not of the sour mind of Solomon, but in Chapter 40 the story he tells exemplifies "The truth of scripture, as found in the sober philosophy of Solomon the wise."

[12] *The Merchant of Venice*, V, *i*, 12–16:

> JESSICA.   In such a night
> Medea gathered the enchanted herbs
> That did renew old Æson.
> LORENZO.   In such a night
> Did Jessica steal from the wealthy Jew,
> And with an unthrift love did run from Venice. . . .

[13] The mythical sorceress Medea, daughter of the King of Colchis, with her magic arts helped Jason to get the Golden Fleece and then fled with him to Corinth. Years later, abandoned by Jason for a daughter of Creon, Medea murdered her rival and her own two sons by Jason. She then fled to Athens, where she had a son, Medus, by Ægeus, the father of Theseus. She tried to murder Theseus, was detected, and fled back to Colchis.

According to most sources, Æson, father of Jason, had committed suicide before Medea ever arrived in Corinth. But Ovid disagrees, and in Book VII of the *Metamorphoses* tells the story used by Shakespeare and Melville, the rejuvenation of Æson by Medea. Medea slits Æson's wrinkled throat, drains his blood, and replaces it with a witches' brew that makes him young again. She then tricks the daughters of Pelias, stepbrother of Æson, into slitting their father's throat under the false belief that she will rejuvenate him too.

and, in a voice that was as the sound of obstructed air gurgling through a maze of broken honey-combs, cried: "Begone! You are all alike. The name of doctor, the dream of helper, condemns you. For years I have been but a gallipot for you experimentizers to rinse your experiments into, and now, in this livid skin, partake of the nature of my contents. Begone! I hate ye."

"I were inhuman, could I take affront at a want of confidence, born of too bitter an experience of betrayers. Yet, permit one who is not without feeling—"

"Begone! Just in that voice talked to me, not six months ago, the German doctor at the water cure, from which I now return six months and sixty pangs nigher my grave."

"The water-cure? Oh, fatal delusion of the well-meaning Preisnitz! [14]—Sir, trust me—"

"Begone!"

"Nay, an invalid should not always have his own way. Ah, sir, reflect how untimely this distrust in one like you. How weak you are; and weakness, is it not the time for confidence? Yes, when through weakness everything bids despair, then is the time to get strength by confidence." [15]

Relenting in his air, the sick man cast upon him a long glance of beseeching, as if saying, "With confidence must come hope; and how can hope be?"

The herb-doctor took a sealed paper box from his surtout pocket, and holding it towards him, said solemnly, "Turn not away. This may be the last time of health's asking. Work upon yourself; invoke confidence, though from ashes; rouse it; for your life, rouse it, and invoke it, I say."

[14] Vincenz Preissnitz (1799–1851), Silesian operator of a center for water cures, author of a book explaining and defending his practice. According to *Nature in Disease* (note 16), "Preissnitz, the prince of modern empirics, himself a robust peasant, died of premature disease at the age of fifty-two, in the midst of his own water-cure."

[15] Cf. Isaiah 30:15: ". . . in quietness and in confidence shall be your strength."

The other trembled, was silent; and then, a little command-ing himself, asked the ingredients of the medicine.

"Herbs."

"What herbs? And the nature of them? And the reason for giving them?"

"It cannot be made known."

"Then I will none of you."

Sedately observant of the juiceless, joyless form before him, the herb-doctor was mute a moment, then said:—"I give up."

"How?"

"You are sick, and a philosopher."

"No, no;—not the last."

"But, to demand the ingredient, with the reason for giving, is the mark of a philosopher; just as the consequence is the penalty of a fool. A sick philosopher is incurable."

"Why?"

"Because he has no confidence."

"How does that make him incurable?"

"Because either he spurns his powder, or, if he take it, it proves a blank cartridge, though the same given to a rustic in like extremity, would act like a charm. I am no materialist; but the mind so acts upon the body, that if the one have no confi-dence, neither has the other."

Again, the sick man appeared not unmoved. He seemed to be thinking what in candid truth could be said to all this. At length, "You talk of confidence. How comes it that when brought low himself, the herb-doctor, who was most confident to prescribe in other cases, proves least confident to prescribe in his own; having small confidence in himself for himself?"

"But he has confidence in the brother he calls in. And that he does so, is no reproach to him, since he knows that when the body is prostrated, the mind is not erect. Yes, in this hour the herb-doctor does distrust himself, but not his art."

The sick man's knowledge did not warrant him to gainsay

this. But he seemed not grieved at it; glad to be confuted in a way tending towards his wish.

"Then you give me hope?" his sunken eye turned up.

"Hope is proportioned to confidence. How much confidence you give me, so much hope do I give you. For this," lifting the box, "if all depended upon this, I should rest. It is nature's own."

"Nature!"

"Why do you start?"

"I know not," with a sort of shudder, "but I have heard of a book entitled 'Nature in Disease.' "[16]

"A title I cannot approve; it is suspiciously scientific. 'Nature in Disease?' As if nature, divine nature, were aught but health; as if through nature disease is decreed! But did I not before hint of the tendency of science, that forbidden tree? Sir, if despondency is yours from recalling that title, dismiss it. Trust me, nature is health; for health is good, and nature cannot work ill. As little can she work error. Get nature, and you get well. Now, I repeat, this medicine is nature's own."

Again the sick man could not, according to his light, conscientiously disprove what was said. Neither, as before, did he seem over-anxious to do so; the less, as in his sensitiveness it seemed to him, that hardly could he offer so to do without something like the appearance of a kind of implied irreligion; nor in his heart was he ungrateful, that since a spirit opposite to that pervaded all the herb-doctor's hopeful words, therefore, for hopefulness, he (the sick man) had not alone medical warrant, but also doctrinal.

"Then you do really think," hectically, "that if I take this medicine," mechanically reaching out for it, "I shall regain my health?"

"I will not encourage false hopes," relinquishing to him the

[16] Jacob Bigelow, M.D., *Nature in Disease* (Boston, 1854), a collection of essays on various diseases and medical subjects including quackery, homeopathy, and the history of medicine. The title refers to a thesis in a number of the essays that some diseases cure themselves and should not be treated. Dr. Bigelow does not seem to be aware of the ambiguity in the title.

box, "I will be frank with you.[17] Though frankness is not always the weakness of the mineral practitioner, yet the herb doctor must be frank, or nothing. Now then, sir, in your case, a radical cure [18]—such a cure, understand, as should make you robust—such a cure, sir, I do not and cannot promise."

"Oh, you need not! only restore me the power of being something else to others than a burdensome care, and to myself a droning grief. Only cure me of this misery of weakness; only make me so that I can walk about in the sun and not draw the flies to me, as lured by the coming of decay. Only do that—but that."

"You ask not much; you are wise; not in vain have you suffered. That little you ask, I think, can be granted. But remember, not in a day, nor a week, nor perhaps a month, but sooner or later; I say not exactly when, for I am neither prophet nor charlatan. Still, if, according to the directions in your box there, you take my medicine steadily, without assigning an especial day, near or remote, to discontinue it, then may you calmly look for some eventual result of good. But again I say, you must have confidence."

Feverishly he replied that he now trusted he had, and hourly should pray for its increase. When suddenly relapsing into one of those strange caprices peculiar to some invalids, he added: "But to one like me, it is so hard, so hard. The most confident hopes so often have failed me, and as often have I vowed never, no, never, to trust them again. Oh," feebly wringing his hands, "you do not know, you do not know."

"I know this, that never did a right confidence come to naught. But time is short; you hold your cure, to retain or reject."

"I retain," with a clinch, "and now how much?"

"As much as you can evoke from your heart and heaven."

"How?—the price of this medicine?"

---

[17] Perhaps a foreshadowing of Frank Goodman, the Cosmopolitan.

[18] With a play on the literal meaning of "radical" ("of" or "to the root"); in this chapter the sick man was first described as "a plant whose hour seems over."

"I thought it was confidence you meant; how much confidence you should have. The medicine,—that is half a dollar a vial. Your box holds six."

The money was paid.

"Now, sir," said the herb-doctor, "my business calls me away, and it may so be that I shall never see you again; if then—"

He paused, for the sick man's countenance fell blank.

"Forgive me," cried the other, "forgive that imprudent phrase 'never see you again.' Though I solely intended it with reference to myself, yet I had forgotten what your sensitiveness might be. I repeat, then, that it may be that we shall not soon have a second interview, so that hereafter, should another of my boxes be needed, you may not be able to replace it except by purchase at the shops; and, in so doing, you may run more or less risk of taking some not salutary mixture. For such is the popularity of the Omni-Balsamic Reinvigorator—thriving not by the credulity of the simple, but the trust of the wise—that certain contrivers have not been idle, though I would not, indeed, hastily affirm of them that they are aware of the sad consequences to the public. Homicides and murderers, some call those contrivers; but I do not; for murder (if such a crime be possible) comes from the heart, and these men's motives come from the purse. Were they not in poverty, I think they would hardly do what they do. Still, the public interests forbid that I should let their needy device for a living succeed. In short, I have adopted precautions. Take the wrapper from any of my vials and hold it to the light, you will see water-marked in capitals the word '*confidence*,' which is the countersign of the medicine, as I wish it was of the world. The wrapper bears that mark or else the medicine is counterfeit. But if still any lurking doubt should remain, pray enclose the wrapper to this address," handing a card, "and by return mail I will answer."

At first the sick man listened, with the air of vivid interest, but gradually, while the other was still talking, another strange caprice came over him, and he presented the aspect of the most calamitous dejection.

"How now?" said the herb-doctor.

"You told me to have confidence, said that confidence was indispensable, and here you preach to me distrust. Ah, truth will out!" [19]

"I told you, you must have confidence, unquestioning confidence, I meant confidence in the genuine medicine, and the genuine *me*."

"But in your absence, buying vials purporting to be yours, it seems I cannot have unquestioning confidence."

"Prove all the vials; trust those which are true." [20]

"But to doubt, to suspect, to prove—to have all this wearing work to be doing continually—how opposed to confidence. It is evil!"

"From evil comes good.[21] Distrust is a stage to confidence. How has it proved in our interview? But your voice is husky; I have let you talk too much. You hold your cure; I leave you. But stay—when I hear that health is yours, I will not, like some I know, vainly make boasts; but, giving glory where all glory is due, say, with the devout herb-doctor, Japus in Virgil, when, in the unseen but efficacious presence of Venus, he with simples healed the wound of Æneas:—

> 'This is no mortal work, no cure of mine,
> Nor art's effect, but done by power divine.' "[22]

[19] In *The Merchant of Venice*, II, *ii*, Launcelot the Clown, servant to Shylock, tells his blind father that Launcelot "is indeed deceased." Then he admits the ruse, kneels, and with these words asks his father's blessing: "Truth will come to light; murder cannot be hid long—a man's son may, but in the end truth will out."

[20] Cf. I Thessalonians 5:21: "Prove all things; hold fast that which is good."

[21] Cf. Romans 3:8: "And not rather, (as we be slanderously reported, and as some affirm that we say,) Let us do evil, that good may come? whose damnation is just."

[22] From Dryden's translation of Virgil's *Aeneid*, XII. 632–633; "power" is a substitute for "hands" in the original.

CHAPTER 17

*Towards the end of which the Herb-Doctor
proves himself a forgiver of injuries.*

In a kind of ante-cabin, a number of respectable looking people, male and female, way-passengers, recently come on board, are listlessly sitting in a mutually shy sort of silence.

Holding up a small, square bottle, ovally labeled with the engraving of a countenance full of soft pity as that of the Romish-painted Madonna,[1] the herb-doctor passes slowly among them, benignly urbane, turning this way and that, saying:—

"Ladies and gentlemen, I hold in my hand here the Samaritan Pain Dissuader, thrice-blessed discovery of that disinterested friend of humanity whose portrait you see. Pure vegetable extract. Warranted to remove the acutest pain within less than ten minutes. Five hundred dollars to be forfeited on failure. Especially efficacious in heart disease and tic-douloureux. Observe the expression of this pledged friend of humanity. —Price only fifty cents."

In vain. After the first idle stare, his auditors—in pretty good health, it seemed—instead of encouraging his politeness, appeared, if anything, impatient of it; and, perhaps, only diffidence, or some small regard for his feelings, prevented them from telling him so. But, insensible to their coldness, or charitably overlooking it, he more wooingly than ever resumed: "May I venture upon a small supposition? Have I your kind leave, ladies and gentlemen?"

To which modest appeal, no one had the kindness to answer a syllable.

"Well," said he, resignedly, "silence is at least not denial,

---

[1] Note the references to Roman Catholicism in this and the following chapter, which ends with a "triangular" discussion of "Jesuit emissaries."

and may be consent. My supposition is this: possibly some lady, here present, has a dear friend at home, a bed-ridden sufferer from spinal complaint. If so, what gift more appropriate to that sufferer than this tasteful little bottle of Pain Dissuader?"

Again he glanced about him, but met much the same reception as before. Those faces, alien alike to sympathy or surprise, seemed patiently to say, "We are travelers; and, as such, must expect to meet, and quietly put up with, many antic fools, and more antic quacks."

"Ladies and gentlemen," (deferentially fixing his eyes upon their now self-complacent faces), "ladies and gentlemen, might I, by your kind leave, venture upon one other small supposition? It is this: that there is scarce a sufferer, this noonday, writhing on his bed, but in his hour he sat satisfactorily healthy and happy; that the Samaritan Pain Dissuader is the one only balm for that to which each living creature—who knows?—may be a draughted victim, present or prospective. In short:—Oh, Happiness on my right hand, and oh, Security on my left, can ye wisely adore a Providence, and not think it wisdom to provide?—Provide!" (Uplifting the bottle.)

What immediate effect, if any, this appeal might have had, is uncertain. For just then the boat touched at a houseless landing, scooped, as by a land-slide, out of sombre forests; back through which led a road, the sole one, which, from its narrowness, and its being walled up with story on story of dusk, matted foliage, presented the vista of some cavernous old gorge in a city, like haunted Cock Lane in London.[2] Issuing

[2] The ghost of 33 Cock Lane, Smithfield, London, turned out to be one of the most famous impostures of the eighteenth century. The knockings of the "ghost" in response to the questions of a Methodist minister formed an elaborate accusation of murder against an innocent man. The hoax was finally exposed by an informal committee including Samuel Johnson, who wrote its report (1762). The final great assault on innocence fomented by this intervention of the "supernatural" in human affairs came when Charles Churchill wrote one of his most powerful

from that road, and crossing that landing, there stooped his
shaggy form in the door-way, and entered the ante-cabin, with
a step so burdensome that shot seemed in his pockets, a kind of
invalid Titan [3] in homespun; his beard blackly pendant, like the
Carolina-moss, and dank with cypress dew; his countenance
tawny and shadowy as an iron-ore country in a clouded day.
In one hand he carried a heavy walking-stick of swamp-oak;
with the other, led a puny girl, walking in moccasins, not
improbably his child, but evidently of alien maternity, perhaps
Creole, or even Camanche. Her eye would have been large for
a woman, and was inky as the pools of falls among mountain-
pines. An Indian blanket, orange-hued, and fringed with lead
tassel-work, appeared that morning to have shielded the child
from heavy showers. Her limbs were tremulous; she seemed a
little Cassandra,[4] in nervousness.

No sooner was the pair spied by the herb-doctor, than with
a cheerful air, both arms extended like a host's, he advanced,

---

poems, *The Ghost*, denouncing Johnson for his supposed belief in the
ghost. Note that in Chapter 2 the lamb-like man was called "Spirit-
rapper."

[3] The Titans, children of Uranus and Gaea (Heaven and Earth),
castrated and dethroned their father, and were then in turn thrust into
Tartarus by one of their sons, Zeus. (See Appendix, "The River.") A
Titan's assaults against heaven form one of the central images of *Pierre*.
Titan was also, in Latin poetry, a name for the sun personified.

It is possible to read "invalid" two ways, and, as Caroline Lury
Karcher points out, this Titan does have certain diabolic associations:
he comes from a seemingly haunted place, brings with him blackness and
an Indian-like girl, speaks with a "voice deep and lonesome enough to
have come from the bottom of an abandoned coal-shaft," and in the next
chapter he is compared to the demon Asmodeus.

[4] Cassandra, daughter of Priam and Hecuba, tried to trick the amorous
Apollo and was therefore doomed always to foretell the future and
always to have her prophecies disbelieved. In the division of spoils at the
fall of Troy, she fell to the lot of Agamemnon, by whom she had two
children. When he, against her advice, returned with her to Mycenae,
they and their children were murdered by his queen Clytemnestra and
her paramour Aegisthus.

and taking the child's reluctant hand, said, trippingly: "On your travels, ah, my little May Queen? [5] Glad to see you. What pretty moccasins. Nice to dance in." Then with a half caper sang—

> "Hey diddle, diddle, the cat and the fiddle;
> The cow jumped over the moon. [6]

Come, chirrup, chirrup, my little robin!"

Which playful welcome drew no responsive playfulness from the child, nor appeared to gladden or conciliate the father; but rather, if anything, to dash the dead weight of his heavy-hearted expression with a smile hypochondriacally scornful.

Sobering down now, the herb-doctor addressed the stranger in a manly, business-like way—a transition which, though it might seem a little abrupt, did not appear constrained, and, indeed, served to show that his recent levity was less the habit of a frivolous nature, than the frolic condescension of a kindly heart.

"Excuse me," said he, "but, if I err not, I was speaking to you the other day;—on a Kentucky boat, wasn't it?"

"Never to me," was the reply; the voice deep and lonesome enough to have come from the bottom of an abandoned coal-shaft.

"Ah!—But am I again mistaken, (his eye falling on the swamp-oak stick,) or don't you go a little lame, sir?"

"Never was lame in my life."

"Indeed? I fancied I had perceived not a limp, but a hitch, a slight hitch;—some experience in these things—divine some hidden cause of the hitch—buried bullet, may be—some dragoons in the Mexican war discharged with such,[7] you

[5] Chief symbolic personage of the May Day vernal festivals.

[6] *The Oxford Dictionary of Nursery Rhymes* calls this "probably the best-known nonsense verse in the language" and lists eleven of its more far-fetched allegorical and mythological interpretations.

[7] Perhaps a cue for the first imposture of Chapter 19.

know.—Hard fate!" he sighed, "little pity for it, for who sees it?—have you dropped anything?"

Why, there is no telling, but the stranger was bowed over, and might have seemed bowing for the purpose of picking up something, were it not that, as arrested in the imperfect posture, he for the moment so remained; slanting his tall stature like a mainmast yielding to the gale, or Adam to the thunder.[8]

The little child pulled him. With a kind of a surge he righted himself, for an instant looked toward the herb-doctor; but, either from emotion or aversion, or both together, withdrew his eyes, saying nothing. Presently, still stooping, he seated himself, drawing his child between his knees, his massy hands tremulous, and still averting his face, while up into the compassionate one of the herb-doctor the child turned a fixed, melancholy glance of repugnance.

The herb-doctor stood observant a moment, then said:

"Surely you have pain, strong pain, somewhere; in strong frames pain is strongest. Try, now, my specific," (holding it up). "Do but look at the expression of this friend of humanity. Trust me, certain cure for any pain in the world. Won't you look?"

"No," choked the other.

"Very good. Merry time to you, little May Queen."

And so, as if he would intrude his cure upon no one, moved pleasantly off, again crying his wares, nor now at last without result. A new-comer, not from the shore, but another part of the boat, a sickly young man, after some questions, purchased a bottle. Upon this, others of the company began a little to wake up as it were; the scales of indifference or prejudice fell from their eyes;[9] now, at last, they seemed to have an inkling that

8 Thunder was a common poetic equivalent for the voice of God; hence the reference is to the voice in the garden (Genesis 3:8–10).

9 Acts 9:18 describes Saul's conversion: "And immediately there fell from his eyes as it had been scales: and he received sight forthwith, and arose, and was baptized."

here was something not undesirable which might be had for the buying.

But while, ten times more briskly bland than ever, the herb-doctor was driving his benevolent trade, accompanying each sale with added praises of the thing traded, all at once the dusk giant, seated at some distance, unexpectedly raised his voice with—

"What was that you last said?"

The question was put distinctly, yet resonantly, as when a great clock-bell—stunning admonisher—strikes one; and the stroke, though single, comes bedded in the belfry clamor.

All proceedings were suspended. Hands held forth for the specific were withdrawn, while every eye turned towards the direction whence the question came. But, no way abashed, the herb-doctor, elevating his voice with even more than wonted self-possession, replied—

"I was saying what, since you wish it, I cheerfully repeat, that the Samaritan Pain Dissuader, which I here hold in my hand, will either cure or ease any pain you please, within ten minutes after its application."

"Does it produce insensibility?"

"By no means. Not the least of its merits is, that it is not an opiate. It kills pain without killing feeling."

"You lie! Some pains cannot be eased but by producing insensibility, and cannot be cured but by producing death."

Beyond this the dusk giant said nothing; neither, for impairing the other's market, did there appear much need to. After eying the rude speaker a moment with an expression of mingled admiration and consternation, the company silently exchanged glances of mutual sympathy under unwelcome conviction. Those who had purchased looked sheepish or ashamed; and a cynical-looking little man, with a thin flaggy beard, and a countenance ever wearing the rudiments of a grin, seated alone in a corner commanding a good view of the scene, held a rusty hat before his face.

But, again, the herb-doctor, without noticing the retort, overbearing though it was, began his panegyrics anew, and in a tone more assured than before, going so far now as to say that his specific was sometimes almost as effective in cases of mental suffering as in cases of physical; or rather, to be more precise, in cases when, through sympathy, the two sorts of pain coöperated into a climax of both—in such cases, he said, the specific had done very well. He cited an example: Only three bottles, faithfully taken, cured a Louisiana widow (for three weeks sleepless in a darkened chamber) of neuralgic sorrow for the loss of husband and child, swept off in one night by the last epidemic.[10] For the truth of this, a printed voucher was produced, duly signed.

While he was reading it aloud, a sudden side-blow all but felled him.

It was the giant, who, with a countenance lividly epileptic with hypochondriac mania, exclaimed—

"Profane fiddler on heart-strings! Snake!"

More he would have added, but, convulsed, could not; so, without another word, taking up the child, who had followed him, went with a rocking pace out of the cabin.

"Regardless of decency, and lost to humanity!" exclaimed the herb-doctor, with much ado recovering himself. Then, after a pause, during which he examined his bruise, not omitting to apply externally a little of his specific, and with some success, as it would seem, plained to himself:

"No, no, I won't seek redress; innocence is my redress. But," turning upon them all, "if that man's wrathful blow provokes me to no wrath, should his evil distrust arouse you to distrust? I do devoutly hope," proudly raising voice and arm, "for the honor of humanity—hope that, despite this coward

[10] This is the third appearance in the book of a man and child somehow separated from wife and mother. The first was in the story of Goneril; the second came with the advent of the Titan and his Cassandra; note what happens to the herb doctor as he now tells of the third.

assault, the Samaritan Pain Dissuader stands unshaken in the confidence of all who hear me!"

But, injured as he was, and patient under it, too, somehow his case excited as little compassion as his oratory now did enthusiasm. Still, pathetic to the last, he continued his appeals, notwithstanding the frigid regard of the company, till, suddenly interrupting himself, as if in reply to a quick summons from without, he said hurriedly, "I come, I come," and so, with every token of precipitate dispatch, out of the cabin the herb-doctor went.

CHAPTER 18

*Inquest into the true character of the
Herb-Doctor.*

"Sha'n't see that fellow again in a hurry," remarked an auburn-haired gentleman, to his neighbor with a hook-nose. "Never knew an operator so completely unmasked."

"But do you think it the fair thing to unmask an operator that way?"

"Fair? It is right."

"Supposing that at high 'change on the Paris Bourse, Asmodeus [1] should lounge in, distributing hand-bills, revealing the true thoughts and designs of all the operators present—would that be the fair thing in Asmodeus? Or, as Hamlet says, were it 'to consider the thing too curiously?' " [2]

"We won't go into that. But since you admit the fellow to be a knave—"

"I don't admit it. Or, if I did, I take it back. Shouldn't wonder if, after all, he is no knave at all, or, but little of one. What can you prove against him?"

"I can prove that he makes dupes."

[1] In Jewish demonology, the giant demon of vanity, a humorously malicious trickster; called "king of the devils" in the Talmud. In Alain René Le Sage's novel *Le Diable Boiteux* (the lame devil) of 1707, Asmodeus flies through the air with Don Cléophas and lifts off the roofs of houses to show him what is going on inside. Note that this is a comparison of the giant lame devil with the "invalid Titan."

[2] It is Horatio who says, " 'Twere to consider too curiously to consider so" (*Hamlet*, V, i, 227), in response to Hamlet's proposal: "Why may not imagination trace the noble dust of Alexander till he find it stopping a bunghole?" To Horatio's objection, Hamlet replies: "No, faith, not a jot. . . ." See Chapter 30 for a discussion of the relations between the characters of *Hamlet* and its author.

"Many held in honor do the same; and many, not wholly knaves, do it too."

"How about that last?"

"He is not wholly at heart a knave, I fancy, among whose dupes is himself. Did you not see our quack friend apply to himself his own quackery? A fanatic quack; essentially a fool, though effectively a knave." [3]

Bending over, and looking down between his knees on the floor, the auburn-haired gentleman meditatively scribbled there awhile with his cane, then, glancing up, said:

"I can't conceive how you, in any way, can hold him a fool. How he talked—so glib, so pat, so well."

"A smart fool always talks well; takes a smart fool to be tonguey."

In much the same strain the discussion continued—the hook-nosed gentleman talking at large and excellently, with a view of demonstrating that a smart fool always talks just so. Ere long he talked to such purpose as almost to convince.

Presently, back came the person of whom the auburn-haired gentleman had predicted that he would not return. Conspic-uous in the door-way he stood, saying, in a clear voice, "Is the agent of the Seminole Widow and Orphan Asylum within here?"

No one replied.

"Is there within here any agent or any member of any chari-table institution whatever?"

No one seemed competent to answer, or, no one thought it worth while to.

"If there be within here any such person, I have in my hand two dollars for him."

Some interest was manifested.

"I was called away so hurriedly, I forgot this part of my duty. With the proprietor of the Samaritan Pain Dissuader it is a rule, to devote, on the spot, to some benevolent purpose, the

[3] The various explanations of the herb doctor offered in this chapter are conventional explanations of the savior gods.

half of the proceeds of sales. Eight bottles were disposed of among this company. Hence, four half-dollars remain to charity. Who, as steward,[4] takes the money?"

One or two pair of feet moved upon the floor, as with a sort of itching; but nobody rose.

"Does diffidence prevail over duty? If, I say, there be any gentleman, or any lady, either, here present, who is in any connection with any charitable institution whatever, let him or her come forward. He or she happening to have at hand no certificate of such connection, makes no difference. Not of a suspicious temper, thank God, I shall have confidence in whoever offers to take the money."

A demure-looking woman, in a dress rather tawdry and rumpled, here drew her veil well down and rose; but, marking every eye upon her, thought it advisable, upon the whole, to sit down again.

"Is it to be believed that, in this Christian company, there is no one charitable person? I mean, no one connected with any charity? Well, then, is there no object of charity here?"

Upon this, an unhappy-looking woman, in a sort of mourning, neat, but sadly worn, hid her face behind a meagre bundle, and was heard to sob. Meantime, as not seeing or hearing her, the herb-doctor again spoke, and this time not unpathetically:

"Are there none here who feel in need of help, and who, in accepting such help, would feel that they, in their time, have given or done more than may ever be given or done to them? Man or woman, is there none such here?"

The sobs of the woman were more audible, though she strove to repress them. While nearly every one's attention was bent upon her, a man of the appearance of a day-laborer, with a white bandage across his face, concealing the side of the nose, and who, for coolness' sake, had been sitting in his red-flannel shirt-sleeves, his coat thrown across one shoulder, the darned cuffs drooping behind—this man shufflingly rose, and, with a

[4] Cf. the references to "steward" in Chapters 3, 7, 9, and 45.

pace that seemed the lingering memento of the lock-step of convicts,[5] went up for a duly-qualified claimant.

"Poor wounded huzzar!" [6] sighed the herb-doctor, and dropping the money into the man's clam-shell of a hand turned and departed.

The recipient of the alms was about moving after, when the auburn-haired gentleman staid him: "Don't be frightened, you; but I want to see those coins. Yes, yes; good silver, good silver. There, take them again, and while you are about it, go bandage the rest of yourself behind something. D'ye hear? Consider yourself, wholly, the scar of a nose, and be off with yourself."

Being of a forgiving nature, or else from emotion not daring to trust his voice, the man silently, but not without some precipitancy, withdrew.

"Strange," said the auburn-haired gentleman, returning to his friend, "the money was good money."

"Aye, and where your fine knavery now? Knavery to devote the half of one's receipts to charity? He's a fool I say again."

"Others might call him an original genius." [7]

"Yes, being original in his folly. Genius? His genius is a cracked pate, and, as this age goes, not much originality about that."

"May he not be knave, fool, and genius altogether?"

"I beg pardon," here said a third person with a gossiping expression who had been listening, "but you are somewhat puzzled by this man, and well you may be."

"Do you know anything about him?" asked the hooked-nosed gentleman.

---

[5] In Chapter 2, one view of the lamb-like man had seen him as an "escaped convict."

[6] See Chapter 16, note 2.

[7] See Chapter 1, note 10.

"No, but I suspect him for something."

"Suspicion. We want knowledge."

"Well, suspect first and know next. True knowledge comes but by suspicion or revelation. That's my maxim."

"And yet," said the auburn-haired gentleman, "since a wise man will keep even some certainties to himself, much more some suspicions, at least he will at all events so do till they ripen into knowledge."

"Do you hear that about the wise man?" said the hook-nosed gentleman, turning upon the new comer. "Now what is it you suspect of this fellow?"

"I shrewdly suspect him," was the eager response, "for one of those Jesuit emissaries prowling all over our country. The better to accomplish their secret designs, they assume, at times, I am told, the most singular masques; sometimes, in appearance, the absurdest." [8]

This, though indeed for some reason causing a droll smile upon the face of the hook-nosed gentleman, added a third angle to the discussion, which now became a sort of triangular duel, and ended, at last, with but a triangular result.

[8] An American Catholic magazine, *Brownson's Quarterly Review*, in 1846 thus caricatured some prevalent views of the Jesuits: "To hear people talk, one would think half the world were Jesuits. They swarm everywhere. One cannot turn over a leaf, but a Jesuit will start up. They are omnipresent. They are omnipotent. They are at the bottom of all movements,—of every intrigue, every outbreak. Nobody is safe."

The narrator of this chapter has used one external physical characteristic to sum up this speaker's identity, referring to him always as "the auburn-haired gentleman"; Chapter 43 discusses the use of auburn hair as a disguise.

CHAPTER 19

A soldier of fortune.

"Mexico? Molino del Rey? Resaca de la Palma?" [1]
"Resaca de la *Tombs!*" [2]

Leaving his reputation to take care of itself, since, as is not seldom the case, he knew nothing of its being in debate, the herb-doctor, wandering towards the forward part of the boat, had there espied a singular character in a grimy old regimental coat, a countenance at once grim and wizened, interwoven paralyzed legs, stiff as icicles, suspended between rude crutches, while the whole rigid body, like a ship's long barometer on gimbals, swung to and fro, mechanically faithful to the motion of the boat. Looking downward while he swung, the cripple seemed in a brown study.

As moved by the sight, and conjecturing that here was some battered hero from the Mexican battle-fields, the herb-doctor had sympathetically accosted him as above, and received the above rather dubious reply. As, with a half moody, half surly sort of air that reply was given, the cripple, by a voluntary jerk, nervously increased his swing (his custom when seized

---

[1] Two battles in the Mexican War, a war vigorously opposed by many of the intellectual and clerical leaders of New England. Resaca de la Palma, near Matamoros, Mexico, was overrun by U.S. troops under Zachary Taylor on May 9, 1846, the day after his victory at Palo Alto and four days before Congress declared war. Molino del Rey, four miles west of Mexico City, was captured, after one of the bloodiest battles of the war, in September, 1847.

[2] Literally, "Dry River Bed (or Undertow) of the Tombs." The Tombs was the so-called Hall of Justice in downtown Manhattan used mainly as a prison. The title character of Melville's *Bartleby* (1853) is taken to the Tombs in a mockery of justice and there dies.

by emotion), so that one would have thought some squall had suddenly rolled the boat and with it the barometer.

"Tombs? my friend," exclaimed the herb-doctor in mild surprise. "You have not descended to the dead,[3] have you? I had imagined you a scarred campaigner, one of the noble children of war, for your dear country a glorious sufferer. But you are Lazarus, it seems."

"Yes, he who had sores."

"Ah, the *other* Lazarus.[4] But I never knew that either of them was in the army," glancing at the dilapidated regimentals.

"That will do now. Jokes enough."

"Friend," said the other reproachfully, "you think amiss. On principle, I greet unfortunates with some pleasant remark, the better to call off their thoughts from their troubles. The physician who is at once wise and humane seldom unreservedly sympathizes with his patient. But come, I am a herb-doctor, and also a natural bone-setter. I may be sanguine, but I think I can do something for you. You look up now. Give me your story. Ere I undertake a cure, I require a full account of the case."

"You can't help me," returned the cripple gruffly. "Go away."

"You seem sadly destitute of—"

"No I ain't destitute; to-day, at least, I can pay my way."

"The Natural Bone-setter is happy, indeed, to hear that. But you were premature. I was deploring your destitution, not of cash, but of confidence. You think the Natural Bone-setter can't help you. Well, suppose he can't, have you any objection to telling him your story? You, my friend, have, in a signal

[3] A play on both Tombs and Resaca (in the sense of "Undertow").

[4] John 11–12 describes the death of Lazarus of Bethany, his resurrection by Christ after being buried four days, and a few hours of his later life. In *Mardi* (Chapter LXXVIII) Melville calls attention to the fact that Lazarus made no revelation after his return. For the other Lazarus, the beggar with sores, see Chapter 9, note 5 and Chapter 15, note 6.

way, experienced adversity. Tell me, then, for my private
good, how, without aid from the noble cripple, Epictetus,[5]
you have arrived at his heroic sang-froid in misfortune."

At these words the cripple fixed upon the speaker the hard
ironic eye of one toughened and defiant in misery, and, in the
end, grinned upon him with his unshaven face like an ogre.

"Come, come, be sociable—be human, my friend. Don't
make that face; it distresses me."

"I suppose," with a sneer, "you are the man I've long heard
of—The Happy Man."

"Happy? my friend. Yes, at least I ought to be. My conscience is peaceful. I have confidence in everybody. I have
confidence that, in my humble profession, I do some little
good to the world. Yes, I think that, without presumption, I
may venture to assent to the proposition that I am the Happy
Man—the Happy Bone-setter."

"Then you shall hear my story. Many a month I have
longed to get hold of the Happy Man, drill him, drop the
powder, and leave him to explode at his leisure."

"What a demoniac unfortunate," exclaimed the herb-doctor
retreating. "Regular infernal machine!"

"Look ye," cried the other, stumping after him, and with his
horny hand catching him by a horn button, "my name is
Thomas Fry. Until my—"

—"Any relation of Mrs. Fry?" interrupted the other. "I still
correspond with that excellent lady on the subject of prisons.
Tell me, are you anyway connected with *my* Mrs. Fry?" [6]

[5] Epictetus, late first- and early second-century Stoic philosopher born
in slavery, supposedly was lamed in this fashion: When his master was
twisting his leg one day, Epictetus said quietly, "You will break it";
when it did break, Epictetus said simply, "Did I not tell you that you
would do so?" The maxim which he said summed up all his teachings
was "bear and forbear."

[6] Mrs. Elizabeth Gurney Fry (1780–1845), an English philanthropist
especially noted for her work in prison reform.

"Blister Mrs. Fry! What do them sentimental souls know of prisons or any other black fact? I'll tell ye a story of prisons. Ha, ha!"

The herb-doctor shrank, and with reason, the laugh being strangely startling.

"Positively, my friend," said he, "you must stop that; I can't stand that; no more of that. I hope I have the milk of kindness, but your thunder will soon turn it."

"Hold, I haven't come to the milk-turning part yet. My name is Thomas Fry. Until my twenty-third year I went by the nickname of Happy Tom—happy—ha, ha! They called me Happy Tom, d'ye see? because I was so good-natured and laughing all the time, just as I am now—ha, ha!"

Upon this the herb-doctor would, perhaps, have run, but once more the hyæna clawed him. Presently, sobering down, he continued:

"Well, I was born in New York, and there I lived a steady, hard-working man, a cooper by trade.[7] One evening I went to a political meeting in the Park—for you must know, I was in those days a great patriot. As bad luck would have it, there was trouble near, between a gentleman who had been drinking wine, and a pavior who was sober. The pavior chewed tobacco, and the gentleman said it was beastly in him, and pushed him, wanting to have his place. The pavior chewed on and pushed back. Well, the gentleman carried a sword-cane, and presently the pavior was down—skewered."

"How was that?"

"Why you see the pavior undertook something above his strength."

"The other must have been a Samson then. 'Strong as a pavior,' is a proverb."

"So it is, and the gentleman was in body a rather weakly man, but, for all that, I say again, the pavior undertook something above his strength."

[7] This cooper from New York may foreshadow Pitch, in part a caricature of James Fenimore Cooper.

"What are you talking about? He tried to maintain his rights, didn't he?"

"Yes; but, for all that, I say again, he undertook something above his strength."

"I don't understand you. But go on."

"Along with the gentleman, I, with other witnesses, was taken to the Tombs. There was an examination, and, to appear at the trial, the gentleman and witnesses all gave bail—I mean all but me."

"And why didn't you?"

"Couldn't get it."

"Steady, hard-working cooper like you; what was the reason you couldn't get bail?"

"Steady, hard-working cooper hadn't no friends. Well, souse I went into a wet cell, like a canal-boat splashing into the lock; locked up in pickle, d'ye see? against the time of the trial."

"But what had you done?"

"Why, I hadn't got any friends, I tell ye. A worse crime than murder, as ye'll see afore long."

"Murder? Did the wounded man die?"

"Died the third night."

"Then the gentleman's bail didn't help him. Imprisoned now, wasn't he?"

"Had too many friends. No, it was *I* that was imprisoned. —But I was going on: They let me walk about the corridor by day; but at night I must into lock. There the wet and the damp struck into my bones. They doctored me, but no use. When the trial came, I was boosted up and said my say."

"And what was that?"

"My say was that I saw the steel go in, and saw it sticking in."

"And that hung the gentleman."

"Hung him with a gold chain! His friends called a meeting in the Park, and presented him with a gold watch and chain upon his acquittal."

"Acquittal?"

"Didn't I say he had friends?"

There was a pause, broken at last by the herb-doctor's saying: "Well, there is a bright side to everything. If this speak prosaically for justice, it speaks romantically for friendship! [8] But go on, my fine fellow."

"My say being said, they told me I might go. I said I could not without help. So the constables helped me, asking *where* would I go? I told them back to the 'Tombs.' I knew no other place. 'But where are your friends?' said they. 'I have none.' So they put me into a hand-barrow with an awning to it, and wheeled me down to the dock and on board a boat, and away to Blackwell's Island to the Corporation Hospital.[9] There I got worse—got pretty much as you see me now. Couldn't cure me. After three years, I grew sick of lying in a grated iron bed alongside of groaning thieves and mouldering burglars. They gave me five silver dollars, and these crutches, and I hobbled off. I had an only brother who went to Indiana, years ago. I begged about, to make up a sum to go to him; got to Indiana at last, and they directed me to his grave. It was on a great plain, in a log-church yard with a stump fence, the old gray roots sticking all ways like moose-antlers. The bier, set over the grave, it being the last dug, was of green hickory; bark on, and green twigs sprouting from it. Someone had planted a bunch of violets on the mound, but it was a poor soil (alway choose the poorest soils for grave-yards), and they were all dried to tinder. I was going to sit and rest myself on the bier and think about my brother in heaven, but the bier broke down, the legs being only tacked. So, after driving some hogs out of the yard that were rooting there, I came away, and, not to make too

[8] See the first cynical cripple's assertion in Chapter 3: ". . . the charitable knave on the stand gives charitable testimony for his friend in the box."

[9] Blackwell's Island (now Welfare Island) in the East River had almshouses and a New York City Hospital (opened in 1853).

long a story of it, here I am, drifting down stream like any other bit of wreck."

The herb-doctor was silent for a time, buried in thought. At last, raising his head, he said: "I have considered your whole story, my friend, and strove to consider it in the light of a commentary on what I believe to be the system of things; but it so jars with all, is so incompatible with all, that you must pardon me, if I honestly tell you, I cannot believe it."

"That don't surprise me."

"How?"

"Hardly anybody believes my story, and so to most I tell a different one."

"How, again?"

"Wait here a bit and I'll show ye."

With that, taking off his rag of a cap, and arranging his tattered regimentals the best he could, off he went stumping among the passengers in an adjoining part of the deck, saying with a jovial kind of air: "Sir, a shilling for Happy Tom, who fought at Buena Vista. Lady, something for General Scott's soldier, crippled in both pins at glorious Contreras." [10]

Now, it so chanced that, unbeknown to the cripple, a prim-looking stranger had overheard part of his story. Beholding him, then, on his present begging adventure, this person, turning to the herb-doctor, indignantly said: "Is it not too bad, sir, that yonder rascal should lie so?"

"Charity never faileth,[11] my good sir," was the reply. "The vice of this unfortunate is pardonable. Consider, he lies not out of wantonness."

"Not out of wantonness. I never heard more wanton lies. In one breath to tell you what would appear to be his true story, and, in the next, away and falsify it."

[10] Buena Vista and Contreras were the sites of two other battles in the Mexican War, the latter coming toward the close of General Winfield Scott's march on Mexico City.

[11] The last of the lamb-like man's inscriptions.

"For all that, I repeat he lies not out of wantonness. A ripe philosopher, turned out of the great Sorbonne of hard times, he thinks that woes, when told to strangers for money, are best sugared. Though the inglorious lock-jaw of his knee-pans in a wet dungeon is a far more pitiable ill than to have been crippled at glorious Contreras, yet he is of opinion that this lighter and false ill shall attract, while the heavier and real one might repel."

"Nonsense; he belongs to the Devil's regiment; and I have a great mind to expose him."

"Shame upon you. Dare to expose that poor unfortunate, and by heaven—don't you do it, sir."

Noting something in his manner, the other thought it more prudent to retire than retort. By-and-by, the cripple came back, and with glee, having reaped a pretty good harvest.

"There," he laughed, "you know now what sort of soldier I am."

"Aye, one that fights not the stupid Mexican, but a foe worthy your tactics—Fortune!"

"Hi, hi!" clamored the cripple, like a fellow in the pit of a sixpenny theatre, then said, "don't know much what you meant, but it went off well."

This over, his countenance capriciously put on a morose ogreness. To kindly questions he gave no kindly answers. Unhandsome notions were thrown out about "free Ameriky," as he sarcastically called his country. These seemed to disturb and pain the herb-doctor, who, after an interval of thoughtfulness, gravely addressed him in these words:

"You, my worthy friend, to my concern, have reflected upon the government under which you live and suffer. Where is your patriotism? Where your gratitude? True, the charitable may find something in your case, as you put it, partly to account for such reflections as coming from you. Still, be the facts how they may, your reflections are none the less unwarrantable. Grant, for the moment, that your experiences are as you give them; in which case I would admit that government might be thought to have more or less to do with what seems undesirable in them. But it is never to be forgotten that human government, being subordinate to the divine, must needs, therefore, in its degree, partake of the characteristics of the divine. That is, while in general efficacious to happiness, the world's law may yet, in some cases, have, to the eye of reason, an unequal operation, just as, in the same imperfect view, some inequalities may appear in the operations of heaven's law; nevertheless, to one who has a right confidence, final benignity is, in every instance, as sure with the one law as the other. I expound the point at some length, because these are the considerations, my poor fellow, which, weighed as they merit, will enable you to sustain with unimpaired trust the apparent calamities which are yours."

"What do you talk your hog-latin to me for?" cried the cripple, who, throughout the address, betrayed the most illiterate obduracy; and, with an incensed look, anew he swung himself.

Glancing another way till the spasm passed, the other continued:

"Charity marvels not that you should be somewhat hard of conviction, my friend, since you, doubtless, believe yourself hardly dealt by; but forget not that those who are loved are chastened." [12]

"Mustn't chasten them too much, though, and too long, because their skin and heart get hard, and feel neither pain nor tickle."

"To mere reason, your case looks something piteous, I grant. But never despond; many things—the choicest—yet remain. You breathe this bounteous air, are warmed by this gracious sun, and, though poor and friendless, indeed, nor so agile as in your youth, yet, how sweet to roam, day by day, through the

[12] Proverbs 13:24: "He that spareth his rod hateth his son: but he that loveth him chasteneth him betimes." Hebrews 12:6: "For whom the Lord loveth he chasteneth, and scourgeth every son whom he receiveth." Revelation 3:19: "As many as I love, I rebuke and chasten. . . ."

groves, plucking the bright mosses and flowers, till forlornness itself becomes a hilarity, and, in your innocent independence, you skip for joy."

"Fine skipping with these 'ere horse-posts—ha ha!"

"Pardon; I forgot the crutches. My mind, figuring you after receiving the benefit of my art, overlooked you as you stand before me."

"Your art? You call yourself a bone-setter—a natural bone-setter, do ye? Go, bone-set the crooked world, and then come bone-set crooked me." [13]

"Truly, my honest friend, I thank you for again recalling me to my original object. Let me examine you," bending down; "ah, I see, I see; much such a case as the negro's. Did you see him? Oh no, you came aboard since. Well, his case was a little something like yours. I prescribed for him, and I shouldn't wonder at all if, in a very short time, he were able to walk almost as well as myself. Now, have you no confidence in my art?"

"Ha, ha!"

The herb-doctor averted himself; but, the wild laugh dying away, resumed:

"I will not force confidence on you. Still, I would fain do the friendly thing by you. Here, take this box; just rub that liniment on the joints night and morning. Take it. Nothing to pay. God bless you. Good-bye."

"Stay," pausing in his swing, not untouched by so unexpected an act; "stay—thank'ee—but will this really do me good? Honor bright, now; will it? Don't deceive a poor fellow," with changed mien and glistening eye.

"Try it. Good-bye."

"Stay, stay! *Sure* it will do me good?"

"Possibly, possibly; no harm in trying. Good-bye."

"Stay, stay; give me three more boxes, and here's the money."

---

[13] Cf. Luke 13:11–17, an account of Jesus making a crippled woman straight.

"My friend," returning towards him with a sadly pleased sort of air, "I rejoice in the birth of your confidence and hopefulness. Believe me that, like your crutches, confidence and hopefulness will long support a man when his own legs will not. Stick to confidence and hopefulness, then, since how mad for the cripple to throw his crutches away. You ask for three more boxes of my liniment. Luckily, I have just that number remaining. Here they are. I sell them at half-a-dollar apiece. But I shall take nothing from you. There; God bless you again; good-bye."

"Stay," in a convulsed voice, and rocking himself, "stay, stay! You have made a better man of me. You have borne with me like a good Christian, and talked to me like one, and all that is enough without making me a present of these boxes. Here is the money. I won't take nay. There, there; and may Almighty goodness go with you."

As the herb-doctor withdrew, the cripple gradually subsided from his hard rocking into a gentle oscillation. It expressed, perhaps, the soothed mood of his reverie.

CHAPTER 20

Reappearance of one who may be remembered.

The herb-doctor had not moved far away, when, in advance of him, this spectacle met his eye. A dried-up old man, with the stature of a boy of twelve, was tottering about like one out of his mind, in rumpled clothes of old moleskin, showing recent contact with bedding, his ferret eyes, blinking in the sunlight of the snowy boat, as imbecilely eager, and, at intervals, coughing, he peered hither and thither as if in alarmed search for his nurse. He presented the aspect of one who, bedrid, has, through overruling excitement, like that of a fire, been stimulated to his feet.

"You seek some one," said the herb-doctor, accosting him. "Can I assist you?"

"Do, do; I am so old and miserable," coughed the old man. "Where is he? This long time I've been trying to get up and find him. But I haven't any friends, and couldn't get up till now. Where is he?"

"Who do you mean?" drawing closer, to stay the further wanderings of one so weakly.

"Why, why, why," now marking the other's dress, "why you, yes you—you, you—ugh, ugh, ugh!"

"I?"

"Ugh, ugh, ugh!—you are the man he spoke of. Who is he?"

"Faith, that is just what I want to know."

"Mercy, mercy!" coughed the old man, bewildered, "ever since seeing him, my head spins round so. I ought to have a guardeean. Is this a snuff-colored surtout of yours, or ain't it? Somehow, can't trust my senses any more, since trusting him —ugh, ugh, ugh!"

"Oh, you have trusted somebody? Glad to hear it. Glad to

140

hear of any instance of that sort. Reflects well upon all men. But you inquire whether this is a snuff-colored surtout. I answer it is; and will add that a herb-doctor wears it."

Upon this the old man, in his broken way, replied that then he (the herb-doctor) was the person he sought—the person spoken of by the other person as yet unknown. He then, with flighty eagerness, wanted to know who this last person was, and where he was, and whether he could be trusted with money to treble it.

"Aye, now, I begin to understand; ten to one you mean my worthy friend, who, in pure goodness of heart, makes people's fortunes for them—their everlasting fortunes, as the phrase goes—only charging his one small commission of confidence. Aye, aye; before intrusting funds with my friend, you want to know about him. Very proper—and, I am glad to assure you, you need have no hesitation; none, none, just none in the world; bona fide, none. Turned me in a trice a hundred dollars the other day into as many eagles." [1]

"Did he? did he? But where is he? Take me to him."

"Pray, take my arm! The boat is large! We may have something of a hunt! Come on! Ah, is that he?"

"Where? where?"

"O, no; I took yonder coat-skirts for his. But no, my honest friend would never turn tail that way. Ah!—"

"Where? where?"

"Another mistake. Surprising resemblance. I took yonder clergyman for him. Come on!"

Having searched that part of the boat without success, they went to another part, and, while exploring that, the boat sided up to a landing, when, as the two were passing by the open guard, the herb-doctor suddenly rushed towards the disembarking throng, crying out: "Mr. Truman, Mr. Truman! There he goes—that's he. Mr. Truman, Mr. Truman!—Confound that steam-pipe. Mr. Truman! for God's sake, Mr. Truman!—No, no.—There, the plank's in—too late—we're off."

[1] Ten-dollar gold coins.

With that, the huge boat, with a mighty, walrus wallow, rolled away from the shore, resuming her course.

"How vexatious!" exclaimed the herb-doctor, returning. "Had we been but one single moment sooner.—There he goes, now, towards yon hotel, his portmanteau following. You see him, don't you?"

"Where? where?"

"Can't see him any more. Wheel-house shot between. I am very sorry. I should have so liked you to have let him have a hundred or so of your money. You would have been pleased with the investment, believe me."

"Oh, I *have* let him have some of my money," groaned the old man.

"You have? My dear sir," seizing both the miser's hands in both his own and heartily shaking them. "My dear sir, how I congratulate you. You don't know."

"Ugh, ugh! I fear I don't," with another groan. His name is Truman, is it?"

"John Truman."

"Where does he live?"

"In St. Louis."

"Where's his office?"

"Let me see. Jones street, number one hundred and—no, no—anyway, it's somewhere or other up-stairs in Jones street."

"Can't you remember the number? Try, now."

"One hundred—two hundred—three hundred—"

"Oh, my hundred dollars! I wonder whether it will be one hundred, two hundred, three hundred, with them! Ugh, ugh! Can't remember the number?"

"Positively, though I once knew, I have forgotten, quite forgotten it. Strange. But never mind. You will easily learn in St. Louis. He is well known there."

"But I have no receipt—ugh, ugh! Nothing to show—don't know where I stand—ought to have a guardeean—ugh, ugh! Don't know anything. Ugh, ugh!"

"Why, you know that you gave him your confidence, don't you?"

"Oh, yes."

"Well, then?"

"But what, what—how, how—ugh, ugh!"

"Why, didn't he tell you?"

"No."

"What! Didn't he tell you that it was a secret, a mystery?"

"Oh—yes."

"Well, then?"

"But I have no bond."

"Don't need any with Mr. Truman. Mr. Truman's word is his bond."

"But how am I to get my profits—ugh, ugh!—and my money back? Don't know anything. Ugh, ugh!"

"Oh, you must have confidence."

"Don't say that word again. Makes my head spin so. Oh, I'm so old and miserable, nobody caring for me, everybody fleecing me, and my head spins so—ugh, ugh!—and this cough racks me so. I say again, I ought to have a guardeean."

"So you ought; and Mr. Truman is your guardian to the extent you invested with him. Sorry we missed him just now. But you'll hear from him. All right. It's imprudent, though, to expose yourself this way. Let me take you to your berth."

Forlornly enough the old miser moved slowly away with him. But, while descending a stairway, he was seized with such coughing that he was fain to pause.

"That is a very bad cough."

"Church-yard—ugh, ugh!—church-yard cough.—Ugh!"

"Have you tried anything for it?"

"Tired of trying. Nothing does me any good—ugh! ugh! Not even the Mammoth Cave.[2] Ugh! ugh! Denned there six

---

[2] In 1843 a group of tubercular patients began living in a colony of huts in Mammoth Cave, Kentucky, hoping to benefit from its constant temperature and rich supply of oxygen. Every patient got worse, and the experiment was quickly abandoned.

months, but coughed so bad the rest of the coughers—ugh! ugh!—black-balled me out. Ugh, ugh! Nothing does me good."

"But have you tried the Omni-Balsamic Reinvigorator, sir?"

"That's what that Truman—ugh, ugh!—said I ought to take. Yarb-medicine; you are that yarb-doctor, too?"

"The same. Suppose you try one of my boxes now. Trust me, from what I know of Mr. Truman, he is not the gentleman to recommend, even in behalf of a friend, anything of whose excellence he is not conscientiously satisfied."

"Ugh!—how much?"

"Only two dollars a box."

"Two dollars? Why don't you say two millions? ugh, ugh! Two dollars, that's two hundred cents; that's eight hundred farthings; that's two thousand mills; and all for one little box of yarb-medicine. My head, my head!—oh, I ought to have a guardeean for my head. Ugh, ugh, ugh, ugh!"

"Well, if two dollars a box seems too much, take a dozen boxes at twenty dollars; and that will be getting four boxes for nothing, and you need use none but those four, the rest you can retail out at a premium, and so cure your cough, and make money by it.[3] Come, you had better do it. Cash down. Can fill an order in a day or two. Here now," producing a box; "pure herbs."

At that moment, seized with another spasm, the miser snatched each interval to fix his half distrustful, half hopeful eye upon the medicine, held alluringly up. "Sure—ugh! Sure it's all nat'ral? Nothing but yarbs? If I only thought it was a purely nat'ral medicine now—all yarbs—ugh, ugh!—oh this cough, this cough—ugh, ugh!—shatters my whole body. Ugh, ugh, ugh!"

"For heaven's sake try my medicine, if but a single box. That it is pure nature you may be confident. Refer you to Mr. Truman."

[3] These are interesting computations.

"Don't know his number—ugh, ugh, ugh, ugh! Oh this cough. He did speak well of this medicine though; said solemnly it would cure me—ugh, ugh, ugh, ugh!—take off a dollar and I'll have a box."

"Can't sir, can't."

"Say a dollar-and-half. Ugh!"

"Can't. Am pledged to the one-price system,[4] only honorable one."

"Take off a shilling—ugh, ugh!"

"Can't."

"Ugh, ugh, ugh—I'll take it.—There."

Grudgingly he handed eight silver coins, but while still in his hand, his cough took him, and they were shaken upon the deck.

One by one, the herb-doctor picked them up, and, examining them, said: "These are not quarters, these are pistareens;[5] and clipped, and sweated,[6] at that."

"Oh don't be so miserly—ugh, ugh!—better a beast than a miser—ugh, ugh!"

"Well, let it go. Anything rather than the idea of your not being cured of such a cough. And I hope, for the credit of humanity, you have not made it appear worse than it is, merely with a view to working upon the weak point of my pity, and so getting my medicine the cheaper. Now, mind, don't take it till night. Just before retiring is the time. There, you can get along now, can't you? I would attend you further, but I land presently, and must go hunt up my luggage."

[4] Compare the price in Chapter 16.

[5] Worth about twenty cents each.

[6] Clipping a silver coin is one way to remove some of its precious metal; sweating, i.e., heating it until the silver melts, is another.

CHAPTER 21

A hard case.

"Yarbs, yarbs; natur, natur; you foolish old file [1] you! He did-
dled you with that hocus-pocus, did he? Yarbs and natur will
cure your incurable cough, you think."

It was a rather eccentric-looking person who spoke; somewhat ursine in aspect; sporting a shaggy spencer of the cloth
called bear's-skin; [2] a high-peaked cap of raccoon-skin, the long
bushy tail switching over behind; raw-hide leggings; grim
stubble chin; and to end, a double-barreled gun in hand—a
Missouri bachelor, a Hoosier [3] gentleman, of Spartan leisure
and fortune, and equally Spartan manners and sentiments; and,
as the sequel may show, not less acquainted, in a Spartan way
of his own, with philosophy and books, than with woodcraft
and rifles.

He must have overheard some of the talk between the miser
and the herb-doctor; for, just after the withdrawal of the one,
he made up to the other—now at the foot of the stairs leaning
against the baluster there—with the greeting above.

"Think it will cure me?" coughed the miser in echo; "why
shouldn't it? The medicine is nat'ral yarbs, pure yarbs; yarbs
must cure me."

"Because a thing is nat'ral, as you call it, you think it must
be good. But who gave you that cough? Was it, or was it not,
nature?"

"Sure, you don't think that natur, Dame Natur, will hurt a
body, do you?"

[1] Wretch.

[2] A coarse shaggy woolen cloth used for overcoats.

[3] In general, a rustic or frontiersman; specifically, a resident or native
of Indiana. Here apparently used in the first sense.

"Natur is good Queen Bess; [4] but who's responsible for the cholera?"

"But yarbs, yarbs; yarbs are good?"

"What's deadly-nightshade? Yarb, ain't it?"

"Oh, that a Christian man should speak agin natur and yarbs —ugh, ugh, ugh!—ain't sick men sent out into the country; sent out to natur and grass?"

"Aye, and poets send out the sick spirit to green pastures, like lame horses turned out unshod to the turf to renew their hoofs. A sort of yarb-doctors in their way, poets have it that for sore hearts, as for sore lungs, nature is the grand cure. But who froze to death my teamster on the prairie? And who made an idiot of Peter the Wild Boy?" [5]

"Then you don't believe in these 'ere yarb-doctors?"

"Yarb-doctors? I remember the lank yarb-doctor I saw once on a hospital-cot in Mobile. One of the faculty passing round and seeing who lay there, said with professional triumph, "Ah, Dr. Green, your yarbs don't help ye now, Dr. Green. Have to come to us and the mercury now, Dr. Green.—Natur! Y-a-r-b-s!" [6]

[4] A popular name for Queen Elizabeth I. In underworld cant, a Bess or Queen Elizabeth was a small instrument used to force open doors or pick locks.

[5] A naked boy, about twelve years old, found in the woods of Hanover in 1725, knowing no language and living as an animal. King George I had him brought to England and placed with Dr. John Arbuthnot, who was then supposed to prove or disprove the existence of innate ideas. Arbuthnot concluded that the boy was an idiot, and evidently wrote, possibly with Swift, a satirical pamphlet on Peter called *The Most Wonderful Wonder that ever appeared to the Wonder of the British Nation*. Later, many authors—Defoe, Linneus, Buffon, DePaauw, J. J. Rousseau, and Monboddo—wrote on the significance of Peter for such concepts as innate ideas, evolution, the great chain of being, and natural man. *It cannot rain but it pours*, a satirical pamphlet probably by Swift, compared him to Orson (see Chapter 26, note 2). Note the resemblance of Peter's case to that of Casper Hauser (Chapter 2, note 2) and its great relevance to the entire argument of Chapter 22.

[6] See Chapter 16, note 5.

"Did I hear something about herbs and herb-doctors?" here said a flute-like voice, advancing.

It was the herb-doctor in person. Carpet-bag in hand, he happened to be strolling back that way.

"Pardon me," addressing the Missourian, "but if I caught your words aright, you would seem to have little confidence in nature; which, really, in my way of thinking, looks like carrying the spirit of distrust pretty far."

"And who of my sublime species may you be?" turning short round upon him, clicking his rifle-lock, with an air which would have seemed half cynic,[7] half wild-cat, were it not for the grotesque excess of the expression, which made its sincerity appear more or less dubious.

"One who has confidence in nature, and confidence in man, with some little modest confidence in himself."

"That's your Confession of Faith, is it? Confidence in man, eh? Pray, which do you think are most, knaves or fools?"

"Having met with few or none of either, I hardly think I am competent to answer."

"I will answer for you. Fools are most."

"Why do you think so?"

"For the same reason that I think oats are numerically more than horses. Don't knaves munch up fools just as horses do oats?"

"A droll, sir; you are a droll. I can appreciate drollery—ha, ha, ha!"

"But I'm in earnest."

"That's the drollery, to deliver droll extravagance with an earnest air—knaves munching up fools as horses oats.—Faith, very droll, indeed, ha, ha, ha! Yes, I think I understand you now, sir. How silly I was to have taken you seriously, in your droll conceits, too, about having no confidence in nature. In reality you have just as much as I have."

"*I* have confidence in nature? *I?* I say again there is nothing I am more suspicious of. I once lost ten thousand dollars by

[7] One of the numerous plays on cynic, literally "dog-like."

nature. Nature embezzled that amount from me; absconded with ten thousand dollars' worth of my property; a plantation on this stream, swept clean away by one of those sudden shiftings of the banks in a freshet; ten thousand dollars' worth of alluvion thrown broad off upon the waters."

"But have you no confidence that by a reverse shifting that soil will come back after many days? [8]—ah, here is my venerable friend," observing the old miser, "not in your berth yet? Pray, if you *will* keep afoot, don't lean against that baluster; take my arm."

It was taken; and the two stood together; the old miser leaning against the herb-doctor with something of that air of trustful fraternity with which, when standing, the less strong of the Siamese twins [9] habitually leans against the other.

The Missourian eyed them in silence, which was broken by the herb-doctor.

"You look surprised, sir. Is it because I publicly take under my protection a figure like this? But I am never ashamed of honesty, whatever his coat."

"Look you," said the Missourian, after a scrutinizing pause, "you are a queer sort of chap. Don't know exactly what to make of you. Upon the whole though, you somewhat remind me of the last boy I had on my place."

"Good, trustworthy boy, I hope?"

"Oh very! I am now started to get me made some kind of machine to do the sort of work which boys are supposed to be fitted for."

"Then you have passed a veto upon boys?"

"And men, too."

"But, my dear sir, does not that again imply more or less lack of confidence?—(Stand up a little, just a very little, my

[8] Cf. Ecclesiastes 11:1: "Cast thy bread upon the waters: for thou shalt find it after many days."

[9] Chang and Eng, the original Siamese twins, were, like the "duck-billed beaver" (Chapter 14) and Calvin Edson (Chapters 16 and 23), among the exhibits at P. T. Barnum's American Museum.

venerable friend; you lean rather hard.)—No confidence in boys, no confidence in men, no confidence in nature. Pray, sir, who or what may you have confidence in?"

"I have confidence in distrust; more particularly as applied to you and your herbs."

"Well," with a forbearing smile, "that is frank. But pray, don't forget that when you suspect my herbs you suspect nature."

"Didn't I say that before?"

"Very good. For the argument's sake I will suppose you are in earnest. Now, can you, who suspect nature, deny, that this same nature not only kindly brought you into being, but has faithfully nursed you to your present vigorous and independent condition? Is it not to nature that you are indebted for that robustness of mind which you so unhandsomely use to her scandal? Pray, is it not to nature that you owe the very eyes by which you criticise her?"

"No! for the privilege of vision I am indebted to an oculist, who in my tenth year operated upon me in Philadelphia. Nature made me blind and would have kept me so. My oculist counterplotted her."

"And yet, sir, by your complexion, I judge you live an out-of-door life; without knowing it, you are partial to nature; you fly to nature, the universal mother."

"Very motherly! Sir, in the passion-fits of nature, I've known birds fly from nature to me, rough as I look; yes, sir, in a tempest, refuge here," smiting the folds of his bearskin. "Fact, sir, fact. Come, come, Mr. Palaverer, for all your palavering, did you yourself never shut out nature of a cold, wet night? Bar her out? Bolt her out? Lint [10] her out?"

"As to that," said the herb-doctor calmly, "much may be said."

"Say it, then," ruffling all his hairs. "You can't, sir, can't." Then, as in apostrophe: "Look you, nature! I don't deny but

[10] Probably meaning to stuff lint into chinks and cracks.

your clover is sweet, and your dandelions don't roar; but whose hailstones smashed my windows?"

"Sir," with unimpaired affability, producing one of his boxes, "I am pained to meet with one who holds nature a dangerous character. Though your manner is refined your voice is rough; in short, you seem to have a sore throat. In the calumniated name of nature, I present you with this box; my venerable friend here has a similar one; but to you, a free gift, sir. Through her regularly-authorized agents, of whom I happen to be one, Nature delights in benefiting those who most abuse her. Pray, take it."

"Away with it! Don't hold it so near. Ten to one there is a torpedo in it. Such things have been. Editors been killed that way. Take it further off, I say."

"Good heavens! my dear sir—"

"I tell you I want none of your boxes," snapping his rifle.

"Oh, take it—ugh, ugh! do take it," chimed in the old miser; "I wish he would give me one for nothing."

"You find it lonely, eh," turning short round; "gulled yourself, you would have a companion."

"How can he find it lonely," returned the herb-doctor, "or how desire a companion, when here I stand by him; I, even I, in whom he has trust. For the gulling, tell me, is it humane to talk so to this poor old man? Granting that his dependence on my medicine is vain, is it kind to deprive him of what, in mere imagination, if nothing more, may help eke out, with hope, his disease? For you, if you have no confidence, and, thanks to your native health, can get along without it, so far, at least, as trusting in my medicine goes; yet, how cruel an argument to use, with this afflicted one here. Is it not for all the world as if some brawny pugilist, aglow in December, should rush in and put out a hospital-fire, because, forsooth, he feeling no need of artificial heat, the shivering patients shall have none? Put it to your conscience, sir, and you will admit, that, whatever be the nature of this afflicted one's trust, you, in opposing it, evince either an erring head or a heart amiss. Come, own, are you not pitiless?"

"Yes, poor soul," said the Missourian, gravely eying the old man—"yes, it *is* pitiless in one like me to speak too honestly to one like you. You are a late sitter-up in this life; past man's usual bed-time; and truth, though with some it makes a wholesome breakfast, proves to all a supper too hearty. Hearty food, taken late, gives bad dreams."

"What, in wonder's name—ugh, ugh!—is he talking about?" asked the old miser, looking up to the herb-doctor.

"Heaven be praised for that!" cried the Missourian.

"Out of his mind, ain't he?" again appealed the old miser.

"Pray, sir," said the herb-doctor to the Missourian, "for what were you giving thanks just now?"

"For this: that, with some minds, truth is, in effect, not so cruel a thing after all, seeing that, like a loaded pistol found by poor devils of savages, it raises more wonder than terror—its peculiar virtue being unguessed, unless, indeed, by indiscreet handling, it should happen to go off of itself."

"I pretend not to divine your meaning there," said the herb-doctor, after a pause, during which he eyed the Missourian with a kind of pinched expression, mixed of pain and curiosity, as if he grieved at his state of mind, and, at the same time, wondered what had brought him to it, "but this much I know," he added, "that the general cast of your thoughts is, to say the least, unfortunate. There is strength in them, but a strength, whose source, being physical, must wither. You will yet recant."

"Recant?"

"Yes, when as with this old man, your evil days of decay come on, when a hoary captive in your chamber, then will you, something like the dungeoned Italian we read of,[11] gladly

[11] Elizabeth Foster guesses that this may be the Abbé Faria in *The Count of Monte Cristo* by Alexander Dumas. After thinking of only revenge through his many years in the dungeon, the Abbé Faria has his youthful feelings of charity restored by Edmond Dantès—who then

seek the breast of that confidence begot in the tender time of your youth, blessed beyond telling if it return to you in age."

"Go back to nurse again, eh? Second childhood, indeed. You are soft."

"Mercy, mercy!" cried the old miser, "what is all this!—ugh, ugh! Do talk sense, my good friends. Ain't you," to the Missourian, "going to buy some of that medicine?"

"Pray, my venerable friend," said the herb-doctor, now trying to straighten himself, "don't lean *quite* so hard; my arm grows numb; abate a little, just a very little."

"Go," said the Missourian, "go lay down in your grave, old man, if you can't stand of yourself. It's a hard world for a leaner."

"As to his grave," said the herb-doctor, "that is far enough off, so he but faithfully take my medicine."

"Ugh, ugh, ugh!—He says true. No, I ain't—ugh! a going to die yet—ugh, ugh, ugh! Many years to live yet, ugh, ugh, ugh!"

"I approve your confidence," said the herb-doctor; "but your coughing distresses me, besides being injurious to you. Pray, let me conduct you to your berth. You are best there. Our friend here will wait till my return, I know."

With which he led the old miser away, and then, coming back, the talk with the Missourian was resumed.

"Sir," said the herb-doctor, with some dignity and more feeling, "now that our infirm friend is withdrawn, allow me, to the full, to express my concern at the words you allowed to escape you in his hearing. Some of those words, if I err not, besides being calculated to beget deplorable distrust in the patient, seemed fitted to convey unpleasant imputations against me, his physician."

"Suppose they did?" with a menacing air.

"Why, then—then, indeed," respectfully retreating, "I fall

spends most of the rest of his own life executing revenge in a series of disguises.

back upon my previous theory of your general facetiousness. I have the fortune to be in company with a humorist—a wag."

"Fall back you had better, and wag it is," cried the Missourian, following him up, and wagging his raccoon tail almost into the herb-doctor's face, "look you!"

"At what?"

"At this coon. Can you, the fox, catch him?"

"If you mean," returned the other, not unselfpossessed, "whether I flatter myself that I can in any way dupe you, or impose upon you, or pass myself off upon you for what I am not, I, as an honest man, answer that I have neither the inclination nor the power to do aught of the kind."

"Honest man? Seems to me you talk more like a craven."

"You in vain seek to pick a quarrel with me, or put any affront upon me. The innocence in me heals me."

"A healing like your own nostrums. But you are a queer man—a very queer and dubious man; upon the whole, about the most so I ever met."

The scrutiny accompanying this seemed unwelcome to the diffidence of the herb-doctor. As if at once to attest the absence of resentment, as well as to change the subject, he threw a kind of familiar cordiality into his air, and said: "So you are going to get some machine made to do your work? Philanthropic scruples, doubtless, forbid your going as far as New Orleans for slaves?"

"Slaves?" morose again in a twinkling, "won't have 'em! Bad enough to see whites ducking and grinning round for a favor, without having those poor devils of niggers congeeing round for their corn. Though, to me, the niggers are the freer of the two.[12] You are an abolitionist, ain't you?" he added, squaring

[12] This eccentric person, who later gives his name as Pitch, has been compared to James Fenimore Cooper by John Seelye, Edwin Fussell, and H. Armstrong Roberts. Aside from his gruff, bluff exterior, his combination of leather-stocking and aristocratic ways, and his disdain for landsmen who don't know the details of a ship's rigging, Pitch's attitude toward slavery constitutes one of the more interesting resemblances.

himself with both hands on his rifle, used for a staff, and gazing in the herb-doctor's face with no more reverence than if it were a target. "You are an abolitionist, ain't you?"

"As to that, I cannot so readily answer. If by abolitionist you mean a zealot, I am none; but if you mean a man, who, being a man, feels for all men, slaves included, and by any lawful act, opposed to nobody's interest, and therefore, rousing nobody's enmity, would willingly abolish suffering (supposing it, in its degree, to exist) from among mankind, irrespective of color, then am I what you say."

"Picked and prudent sentiments. You are the moderate man, the invaluable understrapper of the wicked man. You, the moderate man, may be used for wrong, but are useless for right."

"From all this," said the herb-doctor, still forgivingly, "I infer, that you, a Missourian, though living in a slave-state, are without slave sentiments."

"Aye, but are you? Is not that air of yours, so spiritlessly enduring and yielding, the very air of a slave? Who is your master, pray; or are you owned by a company?" [13]

"*My* master?" [14]

"Aye, for come from Maine or Georgia, you come from a slave-state, and a slave-pen, where the best breeds are to be

---

Roberts, in an unpublished paper, compares Pitch's statement here with Cooper's famous statement: "For near two centuries that my family has been in America we have never held a slave; but, if called upon to give testimony on such a question, I should not hesitate to say that, in my judgement, the American slave is better off, so far as mere animal wants are concerned, than the lower order of the European peasants." Roberts also points out that the actions of Pitch bely his words; he shortly purchases for three dollars the services of a boy described in precisely the terms used for slaves: honesty, age, size, industry, health, and behavior.

[13] A familiar pre-Civil War Southern argument maintained that the workers in the North were also slaves.

[14] Compare the exchange between the drover and Black Guinea in Chapter 3 about Guinea's "massa."

bought up at any price from a livelihood to the Presidency. Abolitionism, ye gods, but expresses the fellow-feeling of slave for slave."

"The back-woods would seem to have given you rather eccentric notions," now with polite superiority smiled the herb-doctor, still with manly intrepidity forbearing each unmanly thrust, "but to return; since, for your purpose, you will have neither man nor boy, bond nor free, truly, then some sort of machine for you is all there is left. My desires for your success attend you, sir.—Ah!" glancing shoreward, "here is Cape Giradeau; [15] I must leave you."

[15] Cape Girardeau, Missouri, about 140 miles downriver from St. Louis and about 50 miles upriver from Cairo, Illinois.

CHAPTER 22

*In the polite spirit of the
Tusculan disputations.* [1]

—" 'PHILOSOPHICAL INTELLIGENCE OFFICE' [2]—novel idea! But how
did you come to dream that I wanted anything in your absurd
line, eh?"

About twenty minutes after leaving Cape Giradeau, the
above was growled out over his shoulder by the Missourian to
a chance stranger who had just accosted him; a round-backed,

[1] A red herring. The *Tusculan Disputations* (45 B.C.) of Marcus
Tullius Cicero (106–43 B.C.) is a book-length series of amiable, more-or-
less philosophical conversations among friends, containing so little give
and take that a reader may for many pages forget that the book is anything but a treatise. The disputations of this chapter are not in the
polite Ciceronian spirit but in the dialectic Socratic spirit of the *Meno*,
one of Plato's most dramatic dialogues.

[2] Intelligence office was the current term for a domestic employment
agency. This "Philosophical" one produces a dialogue that parodies
Plato's *Meno*, which revolves around the question of innate ideas and
innate virtue. (In the *Meno*, Socrates brings an actual boy under
philosophical cross-examination to make his point.) The PIO man himself embodies both Socrates and Plato, particularly as they are
represented by Emerson's essay "Plato; or, The Philosopher" (in
Representative Men). Some of Emerson's assertions provide the basis
for this philosophical comedy: "Plato is philosophy, and philosophy,
Plato"; "According to the old sentence, 'If Jove should descend to the
earth, he would speak in the style of Plato' "; "Socrates and Plato are the
double star, which the most powerful instruments will not entirely
separate." Emerson's description of Socrates very precisely describes the
PIO man: "He was plain as a Quaker in habit and speech, affected low
phrases, and illustrations from cocks and quails, soup-pans and sycamore-
spoons, grooms and farriers, and unnameable offices—"; "under his
hypocritical pretence of knowing nothing, he attacks and brings
down . . . all of the fine philosophers of Athens"; "A pitiless disputant

baker-kneed [3] man, in a mean five-dollar suit, wearing, collar-
wise by a chain, a small brass plate,[4] inscribed P. I. O., and
who, with a sort of canine [5] deprecation, slunk obliquely
behind.

"How did you come to dream that I wanted anything in
your line, eh?"

"Oh, respected sir," whined the other, crouching a pace
nearer, and, in his obsequiousness, seeming to wag his very
coat-tails behind him,[6] shabby though they were, "oh, sir,
from long experience, one glance tells me the gentleman who
is in need of our humble services."

"But suppose I did want a boy—what they jocosely call a
good boy—how could your absurd office help me?—Philosophical Intelligence Office?"

"Yes, respected sir, an office founded on strictly philosophical and physio—"

"Look you—come up here—how, by philosophy or physi-
ology either, make good boys to order? Come up here. Don't
give me a crick in the neck. Come up here, come, sir, come,"
calling as if to his pointer. "Tell me, how put the requisite

---

. . . whose temper was imperturbable; whose dreadful logic was always
leisurely and sportive; so careless and ignorant, as to disarm the wariest,
and draw them, in the pleasantest manner, into horrible doubts and
confusion." Emerson places behind the Socrates-Plato double star the
essence of Hinduism: " 'The whole world is but a manifestation of
Vishnu, who is identical with all things, and is to be regarded by the
wise as not differing from, but as the same as themselves' "; " '. . . light
is whitewash; and durations are deceptive; and form is imprisonment;
and heaven itself is a decoy.' "

.3 Knock-kneed; supposedly an occupational deformity of bakers.

4 In India a child offered for adoption was placed on a brass plate;
this man with a brass plate sells boys.

5 Puns on dog, canine, and cynic permeate this chapter.

6 Compare Pitch's wagging of his raccoon tail in the previous chapter,
and in the chapter before that, the herb doctor's statement about Mr.
Truman: "O, no, I took yonder coat-skirts for his. But no, my honest
friend would never turn tail that way."

assortment of good qualities into a boy, as the assorted mince into the pie?"

"Respected sir, our office—"

"You talk much of that office. Where is it? On board this boat?"

"Oh no, sir, I just came aboard. Our office—"

"Came aboard at that last landing, eh? Pray, do you know a herb-doctor there? Smooth scamp in a snuff-colored surtout?"

"Oh, sir, I was but a sojourner at Cape Giradeau. Though, now that you mention a snuff-colored surtout, I think I met such a man as you speak of stepping ashore as I stepped aboard, and 'pears to me I have seen him somewhere before. Looks like a very mild Christian sort of person, I should say. Do you know him, respected sir?"

"Not much, but better than you seem to. Proceed with your business."

With a low, shabby bow, as grateful for the permission, the other began: "Our office—"

"Look you," broke in the bachelor with ire, "have you the spinal complaint? What are you ducking and groveling about? Keep still. Where's your office?"

"The branch one which I represent, is at Alton,[7] sir, in the free state we now pass," [8] (pointing somewhat proudly ashore).

"Free, eh? You a freeman, you flatter yourself? With those coat-tails and that spinal complaint of servility? Free? Just cast up in your private mind who is your master, will you?"

"Oh, oh, oh! I don't understand—indeed—indeed.[9] But, respected sir, as before said, our office, founded on principles wholly new—"

"To the devil with your principles! Bad sign when a man begins to talk of his principles. Hold, come back, sir; back

[7] Alton, Illinois, on the Mississippi north of St. Louis.

[8] The west bank is Missouri, Pitch's home, a slave state; the east bank is Illinois, the last free state to be passed on the voyage south.

[9] See Chapter 21, note 14.

here, back, sir, back! I tell you no more boys for me. Nay, I'm a Mede and Persian. In my old home in the woods I'm pestered enough with squirrels, weasels, chipmunks, skunks. I want no more wild vermin to spoil my temper and waste my substance. Don't talk of boys; enough of your boys; a plague of your boys; chilblains on your boys! As for Intelligence Offices, I've lived in the East, and know 'em. Swindling concerns kept by low-born cynics, under a fawning exterior wreaking their cynic malice upon mankind. You are a fair specimen of 'em."

"Oh dear, dear, dear!"

"Dear? Yes, a thrice dear purchase one of your boys would be to me. A rot on your boys!"

"But, respected sir, if you will not have boys, might we not, in our small way, accommodate you with a man?"

"Accommodate? Pray, no doubt you could accommodate me with a bosom-friend too, couldn't you? Accommodate! Obliging word accommodate: there's accommodation notes now, where one accommodates another with a loan, and if he don't pay it pretty quickly, accommodates him with a chain to his foot.[10] Accommodate! God forbid that I should ever be accommodated. No, no. Look you, as I told that cousin-german of yours, the herb-doctor, I'm now on the road to get me made some sort of machine to do my work. Machines for me. My cider-mill—does that ever steal my cider? My mowing-machine—does that ever lay a-bed mornings? My corn-husker —does that ever give me insolence? No: cider-mill, mowing-machine, corn-husker—all faithfully attend to their business. Disinterested, too; no board, no wages; yet doing good all their lives long; shining examples that virtue is its own reward—the only practical Christians I know."

"Oh dear, dear, dear, dear!"

"Yes, sir:—boys? Start my soul-bolts, what a difference, in a moral point of view, between a corn-husker and a boy! Sir, a corn-husker, for its patient continuance in well-doing, might

[10] Chapter 40 is a full account of such a loan.

not unfitly go to heaven.[11] Do you suppose a boy will?"

"A corn-husker in heaven! (turning up the whites of his eyes). Respected sir, this way of talking as if heaven were a kind of Washington patent-office museum—oh, oh, oh!—as if mere machine-work and puppet-work went to heaven—oh, oh, oh! Things incapable of free agency, to receive the eternal reward of well-doing—oh, oh, oh!"

"You Praise-God-Barebones [12] you, what are you groaning about? Did I say anything of that sort? Seems to me, though you talk so good, you are mighty quick at a hint the other way, or else you want to pick a polemic quarrel with me."

"It may be so or not, respected sir," was now the demure reply; "but if it be, it is only because as a soldier out of honor is quick in taking affront, so a Christian out of religion is quick, sometimes perhaps a little too much so, in spying heresy."

"Well," after an astonished pause, "for an unaccountable pair, you and the herb-doctor ought to yoke together."

So saying, the bachelor was eying him rather sharply, when he with the brass plate recalled him to the discussion by a hint, not unflattering, that he (the man with the brass plate) was all anxiety to hear him further on the subject of servants.

"About that matter," exclaimed the impulsive bachelor, going off at the hint like a rocket, "all thinking minds are, now-a-days, coming to the conclusion—one derived from an immense hereditary experience—see what Horace and others of the ancients say of servants [13]—coming to the conclusion, I say,

---

[11] Romans 2:7: "To them who by patient continuance in well-doing, seek for glory, and honour, and immortality; eternal life. . . ."

[12] Praisegod Barbon or Barebone (*c.* 1596–1679), Baptist preacher and leather merchant, became a member of Cromwell's "Little Parliament" of 1653, named by its enemies, for him, "Barebone's Parliament." He supposedly had two brothers named "Christ-came-into-the-world-to-save" and "If-Christ-had-not-died-thou-hadst-been-damned."

[13] Quintus Horatius Flaccus (65–8 B.C.), himself the son of a freedman, often tells anecdotes about inefficient, rascally, and downright treacherous slaves. But his most pertinent passage may be the one in which he

that boy or man, the human animal is, for most work-purposes, a losing animal. Can't be trusted; less trustworthy than oxen; for conscientiousness a turn-spit dog excels him. Hence these thousand new inventions—carding machines, horse-shoe machines, tunnel-boring machines, reaping machines, apple-paring machines, boot-blacking machines, sewing machines, shaving machines, run-of-errand machines, dumb-waiter machines, and the Lord-only-knows-what machines; all of which announce the era when that refractory animal, the working or serving man, shall be a buried by-gone, a superseded fossil. Shortly prior to which glorious time, I doubt not that a price will be put upon their peltries as upon the knavish 'possums,' especially the boys. Yes, sir (ringing his rifle down on the deck), I rejoice to think that the day is at hand, when, prompted to it by law, I shall shoulder this gun and go out a boy-shooting."

"Oh, now! Lord, Lord, Lord!—But *our* office, respected sir, conducted as I ventured to observe—"

"No, sir," bristlingly settling his stubble chin in his coon-skins. "Don't try to oil me; the herb-doctor tried that. My experience, carried now through a course—worse than salivation—a course of five and thirty boys, proves to me that boyhood is a natural state of rascality."

"Save us, save us!"

"Yes, sir, yes. My name is Pitch; I stick to what I say. I speak from fifteen years' experience; five and thirty boys; American, Irish, English, German, African, Mulatto; not to speak of that China boy sent me by one who well knew my perplexities, from California; and that Lascar boy from Bombay. Thug! [14] I found him sucking the embryo life from my spring eggs. All rascals, sir, every soul of them; Caucasian or Mongol. Amazing the endless variety of rascality in human

---

compares himself both to a slave-boy and to someone who sells that slave-boy after confessing the boy's faults and promising that his clay can be molded to any master's will (*Epistles* II. 2. 3–16).

[14] See Chapter 1, note 18 for pertinent information on Thugs.

nature of the juvenile sort. I remember, that, having discharged, one after another, twenty-nine boys—each, too, for
some wholly unforeseen species of viciousness peculiar to that
one peculiar boy—I remember saying to myself: Now, then,
surely, I have got to the end of the list, wholly exhausted
it; I have only now to get me a boy, any boy different
from those twenty-nine preceding boys, and he infallibly shall
be that virtuous boy I have so long been seeking. But, bless
me! this thirtieth boy—by the way, having at the time long
forsworn your intelligence offices, I had him sent to me from
the Commissioners of Emigration, all the way from New
York, culled out carefully, in fine, at my particular request,
from a standing army of eight hundred boys, the flowers of all
nations, so they wrote me, temporarily in barracks on an East
River island—I say, this thirtieth boy was in person not un-
graceful; his deceased mother a lady's maid, or something of
that sort; and in manner, why, in a plebeian way, a perfect
Chesterfield; [15] very intelligent, too—quick as a flash. But, such
suavity! 'Please sir! please sir!' always bowing and saying,
'Please sir!' In the strangest way, too, combining a filial affection with a menial respect. Took such warm, singular interest
in my affairs. Wanted to be considered one of the family—sort
of adopted son of mine, I suppose. Of a morning, when I
would go out to my stable, with what childlike good nature he
would trot out my nag, 'Please sir, I think he's getting fatter
and fatter.' 'But, he don't look very clean, does he?' unwilling
to be downright harsh with so affectionate a lad; 'and he seems
a little hollow inside the haunch there, don't he? or no, perhaps
I don't see plain this morning.' 'Oh, please sir, it's just there I
think he's gaining so, please.' Polite scamp! I soon found he
never gave that wretched nag his oats of nights; didn't bed
him either. Was above that sort of chambermaid work. No

[15] The most famous writing of Philip Dormer Stanhope, fourth Earl
of Chesterfield (1694–1773), diplomat and courtier, was a series of
courtesy-book letters to his illegitimate son, Philip, published post-
humously. For Chesterfield, policy was the goal, and the instrument of
policy was manners. Another reference occurs in Chapter 30.

end to his willful neglects. But the more he abused my service, the more polite he grew."

"Oh, sir, some way you mistook him."

"Not a bit of it. Besides, sir, he was a boy who under a Chesterfieldian exterior hid strong destructive propensities. He cut up my horse-blanket for the bits of leather, for hinges to his chest. Denied it point-blank. After he was gone, found the shreds under his mattress. Would slyly break his hoe-handle, too, on purpose to get rid of hoeing. Then be so gracefully penitent for his fatal excess of industrious strength. Offer to mend all by taking a nice stroll to the nighest settlement—cherry-trees in full bearing all the way—to get the broken thing cobbled. Very politely stole my pears, odd pennies, shillings, dollars, and nuts; regular squirrel at it. But I could prove nothing. Expressed to him my suspicions. Said I, moderately enough, 'A little less politeness, and a little more honesty would suit me better.' He fired up; threatened to sue for libel. I won't say anything about his afterwards, in Ohio, being found in the act of gracefully putting a bar across a rail-road track, for the reason that a stoker called him the rogue that he was. But enough: polite boys or saucy boys, white boys or black boys, smart boys or lazy boys, Caucasian boys or Mongol boys—all are rascals."

"Shocking, shocking!" nervously tucking his frayed cravat-end out of sight. "Surely, respected sir, you labor under a deplorable hallucination. Why, pardon again, you seem to have not the slightest confidence in boys. I admit, indeed, that boys, some of them at least, are but too prone to one little foolish foible or other. But, what then, respected sir, when, by natural laws, they finally outgrow such things, and wholly?"

Having until now vented himself mostly in plaintive dissent of canine whines and groans, the man with the brass-plate seemed beginning to summon courage to a less timid encounter. But, upon his maiden essay, was not very encouragingly handled, since the dialogue immediately continued as follows:

"Boys outgrow what is amiss in them? From bad boys

spring good men? Sir, 'the child is father of the man;' [16] hence, as all boys are rascals, so are all men. But, God bless me, you must know these things better than I; keeping an intelligence office as you do; a business which must furnish peculiar facilities for studying mankind. Come, come up here, sir; confess you know these things pretty well, after all. Do you not know that all men are rascals, and all boys, too?"

"Sir," replied the other, spite of his shocked feelings seeming to pluck up some spirit, but not to an indiscreet degree, "Sir, heaven be praised, I am far, very far from knowing what you say. True," he thoughtfully continued, "with my associates, I keep an intelligence office, and for ten years, come October, have, one way or other, been concerned in that line; for no small period in the great city of Cincinnati, too; and though, as you hint, within that long interval, I must have had more or less favorable opportunity for studying mankind—in a business way, scanning not only the faces, but ransacking the lives of several thousands of human beings, male and female, of various nations, both employers and employed, genteel and ungenteel, educated and uneducated; yet—of course, I candidly admit, with some random exceptions, I have, so far as my small observation goes, found that mankind thus domestically viewed, confidentially viewed, I may say; they, upon the whole—making some reasonable allowances for human imperfection—present as pure a moral spectacle as the purest angel could wish. I say it, respected sir, with confidence."

"Gammon! You don't mean what you say. Else you are like a landsman at sea: don't know the ropes, the very things everlastingly pulled before your eyes. Serpent-like, they glide about, traveling blocks too subtle for you. In short, the entire ship is a riddle. Why, you green ones wouldn't know if she were unseaworthy; but still, with thumbs stuck back into your arm-holes, pace the rotten planks, singing, like a fool, words put into your green mouth by the cunning owner, the man who, heavily insuring it, sends his ship to be wrecked—

[16] From William Wordsworth's "My Heart Leaps Up."

'A wet sheet and a flowing sea!'— [17]

and, sir, now that it occurs to me, your talk, the whole of it, is but a wet sheet and a flowing sea, and an idle wind that follows fast, offering a striking contrast to my own discourse."

"Sir," exclaimed the man with the brass-plate, his patience now more or less tasked, "permit me with deference to hint that some of your remarks are injudiciously worded. And thus we say to our patrons, when they enter our office full of abuse of us because of some worthy boy we may have sent them— some boy wholly misjudged for the time. Yes, sir, permit me to remark that you do not sufficiently consider that, though a small man, I may have my small share of feelings."

"Well, well, I didn't mean to wound your feelings at all. And that they are small, very small, I take your word for it. Sorry, sorry. But truth is like a thrashing-machine; tender sensibilities must keep out of the way. Hope you understand me. Don't want to hurt you. All I say is, what I said in the first place, only now I swear it, that all boys are rascals."

"Sir," lowly replied the other, still forbearing like an old lawyer badgered in court, or else like a good-hearted simpleton, the butt of mischievous wags,[18] "Sir, since you come back to the point, will you allow me, in my small, quiet way, to submit to you certain small, quiet views of the subject in hand?"

"Oh, yes!" with insulting indifference, rubbing his chin and looking the other way. "Oh, yes; go on."

"Well, then, respected sir," continued the other, now assuming as genteel an attitude as the irritating set of his pinched five-dollar suit would permit; "well, then, sir, the peculiar principles, the strictly philosophical principles, I may say," guardedly rising in dignity, as he guardedly rose on his toes, "upon which our office is founded, has led me and my associates, in

17 Title line of a poem by Allan Cunningham (1784–1842) in his *The Songs of Scotland, Ancient and Modern* (1825).

18 See the wag who victimizes the lamb-like man in Chapter 1 and the practical jokers who victimize Black Guinea in Chapter 3.

our small, quiet way, to a careful analytical study of man, conducted, too, on a quiet theory, and with an unobtrusive aim wholly our own. That theory I will not now at large set forth. But some of the discoveries resulting from it, I will, by your permission, very briefly mention; such of them, I mean, as refer to the state of boyhood scientifically viewed."

"Then you have studied the thing? expressly studied boys, eh? Why didn't you out with that before?"

"Sir, in my small business way, I have not conversed with so many masters, gentlemen masters, for nothing. I have been taught that in this world there is a precedence of opinions as well as of persons. You have kindly given me your views, I am now, with modesty, about to give you mine."

"Stop flunkying—go on."

"In the first place, sir, our theory teaches us to proceed by analogy from the physical to the moral. Are we right there, sir? Now, sir, take a young boy, a young male infant rather, a man-child in short—what sir, I respectfully ask, do you in the first place remark?"

"A rascal, sir! present and prospective, a rascal!"

"Sir, if passion is to invade, surely science must evacuate. May I proceed? Well, then, what, in the first place, in a general view, do you remark, respected sir, in that male baby or man-child?"

The bachelor privily growled, but this time, upon the whole, better governed himself than before, though not, indeed, to the degree of thinking it prudent to risk an articulate response.

"What do you remark? I respectfully repeat." But, as no answer came, only the low, half-suppressed growl, as of Bruin in a hollow trunk, the questioner continued: "Well, sir, if you will permit me, in my small way, to speak for you, you remark, respected sir, in incipient creation; loose sort of sketchy thing; a little preliminary rag-paper study, or careless cartoon, so to speak, of a man. The idea, you see, respected sir, is there; but, as yet, wants filling out. In a word, respected sir, the man-child is at present but little, every way; I don't pretend to deny it; but, then, he *promises* well, does he not? Yes, promises very well indeed, I may say. (So, too, we say to our patrons in reference to some noble little youngster objected to for being a *dwarf*.[19]) But, to advance one step further," extending his thread-bare leg, as he drew a pace nearer, "we must now drop the figure of the rag-paper cartoon, and borrow one—to use presently, when wanted—from the horticultural kingdom. Some bud, lily-bud, if you please. Now, such points as the new-born man-child has—as yet not all that could be desired, I am free to confess—still, such as they are, there they are, and palpable as those of an adult. But we stop not here," taking another step. "The man-child not only possesses these present points, small though they are, but, likewise—now our horticultural image comes into play—like the bud of the lily, he contains concealed rudiments of others; that is, points at present invisible, with beauties at present dormant."

"Come, come, this talk is getting too horticultural and beautiful altogether. Cut it short, cut it short!"

"Respected sir," with a rustily martial sort of gesture, like a decayed corporal's,[20] "when deploying into the field of discourse the vanguard of an important argument, much more in evolving the grand central forces of a new philosophy of boys, as I may say, surely you will kindly allow scope adequate to the movement in hand, small and humble in its way as that movement may be. Is it worth my while to go on, respected sir?"

"Yes, stop flunkying and go on."

Thus encouraged, again the philosopher with the brass-plate proceeded:

"Supposing, sir, that worthy gentleman (in such terms, to an applicant for service, we allude to some patron we chance to have in our eye), supposing, respected sir, that worthy gen-

[19] The most famous dwarf of the American East was Tom Thumb, displayed in Barnum's American Museum along with the duck-billed beaver, Calvin Edson, and the Siamese twins. The most famous dwarf of the other East was the dwarf avatar of Vishnu.

[20] Perhaps another candidate for the "ge'mman as is a sodjer."

tleman, Adam, to have been dropped overnight in Eden, as a calf in the pasture; supposing that, sir—then how could even the learned serpent himself have foreknown that such a downy-chinned little innocent would eventually rival the goat in a beard? Sir, wise as the serpent was, that eventuality would have been entirely hidden from his wisdom."

"I don't know about that. The devil is very sagacious. To judge by the event, he appears to have understood man better even than the Being who made him."

"For God's sake, don't say that, sir! To the point. Can it now with fairness be denied that, in his beard, the man-child prospectively possesses an appendix, not less imposing than patriarchal; and for this goodly beard, should we not by generous anticipation give the man-child, even in his cradle, credit? Should we not now, sir? respectfully I put it."

"Yes, if like pig-weed he mows it down soon as it shoots," porcinely rubbing his stubble-chin against his coon-skins.

"I have hinted at the analogy," continued the other, calmly disregardful of the digression; "now to apply it. Suppose a boy evince no noble quality. Then generously give him credit for his prospective one. Don't you see? So we say to our patrons when they would fain return a boy upon us as unworthy: 'Madam, or sir, (as the case may be) has this boy a beard?' 'No.' 'Has he, we respectfully ask, as yet, evinced any noble quality?' 'No, indeed.' 'Then, madam, or sir, take him back, we humbly beseech; and keep him till that same noble quality sprouts; for, have confidence, it, like the beard, is in him.' "

"Very fine theory," scornfully exclaimed the bachelor, yet in secret, perhaps, not entirely undisturbed by these strange new views of the matter; "but what trust is to be placed in it?"

"The trust of perfect confidence, sir. To proceed. Once more, if you please, regard the man-child."

"Hold!" paw-like thrusting out his bearskin arm, "don't intrude that man-child upon me too often. He who loves not bread, dotes not on dough. As little of your man-child as your logical arrangements will admit."

"Anew regard the man-child," with inspired intrepidity repeated he with the brass-plate, "in the perspective of his developments, I mean. At first the man-child has no teeth, but about the sixth month—am I right, sir?"

"Don't know anything about it."

"To proceed then: though at first deficient in teeth, about the sixth month the man-child begins to put forth in that particular. And sweet those tender little puttings-forth are."

"Very, but blown out of his mouth directly, worthless enough."

"Admitted. And, therefore, we say to our patrons returning with a boy alleged not only to be deficient in goodness, but redundant in ill: 'The lad, madam or sir, evinces very corrupt qualities, does he?' 'No end to them.' 'But, have confidence, there will be; for pray, madam, in this lad's early childhood, were not those frail first teeth, then his, followed by his present sound, even, beautiful and permanent set. And the more objectionable those first teeth became, was not that, madam, we respectfully submit, so much the more reason to look for their speedy substitution by the present sound, even, beautiful and permanent ones.' 'True, true, can't deny that.' [21] 'Then, madam, take him back, we respectfully beg, and wait till, in the now swift course of nature, dropping those transient moral blemishes you complain of, he replacingly buds forth in the sound, even, beautiful and permanent virtues.' "

"Very philosophical again," was the contemptuous reply—the outward contempt, perhaps, proportioned to the inward misgiving. "Vastly philosophical, indeed, but tell me—to continue your analogy—since the second teeth followed—in fact, came from—the first, is there no chance the blemish may be transmitted?"

[21] Previously the PIO man has asked of Pitch: "permit me . . . to speak for you." Here he uses another Socratic (and Platonic) tactic, creating a figure who reluctantly assents to what he is arguing.

"Not at all." Abating in humility as he gained in the argument. "The second teeth follow, but do not come from, the first; successors, not sons. The first teeth are not like the germ blossom of the apple, at once the father of, and incorporated into, the growth it foreruns; but they are thrust from their place by the independent undergrowth of the succeeding set [22] —an illustration, by the way, which shows more for me than I meant, though not more than I wish."

"What does it show?" Surly-looking as a thundercloud with the inkept unrest of unacknowledged conviction.

"It shows this, respected sir, that in the case of any boy, especially an ill one, to apply unconditionally the saying, that the 'child is father of the man', is, besides implying an uncharitable aspersion of the race, affirming a thing very wide of—"

"—Your analogy," like a snapping turtle.

"Yes, respected sir."

"But is analogy argument? You are a punster."

"Punster, respected sir?" with a look of being aggrieved.

"Yes, you pun with ideas as another man may with words."

"Oh well, sir, whoever talks in that strain, whoever has no confidence in human reason, whoever despises human reason, in vain to reason with him. Still, respected sir," altering his air, "permit me to hint that, had not the force of analogy moved you somewhat, you would hardly have offered to contemn it."

"Talk away," disdainfully; "but pray tell me what has that last analogy of yours to do with your intelligence office business?"

"Everything to do with it, respected sir. From that analogy we derive the reply made to such a patron as, shortly after being supplied by us with an adult servant, proposes to return him upon our hands; not that, while with the patron, said adult has given any cause of dissatisfaction, but the patron has just chanced to hear something unfavorable concerning him from

[22] In other words, like (1) the Titans and their father Uranus, (2) Zeus and his father Cronus, (3) the Missouri and the Mississippi (see Appendix, "The River"), and (4) the psychology of sons and fathers.

some gentleman who employed said adult long before, while a boy. To which too fastidious patron, we, taking said adult by the hand, and graciously reintroducing him to the patron, say: 'Far be it from you, madam, or sir, to proceed in your censure against this adult, in anything of the spirit of an ex-post-facto law. Madam, or sir, would you visit upon the butterfly the sins of the caterpillar? [23] In the natural advance of all creatures, do they not bury themselves over and over again in the endless resurrection of better and better? Madam, or sir, take back this adult; he may have been a caterpillar, but is now a butterfly." [24]

"Pun away; but even accepting your analogical pun, what does it amount to? Was the caterpillar one creature, and is the butterfly another? The butterfly is the caterpillar in a gaudy cloak; stripped of which, there lies the impostor's long spindle of a body, pretty much worm-shaped as before."

"You reject the analogy. To the facts then. You deny that a youth of one character can be transformed into a man of an opposite character. Now then—yes, I have it. There's the founder of La Trappe,[25] and Ignatius Loyola; [26] in boyhood,

[23] Compare God's threat in Exodus 20:5 and elsewhere to visit the sins of the fathers upon the children.

[24] Note that the PIO man is here using precisely the argument and metaphor used by the authorial voice in Chapter 14. The two contexts should be compared in detail to see what is going on. This is the last chapter in which crawls what we might call the Confidence Man as caterpillar, who is to be replaced by the gaudy-colored Cosmopolitan. So the argument between Pitch and the PIO man is an argument about how to read the book.

[25] Armand Jean le Bouthillier de Rancé (1626–1700), abbot of the Cistercian monastery of La Trappe in France (originally founded in the twelfth century), instituted the program of extreme austerity which made the abbey famous; he is therefore known as the founder of the Trappists. A great roué in early life, he was supposedly converted at the age of 29 or 30 by finding the dead body of his mistress.

[26] Saint Ignatius de Loyola (1491–1556), founder of the Society of Jesus. Brought up as a court page, and then a soldier, he was converted

and someway into manhood, both devil-may-care bloods, and yet, in the end, the wonders of the world for anchoritish self-command. These two examples, by-the-way, we cite to such patrons as would hastily return rakish young waiters upon us. 'Madam, or sir—patience; patience,' we say; 'good madam, or sir, would you discharge forth your cask of good wine, because, while working, it riles more or less? Then discharge not forth this young waiter; the good in him is working.' 'But he is a sad rake.' 'Therein is his promise; the rake being crude material for the saint.' "

"Ah, you are a talking man—what I call a wordy man.[27] You talk, talk."

"And with submission, sir, what is the greatest judge, bishop or prophet, but a talking man? He talks, talks. It is the peculiar vocation of a teacher to talk. What's wisdom itself but table-talk? The best wisdom in this world, and the last spoken by its teacher, did it not literally and truly come in the form of table-talk?" [28]

"You, you, you!" rattling down his rifle.

"To shift the subject, since we cannot agree. Pray, what is your opinion, respected sir, of St. Augustine?"

"St. Augustine? What should I, or you either, know of him? Seems to me, for one in such a business, to say nothing of such a coat, that though you don't know a great deal, indeed, yet you know a good deal more than you ought to know, or than you have a right to know, or than it is safe or expedient for you to know, or than, in the fair course of life, you could have honestly come to know. I am of opinion you should be served like a Jew in the middle ages with his gold; this knowledge of yours, which you haven't enough knowledge to know how to

at the age of thirty, while recovering from a severe wound. Under his leadership the Jesuits became one of the main forces of the counter-reformation. See Chapter 18, note 8 on the Jesuits.

[27] Cf. Black Guinea's self-description as "werry well wordy" of confidence.

[28] At Christ's Last Supper.

make a right use of, it should be taken from you. And so I have been thinking all along."

"You are merry, sir. But you have a little looked into St. Augustine I suppose."

"St. Augustine on Original Sin [29] is my text book. But you, I ask again, where do you find time or inclination for these out-of-the-way speculations? In fact, your whole talk, the more I think of it, is altogether unexampled and extraordinary."

"Respected sir, have I not already informed you that the quite new method, the strictly philosophical one, on which our office is founded, has led me and my associates to an enlarged study of mankind. It was my fault, if I did not, likewise, hint, that these studies directed always to the scientific procuring of good servants of all sorts, boys included, for the kind gentlemen, our patrons—that these studies, I say, have been conducted equally among all books of all libraries, as among all men of all nations. Then, you rather like St. Augustine, sir?"

"Excellent genius!"

"In some points he was; yet, how comes it that under his own hand, St. Augustine confesses that, until his thirtieth year, he was a very sad dog?" [30]

"A saint a sad dog?"

---

[29] St. Augustine of Numidia (354–430) wrote no book specifically on original sin, but the concept is central to his system of belief. Man's original sin (which Augustine attributed to the will of Adam even before the Fall) represents his basic deviation from perfection and is both the cause and manifestation of all his sin.

[30] Augustine saw as the three great wickednesses of his earlier life: his Manichean beliefs, his supposed sensualism, and his love and teaching of rhetoric. His obsession with man's sinfulness often took the form of self-loathing. Actually Augustine was about thirty-two at the time of his conversion, but the PIO man suggests that it came precisely at the age when it came to the founder of La Trappe and Ignatius Loyola; this is also the age of a conversion in Chapter 34 and of a convert in Chapter 38.

"Not the saint, but the saint's irresponsible little forerunner
—the boy."

"All boys are rascals, and so are all men," again flying off at
his tangent; "my name is Pitch; I stick to what I say."

"Ah, sir, permit me—when I behold you on this mild summer's eve,[31] thus eccentrically clothed in the skins of wild
beasts, I cannot but conclude that the equally grim and unsuitable habit of your mind is likewise but an eccentric assumption, having no basis in your genuine soul, no more than in
nature herself."

"Well, really, now—really," fidgeted the bachelor, not unaffected in his conscience by these benign personalities,
"really, really, now, I don't know but that I may have been a
little bit too hard upon those five and thirty boys of mine."

"Glad to find you a little softening, sir. Who knows now,
but that flexile gracefulness, however questionable at the time
of that thirtieth boy of yours, might have been the silky husk
of the most solid qualities of maturity. It might have been with
him as with the ear of the Indian corn."

"Yes, yes, yes," excitedly cried the bachelor, as the light of
this new illustration broke in, "yes, yes; and now that I think
of it, how often I've sadly watched my Indian corn in May,
wondering whether such sickly, half-eaten sprouts, could ever
thrive up into the stiff, stately spear of August."

"A most admirable reflection, sir, and you have only, according to the analogical theory first started by our office, to
apply it to that thirtieth boy in question, and see the result.
Had you but kept that thirtieth boy—been patient with his
sickly virtues, cultivated them, hoed round them, why what a
glorious guerdon would have been yours, when at last you
should have had a St. Augustine for an ostler."

"Really, really—well, I am glad I didn't send him to jail, as
at first I intended."

"Oh that would have been too bad. Grant he was vicious.

[31] I.e., appropriate to summer.

The petty vices of boys are like the innocent kicks of colts, as yet imperfectly broken. Some boys know not virtue only for the same reason they know not French; it was never taught them. Established upon the basis of parental charity, juvenile asylums exist by law for the benefit of lads convicted of acts which, in adults, would have received other requital. Why? Because, do what they will, society, like our office, at bottom has a Christian confidence in boys. And all this we say to our patrons."

"Your patrons, sir, seem your marines to whom you may say anything," [32] said the other, relapsing. "Why do knowing employers shun youths from asylums, though offered them at the smallest wages? I'll none of your reformado [33] boys."

"Such a boy, respected sir, I would not get for you, but a boy that never needed reform. Do not smile, for as whooping-cough and measles are juvenile diseases, and yet some juveniles never have them, so are there boys equally free from juvenile vices. True, for the best of boys, measles may be contagious, and evil communications corrupt good manners; but a boy with a sound mind in a sound body [34]—such is the boy I would get you. If hitherto, sir, you have struck upon a peculiarly bad vein of boys, so much the more hope now of your hitting a good one." [35]

[32] The old nautical saying, "You may tell that to the marines, but the sailors won't believe it," was based on the sailors' view of the marines on shipboard as landlubbers.

[33] As a noun "reformado" means (1) a monk who works for the reform of his order, or (2) a disgraced military officer. Hence as an adjective it signifies (1) penitent, reformed, devoted to reformation, or (2) inferior, degraded. Pitch seems to be responding to all the talk about the founder of La Trappe, Ignatius Loyola, and St. Augustine.

[34] From Juvenal, *Satires* 10. 356: *Orandum est, ut sit mens sana in corpore sano.* ("One should pray for a sound mind in a sound body.")

[35] The hope that keeps all prospectors and gamblers going; based on the fallacy that a past deviation from normal probability changes present or future probability.

"That sounds a kind of reasonable, as it were—a little so, really. In fact, though you have said a great many foolish things, very foolish and absurd things, yet, upon the whole, your conversation has been such as might almost lead one less distrustful than I to repose a certain conditional confidence in you, I had almost added in your office, also. Now, for the humor of it, supposing that even I, I myself, really had this sort of conditional confidence, though but a grain, what sort of a boy, in sober fact, could you send me? And what would be your fee?"

"Conducted," replied the other somewhat loftily, rising now in eloquence as his proselyte, for all his pretenses, sunk in conviction, "conducted upon principles involving care, learning, and labor, exceeding what is usual in kindred institutions, the Philosophical Intelligence Office is forced to charges somewhat higher than customary. Briefly, our fee is three dollars in advance. As for the boy, by a lucky chance, I have a very promising little fellow now in my eye—a very likely little fellow, indeed."

"Honest?"

"As the day is long.[36] Might trust him with untold millions. Such, at least, were the marginal observations on the phrenological chart of his head, submitted to me by the mother."

"How old?"

"Just fifteen."

"Tall? Stout?"

"Uncommonly so, for his age, his mother remarked."

"Industrious?"

"The busy bee."

The bachelor fell into a troubled reverie. At last, with much hesitancy, he spoke:

[36] This anonymous old simile has new meaning here. The first half of the book, which takes place between sunrise and twilight, ends with the present chapter; the second half will take place between twilight and shortly after midnight.

"Do you think now, candidly, that—I say candidly—candidly—could I have some small, limited—some faint, conditional degree of confidence in that boy? Candidly, now?"

"Candidly, you could."

"A sound boy? A good boy?"

"Never knew one more so."

The bachelor fell into another irresolute reverie; then said: "Well, now, you have suggested some rather new views of boys, and men, too. Upon those views in the concrete I at present decline to determine. Nevertheless, for the sake purely of a scientific experiment, I will try that boy. I don't think him an angel, mind. No, no. But I'll try him. There are my three dollars, and here is my address. Send him along this day two weeks. Hold, you will be wanting the money for his passage. There," handing it somewhat reluctantly.

"Ah, thank you. I had forgotten his passage;" then, altering in manner, and gravely holding the bills, continued: "Respected sir, never willingly do I handle money not with perfect willingness, nay, with a certain alacrity, paid. Either tell me that you have a perfect and unquestioning confidence in me (never mind the boy now) or permit me respectfully to return these bills."

"Put 'em up, put 'em up!"

"Thank you. Confidence is the indispensable basis of all sorts of business transactions. Without it, commerce between man and man, as between country and country, would, like a watch, run down and stop. And now, supposing that against present expectation the lad should, after all, evince some little undesirable trait, do not, respected sir, rashly dismiss him. Have but patience, have but confidence. Those transient vices will, ere long, fall out, and be replaced by the sound, firm, even and permanent virtues. Ah," glancing shoreward, towards a grotesquely-shaped bluff, "there's the Devil's Joke,[37]

[37] Probably a fictitious place, though local geographical nicknames gave many places to the Devil.

as they call it; the bell for landing will shortly ring. I must go look up the cook I brought for the inn-keeper at Cairo." [38]

[38] This joke, and much of the following chapter, assumes a knowledge of Dickens' *Martin Chuzzlewit* (1844), in which Martin and his servant Mark Tapley are swindled into buying a lot in the "city" of Eden, which turns out to be a deadly swamp (see Chapter 9, note 13). Dickens' model for Eden was Cairo, Illinois, which had been laid out in 1818 by a St. Louis merchant but then undeveloped. In 1837 Cairo was founded anew by the Cairo City and Canal Company, which sold lots and attempted, one way or another, to get settlers. (Because of the name, all of southern Illinois became known as the land of Egypt.) Dickens calls Cairo Eden, and describes it as Hell: the steamboat which takes Martin and Mark there "might have been old Charon's boat"; they learn that "nobody as goes to Eden ever comes back a-live!"; they find themselves damned to:

A flat morass, bestrewn with fallen timber; a marsh on which the good growth of the earth seemed to have been wrecked and cast away, that from its decomposing ashes vile and ugly things might rise; where the very trees took the aspect of huge weeds, begotten of the slime from which they sprung, by the hot sun that burned them up; where fatal maladies, seeking whom they might infect, came forth at night, in misty shapes, and creeping out upon the water, hunted them like spectres until day; where even the blessed sun, shining down on festering elements of corruption and disease, became a horror; this was the realm of Hope through which they moved.

But here Martin, first encountering death and then having the role of servant and master reversed, turns from a sulky, self-centered, arrogant jackanapes to a fine young man—much as the PIO man would have predicted. While Mark is deathly sick, Martin becomes the cook for the in[n]-keeper at Cairo. Then, to pay their passage back to England, Mark engages to be the ship's cook.

The means of Martin's salvation is the "fever and ague" "which was very common in those parts":

"I said you must be ill," returned Mark, tenderly, "and now I'm sure of it. A touch of fever and ague caught on these rivers, I dare say; but bless you, *that's* nothing. It's only a seasoning; and we must all be seasoned, one way or another. That's religion, that is, you know," said Mark.

CHAPTER 23

*In which the powerful effect of natural
scenery is evinced in the case of the
Missourian, who, in view of the
region roundabout Cairo, has a
return of his chilly fit.*

At Cairo,[1] the old established firm of Fever & Ague is still
settling up its unfinished business; that Creole grave-digger,
Yellow Jack [2]—his hand at the mattock and spade has not lost

[1] The voyage began at St. Louis, just below where the Missouri
comes from the West to join the Mississippi. At Cairo, where the Ohio
comes from the East to join the Mississippi, the voyage changes its
nature. Here, where the boat lies still, is the still point which divides
the book precisely into contrasting halves, each composed of twenty-two
chapters.

Cairo, swampy, notorious breeding place of disease, is also the last free
point to be passed on the journey south; from here on the Fidèle will
continually have slave states on both sides. From here on no avatar of
the Confidence Man will appear as listed by the Negro "widout massa,"
Black Guinea; the Cosmopolitan will dominate the rest of the action.

On April First light and darkness endure equally. So here for the
passengers on the Fidèle comes the twilight that ends the day; the rest
of the action will take place in deepening night, concluding shortly after
midnight.

[2] Yellow Fever. The first of Black Guinea's listings not to appear
exactly as described is the "ge'mman in a yaller west." Since vest
meant any vestment, Yellow Jack[et] may well be the missing avatar
and the "ge'mman in a yaller west" may thus be literally an incarnation
of Death himself. In effect, therefore, any passenger boarding at disease-
spawning Cairo may be Death incarnate (cf. Poe's "Masque of the Red
Death") as a form of the Confidence Man.

In the first half of the book there appeared one mute, three cripples,
an invalid Titan, a man with a bandaged nose, and two sick men. In the

its cunning; [3] while Don Saturninus Typhus [4] taking his consti-
tutional with Death, Calvin Edson [5] and three undertakers, in
the morass, snuffs up the mephitic breeze with zest.

In the dank twilight, fanned with mosquitoes, and sparkling
with fire-flies, the boat now lies before Cairo. She has landed
certain passengers, and tarries for the coming of expected ones.
Leaning over the rail on the inshore side, the Missourian eyes
through the dubious medium that swampy and squalid domain;
and over it audibly mumbles his cynical mind to himself, as
Apemantus' dog [6] may have mumbled his bone. He bethinks
him that the man with the brass-plate was to land on this
villainous bank, and for that cause, if no other, begins to suspect him. Like one beginning to rouse himself from a dose of
chloroform treacherously given, he half divines, too, that he,
the philosopher, had unwittingly been betrayed into being an
unphilosophical dupe. To what vicissitudes of light and shade
is man subject! He ponders the mystery of human subjectivity

---

second half everyone on the surface seems well, but there are references
to numerous diseases (including the pip, calentures, distemper, hydrophobia, consumption, glanders, dyspepsia), and there are frequent hints
of the possibly diseased state of both the Cosmopolitan and Charlie
Noble, the riverboat con man, either of whom *may* have come aboard
at Cairo but both of whom give evidence that they were on board
before. In the final chapter, the mysterious boy, who for other reasons
may be an embodiment of Death, wears a yellow coat.

[3] Psalms 137:5: "If I forget thee, O Jerusalem, let my right hand forget her cunning."

[4] This personification links, through etymology, two beings overthrown by Zeus and buried by him in Tartarus: typhus (literally
"smoke") is etymologically identical with the flaming monster Typhoëus;
saturnine literally means born under Saturn (the father of Zeus, usually
identified with Cronus).

[5] See Chapter 16, note 7.

[6] A further development of a tricky word game played by Shakespeare
in *Timon of Athens*; Apemantus the Cynic (i.e., "dog"), friend of
Timon the Cynic, has no dog but himself or Timon. (See I, *i*, 178–180,
203; II, *ii*, 90; IV, *iii*, 198–201, 313–317, 361, 371.)

in general. He thinks he perceives with Crossbones,[7] his favorite author, that, as one may wake up well in the morning, very well, indeed, and brisk as a buck, I thank you, but ere bed-time get under the weather, there is no telling how—so one may wake up wise, and slow of assent, very wise and very slow, I assure you, and for all that, before night, by like trick in the atmosphere, be left in the lurch a ninny. Health and wisdom equally precious, and equally little as unfluctuating possessions to be relied on.

But where was slipped in the entering wedge? Philosophy, knowledge, experience—were those trusty knights of the castle recreant? No, but unbeknown to them, the enemy stole on the castle's south side, its genial one, where Suspicion, the warder, parleyed.[8] In fine, his too indulgent, too artless and companionable nature betrayed him. Admonished by which, he thinks he must be a little splenetic in his intercourse henceforth.

He revolves the crafty process of sociable chat, by which, as he fancies, the man with the brass-plate wormed into him, and made such a fool of him as insensibly to persuade him to waive, in his exceptional case, that general law of distrust systematically applied to the race. He revolves, but cannot comprehend, the operation, still less the operator. Was the man a trickster, it must be more for the love than the lucre. Two or three dirty dollars the motive to so many nice wiles? And yet how full of mean needs his seeming. Before his mental vision the person of that threadbare Talleyrand,[9] that im-

---

[7] An emblem of Death. Pitch may be about to meet, or may have just met, his favorite author in person. The identification of Crossbones and an author suggests one possible set of relations between the "author" of *The Confidence-Man* and his title character.

[8] William Pommer in *Milton and Melville* points to the suggestive resemblance between these last two sentences and the passage in *Paradise Lost* which generalizes about Satan's deception of Uriel, the "sharpest-sighted spirit of all in Heaven" (III, 681–689).

[9] Charles Maurice de Talleyrand-Périgord (1754–1838), French statesman, one of the world's most effective diplomats.

poverished Machiavelli,[10] that seedy Rosicrucian [11]—for something of all these he vaguely deems him—passes now in puzzled review. Fain, in his disfavor, would he make out a logical case. The doctrine of analogies recurs. Fallacious enough doctrine when wielded against one's prejudices, but in corroboration of cherished suspicions not without likelihood. Analogically, he couples the slanting cut of the equivocator's coat-tails with the sinister cast in his eye; he weighs sly-boot's [12] sleek speech in the light imparted by the oblique import of the smooth slope of his worn boot-heels; the insinuator's undulating flunkyisms dovetail into those of the flunky beast that windeth his way on his belly.[13]

From these uncordial reveries he is roused by a cordial slap on the shoulder, accompanied by a spicy volume of tobacco-smoke,[14] out of which came a voice, sweet as a seraph's:

"A penny for your thoughts,[15] my fine fellow."

[10] Niccolo Machiavelli (1469–1527), Florentine statesman and writer whose name has become a symbol of political guile.

[11] A Rosicrucian is a member of any of several secret societies of that name which claim esoteric mystical knowledge of the secrets of nature and the spiritual world. The name literally means Rose-Cross. Melville puns on the first symbol with "seedy" and possibly suggests a relation between the second symbol and Crossbones.

[12] Humorous word for a sly, cunning, or crafty person.

[13] Pitch recognizes the serpent, the beast condemned to going on its belly, but fails to perceive its allegorical union with the dove, here coming about in the word "dovetail." Christ's injunction to his ministers in Matthew 10:16, one of Melville's favorite passages, is relevant here and elsewhere: "Behold, I send you forth as sheep in the midst of wolves: be ye therefore wise as serpents, and harmless as doves."

[14] Perhaps masking the smell of disease, this spicy smoke introduces one of the main images of the second half of the book—smoke as a mask of death.

[15] The Cosmopolitan's first words offer money for words, thus reversing the routine of the first half of the book, in which the Confidence-Man tries to get money for words.

CHAPTER 24

A philanthropist undertakes to convert a
misanthrope, but does not get beyond
confuting [1] *him.*

"Hands off!" cried the bachelor, involuntarily covering dejection with moroseness.

"Hands off? that sort of label won't do in our Fair.[2] Whoever in our Fair has fine feelings loves to feel the nap of fine cloth, especially when a fine fellow wears it."

"And who of my fine-fellow species may you be? From the Brazils, ain't you? Toucan fowl.[3] Fine feathers on foul meat."

This ungentle mention of the toucan was not improbably suggested by the parti-hued, and rather plumagy aspect of the stranger, no bigot it would seem, but a liberalist, in dress, and whose wardrobe, almost anywhere than on the liberal Mississippi, used to all sorts of fantastic informalities, might, even to observers less critical than the bachelor, have looked, if anything, a little out of the common; but not more so perhaps, than, considering the bear and raccoon costume, the bachelor's own appearance. In short, the stranger sported a vesture barred with various hues, that of the cochineal predominating, in style participating of a Highland plaid, Emir's robe, and

[1] Convert and confute are two forms of the con game.

[2] John W. Shroeder ("Sources and Symbols for Melville's *The Confidence-Man*," PMLA, LXVI [1951], 363–380) suggests that this Fair is Vanity Fair of Bunyan's *Pilgrim's Progress*.

[3] Cf. the dove (and the serpent) of the previous chapter.

French blouse; from its plaited sort of front peeped glimpses of a flowered regatta-shirt, while, for the rest, white trowsers of ample duck flowed over maroon-colored slippers, and a jaunty smoking-cap of regal purple crowned him off at top; king of traveled good-fellows, evidently. Grotesque as all was, nothing looked stiff or unused; all showed signs of easy service, the least wonted thing setting like a wonted glove. That genial hand, which had just been laid on the ungenial shoulder, was now carelessly thrust down before him, sailor-fashion, into a sort of Indian belt, confining the redundant vesture; the other held, by its long bright cherry-stem, a Nuremburgh pipe in blast, its great porcelain bowl painted in miniature with linked crests and arms of interlinked nations—a florid show. As by subtle saturations of its mellowing essence the tobacco had ripened the bowl, so it looked as if something similar of the interior spirit came rosily out on the cheek. But rosy pipe-bowl, or rosy countenance, all was lost on that unrosy man, the bachelor, who, waiting a moment till the commotion, caused by the boat's renewed progress, had a little abated, thus continued:

"Hark ye," jeeringly eying the cap and belt, "did you ever see Signor Marzetti in the African pantomime?" [4]

"No;—good performer?"

"Excellent; plays the intelligent ape till he seems it. With such naturalness can a being endowed with an immortal spirit enter into that of a monkey. But where's your tail? In the pantomime, Marzetti, no hypocrite in his monkery, prides himself on that."

The stranger, now at rest, sideways and genially, on one hip, his right leg cavalierly crossed before the other, the toe of his vertical slipper pointed easily down on the deck, whiffed out a long, leisurely sort of indifferent and charitable puff, betokening him more or less of the mature man of the world, a character which, like its opposite, the sincere Christian's, is not always

[4] Joseph Marzetti had played an ape in a skit presented for years in New York (Foster).

swift to take offense; and then, drawing near, still smoking, again laid his hand, this time with mild impressiveness, on the ursine shoulder, and not unamiably said: "That in your address there is a sufficiency of the *fortiter in re* few unbiased observers will question; but that this is duly attempered with the *suaviter in modo* [5] may admit, I think, of an honest doubt. My dear fellow," beaming his eyes full upon him, "what injury have I done you, that you should receive my greeting with a curtailed civility?"

"Off hands;" once more shaking the friendly member from him. "Who in the name of the great chimpanzee, in whose likeness, you, Marzetti, and the other chatterers are made, who in thunder are you?"

"A cosmopolitan, a catholic man; who, being such, ties himself to no narrow tailor or teacher, but federates, in heart as in costume, something of the various gallantries of men under various suns. Oh, one roams not over the gallant globe in vain. Bred by it, is a fraternal and fusing feeling. No man is a stranger. You accost anybody. Warm and confiding, you wait not for measured advances. And though, indeed, mine, in this instance, have met with no very hilarious encouragement, yet the principle of a true citizen of the world is still to return good for ill.—My dear fellow, tell me how I can serve you."

"By dispatching yourself, Mr. Popinjay-of-the-world, into the heart of the Lunar Mountains.[6] You are another of them. Out of my sight!"

"Is the sight of humanity so very disagreeable to you then? Ah, I may be foolish, but for my part, in all its aspects, I love it. Served up à la Pole, or à la Moor, à la Ladrone, or à la

[5] *Fortiter in re, sed suaviter in modo* ("unflinching in act, but gracious in method").

[6] Ptolemy located the source of the Nile as the Mountains of the Moon (Lunae Montes Finis Oriental) in east-central Africa. Generally believed in the nineteenth century to be merely legendary, these Mountains of the Moon have now been identified as the strange Ruwenzori Mountains in Uganda.

Yankee, that good dish, man, still delights me; or rather is man a wine I never weary of comparing and sipping; wherefore am I a pledged cosmopolitan, a sort of London-Dock-Vault connoisseur,[7] going about from Teheran to Natchitoches, a taster of races; in all his vintages, smacking my lips over this racy creature, man, continually. But as there are teetotal palates which have a distaste even for Amontillado, so I suppose there may be teetotal souls which relish not even the very best brands of humanity. Excuse me, but it just occurs to me that you, my dear fellow, possibly lead a solitary life."

"Solitary?" starting as at a touch of divination.

"Yes: in a solitary life one insensibly contracts oddities,—talking to one's self now."

"Been eaves-dropping, eh?"

"Why, a soliloquist in a crowd can hardly but be overheard, and without much reproach to the hearer."

"You are an eaves-dropper."

"Well. Be it so."

"Confess yourself an eaves-dropper?"

"I confess that when you were muttering here I, passing by, caught a word or two, and, by like chance, something previous of your chat with the Intelligence-office man;—a rather sensible fellow, by the way; much of my style of thinking; would, for his own sake, he were of my style of dress. Grief to good minds, to see a man of superior sense forced to hide his light under the bushel [8] of an inferior coat.—Well, from what little I heard, I said to myself, Here now is one with the unprofitable philosophy of disesteem for man. Which disease, in the main, I have observed—excuse me—to spring from a certain lowness, if not sourness, of spirits inseparable from sequestration. Trust me, one had better mix in, and do like others. Sad business, this holding out against having a good time. Life is a

[7] The London dock-vaults contained wines from all over the world.
[8] In the Sermon on the Mount, Christ tells his followers, "Ye are the light of the world," and exhorts them not to hide this light: "Neither do men light a candle, and put it under a bushel, but on a candlestick: and it giveth light unto all that are in the house" (Matthew 5:14-15).

pic-nic *en costume;* one must take a part, assume a character, stand ready in a sensible way to play the fool. To come in plain clothes, with a long face, as a wiseacre, only makes one a discomfort to himself, and a blot upon the scene.[9] Like your jug of cold water among the wine-flasks, it leaves you unelated among the elated ones. No, no. This austerity won't do. Let me tell you too—*en confiance*—that while revelry may not always merge into ebriety, soberness, in too deep potations, may become a sort of sottishness. Which sober sottishness, in my way of thinking, is only to be cured by beginning at the other end of the horn, to tipple a little."

"Pray, what society of vintners and old topers are you hired to lecture for?"

"I fear I did not give my meaning clearly. A little story may help. The story of the worthy old woman of Goshen,[10] a very moral old woman, who wouldn't let her shoats eat fattening apples in fall, for fear the fruit might ferment upon their brains, and so make them swinish. Now, during a green Christmas, inauspicious to the old,[11] this worthy old woman fell into a moping decline, took to her bed, no appetite, and refused to see her best friends. In much concern her good man sent for

---

[9] Charles Lamb, in his essay "All Fools' Day" (1821), asserts the sensibleness of foolishness, the senseless foolishness of the "wise-acre," the trustworthiness of the fool, and cries out, "Beshrew the man who on such a day as this, the *general festival*, should affect to stand aloof."

[10] Goshen was the fertile part of Egypt reserved by God for the Israelites (Genesis 40:10). Because it was the only part of Egypt safe from the plagues described in Exodus 7–9 (see Chapter 16, note 9), its name came to designate any place of plenty, safety, and light. Hence the many towns named Goshen. A number of limericks use the name as the key riming word, and there may well be one about an old woman of Goshen.

[11] Thomas Fuller, "Of Time Serving," *The Holy State*, 1st edition, 1642 (London, 1841): "Frost is as proper for winter, as flowers for spring. Gravity becomes the ancient; and a green Christmas is neither handsome nor healthful."

the doctor, who, after seeing the patient and putting a question or two, beckoned the husband out, and said: 'Deacon, do you want her cured?' 'Indeed I do.' 'Go directly, then, and buy a jug of Santa Cruz.' [12] 'Santa Cruz? my wife drink Santa Cruz?' 'Either that or die.' 'But how much?' 'As much as she can get down.' 'But she'll get drunk!' 'That's the cure.' Wise men, like doctors, must be obeyed. Much against the grain, the sober deacon got the unsober medicine, and, equally against her conscience, the poor old woman took it; but, by so doing, ere long recovered health and spirits, famous appetite, and glad again to see her friends; and having by this experience broken the ice of arid abstinence, never afterwards kept herself a cup too low."

This story had the effect of surprising the bachelor into interest, though hardly into approval.

"If I take your parable right," said he, sinking no little of his former churlishness, "the meaning is, that one cannot enjoy life with gusto unless he renounce the too-sober view of life. But since the too-sober view is, doubtless, nearer true than the too-drunken; I, who rate truth, though cold water, above untruth, though Tokay, will stick to my earthen jug."

"I see," slowly spirting upward a spiral staircase of lazy smoke, "I see; you go in for the lofty."

"How?"

"Oh, nothing! but if I wasn't afraid of prosing, I might tell another story about an old boot in a pieman's loft, contracting there between sun and oven an unseemly, dry-seasoned curl and warp. You've seen such leathery old garretteers, haven't you? Very high, sober, solitary, philosophic, grand, old boots, indeed; but I, for my part, would rather be the pieman's trodden slipper on the ground. Talking of piemen, humble-pie before proud-cake for me. This notion of being lone and lofty is a sad mistake. Men I hold in this respect to be like roosters;

[12] The chief product of the ironically named West Indian island of Santa Cruz was its famous rum.

the one that betakes himself to a lone and lofty perch is the hen-pecked one, or the one that has the pip." [13]

"You are abusive!" cried the bachelor, evidently touched.

"Who is abused? You, or the race? You won't stand by and see the human race abused? Oh, then, you have some respect for the human race."

"I have some respect for *myself*," with a lip not so firm as before.

"And what race may *you* belong to? now don't you see, my dear fellow, in what inconsistencies one involves himself by affecting disesteem for men. To a charm, my little stratagem succeeded. Come, come, think better of it, and, as a first step to a new mind, give up solitude. I fear, by the way, you have at some time been reading Zimmermann, that old Mr. Megrims of a Zimmermann,[14] whose book on Solitude is as vain as Hume's on Suicide,[15] as Bacon's on Knowledge; [16] and, like these, will betray him who seeks to steer soul and body by it, like a false religion. All they, be they what boasted ones you please, who, to the yearning of our kind after a founded rule of content, offer aught not in the spirit of fellowly gladness

[13] Compare this possibly diseased rooster with the images of the toucan and the Popinjay-of-the-world, and, possibly, the image of the alienated Satan in *Paradise Lost*, IV, 194–201, sitting alone, "like a cormorant," on the highest tree in Eden.

[14] Zimmerman's *Über die Einsamkeit* ("On Solitude") was first published in 1755 and revised in 1784–1785. See Chapter 11, note 3.

[15] "Of Suicide," a suppressed essay by the philosopher David Hume (1711–1776), defends suicide as a human right and even in some circumstances as a wise course of action.

[16] Most of Bacon's works could be described as books on knowledge. Perhaps the most relevant passage is that cited by Elizabeth Foster from *The Advancement of Learning* (1605), II, xxi, 9: ". . . it is not possible to join serpentine wisdom with the columbine innocency, except men know exactly all the conditions of the serpent; his baseness and going upon his belly, his volubility and lubricity, his envy and sting, and the rest; that is, all forms and natures of evil." Other references to Bacon occur in Chapters 9 and 37

based on due confidence in what is above, away with them for poor dupes, or still poorer impostors."

His manner here was so earnest that scarcely any auditor, perhaps, but would have been more or less impressed by it, while, possibly, nervous opponents might have a little quailed under it. Thinking within himself a moment, the bachelor replied: "Had you experience, you would know that your tippling theory, take it in what sense you will, is poor as any other. And Rabelais's pro-wine Koran [17] no more trustworthy than Mahomet's anti-wine one." [18]

"Enough," for a finality knocking the ashes from his pipe, "we talk and keep talking, and still stand where we did. What do you say for a walk? My arm, and let's a turn. They are to have dancing on the hurricane-deck to-night. I shall fling them off a Scotch jig, while, to save the pieces, you hold my loose change; and following that, I propose that you, my dear fellow, stack your gun, and throw your bearskins in a sailor's hornpipe—I holding your watch. What do you say?"

At this proposition the other was himself again, all raccoon.

"Look you," thumping down his rifle, "are you Jeremy Diddler No. 3?" [19]

"Jeremy Diddler? I have heard of Jeremy the prophet,[20] and Jeremy Taylor the divine,[21] but your other Jeremy is a gentleman I am unacquainted with."

"You are his confidential clerk, ain't you?"

"*Whose*, pray? Not that I think myself unworthy of being confided in, but I don't understand."

"You are another of them. Somehow I meet with the most

[17] In Book I of Rabelais' *Gargantua and Pantagruel*, Gargantua is born as the climax of a stupendous drinking scene; in Book V the long quest for the oracle of the Holy Bottle consummates with this injunction: "Drink."

[18] The Koran prohibits intoxicating drinks.

[19] See Chapter 3, note 17.

[20] See Chapter 9, note 3.

[21] English bishop and theologian (1613–1667).

extraordinary metaphysical scamps to-day. Sort of visitation of them. And yet that herb-doctor Diddler somehow takes off the raw edge of the Diddlers that come after him."

"Herb-doctor? who is he?"

"Like you—another of them."

"*Who*?" Then drawing near, as if for a good long explanatory chat, his left hand spread, and his pipe-stem coming crosswise down upon it like a ferule,[22] "You think amiss of me. Now to undeceive you, I will just enter into a little argument and—"

"No you don't. No more little arguments for me. Had too many little arguments to-day."

"But put a case. Can you deny—I dare you to deny—that the man leading a solitary life is peculiarly exposed to the sorriest misconceptions touching strangers?"

"Yes, I *do* deny it," again, in his impulsiveness, snapping at the controversial bait, "and I will confute you there in a trice. Look, you—"

"Now, now, now, my dear fellow," thrusting out both vertical palms for double shields, "you crowd me too hard. You don't give one a chance. Say what you will, to shun a social proposition like mine, to shun society in any way, evinces a churlish nature—cold, loveless; as, to embrace it, shows one warm and friendly, in fact, sunshiny."

Here the other, all agog again, in his perverse way, launched forth into the unkindest references to deaf old worldlings keeping in the deafening world; and gouty gluttons limping to their gouty gormandizings; and corseted coquets clasping their corseted cavaliers in the waltz, all for disinterested society's sake; and thousands, bankrupt through lavishness, ruining themselves out of pure love of the sweet company of man—no envies, rivalries, or other unhandsome motive to it.

"Ah, now," deprecating with his pipe, "irony is so unjust;

[22] Note the combination of the figure of a cross and an emblem of punishment.

never could abide irony; something Satanic about irony. God defend me from Irony, and Satire, his bosom friend." [23]

"A right knave's prayer, and a right fool's, too," snapping his rifle-lock.

"Now be frank.[24] Own that was a little gratuitous. But, no, no, you didn't mean it; any way, I can make allowances. Ah, did you but know it, how much pleasanter to puff at this philanthropic pipe, than still to keep fumbling at that misanthropic rifle. As for your worldling, glutton, and coquette, though, doubtless, being such, they may have their little foibles—as who has not?—yet not one of the three can be reproached with that awful sin of shunning society; awful I call it, for not seldom it presupposes a still darker thing than itself—remorse."

"Remorse drives man away from man? How came your fellow-creature, Cain, after the first murder, to go and build the first city? And why is it that the modern Cain dreads nothing so much as solitary confinement?"

"My dear fellow, you get excited. Say what you will, I for one must have my fellow-creatures round me. Thick, too—I must have them thick."

"The pick-pocket, too, loves to have his fellow-creatures round him. Tut, man! no one goes into the crowd but for his end; and the end of too many is the same as the pick-pocket's—a purse."

"Now, my dear fellow, how can you have the conscience to say that, when it is as much according to natural law that men are social as sheep gregarious. But grant that, in being social, each man has his end, do you, upon the strength of that, do you yourself, I say, mix with man, now, immediately, and be your end a more genial philosophy. Come, let's take a turn."

[23] Note the effects of the ambiguous syntax.

[24] Five chapters from now, the Cosmopolitan will say, "call me Frank," thus beginning the games with the names Frank and Charlie played throughout the following thirteen chapters.

Again he offered his fraternal arm; but the bachelor once more flung it off, and, raising his rifle in energetic invocation, cried: "Now the high-constable catch and confound all knaves in towns and rats in grain-bins, and if in this boat, which is a human grain-bin for the time, any sly, smooth, philandering rat be dodging now, pin him, thou high rat-catcher, against this rail."

"A noble burst! shows you at heart a trump. And when a card's that, little matters it whether it be spade or diamond. You are good wine that, to be still better, only needs a shaking up. Come, let's agree that we'll to New Orleans, and there embark for London—I staying with my friends nigh Primrose-hill,[25] and you putting up at the Piazza, Covent Garden [26]— Piazza, Covent Garden; for tell me—since you will not be a disciple to the full—tell me, was not that humor, of Diogenes, which led him to live, a merry-andrew, in the flower-market,[27] better than that of the less wise Athenian, which made him a skulking scare-crow in pine-barrens? [28] An injudicious gentleman, Lord Timon." [29]

"Your hand!" seizing it.

[25] A small hill north of Regent's Park, London. Chalk Farm on the hill was in the first two decades of the century a popular place for duels. Across from the hill were the Zoological Gardens of Regent's Park.

[26] An arcade forming the north and east sides of Covent Garden Market, the main produce market in London.

[27] Diogenes of Sinope (c. 412–323 B.C.), the eccentric Cynic philosopher, supposedly lived in a tub in the market place. He called himself by the same title as the present speaker—"a cosmopolitan," a citizen of the world or cosmos.

In Addison's *Spectator* 69, Mr. Spectator, on a visit to the Royal Exchange in London, thus exalts the merchant as the true cosmopolitan: "I am a *Dane*, *Swede*, or *French-Man* at different times, or rather fancy my self like the old Philosopher, who upon being asked what Countryman he was, replied, That he was a Citizen of the World. . . . I am a great Lover of Mankind."

[28] See Chapter 15, note 1.

[29] See Chapter 3, note 16, and the references in Chapters 23, 30, 42, and 43.

"Bless me, how cordial a squeeze. It is agreed we shall be brothers, then?"

"As much so as a brace of misanthropes can be," with another and terrific squeeze. "I had thought that the moderns had degenerated beneath the capacity of misanthropy. Rejoiced, though but in one instance, and that disguised, to be undeceived."

The other stared in blank amaze.

"Won't do. You are Diogenes, Diogenes in disguise. I say —Diogenes masquerading as a cosmopolitan."

With ruefully altered mien, the stranger still stood mute awhile. At length, in a pained tone, spoke: "How hard the lot of that pleader who, in his zeal conceding too much, is taken to belong to a side which he but labors, however ineffectually, to convert!" Then with another change of air: "To you, an Ishmael,[30] disguising in sportiveness my intent, I came ambassador from the human race,[31] charged with the assurance that for your mislike they bore no answering grudge, but sought to conciliate accord between you and them. Yet you take me not for the honest envoy, but I know not what sort of unheard-of spy. Sir," he less lowly added, "this mistaking of your man should teach you how you may mistake all men. For God's sake," laying both hands upon him, "get you confidence. See how distrust has duped you. I, Diogenes? I he who, going a step beyond misanthropy, was less a man-hater than a man-hooter? Better were I stark and stiff!"

With which the philanthropist moved away less lightsome than he had come, leaving the discomfited misanthrope to the solitude he held so sapient.

---

[30] See Genesis 16:1, 15, 16; 17:18–27; 21:6–21; 25:8–18 for the Biblical account of the outcast Ishmael, about whom it is prophesied, "And he will be a wild man; his hand will be against every man, and every man's hand against him." And, of course, see *Moby-Dick*, in which the narrator's first words are "Call me Ishmael."

[31] Cf. Chapter 2, note 16.

CHAPTER 25

The Cosmopolitan makes an acquaintance.

In the act of retiring, the cosmopolitan was met by a passenger, who, with the bluff *abord* [1] of the West, thus addressed him, though a stranger.

"Queer 'coon, your friend. Had a little skrimmage with him myself.[2] Rather entertaining old 'coon, if he wasn't so deuced analytical. Reminded me somehow of what I've heard about Colonel John Moredock,[3] of Illinois, only your friend ain't quite so good a fellow at bottom, I should think."

It was in the semicircular porch of a cabin, opening a recess from the deck, lit by a zoned lamp swung overhead, and sending its light vertically down, like the sun at noon. Beneath the lamp stood the speaker, affording to any one disposed to it no unfavorable chance for scrutiny; but the glance now resting on him betrayed no such rudeness.

A man neither tall nor stout, neither short nor gaunt; but with a body fitted, as by measure, to the service of his mind. For the rest, one less favored perhaps in his features than his clothes; and of these the beauty may have been less in the fit than the cut; to say nothing of the fineness of the nap, seeming out of keeping with something the reverse of fine in the skin; and the unsuitableness of a violet vest,[4] sending up sunset hues to a countenance betokening a kind of bilious habit.

But, upon the whole, it could not be fairly said that his appearance was unprepossessing; indeed, to the congenial, it

[1] Manner of accosting.

[2] When and where was that?

[3] An historical figure whose life will soon be recounted.

[4] Combining two of the avatars not to appear as described by Guinea, the "ge'mman in a yaller west" and the "ge'mman in a wiolet robe."

would have been doubtless not uncongenial; while to others, it could not fail to be at least curiously interesting, from the warm air of florid cordiality, contrasting itself with one knows not what kind of aguish [5] sallowness of saving discretion lurking behind it. Ungracious critics [6] might have thought that the manner flushed the man, something in the same fictitious way that the vest flushed the cheek. And though his teeth were singularly good, those same ungracious ones might have hinted that they were too good to be true; or rather, were not so good as they might be; since the best false teeth are those made with at least two or three blemishes, the more to look like life. But fortunately for better constructions, no such critics had the stranger now in eye; only the cosmopolitan, who, after, in the first place, acknowledging his advances with a mute salute —in which acknowledgment, if there seemed less of spirit than in his way of accosting the Missourian, it was probably because of the saddening sequel of that late interview—thus now replied: "Colonel John Moredock," repeating the words abstractedly; "that surname recalls reminiscences. Pray," with enlivened air, "was he anyway connected with the Moredocks of Moredock Hall, Northamptonshire, England?" [7]

"I know no more of the Moredocks of Moredock Hall than of the Burdocks of Burdock Hut," [8] returned the other, with the air somehow of one whose fortunes had been of his own making; "all I know is, that the late Colonel John Moredock was a famous one in his time; eye like Lochiel's; [9] finger like a

[5] Perhaps a product of "the old established firm of Fever & Ague" at Cairo.

[6] Note the relations among critics, author, readers, and fiction in this and the following paragraphs.

[7] Northamptonshire is a county in central England; Moredock Hall unidentified.

[8] The burdock is a course weedy plant with burs which commonly grows on waste ground; Burdock Hut unidentified.

[9] Sir Ewan Cameron of Lochiel (1629–1719), ruler of the Cameron Clan, famous hunter and warrior described by Macaulay (in his *History of England*) as "a terrible enemy," the killer of the last wolf of Scotland, and "the Ulysses of the Highlands."

trigger; nerve like a catamount's; and with but two little oddities—seldom stirred without his rifle, and hated Indians like snakes." [10]

"Your Moredock, then, would seem a Moredock of Misanthrope Hall—the Woods. No very sleek creature, the colonel, I fancy."

"Sleek or not, he was no uncombed one, but silky bearded and curly headed, and to all but Indians juicy as a peach. But Indians—how the late Colonel John Moredock, Indian-hater of Illinois, did hate Indians, to be sure!"

"Never heard of such a thing. Hate Indians? Why should he or anybody else hate Indians? *I* admire Indians. Indians I have always heard to be one of the finest of the primitive races, possessed of many heroic virtues. Some noble women, too. When I think of Pocahontas,[11] I am ready to love Indians. Then there's Massasoit,[12] and Philip of Mount Hope,[13] and

[10] Indian-hating, the main subject of the next few chapters, was a ritualized fact of American life and literature. See G. H. Orians, "The Indian-Hater in Early American Fiction," *Journal of American History*, XXVII (1933), 33–44; Roy Harvey Pearce, *The Savages of America* (The Johns Hopkins University Press, 1953); and Edwin Fussell, *Frontier: American Literature and the American West* (Princeton University Press, 1965).

[11] "Pocahontas" or Matoaka (d. 1617), after her legendary rescue of Captain John Smith, was kidnaped by the English, became a Christian convert, and married John Rolfe. "Pocahontas" was a false name which, according to Smith, the Indians gave her to prevent the English from having "the power of casting an evil eye upon her."

[12] A principal chief of the Wampanoag, he befriended the English of Plymouth Plantation and lived peacefully with them until his death in 1662.

[13] Philip of Mount Hope, or King Philip (d. 1676), son and successor of Massasoit, lived at peace with the English for the first nine years of his chieftancy, but was provoked by them into the bloody King Philip's War (1675–1676), in which, after many victories over the colonists, Philip and almost all his tribe were finally exterminated. The Christians exhibited his head in Plymouth and sold his wife and small son into slavery.

Tecumseh,[14] and Red-Jacket,[15] and Logan [16]—all heroes; and there's the Five Nations,[17] and Araucanians [18]—federations and communities of heroes. God bless me; hate Indians? Surely the late Colonel John Moredock must have wandered in his mind."

"Wandered in the woods considerably, but never wandered elsewhere, that I ever heard."

"Are you in earnest? Was there ever one who so made it his particular mission to hate Indians that, to designate him, a special word has been coined—Indian-hater?"

"Even so."

[14] Shawnee chief (1768–1813). Although his father and brothers were killed by the whites, he persuaded his tribe to discontinue the practice of torturing prisoners. He denied the right of the federal government to purchase from one tribe land which belonged to many tribes, and undertook the formation of a great confederacy of all tribes from Florida to the head of the Missouri River. After a defeat in the premature battle of Tippecanoe undertaken by his brother in 1811, Tecumseh led his forces to the British side in the War of 1812, during which he and many of his warriors were slain.

[15] Seneca chief (c. 1756–1830), famous for his gifts of oratory, and so little given to fighting that he was often reproached for cowardice. An ambiguous character throughout his life, Red-Jacket nevertheless maintained a consistent loyalty to the notion of Indian cultural integrity, which he tried to defend by dealing with the white man in terms of European legalism, moralism, and rhetoric.

[16] (c. 1725–1780), son of a white man and Indian woman, lived peacefully in Pennsylvania and Ohio until 1774, when some of his relatives were brutally massacred by a party of white emigrants. He then waged a vicious war on the border settlements.

[17] A confederacy of the Iroquoian tribes (the Mohawk, Oneida, Onondaga, Cayuga, Seneca). After procuring firearms from the Dutch, they drove off or incorporated all other tribes from the Ottawa River to the Tennessee, and from the Kennebec to the Illinois. They became allies of the English against the French and against the American revolutionaries.

[18] A tribal group of Indians of Southern Chile who successfully resisted the Incas in the fifteenth century and the Spaniards in the following two centuries. At the time of *The Confidence-Man*, they were successfully maintaining their independence from Chile.

"Dear me, you take it very calmly.—But really, I would like to know something about this Indian-hating. I can hardly believe such a thing to be. Could you favor me with a little history of the extraordinary man you mentioned?"

"With all my heart," and immediately stepping from the porch, gestured the cosmopolitan to a settee near by, on deck. "There, sir, sit you there, and I will sit here beside you—you desire to hear of Colonel John Moredock. Well, a day in my boyhood is marked with a white stone [19]—the day I saw the colonel's rifle, powder-horn attached, hanging in a cabin on the West bank of the Wabash river. I was going westward a long journey through the wilderness with my father. It was nigh noon, and we had stopped at the cabin to unsaddle and bait. The man at the cabin pointed out the rifle, and told whose it was, adding that the colonel was that moment sleeping on wolf-skins in the corn-loft above, so we must not talk very loud, for the colonel had been out all night hunting (Indians, mind), and it would be cruel to disturb his sleep. Curious to see one so famous, we waited two hours over, in hopes he would come forth; but he did not. So, it being necessary to get to the next cabin before nightfall, we had at last to ride off without the wished-for satisfaction. Though, to tell the truth, I, for one, did not go away entirely ungratified, for, while my father was watering the horses, I slipped back into the cabin, and stepping a round or two up the ladder, pushed my head through the trap, and peered about. Not much light in the loft; but off, in the further corner, I saw what I took to be the wolf-skins, and on them a bundle of something, like a drift of leaves; and at one end, what seemed a moss-ball; and over it, deer-antlers branched; and close by, a small squirrel sprang out from a maple-bowl of nuts, brushed the moss-ball with his tail, through a hole, and vanished, squeaking. That bit of woodland

[19] An allusion to Jacob's vision of a ladder in Genesis 28 (see Chapter 2, note 7). Jacob marked the place of his vision with a stone, called it Beth-el, and promised to build a temple upon it. The vision of a ladder marked by the present white stone is about to be described.

scene was all I saw. No Colonel Moredock there, unless that moss-ball was his curly head, seen in the back view. I would have gone clear up, but the man below had warned me, that though, from his camping habits, the colonel could sleep through thunder, he was for the same cause amazing quick to waken at the sound of footsteps, however soft, and especially if human."

"Excuse me," said the other, softly laying his hand on the narrator's wrist, "but I fear the colonel was of a distrustful nature—little or no confidence. He *was* a little suspicious-minded, wasn't he?"

"Not a bit. Knew too much. Suspected nobody, but was not ignorant of Indians. Well: though, as you may gather, I never fully saw the man, yet, have I, one way and another, heard about as much of him as any other; in particular, have I heard his history again and again from my father's friend, James Hall, the judge,[20] you know. In every company being called upon to give this history, which none could better do, the judge at last fell into a style so methodic, you would have thought he spoke less to mere auditors than to an invisible amanuensis; seemed talking for the press; very impressive way with him indeed. And I, having an equally impressible[21] memory, think that, upon a pinch, I can render you the judge upon the colonel almost word for word."

"Do so, by all means," said the cosmopolitan, well pleased.

"Shall I give you the judge's philosophy, and all?"

[20] James Hall (1793–1868), a circuit judge in Illinois, one of the major literary figures of the West; his fiction, essays, and economic and historical compendia form a valuable repository of information on the American West in the early nineteenth century. Large parts of the following two chapters come directly, often verbatim, from Hall's *Sketches of History, Life, and Manners, in the West* (Philadelphia, 1835), Volume II, Chapter 6, "Indian-hating—Some of the Sources of this Animosity—Brief Account of Col. Moredock." See Fussell's *Frontier* for an account of some of the ways in which Melville is using Hall.

[21] This play on words ("the press . . . impressive . . . impressible") foreshadows the elaborate puns on "press" in Chapters 29–30.

"As to that," rejoined the other gravely, pausing over the pipe-bowl he was filling, "the desirableness, to a man of a certain mind, of having another man's philosophy given, depends considerably upon what school of philosophy that other man belongs to. Of what school or system was the judge, pray?"

"Why, though he knew how to read and write, the judge never had much schooling. But, I should say he belonged, if anything, to the free-school system. Yes, a true patriot, the judge went in strong for free-schools."

"In philosophy? The man of a certain mind, then, while respecting the judge's patriotism, and not blind to the judge's capacity for narrative, such as he may prove to have, might, perhaps, with prudence, waive an opinion of the judge's probable philosophy. But I am no rigorist; proceed, I beg; his philosophy or not, as you please."

"Well, I would mostly skip that part, only, to begin, some reconnoitering of the ground in a philosophical way the judge always deemed indispensable with strangers. For you must know that Indian-hating was no monopoly of Colonel Moredock's but a passion, in one form or other, and to a degree, greater or less, largely shared among the class to which he belonged. And Indian-hating still exists; and, no doubt, will continue to exist, so long as Indians do. Indian-hating, then, shall be my first theme, and Colonel Moredock, the Indian-hater, my next and last."

With which the stranger, settling himself in his seat, commenced—the hearer paying marked regard, slowly smoking, his glance, meanwhile, steadfastly abstracted towards the deck, but his right ear so disposed towards the speaker that each word came through as little atmospheric intervention as possible. To intensify the sense of hearing, he seemed to sink the sense of sight. No complaisance of mere speech could have been so flattering, or expressed such striking politeness as this mute eloquence of thoroughly digesting attention.

CHAPTER 26

*Containing the metaphysics of Indian-hating,
according to the views of one evidently
not so prepossessed as Rousseau[1]
in favor of savages.*

"The judge always began in these words: 'The backwoods-man's hatred of the Indian has been a topic for some remark. In the earlier times of the frontier the passion was thought to be readily accounted for. But Indian rapine having mostly ceased through regions where it once prevailed, the philan-thropist is surprised that Indian-hating has not in like degree ceased with it. He wonders why the backwoodsman still re-gards the red man in much the same spirit that a jury does a murderer, or a trapper a wild cat—a creature, in whose behalf mercy were not wisdom; truce is vain; he must be executed.

" 'A curious point,' the judge would continue, 'which per-haps not everybody, even upon explanation, may fully under-stand; while, in order for any one to approach to an under-standing, it is necessary for him to learn, or if he already know, to bear in mind, what manner of man the backwoods-man is; as for what manner of man the Indian is, many know, either from history or experience.

" 'The backwoodsman is a lonely man. He is a thoughtful man. He is a man strong and unsophisticated. Impulsive, he is what some might call unprincipled. At any rate, he is self-willed; being one who less hearkens to what others may say about things, than looks for himself, to see what are things themselves. If in straits, there are few to help; he must depend

[1] Jean Jacques Rousseau (1712–1778), Swiss-French philosopher, pro-ponent of the ideal of the Noble Savage.

upon himself; he must continually look to himself. Hence self-reliance, to the degree of standing by his own judgment, though it stand alone. Not that he deems himself infallible; too many mistakes in following trails prove the contrary; but he thinks that nature destines such sagacity as she has given him, as she destines it to the 'possum. To these fellow-beings of the wilds their untutored sagacity is their best dependence. If with either it prove faulty, if the 'possum's betray it to the trap, or the backwoodsman's mislead him into ambuscade, there are consequences to be undergone, but no self-blame. As with the 'possum, instincts prevail with the backwoodsman over precepts. Like the 'possum, the backwoodsman presents the spectacle of a creature dwelling exclusively among the works of God, yet these, truth must confess, breed little in him of a godly mind. Small bowing and scraping is his, further than when with bent knee he points his rifle, or picks its flint. With few companions, solitude by necessity his lengthened lot, he stands the trial—no slight one, since, next to dying, solitude, rightly borne, is perhaps of fortitude the most rigorous test. But not merely is the backwoodsman content to be alone, but in no few cases is anxious to be so. The sight of smoke ten miles off is provocation to one more remove from man, one step deeper into nature. Is it that he feels that whatever man may be, man is not the universe? that glory, beauty, kindness, are not all engrossed by him? that as the presence of man frights birds away, so, many bird-like thoughts? Be that how it will, the backwoodsman is not without some fineness to his nature. Hairy Orson [2] as he looks, it may be with him as with the Shetland seal—beneath the bristles lurks the fur.

" 'Though held in a sort a barbarian, the backwoodsman would seem to America what Alexander was to Asia—captain in the vanguard of conquering civilization. Whatever the na-

[2] In the fifteenth-century French romance *Valentin et Orson*, Orson (from Fr. *ourson*, "bear-cub"), carried off by a bear, grows up as a wild man in the forest while his twin brother Valentin, his birth unknown, is raised at Pepin's court. Later versions of the story are legion. Peter the Wild Boy (see Chapter 21, note 5) was called "the modern Orson."

tion's growing opulence or power, does it not lackey his heels? Pathfinder,[3] provider of security to those who come after him, for himself he asks nothing but hardship. Worthy to be compared with Moses in the Exodus, or the Emperor Julian [4] in Gaul, who on foot, and bare-browed, at the head of covered or mounted legions, marched so through the elements, day after day. The tide of emigration, let it roll as it will, never overwhelms the backwoodsman into itself; he rides upon advance, as the Polynesian upon the comb of the surf.

" 'Thus, though he keep moving on through life, he maintains with respect to nature much the same unaltered relation throughout; with her creatures, too, including panthers and Indians. Hence, it is not unlikely that, accurate as the theory of the Peace Congress may be with respect to those two varieties of beings, among others,[5] yet the backwoodsman might be qualified to throw out some practical suggestions.

" 'As the child born to a backwoodsman must in turn lead his father's life—a life which, as related to humanity, is related mainly to Indians—it is thought best not to mince matters, out of delicacy; but to tell the boy pretty plainly what an Indian

[3] One of the nicknames of Natty Bumppo, hero of Cooper's Leatherstocking romances. See note 20 and Chapter 21, note 12.

[4] Julian the Apostate (331–363), Roman emperor 361–363, killed by an arrow in combat against the Persians.

[5] Four international Peace Congresses were held between 1848 and 1851. The theory here referred to may be found in a pamphlet of the American Peace Society, "Safety of Pacific Principles" (reprinted in *The Book of Peace*, edited by George C. Beckwith, Boston, 1845), which asserts that "the peace principle . . . has power over the young and the old, over the refined and the rude, over the bad as well as the good, over savages, maniacs, and even brutes." The pamphlet gives examples of lions responding to kindness and American Indians in war respecting the lives and property of pacific individuals and groups (such as the Quakers under William Penn). Cf. *White-Jacket*, which denounces all war, asserts that "in some things we must turn Quakers," but recognizes that "the boar, the tiger, the cougar, man, the leopard, the ram, the cat" all belong among the "fighting creatures" of "Dame Nature" (Chapters LXXV and LXXXVII).

is, and what he must expect from him. For however charitable
it may be to view Indians as members of the Society of
Friends, yet to affirm them such to one ignorant of Indians,
whose lonely path lies a long way through their lands, this, in
the event, might prove not only injudicious but cruel. At least
something of this kind would seem the maxim upon which
backswoods' education is based. Accordingly, if in youth the
backwoodsman incline to knowledge, as is generally the case,
he hears little from his schoolmasters, the old chroniclers of
the forest, but histories of Indian lying, Indian theft, Indian
double-dealing, Indian fraud and perfidy, Indian want of conscience, Indian blood-thirstiness, Indian diabolism—histories
which, though of wild woods, are almost as full of things
unangelic as the Newgate Calendar [6] or the Annals of Europe.[7]
In these Indian narratives and traditions the lad is thoroughly
grounded. "As the twig is bent the tree's inclined." [8] The instinct of antipathy against an Indian grows in the backwoodsman with the sense of good and bad, right and wrong. In one
breath he learns that a brother is to be loved, and an Indian to
be hated.

    " 'Such are the facts,' the judge would say, 'upon which, if
one seek to moralize, he must do so with an eye to them. It is
terrible that one creature should so regard another, should
make it conscience to abhor an entire race. It is terrible; but is
it surprising? Surprising, that one should hate a race which he
believes to be red from a cause akin to that which makes some
tribes of garden insects green? A race whose name is upon the
frontier a *memento mori*; painted to him in every evil light;

[6] Newgate was the main prison in London. *The Newgate Calendar, or
Malefactor's Bloody Register*, published originally *c.* 1774, described in
detail notorious crimes, criminals, and punishments since 1700. Later
series were issued in the 1820's.

[7] *The Annals of Europe*, an English yearbook, 1739–1744, sought to
give coverage of all the major domestic and foreign events of each year.

[8] Alexander Pope, *Moral Essays* (1732), Epistle 1, 150: "Just as the
twig is bent, the tree's inclined."

now a horse-thief like those in Moyamensing; [9] now an assassin like a New York rowdy; now a treaty-breaker like an Austrian; [10] now a Palmer with poisoned arrows; [11] now a judicial murderer and Jeffries,[12] after a fierce farce of trial condemning his victim to bloody death; or a Jew with hospitable speeches cozening some fainting stranger into ambuscade, there to burk him, and account it a deed grateful to Manitou,[13] his god.

[9] Moyamensing Prison, built in 1832 in the grand Egyptian style; the main prison for Philadelphia County, Pennsylvania.

[10] In the revolutions of 1848–1849, the government of the Austrian Empire made many concessions to liberalism and nationalism; after thus buying time, it retracted each with armed force. See Chapter 29, note 13.

[11] Probably William Palmer (1824–1856), the famous English poisoner who murdered his wife, brother, friend, and many others with poison mysteriously introduced into the body. His trial in the spring of 1856 was an international sensation.

[12] George Jeffreys, first Baron Jeffreys of Wem (1648–1689), Lord Chancellor of England, infamous for his flagrant injustice and brutality in the Bloody Assizes of 1685 (which followed the suppression of Monmouth's Rebellion). He had over three hundred people executed and many hundreds of others tortured.

[13] Among certain American Indians, including the Algonquins, *manito(u)* was a general name for the great good spirit or the great evil spirit. Immediately relevant here is the passage from Longfellow's *Hiawatha* (1855), XIV, which describes the two manitos:

> Gitche Manito the Mighty,
> He, the Master of Life, was painted
> As an egg, with points projecting
> To the four winds of the heavens.
> Everywhere is the Great Spirit,
> Was the meaning of this symbol.
> Mitche Manito the Mighty
> He the dreadful Spirit of Evil,
> As a serpent was depicted,
> As Kenabeek, the great serpent.
> Very crafty, very cunning,
> Is the creeping Spirit of Evil,
> Was the meaning of this symbol.

" 'Still, all this is less advanced as truths of the Indians than as examples of the backwoodsman's impression of them—in which the charitable may think he does them some injustice. Certain it is, the Indians themselves think so; quite unanimously, too. The Indians, in deed, protest against the backwoodsman's view of them; and some think that one cause of their returning his antipathy so sincerely as they do, is their moral indignation at being so libeled by him, as they really believe and say. But whether, on this or any point, the Indians should be permitted to testify for themselves, to the exclusion of other testimony, is a question that may be left to the Supreme Court. At any rate, it has been observed that when an Indian becomes a genuine proselyte to Christianity (such cases, however, not being very many; though, indeed, entire tribes are sometimes nominally brought to the true light,) he will not in that case conceal his enlightened conviction, that his race's portion by nature is total depravity; and, in that way, as much as admits that the backwoodsman's worst idea of it is not very far from true; while, on the other hand, those red men who are the greatest sticklers for the theory of Indian virtue, and Indian loving-kindness, are sometimes the arrantest horse-thieves and tomahawkers among them. So, at least, avers the backwoodsman. And though, knowing the Indian nature, as he thinks he does, he fancies he is not ignorant that an Indian may in some points deceive himself almost as effectually as in bush-tactics he can another, yet his theory and his practice as above contrasted seem to involve an inconsistency so extreme, that the backwoodsman only accounts for it on the supposition that when a tomahawking red-man advances the notion of the benignity of the red race, it is but part and parcel with that subtle strategy which he finds so useful in war, in hunting, and the general conduct of life.'

"In further explanation of that deep abhorrence with which the backwoodsman regards the savage, the judge used to think it might perhaps a little help, to consider what kind of stimulus to it is furnished in those forest histories and traditions before spoken of. In which behalf, he would tell the story of the little

colony of Wrights and Weavers,[14] originally seven cousins
from Virginia, who, after successive removals with their families, at last established themselves near the southern frontier of
the Bloody Ground, Kentucky: [15] 'They were strong, brave
men; but, unlike many of the pioneers in those days, theirs
was no love of conflict for conflict's sake. Step by step they
had been lured to their lonely resting-place by the ever-beck-
oning seductions of a fertile and virgin land, with a singular
exemption, during the march, from Indian molestation. But
clearings made and houses built, the bright shield was soon to
turn its other side. After repeated persecutions and eventual
hostilities, forced on them by a dwindled tribe in their neighborhood—persecutions resulting in loss of crops and cattle;
hostilities in which they lost two of their number, illy to be
spared, besides others getting painful wounds—the five remaining cousins made, with some serious concessions, a kind of treaty
with Mocmohoc, the chief—being to this induced by the harry-
ings of the enemy, leaving them no peace. But they were further prompted, indeed, first incited, by the suddenly changed
ways of Mocmohoc, who, though hitherto deemed a savage almost perfidious as Caesar Borgia, [16] yet now put on a seeming
the reverse of this, engaging to bury the hatchet, smoke the
pipe, and be friends forever; not friends in the mere sense of re-
nouncing enmity, but in the sense of kindliness, active and
familiar.

" 'But what the chief now seemed, did not wholly blind
them to what the chief had been; so that, though in no small
degree influenced by his change of bearing, they still distrusted him enough to covenant with him, among other articles
on their side, that though friendly visits should be exchanged
between the wigwams and the cabins, yet the five cousins
should never, on any account, be expected to enter the chief's

[14] No historical basis for this story has yet been discovered.

[15] Kentucky, an Indian word, was usually translated to mean "the
bloody ground."

[16] Cesare Borgia, Duke of Valentinois (1475-1507), infamous for his
combination of ruthless force and superrefined treachery.

lodge together. The intention was, though they reserved it, that if ever, under the guise of amity, the chief should mean them mischief, and effect it, it should be but partially; so that some of the five might survive, not only for their families' sake, but also for retribution's. Nevertheless, Mocmohoc did, upon a time, with such fine art and pleasing carriage win their confidence, that he brought them all together to a feast of bear's meat, and there, by stratagem, ended them. Years after, over their calcined bones and those of all their families, the chief, reproached for his treachery by a proud hunter whom he had made captive, jeered out, "Treachery? pale face! 'Twas they who broke their covenant first, in coming all together; they that broke it first, in trusting Mocmohoc."'

"At this point the judge would pause, and lifting his hand, and rolling his eyes, exclaim in a solemn enough voice, 'Circling wiles and bloody lusts. The acuteness and genius of the chief but make him the more atrocious.'

"After another pause, he would begin an imaginary kind of dialogue between a backwoodsman and a questioner:

" 'But are all Indians like Mocmohoc?—Not all have proved such; but in the least harmful may lie his germ. There is an Indian nature. "Indian blood is in me," is the half-breed's threat.—But are not some Indians kind?—Yes, but kind Indians are mostly lazy, and reputed simple—at all events, are seldom chiefs; chiefs among the red men being taken from the active, and those accounted wise. Hence, with small promotion, kind Indians have but proportionate influence. And kind Indians may be forced to do unkind biddings. So "beware the Indian, kind or unkind," said Daniel Boone, who lost his sons by them.[17]—But, have all you backwoodsmen been some way

[17] Daniel Boone (1734–1820), frontiersman and explorer of Kentucky, model for Cooper's Natty Bumppo (see note 3), is thus quoted in his spurious "Autobiography" (an ornately literary eighteenth-century work written by John Filson): "Two darling sons, and a brother, have I lost by savage hands. . . ."

victimized by Indians?—No.—Well, and in certain cases may not at least some few of you be favored by them?—Yes, but scarce one among us so self-important, or so selfish-minded, as to hold his personal exemption from Indian outrage such a set-off against the contrary experience of so many others, as that he must needs, in a general way, think well of Indians; or, if he do, an arrow in his flank might suggest a pertinent doubt.

" 'In short,' according to the judge, 'if we at all credit the backwoodsman, his feeling against Indians, to be taken aright, must be considered as being not so much on his own account as on others', or jointly on both accounts. True it is, scarce a family he knows but some member of it, or connection, has been by Indians maimed or scalped. What avails, then, that some one Indian, or some two or three, treat a backwoodsman friendly-like? He fears me, he thinks. Take my rifle from me, give him motive, and what will come? Or if not so, how know I what involuntary preparations may be going on in him for things as unbeknown in present time to him as me—a sort of chemical preparation in the soul for malice, as chemical preparation in the body for malady.'

"Not that the backwoodsman ever used those words, you see, but the judge found him expression for his meaning. And this point he would conclude with saying, that, 'what is called a "friendly Indian" is a very rare sort of creature; and well it was so, for no ruthlessness exceeds that of a "friendly Indian" turned enemy. A coward friend, he makes a valiant foe.

" 'But, thus far the passion in question has been viewed in a general way as that of a community. When to his due share of this the backwoodsman adds his private passion, we have then the stock out of which is formed, if formed at all, the Indian-hater *par excellence.*'

"The Indian-hater *par excellence* the judge defined to be one 'who, having with his mother's milk drank in small love for red men, in youth or early manhood, ere the sensibilities become osseous, receives at their hand some signal outrage, or, which in effect is much the same, some of his kin have, or some friend. Now, nature all around him by her solitudes wooing or bidding him muse upon this matter, he accordingly does so, till the thought develops such attraction, that much as straggling vapors troop from all sides to a storm-cloud, so straggling thoughts of other outrages troop to the nucleus thought, assimilate with it, and swell it. At last, taking counsel with the elements, he comes to his resolution. An intenser Hannibal,[18] he makes a vow, the hate of which is a vortex from whose suction scarce the remotest chip of the guilty race may reasonably feel secure. Next, he declares himself and settles his temporal affairs. With the solemnity of a Spaniard turned monk,[19] he takes leave of his kin; or rather, these leave-takings have something of the still more impressive finality of death-bed adieus. Last, he commits himself to the forest primeval; there, so long as life shall be his, to act upon a calm, cloistered scheme of strategical, implacable, and lonesome vengeance. Ever on the noiseless trail; cool, collected, patient; less seen than felt; snuffing, smelling—a Leather-stocking [20] Nemesis. In the settlements he will not be seen again; in eyes of old companions tears may start at some chance thing that speaks of him; but they never look for him, nor call; they know he will not come. Suns and seasons fleet; the tiger-lily blows and falls; babes are born and leap in their mothers' arms; but, the Indian-hater is good as gone to his long home,[21] and "Terror" is his epitaph.'

"Here the judge, not unaffected, would pause again, but presently resume: 'How evident that in strict speech there can be no biography of an Indian-hater *par excellence*, any more

[18] Hannibal (247–183 B.C.), Carthaginian general and scourge of Rome; his father, Hamilcar, made him swear at the age of nine that he should always be the enemy of the Roman people.

[19] The title character of Melville's *Benito Cereno*, published the year before, is a Spaniard who becomes a monk.

[20] Another nickname of Natty Bumppo (see note 3).

[21] Ecclesiastes 12:5: ". . . man goeth to his long home, and the mourners go about the streets."

than one of a sword-fish, or other deep-sea denizen; or, which is still less imaginable, one of a dead man. The career of the Indian-hater *par excellence* has the impenetrability of the fate of a lost steamer. Doubtless, events, terrible ones, have happened, must have happened; but the powers that be in nature have taken order that they shall never become news.

" 'But, luckily for the curious, there is a species of diluted Indian-hater, one whose heart proves not so steely as his brain. Soft enticements of domestic life too often draw him from the ascetic trail; a monk who apostatizes to the world at times. Like a mariner, too, though much abroad, he may have a wife and family in some green harbor which he does not forget. It is with him as with the Papist converts in Senegal; fasting and mortification prove hard to bear.'

"The judge, with his usual judgment, always thought that the intense solitude to which the Indian-hater consigns himself, has, by its overawing influence, no little to do with relaxing his vow. He would relate instances where, after some months' lonely scoutings, the Indian-hater is suddenly seized with a sort of calenture;[22] hurries openly towards the first smoke, though he knows it is an Indian's, announces himself as a lost hunter, gives the savage his rifle, throws himself upon his charity, embraces him with much affection, imploring the privilege of living a while in his sweet companionship. What is too often the sequel of so distempered a procedure may be best known by those who best know the Indian. Upon the whole, the judge, by two and thirty good and sufficient reasons, would maintain that there was no known vocation whose consistent following calls for such self-containings as that of the Indian-hater *par excellence*. In the highest view, he considered such a soul one peeping out but once an age.

"For the diluted Indian-hater, although the vacations he per-

[22] A delirium characterized by delusions; sailors, from heat or fatigue, are sometimes seized by a calenture which makes the sea seem an inviting meadow—with fatal results.

mits himself impair the keeping of the character, yet, it should not be overlooked that this is the man who, by his very infirmity, enables us to form surmises, however inadequate, of what Indian-hating in its perfection is."

"One moment," gently interrupted the cosmopolitan here, "and let me refill my calumet." [23]

Which being done, the other proceeded:—

[23] The peace pipe of the Indians.

CHAPTER 27

*Some account of a man of questionable
morality, but who, nevertheless, would
seem entitled to the esteem of that
eminent English moralist who said
he liked a good hater.* [1]

"Coming to mention the man to whose story all thus far said
was but the introduction, the judge, who, like you, was a great
smoker, would insist upon all the company taking cigars, and
then lighting a fresh one himself, rise in his place, and, with
the solemnest voice, say—'Gentlemen, let us smoke to the
memory of Colonel John Moredock;' when, after several
whiffs taken standing in deep silence and deeper reverie, he
would resume his seat and his discourse, something in these
words:

" 'Though Colonel John Moredock was not an Indian-hater
par excellence, he yet cherished a kind of sentiment towards
the red man, and in that degree, and so acted out his sentiment
as sufficiently to merit the tribute just rendered to his
memory.

" 'John Moredock was the son of a woman married thrice,
and thrice widowed by a tomahawk. The three successive
husbands of this woman had been pioneers, and with them she
had wandered from wilderness to wilderness, always on the
frontier. With nine children, she at last found herself at a little
clearing, afterwards Vincennes. There she joined a company
about to remove to the new country of Illinois. On the eastern

[1] Samuel Johnson, according to Hester Lynch Piozzi, said that he was
fond of Bathurst because "he was a very good *hater*."

215

side of Illinois there were then no settlements; but on the west side, the shore of the Mississippi, there were, near the mouth of the Kaskaskia, some old hamlets of French. To the vicinity of those hamlets, very innocent and pleasant places, a new Arcadia,[2] Mrs. Moredock's party was destined; for thereabouts, among the vines, they meant to settle. They embarked upon the Wabash in boats, proposing descending that stream into the Ohio, and the Ohio into the Mississippi, and so, northwards, towards the point to be reached. All went well till they made the rock of the Grand Tower [3] on the Mississippi, where they had to land and drag their boats round a point swept by a strong current. Here a party of Indians, lying in wait, rushed out and murdered nearly all of them. The widow was among the victims with her children, John excepted, who, some fifty miles distant, was following with a second party.

" 'He was just entering upon manhood, when thus left in nature sole survivor of his race. Other youngsters might have turned mourners; he turned avenger. His nerves were electric wires—sensitive, but steel. He was one who, from self-possession, could be made neither to flush nor pale. It is said that when the tidings were brought him, he was ashore sitting beneath a hemlock eating his dinner of venison—and as the tidings were told him, after the first start he kept on eating, but slowly and deliberately, chewing the wild news with the wild meat, as if both together, turned to chyle, together should sinew him to his intent. From that meal he rose an Indian-hater. He rose; got his arms, prevailed upon some comrades to join him, and without delay started to discover who were the actual transgressors. They proved to belong to a band of twenty renegades from various tribes, outlaws even among Indians, and who had formed themselves into a maurauding crew. No opportunity for action being at the time presented, he dismissed his friends; told them to go on, thanking them,

[2] Cf. the New Jerusalem of Chapter 9.

[3] A seventy-five-feet high rock standing out into the river from the Missouri shore.

and saying he would ask their aid at some future day. For upwards of a year, alone in the wilds, he watched the crew. Once, what he thought a favorable chance having occurred—it being midwinter, and the savages encamped, apparently to remain so—he anew mustered his friends, and marched against them; but, getting wind of his coming, the enemy fled, and in such panic that everything was left behind but their weapons. During the winter, much the same thing happened upon two subsequent occasions. The next year he sought them at the head of a party pledged to serve him for forty days. At last the hour came. It was on the shore of the Mississippi. From their covert, Moredock and his men dimly descried the gang of Cains in the red dusk of evening, paddling over to a jungled island in mid-stream, there the more securely to lodge; for Moredock's retributive spirit in the wilderness spoke ever to their trepidations now, like the voice calling through the garden.[4] Waiting until dead of night, the whites swam the river, towing after them a raft laden with their arms. On landing, Moredock cut the fastenings of the enemy's canoes, and turned them, with his own raft, adrift; resolved that there should be neither escape for the Indians, nor safety, except in victory, for the whites. Victorious the whites were; but three of the Indians saved themselves by taking to the stream. Moredock's band lost not a man.

" 'Three of the murderers survived. He knew their names and persons. In the course of three years each successively fell by his own hand. All were now dead. But this did not suffice. He made no avowal, but to kill Indians had become his passion. As an athlete, he had few equals; as a shot, none; in single combat, not to be beaten. Master of that woodland-cunning enabling the adept to subsist where the tyro would perish, and expert in all those arts by which an enemy is pursued for

---

[4] Genesis 3:8: "And they heard the voice of the Lord God walking in the garden in the cool of the day: and Adam and his wife hid themselves from the presence of the Lord God amongst the trees of the garden."

weeks, perhaps months, without once suspecting it, he kept to
the forest. The solitary Indian that met him, died. When a
number [5] was descried, he would either secretly pursue their
track for some chance to strike at least one blow; or if, while
thus engaged, he himself was discovered, he would elude them
by superior skill.

" 'Many years he spent thus; and though after a time he was,
in a degree, restored to the ordinary life of the region and
period, yet it is believed that John Moredock never let pass an
opportunity of quenching an Indian. Sins of commission in
that kind may have been his, but none of omission.

" 'It were to err to suppose,' the judge would say, 'that this
gentleman was naturally ferocious, or peculiarly possessed of
those qualities, which, unhelped by provocation of events,
tend to withdraw man from social life. On the contrary,
Moredock was an example of something apparently self-
contradicting, certainly curious, but, at the same time, undeni-
able: namely, that nearly all Indian-haters have at bottom loving hearts; at any rate, hearts, if anything, more generous than
the average. Certain it is, that, to the degree in which he mingled in the life of the settlements, Moredock showed himself
not without humane feelings. No cold husband or colder father, he; and, though often and long away from his household,
bore its needs in mind, and provided for them. He could be
very convivial; told a good story (though never of his more
private exploits), and sung a capital song. Hospitable, not backward to help a neighbor; by report, benevolent, as retributive, in secret; while, in a general manner, though sometimes
grave—as is not unusual with men of his complexion, a sultry
and tragical brown—yet with nobody, Indians excepted,
otherwise than courteous in a manly fashion; a moccasined
gentleman, admired and loved. In fact, no one more popular, as
an incident to follow may prove.

" 'His bravery, whether in Indian fight or any other, was
unquestionable. An officer in the ranging service during the

[5] First edition reads: "When a murder. . . ."

war of 1812, he acquitted himself with more than credit. Of his soldierly character, this anecdote is told: Not long after Hull's dubious surrender at Detroit,[6] Moredock with some of his rangers rode up at night to a log-house, there to rest till morning. The horses being attended to, supper over, and sleeping-places assigned the troop, the host showed the colonel his best bed, not on the ground like the rest, but a bed that stood on legs. But out of delicacy, the guest declined to monopolize it, or, indeed, to occupy it at all; when, to increase the inducement, as the host thought, he was told that a general officer had once slept in that bed. "Who, pray?" asked the colonel. "General Hull." "Then you must not take offense," said the colonel, buttoning up his coat, "but, really, no coward's bed, for me, however comfortable." Accordingly he took up with valor's bed—a cold one on the ground.

" 'At one time the colonel was a member of the territorial council of Illinois, and at the formation of the state government, was pressed to become candidate for governor, but begged to be excused. And, though he declined to give his reasons for declining, yet by those who best knew him the cause was not wholly unsurmised. In his official capacity he might be called upon to enter into friendly treaties with Indian tribes, a thing not to be thought of. And even did no such contingency arise, yet he felt there would be an impropriety in the Governor of Illinois stealing out now and then, during a recess of the legislative bodies, for a few days' shooting at human beings, within the limits of his paternal chief-magistracy. If the governorship offered large honors, from Moredock it demanded larger sacrifices. These were incompatibles. In short, he was not unaware that to be a consistent Indian-hater involves the renunciation of ambition, with its

[6] Brigadier General William Hull (1753–1825), governor of the Michigan territory, surrendered Detroit to the British without a fight in the War of 1812. A court martial sentenced him to execution for cowardice and neglect of duty, but President Madison remanded the sentence.

objects—the pomps and glories of the world; and since religion, pronouncing such things vanities, accounts it merit to
renounce them, therefore, so far as this goes, Indian-hating,
whatever may be thought of it in other respects, may be regarded
as not wholly without the efficacy of a devout sentiment.'"

Here the narrator paused. Then, after his long and irksome
sitting, started to his feet, and regulating his disordered shirt-
frill, and at the same time adjustingly shaking his legs down in
his rumpled pantaloons, concluded: "There, I have done; having given you, not my story, mind, or my thoughts, but another's. And now, for your friend Coonskins, I doubt not,
that, if the judge were here, he would pronounce him a sort of
comprehensive Colonel Moredock, who, too much spreading
his passion, shallows it."

CHAPTER 28

Moot points touching the late
Colonel John Moredock.

"Charity, charity!" exclaimed the cosmopolitan, "never a sound judgment without charity. When man judges man, charity is less a bounty from our mercy than just allowance for the insensible lee-way of human fallibility. God forbid that my eccentric friend should be what you hint. You do not know him, or but imperfectly. His outside deceived you; at first it came near deceiving even me. But I seized a chance, when, owing to indignation against some wrong, he laid himself a little open; I seized that lucky chance, I say, to inspect his heart,[1] and found it an inviting oyster in a forbidding shell. His outside is but put on. Ashamed of his own goodness, he treats mankind as those strange old uncles in romances do their nephews—snapping at them all the time and yet loving them as the apple of their eye."

"Well, my words with him were few. Perhaps he is not what I took him for. Yes, for aught I know, you may be right."

"Glad to hear it. Charity, like poetry, should be cultivated, if only for its being graceful. And now, since you have renounced your notion, I should be happy would you, so to speak, renounce your story, too. That story strikes me with even more incredulity than wonder. To me some parts don't hang together. If the man of hate, how could John Moredock be also the man of love? Either his lone campaigns are fabulous as Hercules'; or else, those being true, what was thrown in

[1] The heart is the central organ of this, and the following, chapter. Both the Cosmopolitan and the stranger seek hearts in every sense.

221

about his geniality is but garnish. In short, if ever there was such a man as Moredock, he, in my way of thinking, was either misanthrope or nothing; and his misanthropy the more intense from being focused on one race of men. Though, like suicide, man-hatred would seem peculiarly a Roman and a Grecian passion—that is, Pagan; yet, the annals of neither Rome nor Greece can produce the equal in man-hatred of Colonel Moredock, as the judge and you have painted him. As for this Indian-hating in general, I can only say of it what Dr. Johnson said of the alleged Lisbon earthquake: 'Sir, I don't believe it.' " [2]

[2] Hester Lynch Piozzi, *Anecdotes of the Late Samuel Johnson*: "I asked him once if he believed the story of the destruction of Lisbon by an earthquake when it first happened: 'Oh! not for six months,' said he, 'at least. I *did* think that story too dreadful to be credited. . . .' "

Sir Thomas Kendrick's *The Lisbon Earthquake* (Philadelphia: J. B. Lippincott, 1957), the latest of many books on the relations between the Lisbon earthquake of All Saints' Day 1755 and the "themes of eighteenth-century earthquake-theology and the end of optimism," gives a precise account of the intellectual violence caused by the earthquake. Those who believed in a just, omnipotent God argued that His wrath had destroyed Lisbon because of its irreligiousness or its Inquisition or its Molinism (called the fourth plague, the caterpillars of Joel 1:4). The optimists saw the earthquake as part of God's great design and therefore good, which provoked Voltaire's famous response, his *Poem on the Lisbon Disaster*. As A. O. Lovejoy points out in *The Great Chain of Being* (New York: Harper and Row, 1960), Voltaire is attacking not the indecent cheerfulness of the optimists so much as their frightening deterministic intensification of evil: "The essence of the optimists' enterprise was to find the evidence of the 'goodness' of the universe not in the paucity but rather in the multiplicity of what to the unphilosophic mind appeared to be evils." Voltaire argued that it would be better to admit an irrational world than the optimists' grotesque mockery—a hopeless rational one.

In Voltaire's *Candide*, Pangloss is hanged and Candide whipped in an auto-da-fe prescribed to make sure the Lisbon earthquake wouldn't repeat itself. But equally pertinent to the present context may be what Kendrick calls "London's most notorious earthquake victim, the Masquerade"; "as Horace Walpole said, 'we have never recovered masquerades since the earthquake at Lisbon.' "

"Didn't believe it? Why not? Clashed with any little prejudice of his?"

"Doctor Johnson had no prejudice; but, like a certain other
person," with an ingenuous smile, "he had sensibilities, and
those were pained."

"Dr. Johnson was a good Christian, wasn't he?"

"He was."

"Suppose he had been something else."

"Then small incredulity as to the alleged earthquake."

"Suppose he had been also a misanthrope?"

"Then small incredulity as to the robberies and murders
alleged to have been perpetrated under the pall of smoke and
ashes. The infidels of the time were quick to credit those re-
ports and worse. So true is it that, while religion, contrary to
the common notion, implies, in certain cases, a spirit of slow
reserve as to assent, infidelity, which claims to despise credulity, is sometimes swift to it."

"You rather jumble together misanthropy and infidelity."

"I do not jumble them; they are coördinates. For misanthropy, springing from the same root with disbelief of religion, is twin with that. It springs from the same root, I say;
for, set aside materialism, and what is an atheist, but one who
does not, or will not, see in the universe a ruling principle of
love; and what a misanthrope, but one who does not, or will
not, see in man a ruling principle of kindness? Don't you see?
In either case the vice consists in a want of confidence."

"What sort of a sensation is misanthropy?"

"Might as well ask me what sort of sensation is hydrophobia.[3] Don't know; never had it. But I have often wondered
what it can be like. Can a misanthrope feel warm, I ask myself;
take ease? be companionable with himself? Can a misanthrope
smoke a cigar and muse? How fares he in solitude? Has the
misanthrope such a thing as an appetite? Shall a peach refresh

[3] Hydrophobia (a morbid revulsion against water) is here appropriately disclaimed by the Cosmopolitan, who repeatedly associates himself with water and maritime things.

him? The effervescence of champagne, with what eye does he behold it? Is summer good to him? Of long winters how much can he sleep? What are his dreams? How feels he, and what does he, when suddenly awakened, alone, at dead of night, by fusilades of thunder?"

"Like you," said the stranger, "I can't understand the misanthrope. So far as my experience goes, either mankind is worthy one's best love, or else I have been lucky. Never has it been my lot to have been wronged, though but in the smallest degree. Cheating, backbiting, superciliousness, disdain, hardheartedness, and all that brood, I know but by report. Cold regards tossed over the sinister shoulder of a former friend, ingratitude in a beneficiary, treachery in a confidant—such things may be; but I must take somebody's word for it. Now the bridge that has carried me so well over, shall I not praise it?"

"Ingratitude to the worthy bridge not to do so. Man is a noble fellow, and in an age of satirists, I am not displeased to find one who has confidence in him, and bravely stands up for him."

"Yes, I always speak a good word for man; and what is more, am always ready to do a good deed for him."

"You are a man after my own heart," responded the cosmopolitan, with a candor which lost nothing by its calmness. "Indeed," he added, "our sentiments agree so, that were they written in a book, whose was whose, few but the nicest critics might determine."

"Since we are thus joined in mind," said the stranger, "why not be joined in hand?"

"My hand is always at the service of virtue," frankly extending it to him as to virtue personified.

"And now," said the stranger, cordially retaining his hand, "you know our fashion here at the West. It may be a little low, but it is kind. Briefly, we being newly-made friends must drink together. What say you?"

"Thank you; but indeed, you must excuse me."

"Why?"

"Because, to tell the truth, I have to-day met so many old friends, all free-hearted, convivial gentlemen, that really, really, though for the present I succeed in mastering it, I am at bottom almost in the condition of a sailor who, stepping ashore after a long voyage, ere night reels with loving welcomes, his head of less capacity than his heart."

At the allusion to old friends, the stranger's countenance a little fell, as a jealous lover's might at hearing from his sweet-heart of former ones. But rallying, he said: "No doubt they treated you to something strong; but wine—surely, that gentle creature, wine; come, let us have a little gentle wine at one of these little tables here. Come, come." Then essaying to roll about like a full pipe in the sea, sang in a voice which had had more of good-fellowship, had there been less of a latent squeak to it:

> "Let us drink of the wine of the vine benign,
> That sparkles warm in Zansovine." [4]

The cosmopolitan, with longing eye upon him, stood as sorely tempted and wavering a moment; then, abruptly stepping towards him, with a look of dissolved surrender, said: "When mermaid songs move figure-heads, then may glory,

[4] From Leigh Hunt's "Bacchus in Tuscany: A Dithyrambic Poem, Translated from the Italian of Francesco Redi" (1825). Bacchus, sitting amidst the Tuscan hills with "his charmer" Ariadne, tastes many wines:

> "A god though I be,
> I too, I too have my deity."   (11.40–41)

> "Oh how widely wandereth he,
> Who in the search for verity
> Keeps aloof from glorious wine!
> Lo the knowledge it bringeth to me!"   (11.156–59)

> "And drink of the wine of the vine benign
> That sparkles warm in Sansovine."   (11.246-247)

gold, and women try their blandishments on me. But a good fellow, singing a good song, he woos forth my every spike, so that my whole hull, like a ship's, sailing by a magnetic rock, caves in with acquiescence.[5] Enough: when one has a heart of a certain sort, it is in vain trying to be resolute."

[5] The Cosmopolitan's nautical metaphors here reach a strange climax: he likens the present situation to a sexual seduction and his role in it to that of a ship which disintegrates when all its spikes are drawn out by a magnetic rock. Note also the relation to General Hull and the bed he slept in.

228

T
lit
str
rec
bou
wit
con
it?"

said
only
Wh
stran

"R
ways
shoul

"Charles Arnold Noble. But do you call me Ch

"I will, Charlie; nothing like preserving in

ternal familiarities of youth. It proves the

the last."

"My sentiments again. Ah!"

It was a smiling waiter, with

drawn; a common quart bottle

bottom into a little bark bas

gayly tinted in the India

entertainer, he regard

seemed not to und

some red label p

P. W.

"P. W.

poser, "

"S

...y, friends

...each other's names. What is yours, pray?"

"Francis Goodman.² But those who love me, call me Frank. And yours?"

¹ The organ of this chapter, like the last, is the heart; from it, into it, and around it flows wine sacramentally transformed into blood, but possibly poisonous in either form.

² "Francis" may point toward France; this chapter includes references to the Marquise de Brinvilliers, Rochefoucauld, an anonymous "irreligious Parisian wit," and "eau-de-vie"; later the Cosmopolitan will bait Charlie with the tale of Charlemont, "a young merchant of French descent, living in St. Louis," and his possible adventures in France; the Fidèle is bound for New Orleans. "Frank" (literally "free") has obvious significances. "Goodman" was the Puritan title of address; later the Cosmopolitan insists that no aspersions be cast on the sons of the Puritans in his presence. "Goodman" is also a cant term for a thief, roisterer, or Don Juan, and a Scottish title for the Devil.

rlie." [3]

anhood the fra-

eart a rosy boy to

he smiling bottle, the cork
, but for the occasion fitted at
et, braided with porcupine quills,
fashion. This being set before the
ed it with affectionate interest, but
rstand, or else to pretend not to, a hand-
sted on the bottle, bearing the capital letters,

said he at last, perplexedly eying the pleasing
ow what does P. W. mean?"

ouldn't wonder," said the cosmopolitan gravely, "if it
od for port wine. You called for port wine, didn't you?"

"Why so it is, so it is!"

"I find some little mysteries not very hard to clear up," said the other, quietly crossing his legs.

This commonplace seemed to escape the stranger's hearing, for, full of his bottle, he now rubbed his somewhat sallow

[3] "CHARLEY NOBLE, the enlisted man's name for the galley smoke pipe. It is quite the custom to send each landsman to find Charley Noble, a hunt which causes endless amusement for the older men" (Gersham Bradford, *A Glossary of Sea Terms*, New York, 1946). "Charlie Noble is said to have been a Commander in the Mediterranean Fleet about 1840, one of whose fads was the keeping of the copper bowl of the galley funnel extra bright and shiny" (Edward Fraser and John Gibbons, *Soldier and Sailor Words and Phrases*, London, 1925). See also Frank Shay, *A Sailor's Treasury*, New York, 1951.
John Seelye has pointed out to me that Poe's "Thou Art the Man" presents a mysterious stranger whose name, Charley Goodfellow, combines parts of these two characters' names, and who is revealed by a corpse in a supposed case of wine to be the murderer of his "bosom friend." Poe discusses the significance of this character's first name: ". . . there never yet was any person named Charles who was not an open, manly, honest, good-natured and frank-hearted fellow. . . ."

hands over it, and with a strange kind of cackle, meant to be a chirrup, cried: "Good wine, good wine; is it not the peculiar bond of good feeling?" Then brimming both glasses, pushed one over, saying, with what seemed intended for an air of fine disdain: "Ill betide those gloomy skeptics who maintain that now-a-days pure wine is unpurchasable; that almost every variety on sale is less the vintage of vineyards than laboratories; that most bar-keepers are but a set of male Brinvilliarses,[4] with complaisant arts practicing against the lives of their best friends, their customers."

A shade passed over the cosmopolitan. After a few minutes' down-cast musing, he lifted his eyes and said: "I have long thought, my dear Charlie, that the spirit in which wine is regarded by too many in these days is one of the most painful examples of want of confidence. Look at these glasses. He who could mistrust poison in this wine would mistrust consumption in Hebe's cheek.[5] While, as for suspicions against the dealers in wine and sellers of it, those who cherish such suspicions can

[4] Marie d'Aubrey, Marquise de Brinvilliers (*c.* 1630–1676), infamous French poisoner. Instructed by her lover in the use of a subtle poison, probably Aqua Tofana (a masked form of arsenic), which she purchased from the infamous pharmacy known as The Red Rose, she murdered her father, sister, and two brothers in order to finance her adventures. She supposedly visited hospitals on errands of seeming charity—to experiment with her poison. In Melville's later poem, "The Marchioness of Brinvilliers," he describes her apparent "sweetness" and "fathomless mild eyes" as the artwork of an ambiguous "He" who created all "light and shade."

[5] Hebe, Greek goddess of youth and spring, daughter of Zeus and Hera, who gave her as a wife to Hercules in reward for his great feats (in the previous chapter the Cosmopolitan had objected that Moredock's feats might be "as fabulous as Hercules'"). Hebe had the job of passing the cup of nectar round among the gods, which offers an interesting comparison to the Marquise de Brinvilliers. According to one story, Hebe was dismissed from her office because she awkwardly fell while performing it; in Thomas Moore's poem "The Fall of Hebe," she is indecorously exposed by her fall and her spilled cup causes a rain of wine upon the earth.

have but limited trust in the human heart. Each human heart they must think to be much like each bottle of port, not such port as this, but such port as they hold to. Strange traducers, who see good faith in nothing, however sacred. Not medicines, not the wine in sacraments, has escaped them. The doctor with his phial, and the priest with his chalice, they deem equally the unconscious dispensers of bogus cordials to the dying."

"Dreadful!"

"Dreadful indeed," said the cosmopolitan solemnly. "These distrusters stab at the very soul of confidence. If this wine," impressively holding up his full glass, "if this wine with its bright promise be not true, how shall man be, whose promise can be no brighter? But if wine be false, while men are true, whither shall fly convivial geniality? To think of sincerely-genial souls drinking each other's health at unawares in perfidious and murderous drugs!"

"Horrible!"

"Much too much so to be true, Charlie. Let us forget it. Come, you are my entertainer on this occasion, and yet you don't pledge me. I have been waiting for it."

"Pardon, pardon," half confusedly and half ostentatiously lifting his glass. "I pledge you, Frank, with my whole heart, believe me," taking a draught too decorous to be large, but which, small though it was, was followed by a slight involuntary wryness to the mouth.

"And I return you the pledge, Charlie, heart-warm as it came to me, and honest as this wine I drink it in," reciprocated the cosmopolitan with princely kindliness in his gesture, taking a generous swallow, concluding in a smack, which, though audible, was not so much so as to be unpleasing.

"Talking of alleged spuriousness of wines," said he, tranquilly setting down his glass, and then sloping back his head and with friendly fixedness eying the wine, "perhaps the strangest part of those allegings is, that there is, as claimed, a kind of man who, while convinced that on this continent most wines are shams, yet still drinks away at them; accounting wine so fine a thing, that even the sham article is better than none at all. And if the temperance people urge that, by this course, he will sooner or later be undermined in health, he answers, 'And do you think I don't know that? But health without cheer I hold a bore; and cheer, even of the spurious sort, has its price, which I am willing to pay.' "

"Such a man, Frank, must have a disposition ungovernably bacchanalian."

"Yes, if such a man there be, which I don't credit. It is a fable, but a fable from which I once heard a person of less genius than grotesqueness draw a moral even more extravagant than the fable itself. He said that it illustrated, as in a parable, how that a man of a disposition ungovernably good-natured might still familiarly associate with men, though, at the same time, he believed the greater part of men false-hearted—accounting society so sweet a thing that even the spurious sort was better than none at all. And if the Rochefoucaultites [6] urge that, by this course, he will sooner or later be undermined in security, he answers, 'And do you think I don't know that? But security without society I hold a bore; and society, even of the spurious sort, has its price, which I am willing to pay.' "

"A most singular theory," said the stranger with a slight fidget, eying his companion with some inquisitiveness, "indeed, Frank, a most slanderous thought," he exclaimed in sudden heat and with an involuntary look almost of being personally aggrieved.

"In one sense it merits all you say, and more," rejoined the other with wonted mildness, "but, for a kind of drollery in it, charity might, perhaps, overlook something of the wickedness. Humor is, in fact, so blessed a thing, that even in the least virtuous product of the human mind, if there can be found but nine good jokes, some philosophers are clement enough to

[6] François, Duke of La Rochefoucauld, Prince of Marcillac (1613–1680), French moralist famous for his worldly maxims.

affirm that those nine good jokes should redeem all the wicked thoughts, though plenty as the populace of Sodom.[7] At any rate, this same humor has something, there is no telling what, of beneficence in it, it is such a catholicon and charm—nearly all men agreeing in relishing it, though they may agree in little else—and in its way it undeniably does such a deal of familiar good in the world, that no wonder it is almost a proverb, that a man of humor, a man capable of a good loud laugh—seem how he may in other things—can hardly be a heartless scamp."

"Ha, ha, ha!" laughed the other, pointing to the figure of a pale pauper-boy on the deck below, whose pitiableness was touched, as it were, with ludicrousness by a pair of monstrous boots, apparently some mason's discarded ones, cracked with drouth, half eaten by lime, and curled up about the toe like a bassoon. "Look—ha, ha, ha!"

"I see," said the other, with what seemed quiet appreciation, but of a kind expressing an eye to the grotesque, without blindness to what in this case accompanied it, "I see; and the way in which it moves you, Charlie, comes in very apropos to point the proverb I was speaking of. Indeed, had you intended this effect, it could not have been more so. For who that heard that laugh, but would as naturally argue from it a sound heart as sound lungs? True, it is said that a man may smile, and smile, and smile, and be a villain;[8] but it is not said that a man

[7] Genesis 18:23–32 tells how Abraham extracted a promise from God that He would not destroy Sodom if ten righteous persons should be found there. Genesis 19 then describes the destruction of Sodom and Gomorrah, the saving of Lot and his two daughters, and, particularly relevant here, how these two daughters keep their race from extinction: they inebriate their father with wine, lie with him, and conceive by him.

The "nine good jokes" is one short of the figure demanded by the Jewish God, but exactly matches the number of Vishnu's major avatars which have come; it may also refer to the number of avatars of the Confidence Man, and the number of jokes on the reader in this chapter.

[8] After learning how Claudius poisoned Hamlet's father, Hamlet says, "Meet it is I set it down/That one may smile, and smile, and be a villain" (I, v, 107f). Hamlet becomes wise enough to avoid the poisoned

may laugh, and laugh, and laugh, and be one, is it, Charlie?"

"Ha, ha, ha!—no no, no no."

"Why Charlie, your explosions illustrate my remarks almost as aptly as the chemist's imitation volcano did his lectures. But even if experience did not sanction the proverb, that a good laugher cannot be a bad man, I should yet feel bound in confidence to believe it, since it is a saying current among the people, and I doubt not originated among them, and hence *must* be true; for the voice of the people is the voice of truth.[9] Don't you think so?"

"Of course I do. If Truth don't speak through the people, it never speaks at all; so I heard one say."

"A true saying. But we stray. The popular notion of humor, considered as index to the heart, would seem curiously confirmed by Aristotle—I think, in his "Politics," (a work, by-the-by, which, however it may be viewed upon the whole, yet, from the tenor of certain sections, should not, without precaution, be placed in the hands of youth)—who remarks that the least lovable men in history seem to have had for humor not only a disrelish, but a hatred; and this, in some cases, along with an extraordinary dry taste for practical punning. I remember it is related of Phalaris, the capricious tyrant of Sicily, that he once caused a poor fellow to be beheaded on a horse-block, for no other cause than having a horse-laugh." [10]

------

wine which King Claudius has prepared for him, but succumbs to poison in another form while his mother dies of the poisoned wine. The next chapter deals at length with *Hamlet*.

[9] The Latin proverb, *Vox populi, vox Dei* ("the voice of the people, the voice of God"), supposedly based on a misunderstanding of Isaiah 66:6, "*Vox populi de civitate . . . vox Domini reddentis retributionem inimicis*," had been for over a thousand years a slogan in the fight against political authoritarianism.

[10] Both references in this paragraph are All Fools' jokes: Aristotle says no such thing in the *Politics*, and the story about Phalaris has no apparent source whatsoever. A reader looking for the first is merely like a green sailor looking for Charlie Noble; but a reader looking for the second becomes enmeshed in a most pertinent web of relationships.

"Funny Phalaris!"

"Cruel Phalaris!"

As after fire-crackers, there was a pause, both looking downward on the table as if mutually struck by the contrast of exclamations, and pondering upon its significance, if any. So, at least, it seemed; but on one side it might have been otherwise: for presently glancing up, the cosmopolitan said: "In the instance of the moral, drolly cynic, drawn from the queer bacchanalian fellow we were speaking of, who had his reasons for still drinking spurious wine, though knowing it to be such—there, I say, we have an example of what is certainly a wicked thought, but conceived in humor. I will now give you one of a wicked thought conceived in wickedness. You shall compare the two, and answer, whether in the one case the sting is not neutralized by the humor, and whether in the other the absence of humor does not leave the sting free play. I once

---

Phalaris, the notoriously cruel tyrant of Sicily from about 570 to about 550 B.C., whose cruel jokes supposedly destroyed vast numbers of human victims, became, twenty-three centuries later, part of one of the most far-reaching literary hoaxes. In 1695 Charles Boyle edited the spurious *Epistles of Phalaris*, which were extravagantly praised by Sir William Temple. The great classical scholar Richard Bentley argued for their spuriousness, was viciously attacked for it, and finally demonstrated that they were modern forgeries. Swift, however, in *The Battle of the Books* (1704) takes the side of Temple (who aids Aristotle and the other ancients) and Boyle (who spears Bentley). The present context is a new battle of the books, with a spurious Aristotle and a spurious Phalaris representing the ancients.

To see the reader's position, one must first recognize that the context is all about the relation between laughter and character. If the reader laughs, or if he doesn't laugh, he puts himself within this context. The reader has just been given the suggestion that "nine good jokes" might redeem all wicked thoughts; now he encounters an array of jokesters stretching from Phalaris through the author of his supposed epistles and Swift to the Cosmopolitan and Melville.

This is the groundwork for the following chapter, with its dialectical discussion of the relations among fictions, characters, creators, and perceivers.

heard a wit, a mere wit, mind, an irreligious Parisian wit, say, with regard to the temperance movement, that none, to their personal benefit, joined it sooner than niggards and knaves; because, as he affirmed, the one by it saved money and the other made money, as in ship-owners cutting off the spirit ration without giving its equivalent, and gamblers and all sorts of subtle tricksters sticking to cold water, the better to keep a cool head for business."

"A wicked thought, indeed!" cried the stranger, feelingly.

"Yes," leaning over the table on his elbow and genially gesturing at him with his forefinger: "yes, and, as I said, you don't remark the sting of it?"

"I do, indeed. Most calumnious thought, Frank!"

"No humor in it?"

"Not a bit!"

"Well now, Charlie," eying him with moist regard, "let us drink. It appears to me you don't drink freely."

"Oh, oh—indeed, indeed—I am not backward there. I protest, a freer drinker than friend Charlie you will find nowhere," with feverish zeal snatching his glass, but only in the sequel to dally with it. "By-the-way, Frank," said he, perhaps, or perhaps not, to draw attention from himself, "by-the-way, I saw a good thing the other day; capital thing; a panegyric on the press. It pleased me so, I got it by heart at two readings. It is a kind of poetry, but in a form which stands in something the same relation to blank verse which that does to rhyme.[11] A sort of free-and-easy chant with refrains to it. Shall I recite it?"

"Anything in praise of the press I shall be happy to hear," rejoined the cosmopolitan, "the more so," he gravely proceeded, "as of late I have observed in some quarters a disposition to disparage the press."

"Disparage the press?"

"Even so; some gloomy souls affirming that it is proving

[11] The first edition of Walt Whitman's *Leaves of Grass* had appeared in 1855, the second, greatly enlarged, in 1856.

with that great invention as with brandy or eau-de-vie, which, upon its first discovery, was believed by the doctors to be, as its French name implies, a panacea—a notion which experience, it may be thought, has not fully verified."

"You surprise me, Frank. Are there really those who so decry the press? Tell me more. Their reasons."

"Reasons they have none, but affirmations they have many; among other things affirming that, while under dynastic despotisms, the press is to the people little but an improvisatore, under popular ones it is too apt to be their Jack Cade.[12] In fine, these sour sages regard the press in the light of a Colt's revolver, pledged to no cause but his in whose chance hands it may be; deeming the one invention an improvement upon the pen, much akin to what the other is upon the pistol; involving, along with the multiplication of the barrel, no consecration of the aim. The term 'freedom of the press' they consider on a par with *freedom of Colt's revolver*. Hence, for truth and the right, they hold, to indulge hopes from the one is little more sensible than for Kossuth and Mazzini [13] to indulge hopes from the other. Heart-breaking views enough, you think; but their refutation is in every true reformer's contempt. Is it not so?"

"Without doubt. But go on, go on. I like to hear you," flatteringly brimming up his glass for him.

"For one," continued the cosmopolitan, grandly swelling his chest, "I hold the press to be neither the people's improvisatore, nor Jack Cade; neither their paid fool, nor conceited drudge. I think interest never prevails with it over duty. The

[12] An English peasant who led a peasants' rebellion against King Henry VI in 1450; Shakespeare's *Henry VI, Part II* presents him as a kind of Tamburlaine *manqué*.

[13] Lajos Kossuth (1802–1894) and Giuseppi Mazzini (1805–1872), two of the liberal nationalist leaders of the revolutions of 1848–1849. Kossuth's Hungarian revolution against the Austrian Empire was crushed when, at the invitation of Austria, a hundred thousand Russian troops overwhelmed the country (see Chapter 26, note 10). Mazzini's antipapal Roman Republic was overthrown by the French army, which occupied Rome and restored the pope.

press still speaks for truth though impaled, in the teeth of lies though intrenched. Disdaining for it the poor name of cheap diffuser of news, I claim for it the independent apostleship of Advancer of Knowledge:—the iron Paul! [14] Paul, I say; for not only does the press advance knowledge, but righteousness. In the press, as in the sun, resides, my dear Charlie, a dedicated principle of beneficent force and light. For the Satanic press, by its coappearance with the apostolic, it is no more an aspersion to that, than to the true sun is the coappearance of the mock one. For all the baleful-looking parhelion,[15] god Apollo dispenses the day. In a word, Charlie, what the sovereign of England is titularly, I hold the press to be actually—Defender of the Faith!—defender of the faith in the final triumph of truth over error, metaphysics over superstition, theory over falsehood, machinery over nature, and the good man over the bad. Such are my views, which, if stated at some length, you, Charlie, must pardon, for it is a theme upon which I cannot speak with cold brevity. And now I am impatient for your panegyric, which, I doubt not, will put mine to the blush."

"It is rather in the blush-giving vein," smiled the other; "but such as it is, Frank, you shall have it."

"Tell me when you are about to begin," said the cosmopolitan, "for, when at public dinners the press is toasted, I always drink the toast standing, and shall stand while you pronounce the panegyric."

"Very good, Frank; you may stand up now."

He accordingly did so, when the stranger likewise rose, and uplifting the ruby wine-flask, began.

[14] The scriptural text published by the lamb-like man in Chapter 1 comes from Paul.

[15] A parhelion is a mock sun produced by ice crystals refracting the sun's rays. When they form, there are usually several, they are often very bright, and they may be in either a horizontal or vertical line with the sun. This figure, perhaps more than any other, emblematically displays the possible incarnations of the sun in *The Confidence-Man: His Masquerade*. Mock suns can only appear in the presence of the true sun.

CHAPTER 30

*Opening with a poetical eulogy of the Press
and continuing with talk inspired
by the same.*

" 'Praise be unto the press,[1] not Faust's,[2] but Noah's; [3] let us extol and magnify the press, the true press of Noah, from which breaketh the true morning. Praise be unto the press, not the black press but the red; let us extol and magnify the press, the red press of Noah, from which cometh inspiration. Ye pressmen of the Rhineland and the Rhine, join in with all ye who tread out the glad tidings on isle Madeira or Mitylene.[4]—

[1] This entire paragraph, as Nathalia Wright demonstrates in *Melville's Use of the Bible* (Duke University Press, 1949), imitates the form of some of the more choric Psalms while giving a reversed version of Proverbs 23:29–30:

> Who hath woe? who hath sorrow? who hath contentions? who hath babbling? who hath wounds without cause? who hath redness of eyes?
> They that tarry long at the wine. . . .

Miss Wright resets the passage as poetry, and also points out the Psalmists' vocabulary ("extol," "magnify," "praise be unto," etc.), the echo of Isaiah 58, "Then shall thy light break forth as morning," and use of "glad tidings" from Luke and Paul.

[2] Johann Faust or Fust (d. 1467), German printer, partner of Gutenberg; when the partnership dissolved, he obtained possession of Gutenberg's press.

[3] Genesis 9:20–27 describes Noah's drunkenness on his own wine and his resulting curse of Ham for mocking his nakedness. Noah has often been presented as a toper. The Fidèle has many resemblances to his ark.

[4] Madeira, a Portugese island about 800 miles southeast of Gibraltar, famous for its sherry; Mitylene (or Mytilene or Lesbos), a Turkish island just south of the Dardanelles, famous since ancient times for its wine.

Who giveth redness of eyes by making men long to tarry at the fine print?—Praise be unto the press, the rosy press of Noah, which giveth rosiness of hearts, by making men long to tarry at the rosy wine.—Who hath babblings and contentions? Who, without cause, inflicteth wounds? Praise be unto the press, the kindly press of Noah, which knitteth friends, which fuseth foes.—Who may be bribed?—Who may be bound?— Praise be unto the press, the free press of Noah, which will not lie for tyrants, but make tyrants speak the truth.—Then praise be unto the press, the frank old press of Noah; then let us extol and magnify the press, the brave old press of Noah; then let us with roses garland and enwreath the press, the grand old press of Noah, from which flow streams of knowledge which give man a bliss no more unreal than his pain.' "

"You deceived me," smiled the cosmopolitan, as both now resumed their seats; "you roguishly took advantage of my simplicity; you archly played upon my enthusiasm. But never mind; the offense, if any, was so charming, I almost wish you would offend again. As for certain poetic left-handers in your panegyric, those I cheerfully concede to the indefinite privileges of the poet. Upon the whole, it was quite in the lyric style—a style I always admire on account of that spirit of Sibyllic confidence and assurance which is, perhaps, its prime ingredient. But come," glancing at his companion's glass, "for a lyrist, you let the bottle stay with you too long."

"The lyre and the vine forever!" cried the other in his rapture, or what seemed such, heedless of the hint, "the vine, the vine! is it not the most graceful and bounteous of all growths? And, by its being such, is not something meant—divinely meant? As I live, a vine, a Catawba vine,[5] shall be planted on my grave!"

"A genial thought; but your glass there."

[5] A famous wine was made from the Catawba grape, which took its name from the Catawba River in the Carolinas, along whose banks lived the Catawba Indians. Longfellow celebrated it in the poem "Catawba Wine."

"Oh, oh," taking a moderate sip, "but you, why don't you drink?"

"You have forgotten, my dear Charlie, what I told you of my previous convivialities to-day."

"Oh," cried the other, now in manner quite abandoned to the lyric mood, not without contrast to the easy sociability of his companion. "Oh, one can't drink too much of good old wine—the genuine, mellow old port. Pooh, pooh! drink away."

"Then keep me company."

"Of course," with a flourish, taking another sip—"suppose we have cigars. Never mind your pipe there; a pipe is best when alone. I say, waiter, bring some cigars—your best."

They were brought in a pretty little bit of western pottery, representing some kind of Indian utensil, mummy-colored, set down in a mass of tobacco leaves, whose long, green fans, fancifully grouped, formed with peeps of red the sides of the receptacle.

Accompanying it were two accessories, also bits of pottery, but smaller, both globes; one in guise of an apple flushed with red and gold to the life, and, through a cleft at top, you saw it was hollow. This was for the ashes.[6] The other, gray, with wrinkled surface, in the likeness of a wasp's nest, was the match-box.

"There," said the stranger, pushing over the cigar-stand, "help yourself, and I will touch you off," taking a match. "Nothing like tobacco," he added, when the fumes of the cigar began to wreathe, glancing from the smoker to the pottery, "I will have a Virginia tobacco-plant set over my grave beside the Catawba vine."

[6] Apples of Sodom, or Dead Sea Fruit, supposedly found at the site of Sodom, had the external appearance of beautiful apples but inside were nothing but ashes. This apple of Sodom and the other two pieces of pottery suggest "the populace of Sodom" mentioned in the previous chapter.

"Improvement upon your first idea, which by itself was good—but you don't smoke."

"Presently, presently—let me fill your glass again. You don't drink."

"Thank you; but no more just now. Fill *your* glass."

"Presently, presently; do you drink on. Never mind me. Now that it strikes me, let me say, that he who, out of super-fine gentility or fanatic morality, denies himself tobacco, suffers a more serious abatement in the cheap pleasures of life than the dandy in his iron boot, or the celibate on his iron cot. While for him who would fain revel in tobacco, but cannot, it is a thing at which philanthropists must weep, to see such an one, again and again, madly returning to the cigar, which, for his incompetent stomach, he cannot enjoy, while still, after each shameful repulse, the sweet dream of the impossible good goads him on to his fierce misery once more—poor eunuch!"

"I agree with you," said the cosmopolitan, still gravely social, "but you don't smoke."

"Presently, presently, do you smoke on. As I was saying about—"

"But *why* don't you smoke—come. You don't think that tobacco, when in league with wine, too much enhances the latter's vinous quality—in short, with certain constitutions tends to impair self-possession, do you?"

"To think that, were treason to good fellowship," was the warm disclaimer. "No, no. But the fact is, there is an unpropitious flavor in my mouth just now. Ate of a diabolical ragout at dinner,[7] so I shan't smoke till I have washed away the lingering memento of it with wine. But smoke away, you, and pray, don't forget to drink. By-the-way, while we sit here so companionably, giving loose to any companionable nothing, your uncompanionable friend, Coonskins, is, by pure contrast, brought to recollection. If he were but here now, he would see how much of real heart-joy he denies himself by not hob-a-nobbing with his kind."

[7] The Devil's favorite dish is man.

"Why," with loitering emphasis, slowly withdrawing his cigar, "I thought I had undeceived you there. I thought you had come to a better understanding of my eccentric friend."

"Well, I thought so, too; but first impressions will return, you know. In truth, now that I think of it, I am led to conjecture from chance things which dropped from Coonskins, during the little interview I had with him, that he is not a Missourian by birth, but years ago came West here, a young misanthrope from the other side of the Alleghanies, less to make his fortune, than to flee man.[8] Now, since they say trifles sometimes effect great results, I shouldn't wonder, if his history were probed, it would be found that what first indirectly gave his sad bias to Coonskins was his disgust at reading in boyhood the advice of Polonius to Laertes[9]—advice which, in the self-

[8] Pitch had disclosed his Eastern background to the herb doctor and the PIO man.

[9] Polonius' entire speech to Laertes is the basic subject of the next few pages. The text used is Pope's; most modern editions locate the passage as I, *iii*, 54–81.

> Yet here, *Laertes!* get abroad for shame,
> The wind sits in the shoulder of your sail,
> And you are staid for there. My blessing with you;
> And these few precepts in thy memory
> See thou character. 'Give thy thoughts no tongue,
> 'Nor any unproportion'd thought his act:
> 'Be thou familiar, but by no means vulgar;
> 'The friends thou hast, and their adoption try'd,
> 'Grapple them to thy soul with hooks of steel:
> 'But do not dull thy palm with entertainment
> 'Of each new-hatch'd, unfledg'd comrade. Beware
> 'Of Entrance to a quarrel: but being in,
> 'Bear't that th'opposed may beware of thee.
> 'Give ev'ry man thine ear; but few thy voice.
> 'Take each man's censure; but reserve thy judgment.
> Costly thy habit as thy purse can buy,
> But not exprest in fancy; rich, not gaudy:
> For the apparel oft proclaims the man,
> And they in *France* of the best rank and station
> Are most select and generous, chief in that.

ishness it inculcates, is almost on a par with a sort of ballad upon the economies of money-making, to be occasionally seen pasted against the desk of small retail traders in New England."

"I do hope now, my dear fellow," said the cosmopolitan with an air of bland protest, "that, in my presence at least, you will throw out nothing to the prejudice of the sons of the Puritans." [10]

"Hey-day and high times indeed," exclaimed the other, nettled, "sons of the Puritans forsooth! And who be Puritans, that I, an Alabamaian, must do them reverence? A set of sourly conceited old Malvolios, whom Shakespeare laughs his fill at in his comedies." [11]

"Pray, what were you about to suggest with regard to Polonius," observed the cosmopolitan with quiet forbearance, expressive of the patience of a superior mind at the petulance of an inferior one; "how do you characterize his advice to Laertes?"

"As false, fatal, and calumnious," exclaimed the other, with a degree of ardor befitting one resenting a stigma upon the family escutcheon, "and for a father to give his son—monstrous. The case you see is this: The son is going abroad, and for the

---

> Neither a borrower, nor a lender be;
> For loan oft loses both it self and friend:
> A borrowing dulls the edge of husbandry.
> This above all; to thine own self be true;
> And it must follow, as the night the day,
> Thou canst not then be false to any man.
> Farewell; my blessing season this in thee!

[10] John Seelye (in a paper presented to the Modern Language Association in 1964) has argued that the Cosmopolitan in some ways represents Hawthorne.

[11] Malvolio, Olivia's self-righteous steward in *Twelfth Night*, is characterized by Maria, Olivia's woman, as being sometimes "a kind of Puritan"; in fact, she says, "The devil a Puritan he is . . ." (II, *iii*, 151–160). Puritans are mocked in *All's Well that Ends Well* (I, *iii*, 98) and *The Winter's Tale* (IV, *iii*, 45–46), but in *Pericles* (IV, *vi*, 9–10) a Puritan is offered as the opposite of the devil.

first. What does the father? Invoke God's blessing upon him? Put the blessed Bible in his trunk? No. Crams him with maxims smacking of my Lord Chesterfield,[12] with maxims of France, with maxims of Italy."

"No, no, be charitable, not that. Why, does he not among other things say:—

> 'The friends thou hast, and their adoption tried,
> Grapple them to thy soul with hooks of steel'?

Is that compatible with maxims of Italy?"

"Yes it is, Frank. Don't you see? Laertes is to take the best of care of his friends—his proved friends, on the same principle that a wine-corker takes the best of care of his proved bottles. When a bottle gets a sharp knock and don't break, he says, 'Ah, I'll keep that bottle.' Why? Because he loves it? No, he has particular use for it."

"Dear, dear!" appealingly turning in distress, "that—that kind of criticism is—is—in fact—it won't do."

"Won't truth do, Frank? You are so charitable with everybody, do but consider the tone of the speech. Now I put it to you, Frank; is there anything in it hortatory to high, heroic, disinterested effort? Anything like 'sell all thou hast and give to the poor?'[13] And, in other points, what desire seems most in the father's mind, that his son should cherish nobleness for himself, or be on his guard against the contrary thing in others? An irreligious warner, Frank—no devout counselor, is Polonius. I hate him. Nor can I bear to hear your veterans of the world affirm, that he who steers through life by the advice of old Polonius will not steer among the breakers."

"No, no—I hope nobody affirms that," rejoined the cosmo-

---

12 See Chapter 22, note 15.

13 Matthew 19:21: "If thou wilt be perfect, go and sell that thou hast, and give it to the poor. . . ." In Matthew 26, when a woman anoints Christ's head with a precious ointment, the disciples, recalling this injunction, say that "this ointment might have been sold for much, and given to the poor." Christ denies this: "For ye have the poor always with you; but me ye have not always."

politan, with tranquil abandonment; sideways reposing his arm
at full length upon the table. "I hope nobody affirms that;
because, if Polonius' advice be taken in your sense, then the
recommendation of it by men of experience would appear to
involve more or less of an unhandsome sort of reflection upon
human nature. And yet," with a perplexed air, "your suggestions have put things in such a strange light to me as in fact a
little to disturb my previous notions of Polonius and what he
says. To be frank, by your ingenuity you have unsettled me
there, to that degree that were it not for our coincidence of
opinion in general, I should almost think I was now at length
beginning to feel the ill effect of an immature mind, too much
consorting with a mature one, except on the ground of first
principles in common."

"Really and truly," cried the other with a kind of tickled
modesty and pleased concern, "mine is an understanding too
weak to throw out grapnels and hug another to it. I have
indeed heard of some great scholars in these days, whose boast
is less that they have made disciples than victims. But for me,
had I the power to do such things, I have not the heart to
desire."

"I believe you, my dear Charlie. And yet, I repeat, by your
commentaries on Polonius you have, I know not how, unsettled
me; so that now I don't exactly see how Shakespeare meant the
words he puts in Polonius' mouth." [14]

"Some say that he meant them to open people's eyes; but I
don't think so."

"Open their eyes?" echoed the cosmopolitan, slowly expanding his; "what is there in this world for one to open his
eyes to? I mean in the sort of invidious sense you cite?"

"Well, others say he meant to corrupt people's morals; and

[14] Cf. the view of Shakespeare expressed in Melville's "Hawthorne and
His Mosses" (1849): "Through the mouths of the dark characters of
Hamlet, Timon, Lear, and Iago, he craftily says, or sometimes insinuates,
the things which we feel to be so terrifically true, that it were all but
madness for any good man, in his own proper character, to utter, or even
hint of them."

still others, that he had no express intention at all, but in effect opens their eyes and corrupts their morals in one operation. All of which I reject."

"Of course you reject so crude an hypothesis; and yet, to confess, in reading Shakespeare in my closet, struck by some passage, I have laid down the volume, and said: 'This Shakespeare is a queer man.' At times seeming irresponsible, he does not always seem reliable. There appears to be a certain—what shall I call it?—hidden sun, say, about him, at once enlightening and mystifying. Now, I should be afraid to say what I have sometimes thought that hidden sun might be."

"Do you think it was the true light?" with clandestine geniality again filling the other's glass.

"I would prefer to decline answering a categorical question there. Shakespeare has got to be a kind of deity. Prudent minds, having certain latent thoughts concerning him, will reserve them in a condition of lasting probation. Still, as touching avowable speculations, we are permitted a tether. Shakespeare himself is to be adored, not arraigned; but, so we do it with humility, we may a little canvass his characters. There's his Autolycus [15] now, a fellow that always puzzled me. How is one to take Autolycus? A rogue so happy, so lucky, so triumphant, of so almost captivatingly vicious a career that a virtuous man reduced to the poor-house (were such a contingency conceivable), might almost long to change sides with him. And yet, see the words put into his mouth: 'Oh,' cries Autolycus, as he comes galloping, gay as a buck, upon the stage, 'oh,' he laughs, 'oh what a fool is Honesty, and Trust, his sworn brother, a very simple gentleman.' [16] Think of that. Trust, that is, confidence—that is, the thing in this universe the sacredest —is rattlingly pronounced just the simplest. And the scenes in which the rogue figures seem purposely devised for verification of his principles. Mind, Charlie, I do not say it *is* so, far

[15] Pickpocket and peddler of puns, ballads, counterfeit jewels, and trash in *The Winter's Tale*.

[16] *The Winter's Tale*, IV, iv, 606–607.

from it; but I *do* say it seems so. Yes, Autolycus would seem a needy varlet acting upon the persuasion that less is to be got by invoking pockets than picking them, more to be made by an expert knave than a bungling beggar; and for this reason, as he thinks, that the soft heads outnumber the soft hearts. The devil's drilled recruit, Autolycus is joyous as if he wore the livery of heaven. When disturbed by the character and career of one thus wicked and thus happy, my sole consolation is in the fact that no such creature ever existed, except in the powerful imagination which evoked him. And yet, a creature, a living creature, he is, though only a poet was his maker. It may be, that in that paper-and-ink investiture of his, Autolycus acts more effectively upon mankind than he would in a flesh-and-blood one. Can his influence be salutary? True, in Autolycus there is humor; but though, according to my principle, humor is in general to be held a saving quality, yet the case of Autolycus is an exception; because it is his humor which, so to speak, oils his mischievousness. The bravadoing mischievousness of Autolycus is slid into the world on humor, as a pirate schooner, with colors flying, is launched into the sea on greased ways."

"I approve of Autolycus as little as you," said the stranger, who, during his companion's commonplaces, had seemed less attentive to them than to maturing within his own mind the original conceptions destined to eclipse them. "But I cannot believe that Autolycus, mischievous as he must prove upon the stage, can be near so much so as such a character as Polonius."

"I don't know about that," bluntly, and yet not impolitely, returned the cosmopolitan; "to be sure, accepting your view of the old courtier, then if between him and Autolycus you raise the question of unprepossessingness, I grant you the latter comes off best. For a moist rogue may tickle the midriff, while a dry worldling may but wrinkle the spleen."

"But Polonius is not dry," said the other excitedly; "he drules. One sees the fly-blown old fop drule and look wise. His vile wisdom is made the viler by his vile rheuminess. The

bowing and cringing, time-serving old sinner—is such an one
to give manly precepts to youth? The discreet, decorous, old
dotard-of-state; senile prudence; fatuous soullessness! The
ribanded old dog is paralytic all down one side, and that the
side of nobleness. His soul is gone out. Only nature's auto-
matonism keeps him on his legs. As with some old trees, the
bark survives the pith, and will still stand stiffly up, though but
to rim round punk, so the body of old Polonius has outlived
his soul."

"Come, come," said the cosmopolitan with serious air, almost displeased; "though I yield to none in admiration of earnestness, yet, I think, even earnestness may have limits. To
human minds, strong language is always more or less distressing. Besides, Polonius is an old man—as I remember him upon
the stage—with snowy locks. Now charity requires that such a
figure—think of it how you will—should at least be treated
with civility. Moreover, old age is ripeness, and I once heard
say, 'Better ripe than raw.' "

"But not better rotten than raw!" bringing down his hand
with energy on the table.

"Why, bless me," in mild surprise contemplating his heated
comrade, "how you fly out against this unfortunate Polonius
—a being that never was, nor will be. And yet, viewed in a
Christian light," he added pensively, "I don't know that anger
against this man of straw is a whit less wise than anger against a
man of flesh. Madness, to be mad with anything." [17]

"That may be, or may not be," returned the other, a little
testily, perhaps; "but I stick to what I said, that it is better to
be raw than rotten. And what is to be feared on that head, may
be known from this: that it is with the best of hearts as with
the best of pears—a dangerous experiment to linger too long
upon the scene. This did Polonius. Thank fortune, Frank, I am

[17] See Starbuck's speech in the chapter "The Quarter-Deck" in *Moby-
Dick*: "Madness! To be enraged with a dumb thing, Captain Ahab,
seems blasphemous."

young, every tooth sound in my head, and if good wine can keep me where I am, long shall I remain so."

"True," with a smile. "But wine, to do good, must be drunk. You have talked much and well, Charlie; but drunk little and indifferently—fill up."

"Presently, presently," with a hasty and preoccupied air. "If I remember right, Polonius hints as much as that one should, under no circumstances, commit the indiscretion of aiding in a pecuniary way an unfortunate friend. He drules out some stale stuff about 'loan losing both itself and friend,' don't he? But our bottle; is it glued fast? Keep it moving, my dear Frank. Good wine, and upon my soul I begin to feel it, and through me old Polonius—yes, this wine, I fear, is what excites me so against that detestable old dog without a tooth."

Upon this, the cosmopolitan, cigar in mouth, slowly raised the bottle, and brought it slowly to the light, looking at it steadfastly, as one might at a thermometer in August, to see not how low it was, but how high. Then whiffing out a puff, set it down, and said: "Well, Charlie, if what wine you have drunk came out of this bottle, in that case I should say that if—supposing a case—that if one fellow had an object in getting another fellow fuddled, and this fellow to be fuddled was of your capacity, the operation would be comparatively inexpensive. What do you think, Charlie?"

"Why, I think I don't much admire the supposition," said Charlie, with a look of resentment; "it ain't safe, depend upon it, Frank, to venture upon too jocose suppositions with one's friends."

"Why, bless you, Frank,[18] my supposition wasn't personal, but general. You mustn't be so touchy."

"If I am touchy it is the wine. Sometimes, when I freely drink, it has a touchy effect on me, I have observed."

"Freely drink? you haven't drunk the perfect measure of

[18] This apparent mistake appears in both the first American and first English editions.

one glass, yet. While for me, this must be my fourth or fifth, thanks to your importunity; not to speak of all I drank this morning, for old acquaintance' sake. Drink, drink; you must drink."

"Oh, I drink while you are talking," laughed the other; "you have not noticed it, but I have drunk my share. Have a queer way I learned from a sedate old uncle, who used to tip off his glass unperceived. Do you fill up, and my glass, too. There! Now away with that stump, and have a new cigar. Good fellowship forever!" again in the lyric mood. "Say, Frank, are we not men? I say are we not human? Tell me, were they not human who engendered us, as before heaven I believe they shall be whom we shall engender? [19] Fill up, up, up, my friend. Let the ruby tide aspire, and all ruby aspirations with it! Up, fill up! Be we convivial. And conviviality, what is it? The word, I mean; what expresses it? A living together. But bats live together, and did you ever hear of convivial bats?"

"If I ever did," observed the cosmopolitan, "it has quite slipped my recollection."

"But *why* did you never hear of convivial bats, nor anybody else? Because bats, though they live together, live not together genially. Bats are not genial souls. But men are; and how delightful to think that the word which among men signifies the highest pitch of geniality, implies, as indispensable auxiliary, the cheery benediction of the bottle. Yes, Frank, to live together in the finest sense, we must drink together. And so, what wonder that he who loves not wine, that sober wretch has a lean heart—a heart like a wrung-out old bluing-bag, and loves not his kind? Out upon him, to the rag-house with him, hang him—the ungenial soul!"

"Oh, now, now, can't you be convivial without being censorious? I like easy, unexcited conviviality. For the sober man, really, though for my part I naturally love a cheerful glass, I will not prescribe my nature as the law to other natures. So

[19] Note relations to both author and reader.

don't abuse the sober man. Conviviality is one good thing, and
sobriety is another good thing. So don't be one-sided."

"Well, if I am one-sided, it is the wine. Indeed, indeed, I
have indulged too genially.[20] My excitement upon slight provocation shows it. But yours is a stronger head; drink you. By
the way, talking of geniality, it is much on the increase in
these days, ain't it?"

"It is, and I hail the fact. Nothing better attests the advance
of the humanitarian spirit. In former and less humanitarian
ages—the ages of amphitheatres and gladiators—geniality was
mostly confined to the fireside and table. But in our age—the
age of joint-stock companies and free-and-easies [21]—it is with
this precious quality as with precious gold in old Peru, which
Pizarro [22] found making up the scullion's sauce-pot as the
Inca's crown.[23] Yes, we golden boys, the moderns, have geniality everwhere—a bounty broadcast like noonlight."

"True, true; my sentiments again. Geniality has invaded
each department and profession. We have genial senators,
genial authors, genial lecturers, genial doctors, genial clergymen, genial surgeons, and the next thing we shall have genial
hangmen."

"As to the last-named sort of person," said the cosmopolitan,

[20] The rest of this chapter contains thirty usages of the term "genial"
and its associated forms. "Genial" meant literally pertaining to genius
(in the root sense of birth or nature) or to generation. Hence it came
to be associated first with sexual activity (as in the Latin *lectus genialis*,
the genial bed), then with gods, goddesses, or angels presiding over
marriage or sexual activity, and next with the sun as the source of all
fertility and growth. At the same time, it was acquiring its more modern
meanings of cheerful, jovial, kindly.

[21] Informal gatherings, often in saloons, for the purpose of singing,
smoking, and drinking.

[22] Francisco Pizarro (*c.* 1471–1541), one of the most rapacious of the
Spanish conquistadores, devastated almost the entire Incan empire.

[23] Because the Inca was considered the Sun incarnate, even the cooking
vessels in all palaces were made of gold, his symbol. The Cosmopolitan here relates himself and other "golden boys" to the being who
appears "suddenly as Manco Capac" in the first sentence of the book.

"I trust that the advancing spirit of geniality will at last enable us to dispense with him. No murderers—no hangmen. And surely, when the whole world shall have been genialized, it will be as out of place to talk of murderers, as in a Christianized world to talk of sinners."

"To pursue the thought," said the other, "every blessing is attended with some evil, and—"

"Stay," said the cosmopolitan, "that may be better let pass for a loose saying, than for hopeful doctrine."

"Well, assuming the saying's truth, it would apply to the future supremacy of the genial spirit, since then it will fare with the hangman as it did with the weaver when the spinning-jenny whizzed into the ascendant. Thrown out of employment, what could Jack Ketch [24] turn his hand to? Butchering?"

"That he could turn his hand to it seems probable; but that, under the circumstances, it would be appropriate, might in some minds admit of a question. For one, I am inclined to think—and I trust it will not be held fastidiousness—that it would hardly be suitable to the dignity of our nature, that an individual, once employed in attending the last hours of human unfortunates, should, that office being extinct, transfer himself to the business of attending the last hours of unfortunate cattle. I would suggest that the individual turn valet—a vocation to which he would, perhaps, appear not wholly inadapted by his familiar dexterity about the person. In particular, for giving a finishing tie to a gentleman's cravat, I know few who would in all likelihood, be, from previous occupation, better fitted than the professional person in question."

"Are you in earnest?" regarding the serene speaker with unaffected curiosity; "are you really in earnest?"

"I trust I am never otherwise," was the mildly earnest reply; "but talking of the advance of geniality, I am not without

[24] A seventeenth-century headsman infamous for some of his clumsy executions. The puppet-show "Punchinello" or "Punch and Judy" came into England at about the time of his death in 1686, and Ketch's name thus passed naturally to the puppet executioner.

hopes that it will eventually exert its influence even upon so difficult a subject as the misanthrope."

"A genial misanthrope! I thought I had stretched the rope pretty hard in talking of genial hangmen. A genial misanthrope is no more conceivable than a surly philanthropist."

"True," lightly depositing in an unbroken little cylinder the ashes of his cigar, "true, the two you name are well opposed."

"Why, you talk as if there *was* such a being as a surly philanthropist."

"I do. My eccentric friend, whom you call Coonskins, is an example. Does he not, as I explained to you, hide under a surly air a philanthropic heart? Now, the genial misanthrope, when, in the process of eras, he shall turn up, will be the converse of this; under an affable air, he will hide a misanthropical heart. In short, the genial misanthrope will be a new kind of monster, but still no small improvement upon the original one, since, instead of making faces and throwing stones at people, like that poor old crazy man, Timon,[25] he will take steps, fiddle in hand, and set the tickled world a'dancing. In a word, as the progress of Christianization mellows those in manner whom it cannot mend in mind, much the same will it prove with the progress of genialization. And so, thanks to geniality, the misanthrope, reclaimed from his boorish address, will take on refinement and softness—to so genial a degree, indeed, that it may possibly fall out that the misanthrope of the coming century will be almost as popular as, I am sincerely sorry to say, some philanthropists of the present time would seem not to be, as witness my eccentric friend named before."

"Well," cried the other, a little weary, perhaps, of a speculation so abstract, "well, however it may be with the century to come, certainly in the century which is, whatever else one may be, he must be genial or he is nothing. So fill up, fill up, and be genial!"

"I am trying my best," said the cosmopolitan, still calmly

[25] In Lucian's Greek dialogue, Timon throws stones not only at people but even at the gods who come to help him.

companionable. "A moment since, we talked of Pizarro, gold, and Peru; no doubt, now, you remember that when the Spaniard first entered Atahalpa's treasure-chamber,[26] and saw such profusion of plate stacked up, right and left, with the wantonness of old barrels in a brewer's yard, the needy fellow felt a twinge of misgiving, of want of confidence, as to the genuineness of an opulence so profuse. He went about rapping the shining vases with his knuckles. But it was all gold, pure gold, good gold, sterling gold, which how cheerfully would have been stamped such at Goldsmiths' Hall. And just so those needy minds, which, through their own insincerity, having no confidence in mankind, doubt lest the liberal geniality of this age be spurious. They are small Pizarros in their way—by the very princeliness of men's geniality stunned into distrust of it."

"Far be such distrust from you and me, my genial friend," cried the other fervently; "fill up, fill up!"

"Well, this all along seems a division of labor," smiled the cosmopolitan. "I do about all the drinking, and you do about all—the genial. But yours is a nature competent to do that to a large population. And now, my friend," with a peculiarly grave air, evidently foreshadowing something not unimportant, and very likely of close personal interest; "wine, you know, opens the heart, and—"

"Opens it!" with exultation, "it thaws it right out. Every heart is ice-bound till wine melt it, and reveal the tender grass and sweet herbage budding below, with every dear secret, hidden before like a dropped jewel in a snow-bank, lying there unsuspected through winter till spring."

"And just in that way, my dear Charlie, is one of my little secrets now to be shown forth."

[26] Pizarro treacherously massacred hundreds of unarmed attendants of Atahualpa (c. 1493–1533), and then seized this Incan king. Atahualpa then had a large room half filled with gold as a ransom; Pizarro took the gold and killed the king. Whether he thus slew the son of the Sun was debatable, because the question of Atahualpa's legitimacy had already split the Incan empire in two.

"Ah!" eagerly moving round his chair, "what is it?"

"Be not so impetuous, my dear Charlie. Let me explain. You see, naturally, I am a man not overgifted with assurance; in general, I am, if anything, diffidently reserved; so, if I shall presently seem otherwise, the reason is, that you, by the geniality you have evinced in all your talk, and especially the noble way in which, while affirming your good opinion of men, you intimated that you never could prove false to any man, but most by your indignation at a particularly illiberal passage in Polonius' advice—in short, in short," with extreme embarrassment, "how shall I express what I mean, unless I add that by your whole character you impel me to throw myself upon your nobleness; in one word, put confidence in you, a generous confidence?"

"I see, I see," with heightened interest, "something of moment you wish to confide. Now, what is it, Frank? Love affair?"

"No, not that."

"What, then, my *dear* Frank? Speak—depend upon me to the last. Out with it."

"Out it shall come, then," said the cosmopolitan. "I am in want, urgent want, of money."

CHAPTER 31

*A metamorphosis more surprising than any
in Ovid.* [1]

"In want of money!" pushing back his chair as from a suddenly-disclosed man-trap or crater.

"Yes," naïvely assented the cosmopolitan, "and you are going to loan me fifty dollars. I could almost wish I was in need of more, only for your sake. Yes, my dear Charlie, for your sake; that you might the better prove your noble kindliness, my dear Charlie."

"None of your dear Charlies," cried the other, springing to his feet, and buttoning up his coat, as if hastily to depart upon a long journey.

"Why, why, why?" painfully looking up.

"None of your why, why, whys!" tossing out a foot, "go to the devil, sir! Beggar, impostor!—never so deceived in a man in my life."

[1] Ovid's *Metamorphoses*, poetic retellings of many of the classical myths, underlies much of *The Confidence-Man*.

CHAPTER 32

*Showing that the age of magic and magicians
is not yet over.*

While speaking or rather hissing those words, the boon companion underwent much such a change as one reads of in fairy-
books. Out of old materials sprang a new creature. Cadmus
glided into the snake.[1]

The cosmopolitan rose, the traces of previous feeling vanished; looked steadfastly at his transformed friend a moment,
then, taking ten half-eagles [2] from his pocket, stooped down,
and laid them, one by one, in a circle round him; and, retiring
a pace, waved his long tasseled pipe with the air of a necromancer, an air heightened by his costume, accompanying each
wave with a solemn murmur of cabalistical words.

Meantime, he within the magic-ring stood suddenly rapt,
exhibiting every symptom of a successful charm—a turned
cheek, a fixed attitude, a frozen eye; spellbound, not more by
the waving wand than by the ten invincible talismans on the
floor.

"Reappear, reappear, reappear, oh, my former friend! Replace this hideous apparition with thy blest shape, and be the
token of thy return the words, 'My dear Frank.'"

"My dear Frank," now cried the restored friend, cordially
stepping out of the ring, with regained self-possession regain-

[1] Cadmus, who had killed a giant serpent sacred to Mars, sowed the
serpent's teeth, and garnered a harvest of armed warriors (Ovid, *Metamorphoses* III. 1–137), later finds himself enmeshed in troubles. He
cries out that if the gods are angry because he slew the serpent, may he
become one too; even as he speaks he metamorphoses into a serpent
(*Metamorphoses* IV. 563–603).

[2] The sum he had just requested.

ing lost identity, "My dear Frank, what a funny man you are; full of fun as an egg of meat. How could you tell me that absurd story of your being in need? But I relish a good joke too well to spoil it by letting on. Of course, I humored the thing; and, on my side, put on all the cruel airs you would have me. Come, this little episode of fictitious estrangement will but enhance the delightful reality. Let us sit down again, and finish our bottle."

"With all my heart," said the cosmopolitan, dropping the necromancer with the same facility with which he had assumed it. "Yes," he added, soberly picking up the gold pieces, and returning them with a chink to his pocket, "yes, I am something of a funny man now and then; while for you, Charlie," eying him in tenderness, "what you say about your humoring the thing is true enough; never did man second a joke better than you did just now. You played your part better than I did mine; you played it, Charlie, to the life."

"You see, I once belonged to an amateur play company; that accounts for it. But come, fill up, and let's talk of something else."

"Well," acquiesced the cosmopolitan, seating himself, and quietly brimming his glass, "what shall we talk about?"

"Oh, anything you please," a sort of nervously accommodating.

"Well, suppose we talk about Charlemont?"

"Charlemont? What's Charlemont? Who's Charlemont?"

"You shall hear, my dear Charlie," answered the cosmopolitan. "I will tell you the story of Charlemont, the gentleman-madman."

CHAPTER 33

*Which may pass for whatever it may prove
to be worth.*

But ere be given the rather grave story of Charlemont, a reply
must in civility be made to a certain voice which methinks I
hear, that, in view of past chapters, and more particularly the
last, where certain antics appear, exclaims: How unreal all this
is! Who did ever dress or act like your cosmopolitan? And
who, it might be returned, did ever dress or act like harlequin?

Strange, that in a work of amusement, this severe fidelity [1] to
real life should be exacted by any one, who, by taking up such
a work, sufficiently shows that he is not unwilling to drop real
life, and turn, for a time, to something different. Yes, it is,
indeed, strange that any one should clamor for the thing he is
weary of; that any one, who, for any cause, finds real life dull,
should yet demand of him who is to divert his attention from
it, that he should be true to that dullness.

There is another class, and with this class we side, who sit
down to a work of amusement tolerantly as they sit at a play,
and with much the same expectations and feelings. They look
that fancy shall evoke scenes different from those of the same
old crowd round the custom-house counter, and same old
dishes on the boarding-house table, with characters unlike
those of the same old acquaintances they meet in the same old
way every day in the same old street. And as, in real life, the
proprieties will not allow people to act out themselves with
that unreserve permitted to the stage; so, in books of fiction,
they look not only for more entertainment, but, at bottom,

[1] In this word *The Confidence-Man* as a fiction merges with the
characters aboard the Fidèle.

even for more reality, than real life itself can show. Thus, though they want novelty, they want nature, too; but nature unfettered, exhilarated, in effect transformed. In this way of thinking, the people in a fiction, like the people in a play, must dress as nobody exactly dresses, talk as nobody exactly talks, act as nobody exactly acts. It is with fiction as with religion: it should present another world, and yet one to which we feel the tie.

If, then, something is to be pardoned to well-meant endeavor, surely a little is to be allowed to that writer who, in all his scenes, does but seek to minister to what, as he understands it, is the implied wish of the more indulgent lovers of entertainment, before whom harlequin can never appear in a coat too parti-colored, or cut capers too fantastic.

One word more. Though every one knows how bootless it is to be in all cases vindicating one's self, never mind how convinced one may be that he is never in the wrong; yet, so precious to man is the approbation of his kind, that to rest, though but under an imaginary censure applied to but a work of imagination, is no easy thing. The mention of this weakness will explain why all such readers as may think they perceive something inharmonious between the boisterous hilarity of the cosmopolitan with the bristling cynic, and his restrained good-nature with the boon-companion, are now referred to that chapter where some similar apparent inconsistency in another character is, on general principles, modestly endeavored to be apologized for.

CHAPTER 34

*In which the Cosmopolitan tells the story of
the gentleman-madman.*

"Charlemont [1] was a young merchant of French descent, living
in St. Louis [2]—a man not deficient in mind, and possessed of
that sterling and captivating kindliness, seldom in perfection
seen but in youthful bachelors, united at times to a remarkable
sort of gracefully devil-may-care and witty good-humor. Of
course, he was admired by everybody, and loved, as only mankind can love, by not a few. But in his twenty-ninth year a
change came over him. [3] Like one whose hair turns gray in a
night, so in a day Charlemont turned from affable to morose.
His acquaintances were passed without greeting; while, as for
his confidential friends, them he pointedly, unscrupulously,
and with a kind of fierceness, cut dead.

"One, provoked by such conduct, would fain have resented
it with words as disdainful; while another, shocked by the
change, and, in concern for a friend, magnanimously overlooking affronts, implored to know what sudden, secret grief had
distempered him. But from resentment and from tenderness
Charlemont alike turned away.

"Ere long, to the general surprise, the merchant Charlemont
was gazetted, [4] and the same day it was reported that he had

[1] The primary significance of this name I take to refer not to the
Earls of Charlemont, the French fortress of Charlemont, William Gil-
more Simms' 1856 romance *Charlemont*, or Charlemagne, but, in a pun,
to the relationship between Charlie and the Cosmopolitan.

[2] The city from which the voyage of the Fidèle began.

[3] See Chapter 22, note 30, and Carolyn Lury Karcher, "The Story of
Charlemont," *Nineteenth-Century Fiction*, XXI (1966), 73–84.

[4] Had his bankruptcy officially announced.

withdrawn from town, but not before placing his entire property in the hands of responsible assignees for the benefit of creditors.

"Whither he had vanished, none could guess. At length, nothing being heard, it was surmised that he must have made away with himself—a surmise, doubtless, originating in the remembrance of the change some months previous to his bankruptcy—a change of a sort only to be ascribed to a mind suddenly thrown from its balance.

"Years passed. It was spring-time, and lo, one bright morning, Charlemont lounged into the St. Louis coffee-houses— gay, polite, humane, companionable, and dressed in the height of costly elegance. Not only was he alive, but he was himself again. Upon meeting with old acquaintances, he made the first advances, and in such a manner that it was impossible not to meet him half-way. Upon other old friends, whom he did not chance casually to meet, he either personally called, or left his card and compliments for them; and to several, sent presents of game or hampers of wine.

"They say the world is sometimes harshly unforgiving, but it was not so to Charlemont. The world feels a return of love for one who returns to it as he did. Expressive of its renewed interest was a whisper, an inquiring whisper, how now, exactly, so long after his bankruptcy, it fared with Charlemont's purse. Rumor, seldom at a loss for answers, replied that he had spent nine years in Marseilles in France, and there acquiring a second fortune, had returned with it, a man devoted henceforth to genial friendships.

"Added years went by, and the restored wanderer still the same; or rather, by his noble qualities, grew up like golden maize in the encouraging sun of good opinions. But still the latent wonder was, what had caused that change in him at a period when, pretty much as now, he was, to all appearance, in the possession of the same fortune, the same friends, the same popularity. But nobody thought it would be the thing to question him here.

"At last, at a dinner at his house, when all the guests but one had successively departed; this remaining guest, an old acquaintance, being just enough under the influence of wine to set aside the fear of touching upon a delicate point, ventured, in a way which perhaps spoke more favorably for his heart than his tact, to beg of his host to explain the one enigma of his life. Deep melancholy overspread the before cheery face of Charlemont; he sat for some moments tremulously silent; then pushing a full decanter towards the guest, in a choked voice, said: 'No, no! when by art, and care, and time, flowers are made to bloom over a grave, who would seek to dig all up again only to know the mystery?—The wine.' When both glasses were filled, Charlemont took his, and lifting it, added lowly: 'If ever, in days to come, you shall see ruin at hand, and, thinking you understand mankind, shall tremble for your friendships, and tremble for your pride; and, partly through love for the one and fear for the other, shall resolve to be beforehand with the world, and save it from a sin by prospectively taking that sin to yourself,[5] then will you do as one I now dream of once did, and like him will you suffer; but how fortunate and how grateful should you be, if like him, after all that had happened, you could be a little happy again.'

"When the guest went away, it was with the persuasion, that though outwardly restored in mind as in fortune, yet, some taint of Charlemont's old malady survived, and that it was not well for friends to touch one dangerous string."

[5] See Chapter 7, note 2.

CHAPTER 35

*In which the Cosmopolitan strikingly evinces
the artlessness of his nature.*

"Well, what do you think of the story of Charlemont?"
mildly asked he who had told it.

"A very strange one," answered the auditor, who had been
such not with perfect ease, "but is it true?"

"Of course not; it is a story which I told with the purpose
of every story-teller—to amuse. Hence, if it seem strange to
you, that strangeness is the romance; it is what contrasts it
with real life; it is the invention, in brief, the fiction as opposed
to the fact. For do but ask yourself, my dear Charlie," lovingly
leaning over towards him, "I rest it with your own heart now,
whether such a forereaching motive as Charlemont hinted he
had acted on in his change—whether such a motive, I say,
were a sort of one at all justified by the nature of human
society? Would you, for one, turn the cold shoulder to a
friend—a convivial one, say, whose pennilessness should be
suddenly revealed to you?"

"How can you ask me, my dear Frank? You know I would
scorn such meanness." But rising somewhat disconcerted—
"really, early as it is, I think I must retire; my head," putting up
his hand to it, "feels unpleasantly; this confounded elixir of
logwood, little as I drank of it, has played the deuce with
me."

"Little as you drank of this elixir of logwood? Why, Charlie, you are losing your mind. To talk so of the genuine, mellow old port. Yes, I think that by all means you had better
away, and sleep it off. There—don't apologize—don't explain—
go, go—I understand you exactly. I will see you to-morrow."

CHAPTER 36

In which the Cosmopolitan is accosted by a
mystic, whereupon ensues pretty much
such talk as might be expected.

As, not without some haste, the boon companion withdrew, a
stranger advanced, and touching the cosmopolitan, said: "I
think I heard you say you would see that man again. Be
warned; don't you do so."

He turned, surveying the speaker; a blue-eyed man, sandy-
haired, and Saxon-looking; perhaps five and forty; tall, and,
but for a certain angularity, well made; little touch of the
drawing-room about him, but a look of plain propriety of a
Puritan sort, with a kind of farmer dignity. His age seemed
betokened more by his brow, placidly thoughtful, than by his
general aspect, which had that look of youthfulness in maturity, peculiar sometimes to habitual health of body, the original gift of nature, or in part the effect or reward of steady
temperance of the passions, kept so, perhaps, by constitution as
much as morality. A neat, comely, almost ruddy cheek, coolly
fresh, like a red clover-blossom at coolish dawn—the color of
warmth preserved by the virtue of chill. Toning the whole
man, was one-knows-not-what of shrewdness and mythiness,
strangely jumbled; in that way, he seemed a kind of cross
between a Yankee peddler [1] and a Tartar [2] priest, though it
seemed as if, at a pinch, the first would not in all probability
play second fiddle to the last. [3]

[1] The Yankee peddler, a folklore figure; a crafty rogue who loves
wearing disguises and playing new roles and sharp tricks.

[2] See Chapter 2, note 17.

[3] This stranger, as Egbert S. Oliver first demonstrated in "Melville's
Picture of Emerson and Thoreau in *The Confidence-Man*," *College*

"Sir," said the cosmopolitan, rising and bowing with slow dignity, "if I cannot with unmixed satisfaction hail a hint pointed at one who has just been clinking the social glass with me, on the other hand, I am not disposed to underrate the motive which, in the present case, could alone have prompted such an intimation. My friend, whose seat is still warm, has retired for the night, leaving more or less in his bottle here. Pray, sit down in his seat, and partake with me; and then, if you choose to hint aught further unfavorable to the man, the genial warmth of whose person in part passes into yours, and whose genial hospitality meanders through you—be it so."

"Quite beautiful conceits," said the stranger, now scholastically and artistically eying the picturesque speaker, as if he were a statue in the Pitti Palace; [4] "very beautiful:" then with the gravest interest, "yours, sir, if I mistake not, must be a beautiful soul—one full of all love and truth; for where beauty is, there must those be."

"A pleasing belief," rejoined the cosmopolitan, beginning with an even air, "and to confess, long ago it pleased me. Yes, with you and Schiller,[5] I am pleased to believe that beauty is at bottom incompatible with ill, and therefore am so eccentric as to have confidence in the latent benignity of that beautiful creature, the rattle-snake, whose lithe neck and burnished maze of tawny gold, as he sleekly curls aloft in the sun, who on the prairie can behold without wonder?"

As he breathed these words, he seemed so to enter into their spirit—as some earnest descriptive speakers will—as uncon-

---

English, VIII (1946), 61–72, is in body, word, and deed a comic embodiment of Ralph Waldo Emerson. Because the parody is extremely detailed and pervades the next two chapters, only a few of its more striking strokes are annotated.

[4] A Florentine palace containing a world-famous collection of paintings and statuary.

[5] Johann Cristoph Friedrich von Schiller (1759–1805), German poet, dramatist, essayist, and historian, held that beauty is essentially a way of perceiving the external world.

sciously to wreathe his form and sidelong crest his head,[6] till he all but seemed the creature described. Meantime, the stranger regarded him with little surprise, apparently, though with much contemplativeness of a mystical sort, and presently said: "When charmed by the beauty of that viper, did it never occur to you to change personalities with him? to feel what it was to be a snake? to glide unsuspected in grass? to sting, to kill at a touch; your whole beautiful body one iridescent scabbard of death? In short, did the wish never occur to you to feel yourself exempt from knowledge, and conscience, and revel for a while in the care-free, joyous life of a perfectly instinctive, unscrupulous, and irresponsible creature?"

"Such a wish," replied the other, not perceptibly disturbed, "I must confess, never consciously was mine. Such a wish, indeed, could hardly occur to ordinary imaginations, and mine I cannot think much above the average."

"But now that the idea is suggested," said the stranger, with infantile intellectuality, "does it not raise the desire?"

"Hardly. For though I do not think I have any uncharitable prejudice against the rattle-snake, still, I should not like to be one. If I were a rattle-snake now, there would be no such thing as being genial with men—men would be afraid of me, and then I should be a very lonesome and miserable rattle-snake."

"True, men would be afraid of you. And why? Because of your rattle, your hollow rattle—a sound, as I have been told, like the shaking together of small, dry skulls in a tune of the

[6] Cf. the description of Satan as the serpent tempting Eve in *Paradise Lost*, IX, 499-525 (a source first pointed out by Elizabeth Foster):

> Fold above fold, a surging maze! his head
> Crested aloft, and carbuncle his eyes;
> With burnished neck of verdant gold, erect
> Amidst his circling spires . . .
> . . . sidelong he works his way.
> . . . of his tortuous train
> Curl'd many a wanton wreath in sight of Eve . . .
> . . . Oft he bow'd
> His turret crest and sleek enamelled neck . . .

Waltz of Death.[7] And here we have another beautiful truth. When any creature is by its make inimical to other creatures, nature in effect labels that creature, much as an apothecary does a poison. So that whoever is destroyed by a rattle-snake, or other harmful agent, it is his own fault. He should have respected the label. Hence that significant passage in Scripture, 'Who will pity the charmer that is bitten with a serpent?' " [8]

"*I* would pity him," said the cosmopolitan, a little bluntly, perhaps.

"But don't you think," rejoined the other, still maintaining his passionless air, "don't you think, that for a man to pity where nature is pitiless, is a little presuming?"

"Let casuists decide the casuistry, but the compassion the heart decides for itself. But, sir," deepening in seriousness, "as I now for the first realize, you but a moment since intro-duced the word irresponsible in a way I am not used to. Now, sir, though, out of a tolerant spirit, as I hope, I try my best never to be frightened at any speculation, so long as it is pur-sued in honesty, yet, for once, I must acknowledge that you do really, in the point cited, cause me uneasiness; because a proper view of the universe, that view which is suited to breed a proper confidence, teaches, if I err not, that since all things are justly presided over, not very many living agents but must be some way accountable."

"Is a rattle-snake accountable?" asked the stranger with such a preternaturally cold, gemmy glance out of his pellucid

[7] The Dance of Death burst into European literature and art in the fourteenth century and rapidly became a familiar tradition that still endures. The most conventional versions show Death as a skeleton seizing representative living people of different types and classes and leading them in a grotesque dance, often to the accompaniment of skeleton musicians. See Chapter 23, note 2.

[8] Ecclesiasticus 12:13: "Who will pity the charmer that is bitten with a serpent . . . ? " In Chapter 43 William Cream quotes from the same and following chapter of this apocryphal book, and Chapter 45 refers directly to it.

blue eye, that he seemed more a metaphysical merman than a feeling man; "is a rattle-snake accountable?"

"If I will not affirm that it is," returned the other, with the caution of no inexperienced thinker, "neither will I deny it. But if we suppose it so, I need not say that such accountability is neither to you, nor me, nor the Court of Common Pleas,[9] but to something superior."

He was proceeding, when the stranger would have interrupted him; but as reading his argument in his eye, the cosmopolitan, without waiting for it to be put into words, at once spoke to it: "You object to my supposition, for but such it is, that the rattle-snake's accountability is not by nature manifest; but might not much the same thing be urged against man's? A *reductio ad absurdum*, proving the objection vain. But if now," he continued, "you consider what capacity for mischief there is in a rattle-snake (observe, I do not charge it with being mischievous, I but say it has the capacity), could you well avoid admitting that that would be no symmetrical view of the universe which should maintain that, while to man it is forbidden to kill, without judicial cause, his fellow, yet the rattle-snake has an implied permit of unaccountability to murder any creature it takes capricious umbrage at—man included?—But," with a wearied air, "this is no genial talk; at least it is not so to me. Zeal at unawares embarked me in it. I regret it. Pray, sit down, and take some of this wine."

"Your suggestions are new to me," said the other, with a kind of condescending appreciativeness, as of one who, out of devotion to knowledge, disdains not to appropriate the least crumb of it, even from a pauper's board; "and, as I am a very Athenian [10] in hailing a new thought, I cannot consent to let it drop so abruptly. Now, the rattle-snake—"

[9] Originally, in England, a court for the trial of civil actions between citizens. Several of the United States had a Court of Common Pleas having criminal as well as civil jurisdiction over the entire state.

[10] Melville called Emerson (in a famous letter to Evert Duyckinck) "this Plato who talks thro' his nose."

"Nothing more about rattle-snakes, I beseech," in distress; "I must positively decline to reënter upon that subject. Sit down, sir, I beg, and take some of this wine."

"To invite me to sit down with you is hospitable," collectedly acquiescing now in the change of topics; "and hospitality being fabled to be of oriental origin,[11] and forming, as it does, the subject of a pleasing Arabian romance,[12] as well as being a very romantic thing in itself—hence I always hear the expressions of hospitality with pleasure. But, as for the wine, my regard for that beverage is so extreme, and I am so fearful of letting it sate me, that I keep my love for it in the lasting condition of an untried abstraction. Briefly, I quaff immense draughts of wine from the page of Hafiz,[13] but wine from a cup I seldom as much as sip."

The cosmopolitan turned a mild glance upon the speaker, who, now occupying the chair opposite him, sat there purely and coldly radiant as a prism. It seemed as if one could almost hear him vitreously chime and ring. That moment a waiter passed, whom, arresting with a sign, the cosmopolitan bid go bring a goblet of ice-water. "Ice it well, waiter," said he; "and now," turning to the stranger, "will you, if you please, give me your reason for the warning words you first addressed to me?"

[11] See Chapter 1, note 10.

[12] In his 1841 essay "Heroism," Emerson relates a tale told by Ibn Hankal, the Arabian geographer, about the "heroic extreme in the hospitality of Sogd, in Bukharia": "'. . . a great building, like a palace . . . had not been shut, night or day, for a hundred years. Strangers may present themselves at any hour, and in whatever number; the master has amply provided for the reception of the men and their animals, and is never happier than when they tarry for some time.'"

[13] Shams ed-din Muhammad Hafiz, fourteenth-century Persian theologian, philosopher, grammarian, and poet. Hafiz (Arabic: "he who knows by heart," referring to the Koran) in his lyric poetry celebrates wine, love, nightingales, flowers, Allah, and the Prophet. Emerson translated some of Hafiz' poetry from German and wrote an essay entitled "Persian Poetry."

"I hope they were not such warnings as most warnings are," said the stranger; "warnings which do not forewarn, but in mockery come after the fact. And yet something in you bids me think now, that whatever latent design your impostor friend might have had upon you, it as yet remains unaccomplished. You read his label."

"And what did it say? 'This is a genial soul.' So you see you must either give up your doctrine of labels, or else your prejudice against my friend. But tell me," with renewed earnestness, "what do you take him for? What is he?"

"What are you? What am I? Nobody knows who anybody is. The data which life furnishes, towards forming a true estimate of any being, are as insufficient to that end as in geometry one side given would be to determine the triangle."

"But is not this doctrine of triangles someway inconsistent with your doctrine of labels?"

"Yes; but what of that? I seldom care to be consistent.[14] In a philosophical view, consistency is a certain level at all times, maintained in all the thoughts of one's mind. But, since nature is nearly all hill and dale, how can one keep naturally advancing in knowledge without submitting to the natural inequalities in the progress? Advance into knowledge is just like advance upon the grand Erie canal, where, from the character of the country, change of level is inevitable; you are locked up and locked down with perpetual inconsistencies, and yet all the time you get on; while the dullest part of the whole route is what the boatmen call the 'long level'—a consistently-flat surface of sixty miles through stagnant swamps."

"In one particular," rejoined the cosmopolitan, "your simile is, perhaps, unfortunate. For, after all these weary lockings-up and lockings-down, upon how much of a higher plain do you finally stand? Enough to make it an object? Having from youth been taught reverence for knowledge, you must pardon

[14] Emerson, "Self-Reliance" (1841): "A foolish consistency is the hobgoblin of little minds. . . . With consistency a great mind has simply nothing to do."

me if, on but this one account, I reject your analogy. But
really you someway bewitch me with your tempting discourse, so that I keep straying from my point unawares. You
tell me you cannot certainly know who or what my friend is;
pray, what do you conjecture him to be?"

"I conjecture him to be what, among the ancient Egyptians,
was called a ———" using some unknown word.

"A ———! And what is that?"

"A ——— is what Proclus,[15] in a little note to his third
book on the theology of Plato, defines as ——— ———" coming out with a sentence of Greek.

Holding up his glass, and steadily looking through its transparency, the cosmopolitan rejoined: "That, in· so defining the
thing, Proclus set it to modern understandings in the most
crystal light it was susceptible of, I will not rashly deny; still,
if you could put the definition in words suited to perceptions
like mine, I should take it for a favor."

"A favor!" slightly lifting his cool eyebrows; "a bridal favor
I understand, a knot of white ribands, a very beautiful type of
the purity of true marriage; but of other favors I am yet to
learn; and still, in a vague way, the word, as you employ it,
strikes me as unpleasingly significant in general of some poor,
unheroic submission to being done good to."

Here the goblet of iced-water was brought, and, in compli-
ance with a sign from the cosmopolitan, was placed before the
stranger, who, not before expressing acknowledgments, took a
draught, apparently refreshing—its very coldness, as with
some is the case, proving not entirely uncongenial.

At last, setting down the goblet, and gently wiping from his
lips the beads of water freshly clinging there as to the valve of
a coral-shell upon a reef, he turned upon the cosmopolitan,
and, in a manner the most cool, self-possessed, and matter-of-
fact possible, said: "I hold to the metempsychosis; and who-

---

[15] The neo-Platonic philosopher Proclus (412–485) saw the Orphic
Hymns and Chaldean Oracles as divine revelation, and allegorized them
in terms of an arcane system. Emerson read and was influenced by him.

ever I may be now, I feel that I was once the stoic Arrian,[16] and have inklings of having been equally puzzled by a word in the current language of that former time, very probably answering to your word *favor*."

"Would you favor me by explaining?" said the cosmopolitan, blandly.

"Sir," responded the stranger, with a very slight degree of severity, "I like lucidity, of all things, and am afraid I shall hardly be able to converse satisfactorily with you, unless you bear it in mind."

The cosmopolitan ruminatingly eyed him awhile, then said: "The best way, as I have heard, to get out of a labyrinth, is to retrace one's steps. I will accordingly retrace mine, and beg you will accompany me. In short, once again to return to the point: for what reason did you warn me against my friend?"

"Briefly, then, and clearly, because, as before said, I conjecture him to be what, among the ancient Egyptians—"

"Pray, now," earnestly deprecated the cosmopolitan, "pray, now, why disturb the repose of those ancient Egyptians? What to us are their words or their thoughts? Are we pauper Arabs, without a house of our own, that, with the mummies, we must turn squatters among the dust of the Catacombs?"

"Pharaoh's poorest brick-maker lies proudlier in his rags than the Emperor of all the Russias in his hollands," oracularly said the stranger; "for death, though in a worm, is majestic; while life, though in a king, is contemptible. So talk not against mummies. It is a part of my mission to teach mankind a due reverence for mummies."

Fortunately, to arrest these incoherencies, or rather, to vary them, a haggard, inspired-looking man now approached—a crazy beggar, asking alms under the form of peddling a rhapsodical tract, composed by himself, and setting forth his claims to some rhapsodical apostleship. Though ragged and dirty, there was about him no touch of vulgarity; for, by nature, his

[16] Flavius Arrianus, second-century Greek historian and philosopher, became a citizen of Rome and a disciple of Epictetus.

manner was not unrefined, his frame slender, and appeared the more so from the broad, untanned frontlet of his brow, tangled over with a disheveled mass of raven curls, throwing a still deeper tinge upon a complexion like that of a shriveled berry. Nothing could exceed his look of picturesque Italian ruin and dethronement, heightened by what seemed just one glimmering peep of reason, insufficient to do him any lasting good, but enough, perhaps, to suggest a torment of latent doubts at times, whether his addled dream of glory were true.[17]

Accepting the tract offered him, the cosmopolitan glanced over it, and, seeming to see just what it was, closed it, put it in his pocket, eyed the man a moment, then, leaning over and presenting him with a shilling, said to him, in tones kind and considerate: "I am sorry, my friend, that I happen to be engaged just now; but, having purchased your work, I promise myself much satisfaction in its perusal at my earliest leisure."

In his tattered, single-breasted frock-coat, buttoned meagerly up to his chin, the shatter-brain made him a bow, which, for courtesy, would not have misbecome a viscount, then turned with silent appeal to the stranger. But the stranger sat more like a cold prism than ever, while an expression of keen Yankee cuteness, now replacing his former mystical one, lent added icicles to his aspect. His whole air said: "Nothing from me." The repulsed petitioner threw a look full of resentful pride and cracked disdain upon him, and went his way.

"Come, now," said the cosmopolitan, a little reproachfully, "you ought to have sympathized with that man; tell me, did you feel no fellow-feeling? Look at his tract here, quite in the transcendental vein."

"Excuse me," said the stranger, declining the tract, "I never patronize scoundrels."

"Scoundrels?"

[17] This madman, as demonstrated by Harrison Hayford in "Poe in *The Confidence-Man*," *Nineteenth-Century Fiction*, XIV (1959), 207–218, is a caricature of Edgar Allan Poe.

"I detected in him, sir, a damning peep of sense—damning, I say; for sense in a seeming madman is scoundrelism. I take him for a cunning vagabond, who picks up a vagabond living by adroitly playing the madman. Did you not remark how he flinched under my eye?"

"Really," drawing a long, astonished breath, "I could hardly have divined in you a temper so subtly distrustful. Flinched? to be sure he did, poor fellow; you received him with so lame a welcome. As for his adroitly playing the madman, invidious critics might object the same to some one or two strolling magi of these days. But that is a matter I know nothing about. But, once more, and for the last time, to return to the point: why sir, did you warn me against my friend? I shall rejoice, if, as I think it will prove, your want of confidence in my friend rests upon a basis equally slender with your distrust of the lunatic. Come, why did you warn me? Put it, I beseech, in few words, and those English."

"I warned you against him because he is suspected for what on these boats is known—so they tell me—as a Mississippi operator."

"An operator, ah? he operates, does he? My friend, then, is something like what the Indians call a Great Medicine, is he? He operates, he purges, he drains off the repletions."

"I perceive, sir," said the stranger, constitutionally obtuse to the pleasant drollery, "that your notion, of what is called a Great Medicine, needs correction. The Great Medicine among the Indians is less a bolus than a man in grave esteem for his politic sagacity."

"And is not my friend politic? Is not my friend sagacious? By your own definition, is not my friend a Great Medicine?"

"No, he is an operator, a Mississippi operator; an equivocal character. That he is such, I little doubt, having had him pointed out to me as such by one desirous of initiating me into any little novelty of this western region, where I never before traveled. And, sir, if I am not mistaken, you also are a stranger here (but, indeed, where in this strange universe is not one a stranger?) and that is a reason why I felt moved to warn you against a companion who could not be otherwise than perilous to one of a free and trustful disposition. But I repeat the hope, that, thus far at least, he has not succeeded with you, and trust that, for the future, he will not."

"Thank you for your concern; but hardly can I equally thank you for so steadily maintaining the hypothesis of my friend's objectionableness. True, I but made his acquaintance for the first to-day, and know little of his antecedents; but that would seem no just reason why a nature like his should not of itself inspire confidence. And since your own knowledge of the gentleman is not, by your account, so exact as it might be, you will pardon me if I decline to welcome any further suggestions unflattering to him. Indeed, sir," with friendly decision, "let us change the subject."

CHAPTER 37

*The mystical master introduces the
practical disciple.*

"Both, the subject and the interlocutor," replied the stranger rising, and waiting the return towards him of a promenader, that moment turning at the further end of his walk.

"Egbert!" said he, calling.

Egbert, a well-dressed, commercial-looking gentleman of about thirty,[1] responded in a way strikingly deferential, and in a moment stood near, in the attitude less of an equal companion apparently than a confidential follower.[2]

"This," said the stranger, taking Egbert by the hand and leading him to the cosmopolitan, "this is Egbert, a disciple. I wish you to know Egbert. Egbert was the first among mankind to reduce to practice the principles of Mark Winsome—principles previously accounted as less adapted to life than the closet. Egbert," turning to the disciple, who, with seeming modesty, a little shrank under these compliments, "Egbert, this," with a salute towards the cosmopolitan, "is, like all of us, a stranger. I wish you, Egbert, to know this brother stranger; be communicative with him. Particularly if, by anything hitherto dropped, his curiosity has been roused as to the precise nature of my philosophy, I trust you will not leave such curiosity ungratified. You, Egbert, by simply setting forth your

---

[1] See Chapter 22, note 30.

[2] Winsome's confidential follower, as Egbert S. Oliver first pointed out in "Melville's Picture of Emerson and Thoreau in *The Confidence-Man*," seems to be Melville's caricature of Henry David Thoreau. Winsome was pointedly described as "perhaps five and forty"; Egbert is "about thirty." Since Emerson was born in 1803, Thoreau in 1817, they both appear here as they would around 1848.

practice, can do more to enlighten one as to my theory, than I myself can by mere speech. Indeed, it is by you that I myself best understand myself. For to every philosophy are certain rear parts, very important parts, and these, like the rear of one's head, are best seen by reflection. Now, as in a glass, you, Egbert, in your life, reflect to me the more important part of my system. He, who approves you, approves the philosophy of Mark Winsome."

Though portions of this harangue may, perhaps, in the phraseology seem self-complaisant, yet no trace of self-complacency was perceptible in the speaker's manner, which throughout was plain, unassuming, dignified, and manly; the teacher and prophet seemed to lurk more in the idea, so to speak, than in the mere bearing of him who was the vehicle of it.

"Sir," said the cosmopolitan, who seemed not a little interested in this new aspect of matters, "you speak of a certain philosophy, and a more or less occult one it may be, and hint of its bearing upon practical life; pray, tell me, if the study of this philosophy tends to the same formation of character with the experiences of the world?"

"It does; and that is the test of its truth; for any philosophy that, being in operation contradictory to the ways of the world, tends to produce a character at odds with it, such a philosophy must necessarily be but a cheat and a dream."

"You a little surprise me," answered the cosmopolitan; "for, from an occasional profundity in you, and also from your allusions to a profound work on the theology of Plato, it would seem but natural to surmise that, if you are the originator of any philosophy, it must needs so partake of the abstruse, as to exalt it above the comparatively vile uses of life."

"No uncommon mistake with regard to me," rejoined the other. Then meekly standing like a Raphael: [3] "If still in

---

[3] In the dialogue between Raphael and Adam in *Paradise Lost*, the archangel is described as "heavenly meek" (VII, 217).

golden accents old Memnon murmurs his riddle,[4] none the less does the balance-sheet of every man's ledger unriddle the profit or loss of life. Sir," with calm energy, "man came into this world, not to sit down and muse, not to befog himself with vain subtleties, but to gird up his loins and to work.[5] Mystery is in the morning, and mystery in the night, and the beauty of mystery is everywhere; but still the plain truth remains, that mouth and purse must be filled. If, hitherto, you have supposed me a visionary, be undeceived. I am no one-ideaed one, either; no more than the seers before me. Was not Seneca a usurer? [6] Bacon a courtier? [7] and Swedenborg, though with one eye on the invisible, did he not keep the other on the

[4] Melville, *Pierre* (1852), VII, *vi*: ". . . Memnon was that dewy, royal boy, son of Aurora, born King of Egypt . . . [who] met his boyish and most dolorous death beneath the walls of Troy. His wailing subjects built a monument in Egypt to commemorate his untimely fate. Touched by the breath of the bereaved Aurora, every sunrise that statue gave forth a mournful broken sound, as of a harp-string suddenly sundered, being too harshly wound. . . . Memnon's sculptured woes did once melodiously resound; now all is mute." Some ancient authorities thought the sound was caused by the rising sun's warmth; others thought it a trick of the priests.

[5] Cf. the chapter "Labour" in Thomas Carlyle's *Past and Present* (1843).

[6] See Chapter 9, note 7. Seneca's usury was enormous and infamous. Elizabeth Foster points out two relevant accusations: Tacitus repeats the charge that "At Rome the wills of the childless were, so to say, caught in his snare, while Italy and the provinces were drained by a boundless usury"; Dio blames the British uprising of A.D. 61 partly on "the fact that Seneca, in the hope of receiving a good rate of interest, had lent to the islanders 40,000,000 sesterces that they did not want, and had afterwards called in this loan all at once and had resorted to severe measures in exacting it." Compare the story of China Aster shortly to be narrated by Egbert.

[7] Bacon was knighted in 1603, became solicitor-general in 1607, attorney-general in 1613, privy-councilor in 1616, lord keeper in 1617, and lord chancellor in 1618. In 1621 he was condemned for bribery and stripped of his offices. See Chapetr 9, note 8 and Chapter 24, note 16.

main chance? [8] Along with whatever else it may be given me
to be, I am a man of serviceable knowledge, and a man of the
world. Know me for such. And as for my disciple here," turning towards him, "if you look to find any soft Utopianisms and
last year's sunsets in him, I smile to think how he will set you
right. The doctrines I have taught him will, I trust, lead him
neither to the mad-house nor the poor-house, as so many other
doctrines have served credulous sticklers. Furthermore,"
glancing upon him paternally, "Egbert is both my disciple and
my poet. For poetry is not a thing of ink and rhyme, but of
thought and act, and, in the latter way, is by any one to be
found anywhere, when in useful action sought. In a word, my
disciple here is a thriving young merchant, a practical poet in
the West India trade.[9] There," presenting Egbert's hand to the
cosmopolitan, "I join you, and leave you." With which words,
and without bowing, the master withdrew.

[8] Emanuel Swedenborg (1688–1772), Swedish philosopher and
theosophist, before his first mystical visions in 1743 was a noted engineer
and inventor of machines. Emerson gave his view of him in "Swedenborg; or, The Mystic," in *Representative Men* (1850).

[9] The "West India trade" may include rum, slavery, and its own
initials. In the chapter "Economy" in *Walden,* Thoreau metaphorically
describes his activities at Walden Pond as a business, in which he
succeeded partly because "I have always endeavored to acquire strict
business habits."

CHAPTER 38

*The disciple unbends, and consents to act a
social part.*

In the master's presence the disciple had stood as one not ignorant of his place; modesty was in his expression, with a sort of
reverential depression. But the presence of the superior withdrawn, he seemed lithely to shoot up erect from beneath it,
like one of those wire men from a toy snuff-box.

He was, as before said, a young man of about thirty. His
countenance of that neuter sort, which, in repose, is neither
prepossessing nor disagreeable; so that it seemed quite uncertain how he would turn out. His dress was neat, with just
enough of the mode to save it from the reproach of originality; in which general respect, though with a readjustment of
details, his costume seemed modeled upon his master's. But,
upon the whole, he was, to all appearances, the last person in
the world that one would take for the disciple of any transcendental philosophy; though, indeed, something about his
sharp nose and shaved chin seemed to hint that if mysticism, as
a lesson, ever came in his way, he might, with the characteristic knack of a true New-Englander, turn even so profitless a
thing to some profitable account.

"Well," said he, now familiarly seating himself in the va-
cated chair, "what do you think of Mark? Sublime fellow,
ain't he?"

"That each member of the human guild is worthy respect
my friend," rejoined the cosmopolitan, "is a fact which no
admirer of that guild will question; but that, in view of higher
natures, the word sublime, so frequently applied to them, can,
without confusion, be also applied to man, is a point which
man will decide for himself; though, indeed, if he decide it in
the affirmative, it is not for me to object. But I am curious to

know more of that philosophy of which, at present, I have but inklings. You, its first disciple among men, it seems, are peculiarly qualified to expound it. Have you any objections to begin now?"

"None at all," squaring himself to the table. "Where shall I begin? At first principles?"

"You remember that it was in a practical way that you were represented as being fitted for the clear exposition. Now, what you call first principles, I have, in some things, found to be more or less vague. Permit me, then, in a plain way, to suppose some common case in real life, and that done, I would like you to tell me how you, the practical disciple of the philosophy I wish to know about, would, in that case, conduct."

"A business-like view. Propose the case."

"Not only the case, but the persons. The case is this: There are two friends, friends from childhood, bosom-friends; one of whom, for the first time, being in need, for the first time seeks a loan from the other, who, so far as fortune goes, is more than competent to grant it. And the persons are to be you and I: you, the friend from whom the loan is sought—I, the friend who seeks it; you, the disciple of the philosophy in question—I, a common man, with no more philosophy than to know that when I am comfortably warm I don't feel cold, and when I have the ague I shake.[1] Mind, now, you must work up your imagination, and, as much as possible, talk and behave just as if the case supposed were a fact. For brevity, you shall call me Frank, and I will call you Charlie. Are you agreed?"

"Perfectly. You begin."

The cosmopolitan paused a moment, then, assuming a serious and care-worn air, suitable to the part to be enacted, addressed his hypothesized friend.

[1] In the first chapter of *Walden*, Thoreau reduces the necessities of life—"Food, Shelter, Clothing, and Fuel"—to one common need: "The grand necessity, then, for our bodies, is to keep warm, to keep the vital heat in us." The Cosmopolitan's reference to "ague" recalls the "firm of Fever & Ague" of Chapter 23, and his references to bodily warmth foreshadow his final words to Egbert (in Chapter 41).

CHAPTER 39

The hypothetical friends.

"Charlie, I am going to put confidence in you."

"You always have, and with reason. What is it Frank?"

"Charlie, I am in want—urgent want of money."

"That's not well."

"But it *will* be well, Charlie, if you loan me a hundred dollars. I would not ask this of you, only my need is sore, and you and I have so long shared hearts and minds together, however unequally on my side, that nothing remains to prove our friendship than, with the same inequality on my side, to share purses. You will do me the favor, won't you?"

"Favor? What do you mean by asking me to do you a favor?"

"Why, Charlie, you never used to talk so."

"Because, Frank, you on your side, never used to talk so."

"But won't you loan me the money?"

"No, Frank."

"Why?"

"Because my rule forbids. I give away money, but never loan it; and of course the man who calls himself my friend is above receiving alms.[1] The negotiation of a loan is a business transaction. And I will transact no business with a friend. What a friend is, he is socially and intellectually; and I rate

[1] This conversation satirizes the section on friendship in Thoreau's "Wednesday," *A Week on the Concord and Merrimack Rivers* (1849). For instance, compare the last sentence with this passage: "When the Friend . . . treats his Friend like a Christian . . . then Friendship ceases to be Friendship, and becomes Charity; that principle which established the almshouse is now beginning with its charity at home, and establishing an almshouse and pauper relations there."

social and intellectual friendship too high to degrade it on either side into a pecuniary make-shift. To be sure there are, and I have, what is called business friends; that is, commercial acquaintances, very convenient persons. But I draw a red-ink line between them and my friends in the true sense—my friends social and intellectual. In brief, a true friend has nothing to do with loans; he should have a soul above loans. Loans are such unfriendly accommodations as are to be had from the soulless corporation of a bank, by giving the regular security and paying the regular discount."

"An *unfriendly* accommodation? Do those words go together handsomely?"

"Like the poor farmer's team, of an old man and a cow—not handsomely, but to the purpose. Look, Frank, a loan of money on interest is a sale of money on credit. To sell a thing on credit may be an accommodation, but where is the friendliness? Few men in their senses, except operators, borrow money on interest, except upon a necessity akin to starvation. Well, now, where is the friendliness of my letting a starving man have, say, the money's worth of a barrel of flour upon the condition that, on a given day, he shall let me have the money's worth of a barrel and a half of flour; especially if I add this further proviso, that if he fail so to do, I shall then, to secure to myself the money's worth of my barrel and his half barrel, put his heart up at public auction, and, as it is cruel to part families, throw in his wife's and children's?"

"I understand," with a pathetic shudder; "but even did it come to that, such a step on the creditor's part, let us, for the honor of human nature, hope, were less the intention than the contingency."

"But, Frank, a contingency not unprovided for in the taking beforehand of due securities."

"Still, Charlie, was not the loan in the first place a friend's act?"

"And the auction in the last place an enemy's act. Don't you see? The enmity lies couched in the friendship, just as the ruin in the relief."

"I must be very stupid to-day, Charlie, but really, I can't understand this. Excuse me, my dear friend, but it strikes me that in going into the philosophy of the subject, you go somewhat out of your depth."

"So said the incautious wader-out to the ocean; but the ocean replied: 'It is just the other way, my wet friend,' and drowned him."

"That, Charlie, is a fable about as unjust to the ocean, as some of Æsop's are to the animals. The ocean is a magnanimous element, and would scorn to assassinate a poor fellow, let alone taunting him in the act. But I don't understand what you say about enmity couched in friendship, and ruin in relief."

"I will illustrate, Frank. The needy man is a train slipped off the rail. He who loans him money on interest is the one who, by way of accommodation, helps get the train back where it belongs; but then, by way of making all square, and a little more, telegraphs to an agent, thirty miles a-head by a precipice, to throw just there, on his account, a beam across the track. Your needy man's principle-and-interest friend is, I say again, a friend with an enmity in reserve. No, no, my dear friend, no interest for me. I scorn interest."

"Well, Charlie, none need you charge. Loan me without interest."

"That would be alms again."

"Alms, if the sum borrowed is returned?"

"Yes: an alms, not of the principle, but the interest."

"Well, I am in sore need, so I will not decline the alms. Seeing that it is you, Charlie, gratefully will I accept the alms of the interest. No humiliation between friends."

"Now, how in the refined view of friendship can you suffer yourself to talk so, my dear Frank. It pains me. For though I am not of the sour mind of Solomon, that, in the hour of need, a stranger is better than a brother; [2] yet, I entirely agree with

[2] Proverbs 18:24: ". . . there is a friend that sticketh closer than a brother," and Proverbs 27:10: "Thine own friend, and thy father's friend, foresake not; neither go into thy brother's house in the day of thy calamity; for better is a neighbour that is near, than a brother far off."

my sublime master, who, in his Essay on Friendship, says so nobly, that if he want a terrestrial convenience, not to his friend celestial (or friend social and intellectual) would he go; no: for his terrestrial convenience, to his friend terrestrial (or humbler business-friend) he goes. Very lucidly he adds the reason: Because, for the superior nature, which on no account can ever descend to do good, to be annoyed with requests to do it, when the inferior one, which by no instruction can ever rise above that capacity, stands always inclined to it—this is unsuitable." [3]

"Then I will not consider you as my friend celestial, but as the other."

"It racks me to come to that; but, to oblige you, I'll do it. We are business friends; business is business. You want to negotiate a loan. Very good. On what paper? Will you pay three per cent. a month? Where is your security?"

"Surely, you will not exact those formalities from your old schoolmate—him with whom you have so often sauntered down the groves of Academe, discoursing of the beauty of virtue, and the grace that is in kindliness—and all for so paltry a sum. Security? Our being fellow-academics, and friends from childhood up, is security."

"Pardon me, my dear Frank, our being fellow-academics is the worst of securities; while, our having been friends from childhood up is just no security at all. You forget we are now business friends."

The book of Proverbs was traditionally attributed to Solomon. See Chapter 16, note 11 and the epitaph toward the end of Chapter 40 for other references to Solomon.

[3] Cf. Emerson's essay "Friendship": "Why insist on rash personal relations with your friend? . . . Leave this touching and clawing. Let him be to me a spirit. A message, a thought, a sincerity, a glance from him, I want, but not news or pottage. I can get politics, and chat, and neighborly conveniences from cheaper companions. Should not the society of my friend be to me poetic, pure, universal, and great as nature itself?" In *Pierre* Melville uses the terms terrestrial and celestial as poles to chart Emersonian and most other ethics.

"And you, on your side, forget, Charlie, that as your business friend I can give you no security; my need being so sore that I cannot get an indorser."

"No indorser, then, no business loan."

"Since then, Charlie, neither as the one nor the other sort of friend you have defined, can I prevail with you; how if, combining the two, I sue as both?"

"Are you a centaur?"

"When all is said then, what good have I of your friendship, regarded in what light you will?"

"The good which is in the philosophy of Mark Winsome, as reduced to practice by a practical disciple."

"And why don't you add, much good may the philosophy of Mark Winsome do me? Ah," turning invokingly, "what is friendship, if it be not the helping hand and the feeling heart, the good Samaritan pouring out at need the purse as the vial!" [4]

"Now, my dear Frank, don't be childish. Through tears never did man see his way in the dark. I should hold you unworthy that sincere friendship I bear you, could I think that friendship in the ideal is too lofty for you to conceive. And let me tell you, my dear Frank, that you would seriously shake the foundations of our love, if ever again you should repeat the present scene. The philosophy, which is mine in the strongest way, teaches plain-dealing. Let me, then, now, as at the most suitable time, candidly disclose certain circumstances you seem in ignorance of. Though our friendship began in boyhood, think not that, on my side at least, it began injudiciously. Boys are little men, it is said. You, I juvenilely picked out for my friend, for your favorable points at the time; not the least of which were your good manners, handsome dress, and your parents' rank and repute of wealth. In short, like any grown man, boy though I was, I went into the market and chose me my mutton, not for its leanness, but its fatness. In other words, there seemed in you, the schoolboy who always

[4] In Chapter 16 the herb doctor, with his vials, had referred to mineral doctors as "good Samaritans erring."

had silver in his pocket, a reasonable probability that you would never stand in lean need of fat succor; and if my early impression has not been verified by the event, it is only because of the caprice of fortune producing a fallibility of human expectations, however discreet."

"Oh, that I should listen to this cold-blooded disclosure!"

"A little cold blood in your ardent veins, my dear Frank, wouldn't do you any harm, let me tell you. Cold-blooded? You say that, because my disclosure seems to involve a vile prudence on my side. But not so. My reason for choosing you in part for the points I have mentioned, was solely with a view of preserving inviolate the delicacy of the connection. For—do but think of it—what more distressing to delicate friendship, formed early, than your friend's eventually, in manhood, dropping in of a rainy night for his little loan of five dollars or so? Can delicate friendship stand that? And, on the other side, would delicate friendship, so long as it retained its delicacy, do that? Would you not instinctively say of your dripping friend in the entry, 'I have been deceived, fraudulently deceived, in this man; he is no true friend that, in platonic love to demand love-rites?'"

"And rites, doubly rights, they are, cruel Charlie!"

"Take it how you will, heed well how, by too importunately claiming those rights, as you call them, you shake those foundations I hinted of. For though, as it turns out, I, in my early friendship, built me a fair house on a poor site; yet such pains and cost have I lavished on that house, that, after all, it is dear to me. No, I would not lost the sweet boon of your friendship, Frank. But beware."

"And of what? Of being in need? Oh, Charlie! you talk not to a god, a being who in himself holds his own estate, but to a man who, being a man, is the sport of fate's wind and wave, and who mounts towards heaven or sinks towards hell, as the billows roll him in trough or on crest."

"Tut! Frank. Man is no such poor devil as that comes to—no poor drifting sea-weed of the universe. Man has a soul;

which, if he will, puts him beyond fortune's finger and the future's spite. Don't whine like fortune's whipped dog, Frank, or by the heart of a true friend, I will cut ye."

"Cut me you have already, cruel Charlie, and to the quick. Call to mind the days we went nutting, the times we walked in the woods, arms wreathed about each other, showing trunks invined like the trees:—oh, Charlie!"

"Pish! we were boys."

Then lucky the fate of the first-born of Egypt,[5] cold in the grave ere maturity struck them with a sharper frost.—Charlie?"

"Fie! you're a girl."

"Help, help, Charlie, I want help!"

"Help? to say nothing of the friend, there is something wrong about the man who wants help. There is somewhere a defect, a want, in brief, a need, a crying need, somewhere about that man."

"So there is, Charlie.—Help, Help!"

"How foolish a cry, when to implore help, is itself the proof of undesert of it."

"Oh, this, all along, is not you, Charlie, but some ventriloquist who usurps your larynx. It is Mark Winsome that speaks, not Charlie."

"If so, thank heaven, the voice of Mark Winsome is not alien but congenial to my larynx. If the philosophy of that illustrious teacher find little response among mankind at large, it is less that they do not possess teachable tempers, than because they are so unfortunate as not to have natures predisposed to accord with him."

"Welcome, that compliment to humanity," exclaimed Frank with energy, "the truer because unintended. And long in this respect may humanity remain what you affirm it. And long it will; since humanity, inwardly feeling how subject it is to straits, and hence how precious is help, will, for selfishness'

[5] Exodus 12:29.

sake, if no other, long postpone ratifying a philosophy that banishes help from the world. But Charlie, Charlie! speak as you used to; tell me you will help me. Were the case reversed, not less freely would I loan you the money than you would ask me to loan it."

"*I* ask? *I* ask a loan? Frank, by this hand, under no circumstances would I accept a loan, though without asking pressed on me. The experience of China Aster might warn me."

"And what was that?"

"Not very unlike the experience of the man that built himself a palace of moon-beams, and when the moon set was surprised that his palace vanished with it. I will tell you about China Aster. I wish I could do so in my own words, but unhappily the original story-teller here has so tyrannized over me, that it is quite impossible for me to repeat his incidents without sliding into his style. I forewarn you of this, that you may not think me so maudlin as, in some parts, the story would seem to make its narrator. It is too bad that any intellect, especially in so small a matter, should have such power to impose itself upon another, against its best exerted will, too. However, it is satisfaction to know that the main moral, to which all tends, I fully approve. But, to begin."

CHAPTER 40

*In which the story of China Aster¹ is at
second-hand told by one who, while not
disapproving the moral, disclaims the
spirit of the style.*

"China Aster was a young candle-maker of Marietta,² at the
mouth of the Muskingum³—one whose trade would seem a
kind of subordinate branch of that parent craft and mystery of
the hosts of heaven, to be the means, effectively or otherwise,
of shedding some light through the darkness of a planet benighted. But he made little money by the business. Much ado
had poor China Aster and his family to live; he could, if he
chose, light up from his stores a whole street, but not so easily
could he light up with prosperity the hearts of his household.

"Now, China Aster, it so happened, had a friend, Orchis,⁴ a

¹ Aster ("star") suggests one role of this candlemaker who should be
a means of "shedding some light through the darkness of a planet
benighted"; another role is as the common little China Aster in this fable
of the flowers with the exotic Orchis.

² The oldest community in Ohio; named for Marie Antoinette.

³ Marietta is to the junction of the Muskingum and the Ohio as Cairo
is to the junction of the Ohio and the Mississippi. Although Muskingum
is an American Indian word, it may be mentioned here because "musk"
comes from Sanskrit *mushka*, "testicle" (see next note).

⁴ "Orchis. [a. L. *orchis* (Pliny), the plant, a. Gr. ὄρχις] testicle, also
the plant orchis (so called from the shape of the tubers in most species:
cf. Ballocks, Dogstones)" (*NED*). In this sexual allegory, Orchis forces
the candlemaker to produce candles made of spermaceti, thus producing
sterility and death. Together with the book's many sexual jokes and
names, phallic symbols and hints of sexual perversion, this story is part
of the great vernal fertility festival being celebrated on the Fidèle. It
relates to the various forms of conception and reproduction—the seeds of

shoemaker; one whose calling it is to defend the understandings of men from naked contact with the substance of things:
a very useful vocation, and which, spite of all the wiseacres
may prophesy, will hardly go out of fashion so long as rocks
are hard and flints will gall. All at once, by a capital prize in a
lottery, this useful shoemaker was raised from a bench to a
sofa. A small nabob was the shoemaker now, and the understandings of men, let them shift for themselves. Not that
Orchis was, by prosperity, elated into heartlessness. Not at all.
Because, in his fine apparel, strolling one morning into the
candlery, and gayly switching about at the candle-boxes with
his gold-headed cane—while poor China Aster, with his greasy
paper cap and leather apron, was selling one candle for one
penny to a poor orange-woman, who, with the patronizing
coolness of a liberal customer, required it to be carefully rolled
up and tied in a half sheet of paper—lively Orchis, the woman
being gone, discontinued his gay switchings and said: 'This is
poor business for you, friend China Aster; your capital is too
small. You must drop this vile tallow and hold up pure spermaceti to the world. I tell you what it is, you shall have one
thousands dollars to extend with. In fact, you must make
money, China Aster. I don't like to see your little boy paddling
about without shoes, as he does.'

" 'Heaven bless your goodness, friend Orchis,' replied the
candle-maker, 'but don't take it illy if I call to mind the word

---

the Canada thistle, the egg that engenders an original character (see
Chapter 44), the metamorphoses of the caterpillar, the printing-press,
wine, the sun, the human incarnation of beneficent light. Orchis, whose
symbol is his "gold-headed cane," ends by destroying the lightgiver; his
function resembles that of Siva the Destroyer, the Hindu fertility god
whose principal symbol is the lingam, ritually anointed with oil in his
temples (see Introduction, pp. xxv–xxvii).

The name Orchis may also evoke the old Roman god of the underworld, Orcus (mentioned in Melville's *Clarel*, II, *xxxix*, 78). Edwin
Fussell conjectures that Orchis represents Hawthorne in what he takes
to be "a rather transparent allegorical parody of Melville's disastrous
literary career and of its relations to Hawthorne's."

of my uncle, the blacksmith, who, when a loan was offered him, declined it, saying: "To ply my own hammer, light though it be, I think best, rather than piece it out heavier by welding to it a bit off a neighbor's hammer, though that may have some weight to spare; otherwise, were the borrowed bit suddenly wanted again, it might not split off at the welding, but too much to one side or the other." '

" 'Nonsense, friend China Aster, don't be so honest; your boy is barefoot. Besides, a rich man lose by a poor man? Or a friend be the worse by a friend? China Aster, I am afraid that, in leaning over into your vats here, this morning, you have spilled out your wisdom. Hush! I won't hear any more. Where's your desk? Oh, here.' With that, Orchis dashed off a check on his bank, and off-handedly presenting it, said: 'There, friend China Aster, is your one thousand dollars; when you make it ten thousand, as you soon enough will (for experience, the only true knowledge,[5] teaches me that, for every one, good luck is in store), then, China Aster, why, then you can return me the money or not, just as you please. But, in any event, give yourself no concern, for I shall never demand payment.'

"Now, as kind heaven will so have it that to a hungry man bread is a great temptation, and, therefore, he is not too harshly to be blamed, if, when freely offered, he take it, even though it be uncertain whether he shall ever be able to reciprocate; so, to a poor man, proffered money is equally enticing, and the worst that can be said of him, if he accept it, is just what can be said in the other case of the hungry man. In short, the poor candle-maker's scrupulous morality succumbed to his unscrupulous necessity, as is now and then apt to be the case. He took the check, and was about carefully putting it away for the present, when Orchis, switching about again with his gold-headed cane, said: 'By-the-way, China Aster, it don't mean anything, but suppose you make a little memorandum of this; won't do any harm, you know.' So China Aster gave Orchis his note for one thousand dollars on demand. Orchis

[5] See Chapter 14, note 4.

took it, and looked at it a moment, 'Pooh, I told you, friend China Aster, I wasn't going ever to make any *demand*.' Then tearing up the note, and switching away again at the candleboxes, said, carelessly; 'Put it at four years.' So China Aster gave Orchis his note for one thousand dollars at four years. 'You see I'll never trouble you about this,' said Orchis, slipping it in his pocket-book, 'give yourself no further thought, friend China Aster, than how best to invest your money. And don't forget my hint about spermaceti. Go into that, and I'll buy all my light of you,' with which encouraging words, he, with wonted, rattling kindness, took leave.

"China Aster remained standing just where Orchis had left him; when, suddenly, two elderly friends, having nothing better to do, dropped in for a chat. The chat over, China Aster, in greasy cap and apron, ran after Orchis, and said: 'Friend Orchis, heaven will reward you for your good intentions, but here is your check, and now give me my note.'

" 'Your honesty is a bore, China Aster,' said Orchis, not without displeasure. 'I won't take the check from you.'

" 'Then you must take it from the pavement, Orchis,' said China Aster; and, picking up a stone, he placed the check under it on the walk.

" 'China Aster,' said Orchis, inquisitively eying him, 'after my leaving the candlery just now, what asses dropped in there to advise with you, that now you hurry after me, and act so like a fool? Shouldn't wonder if it was those two old asses that the boys nickname Old Plain Talk and Old Prudence.'

" 'Yes, it was those two, Orchis, but don't call them names.'

" 'A brace of spavined old croakers. Old Plain Talk had a shrew for a wife, and that's made him shrewish; and Old Prudence, when a boy, broke down in an apple-stall, and that discouraged him for life. No better sport for a knowing spark like me than to hear Old Plain Talk wheeze out his sour old saws, while Old Prudence stands by, leaning on his staff, wagging his frosty old pow, and chiming in at every clause.'

" 'How can you speak so, friend Orchis, of those who were my father's friends?'

" 'Save me from my friends, if those old croakers were Old Honesty's friends. I call your father so, for every one used to. Why did they let him go in his old age on the town? Why, China Aster, I've often heard from my mother, the chronicler, that those two old fellows, with Old Conscience—as the boys called the crabbed old quaker, that's dead now—they three used to go to the poor-house when your father was there, and get round his bed, and talk to him for all the world as Eliphaz, Bildad, and Zophar did to poor old pauper Job.[6] Yes, Job's comforters were Old Plain Talk, and Old Prudence, and Old Conscience, to your poor old father. Friends? I should like to know who you call foes? With their everlasting croaking and reproaching they tormented poor Old Honesty, your father, to death.'

"At these words, recalling the sad end of his worthy parent, China Aster could not restrain some tears. Upon which Orchis said: 'Why, China Aster, you are the dolefulest creature. Why don't you, China Aster, take a bright view of life? You will never get on in your business or anything else, if you don't take the bright view of life. It's the ruination of a man to take the dismal one.' Then, gayly poking at him with his gold-headed cane, 'Why don't you, then? Why don't you be bright and hopeful, like me? Why don't you have confidence, China Aster?'

" 'I'm sure I don't know, friend Orchis,' soberly replied China Aster, 'but may be my not having drawn a lottery-prize, like you, may make some difference.'

" 'Nonsense! before I knew anything about the prize I was gay as a lark, just as gay as I am now. In fact, it has always been a principle with me to hold to the bright view.'

"Upon this, China Aster looked a little hard at Orchis, because the truth was, that until the lucky prize came to him,

[6] Job 2:11–32:5.

Orchis had gone under the nickname of Doleful Dumps, he
having been beforetimes of a hypochondriac turn, so much so
as to save up and put by a few dollars of his scanty earnings
against that rainy day he used to groan so much about.

" 'I tell you what it is, now, friend China Aster,' said Orchis,
pointing down to the check under the stone, and then slapping
his pocket, 'the check shall lie there if you say so, but your
note shan't keep it company. In fact, China Aster, I am too
sincerely your friend to take advantage of a passing fit of the
blues in you. You *shall* reap the benefit of my friendship.'
With which, buttoning up his coat in a jiffy, away he ran,
leaving the check behind.

"At first, China Aster was going to tear it up, but thinking
that this ought not to be done except in the presence of the
drawer of the check, he mused a while, and picking it up,
trudged back to the candlery, fully resolved to call upon
Orchis soon as his day's work was over, and destroy the check
before his eyes. But it so happened that when China Aster
called, Orchis was out, and, having waited for him a weary
time in vain, China Aster went home, still with the check, but
still resolved not to keep it another day. Bright and early next
morning he would a second time go after Orchis, and would,
no doubt, make a sure thing of it, by finding him in his bed;
for since the lottery-prize came to him, Orchis, besides becoming more cheery, had also grown a little lazy. But as destiny
would have it, that same night China Aster had a dream, in
which a being in the guise of a smiling angel, and holding a
kind of cornucopia in her hand, hovered over him, pouring
down showers of small gold dollars, thick as kernels of corn. 'I
am Bright Future, friend China Aster,' said the angel, 'and if
you do what friend Orchis would have you do, just see what
will come of it.' With which Bright Future, with another
swing of her cornucopia, poured such another shower of small
gold dollars upon him, that it seemed to bank him up all round,
and he waded about in it like a maltster in malt.

"Now, dreams are wonderful things, as everybody knows—

so wonderful, indeed, that some people stop not short of ascribing them directly to heaven; and China Aster, who was of a proper turn of mind in everything, thought that in consideration of the dream, it would be but well to wait a little, ere seeking Orchis again. During the day, China Aster's mind dwelling continually upon the dream, he was so full of it, that when Old Plain Talk dropped in to see him, just before dinnertime, as he often did, out of the interest he took in Old Honesty's son, China Aster told all about his vision, adding that he could not think that so radiant an angel could deceive; and, indeed, talked at such a rate that one would have thought he believed the angel some beautiful human philanthropist. Something in this sort Old Plain Talk understood him, and, accordingly, in his plain way, said: 'China Aster, you tell me that an angel appeared to you in a dream. Now, what does that amount to but this, that you dreamed an angel appeared to you? Go right away, China Aster, and return the check, as I advised you before. If friend Prudence were here, he would say just the same thing.' With which words Old Plain Talk went off to find friend Prudence, but not succeeding, was returning to the candlery himself, when, at distance mistaking him for a dun who had long annoyed him, China Aster in a panic barred all his doors, and ran to the back part of the candlery, where no knock could be heard.

"By this sad mistake, being left with no friend to argue the other side of the question, China Aster was so worked upon at last, by musing over his dream, that nothing would do but he must get the check cashed, and lay out the money the very same day in buying a good lot of spermaceti to make into candles, by which operation he counted upon turning a better penny than he ever had before in his life; in fact, this he believed would prove the foundation of that famous fortune which the angel had promised him.

"Now, in using the money, China Aster was resolved punctually to pay the interest every six months till the principal should be returned, howbeit not a word about such a thing had been breathed by Orchis; though, indeed, according to custom, as well as law, in such matters, interest would legitimately accrue on the loan, nothing to the contrary having been put in the bond. Whether Orchis at the time had this in mind or not, there is no sure telling; but, to all appearance, he never so much as cared to think about the matter, one way or other.

"Though the spermaceti venture rather disappointed China Aster's sanguine expectations, yet he made out to pay the first six months' interest, and though his next venture turned out still less prosperously, yet by pinching his family in the matter of fresh meat, and, what pained him still more, his boys' schooling, he contrived to pay the second six months' interest, sincerely grieved that integrity, as well as its opposite, though not in an equal degree, costs something, sometimes.

"Meanwhile, Orchis had gone on a trip to Europe by advice of a physician; it so happening that, since the lottery-prize came to him, it had been discovered to Orchis that his health was not very firm, though he had never complained of anything before but a slight ailing of the spleen, scarce worth talking about at the time. So Orchis, being abroad, could not help China Aster's paying his interest as he did, however much he might have been opposed to it; for China Aster paid it to Orchis's agent, who was of too business-like a turn to decline interest regularly paid in on a loan.

"But overmuch to trouble the agent on that score was not again to be the fate of China Aster; for, not being of that skeptical spirit which refuses to trust customers, his third venture resulted, through bad debts, in almost a total loss—a bad blow for the candle-maker. Neither did Old Plain Talk, and Old Prudence neglect the opportunity to read him an uncheerful enough lesson upon the consequences of his disregarding their advice in the matter of having nothing to do with borrowed money. 'It's all just as I predicted,' said Old Plain Talk, blowing his old nose with his old bandana. 'Yea, indeed is it,' chimed in Old Prudence, rapping his staff on the floor, and

then leaning upon it, looking with solemn forebodings upon
China Aster. Low-spirited enough felt the poor candle-maker;
till all at once who should come with a bright face to him but
his bright friend, the angel, in another dream. Again the cornucopia poured out its treasure, and promised still more. Revived by the vision, he resolved not to be down-hearted, but
up and at it once more—contrary to the advice of Old Plain
Talk, backed as usual by his crony, which was to the effect,
that, under present circumstances, the best thing China Aster
could do, would be to wind up his business, settle, if he could,
all his liabilities, and then go to work as a journeyman, by
which he could earn good wages, and give up, from that time
henceforth, all thoughts of rising above being a paid subordinate to men more able than himself, for China Aster's career
thus far plainly proved him the legitimate son of Old Honesty,
who, as every one knew, had never shown much business-
talent, so little, in fact, that many said of him that he had no
business to be in business. And just this plain saying Plain Talk
now plainly applied to China Aster, and Old Prudence never
disagreed with him. But the angel in the dream did, and,
maugre Plain Talk, put quite other notions into the candle-
maker.

"He considered what he should do towards reëstablishing
himself. Doubtless, had Orchis been in the country, he would
have aided him in this strait. As it was, he applied to others;
and as in the world, much as some may hint to the contrary, an
honest man in misfortune still can find friends to stay by him
and help him, even so it proved with China Aster, who at last
succeeded in borrowing from a rich old farmer the sum of six
hundred dollars, at the usual interest of money-lenders, upon
the security of a secret bond signed by China Aster's wife and
himself, to the effect that all such right and title to any property that should be left her by a well-to-do childless uncle, an
invalid tanner, such property should, in the event of China
Aster's failing to return the borrowed sum on the given day,
be the lawful possession of the money-lender. True, it was just

as much as China Aster could possibly do to induce his wife, a careful woman, to sign this bond; because she had always regarded her promised share in her uncle's estate as an anchor well to windward of the hard times in which China Aster had always been more or less involved, and from which, in her bosom, she never had seen much chance of his freeing himself. Some notion may be had of China Aster's standing in the heart and head of his wife, by a short sentence commonly used in reply to such persons as happened to sound her on the point. 'China Aster,' she would say, 'is a good husband, but a bad business man!' Indeed, she was a connection on the maternal side of Old Plain Talk's. But had not China Aster taken good care not to let Old Plain Talk and Old Prudence hear of his dealings with the old farmer, ten to one they would, in some way, have interfered with his success in that quarter.

"It has been hinted that the honesty of China Aster was what mainly induced the money-lender to befriend him in his misfortune, and this must be apparent; for, had China Aster been a different man, the money-lender might have dreaded lest, in the event of his failing to meet his note, he might some way prove slippery—more especially as, in the hour of distress, worked upon by remorse for so jeopardizing his wife's money, his heart might prove a traitor to his bond, not to hint that it was more than doubtful how such a secret security and claim, as in the last resort would be the old farmer's, would stand in a court of law. But though one inference from all this may be, that had China Aster been something else than what he was, he would not have been trusted, and, therefore, he would have been effectually shut out from running his own and wife's head into the usurer's noose; yet those who, when everything at last came out, maintained that, in this view and to this extent, the honesty of the candle-maker was no advantage to him, in so saying, such persons said what every good heart must deplore, and no prudent tongue will admit.

"It may be mentioned, that the old farmer made China Aster take part of his loan in three old dried-up cows and one lame horse, not improved by the glanders. These were thrown in at a pretty high figure, the old money-lender having a singular prejudice in regard to the high value of any sort of stock raised on his farm. With a great deal of difficulty, and at more loss, China Aster disposed of his cattle at public auction, no private purchaser being found who could be prevailed upon to invest. And now, raking and scraping in every way, and working early and late, China Aster at last started afresh, nor without again largely and confidently extending himself. However, he did not try his hand at the spermaceti again, but, admonished by experience, returned to tallow. But, having bought a good lot of it, by the time he got it into candles, tallow fell so low, and candles with it, that his candles per pound barely sold for what he had paid for the tallow. Meantime, a year's unpaid interest had accrued on Orchis'-loan, but China Aster gave himself not so much concern about that as about the interest now due to the old farmer. But he was glad that the principal there had yet some time to run. However, the skinny old fellow gave him some trouble by coming after him every day or two on a scraggy old white horse, furnished with a musty old saddle, and goaded into his shambling old paces with a withered old raw hide. All the neighbors said that surely Death himself on the pale horse [7] was after poor China Aster now. And something so it proved; for, ere long, China Aster found himself involved in troubles mortal enough.

"At this juncture Orchis was heard of. Orchis, it seemed, had returned from his travels, and clandestinely married, and, in a kind of queer way, was living in Pennsylvania among his wife's relations, who, among other things, had induced him to join a church, or rather semi-religious school, of Come-Outers; [8] and what was still more, Orchis, without coming to

[7] Revelation 6:8: "And I looked, and behold, a pale horse; and his name that sat on him was Death, and hell followed with him." See the several incarnations of Death in Chapter 23, the reference to the Waltz of Death in Chapter 36, and Introduction, pp. xxiii–xxvii.

[8] A come-outer is, in general, anyone who dissents violently from an established creed, particularly religious, and who seeks for radical

the spot himself, had sent word to his agent to dispose of some of his property in Marietta, and remit him the proceeds. Within a year after, China Aster received a letter from Orchis, commending him for his punctuality in paying the first year's interest, and regretting the necessity that he (Orchis) was now under of using all his dividends; so he relied upon China Aster's paying the next six months' interest, and of course with the back interest. Not more surprised than alarmed, China Aster thought of taking steamboat to go and see Orchis, but he was saved that expense by the unexpected arrival in Marietta of Orchis in person, suddenly called there by that strange kind of capriciousness lately characterizing him. No sooner did China Aster hear of his old friend's arrival than he hurried to call upon him. He found him curiously rusty in dress, sallow in cheek, and decidedly less gay and cordial in manner, which the more surprised China Aster, because, in former days, he had more than once heard Orchis, in his light rattling way, declare that all he (Orchis) wanted to make him a perfectly happy, hilarious, and benignant man, was a voyage to Europe and a wife, with a free development of his inmost nature.

"Upon China Aster's stating his case, his rusted friend was silent for a time; then, in an odd way, said that he would not crowd China Aster, but still his (Orchis') necessities were urgent. Could not China Aster mortgage the candlery? He was honest, and must have moneyed friends; and could he not press his sales of candles? Could not the market be forced a little in that particular? The profits on candles must be very great. Seeing, now, that Orchis had the notion that the candle-making business was a very profitable one, and knowing sorely enough what an error was here, China Aster tried to undeceive him. But he could not drive the truth into Orchis—Orchis being very obtuse here, and, at the same time, strange to say, very melancholy. Finally, Orchis glanced off from so unpleasing a subject into the most unexpected reflections, taken from a religious point of view, upon the unstableness and deceitfulness

reform. The early-nineteenth-century sects known as come-outers were opposed to most religious institutions.

of the human heart. But having, as he thought, experienced something of that sort of thing, China Aster did not take exception to his friend's observations, but still refrained from so doing, almost as much for the sake of sympathetic sociality as anything else. Presently, Orchis, without much ceremony, rose, and saying he must write a letter to his wife, bade his friend good-bye, but without warmly shaking him by the hand as of old.

"In much concern at the change, China Aster made earnest inquiries in suitable quarters, as to what things, as yet unheard of, had befallen Orchis, to bring about such a revolution; and learned at last that, besides traveling, and getting married, and joining the sect of Come-Outers, Orchis had somehow got a bad dyspepsia, and lost considerable property through a breach of trust on the part of a factor in New York. Telling these things to Old Plain Talk, that man of some knowledge of the world shook his old head, and told China Aster that, though he hoped it might prove otherwise, yet it seemed to him that all he had communicated about Orchis worked together for bad omens as to his future forbearance—especially, he added with a grim sort of smile, in view of his joining the sect of Come-Outers; for, if some men knew what was their inmost natures, instead of coming out with it, they would try their best to keep it in, which, indeed, was the way with the prudent sort. In all which sour notions Old Prudence, as usual, chimed in.

"When interest-day came again, China Aster, by the utmost exertions, could only pay Orchis' agent a small part of what was due, and a part of that was made up by his children's gift money (bright tenpenny pieces and new quarters, kept in their little money-boxes), and pawning his best clothes, with those of his wife and children, so that all were subjected to the hardship of staying away from church. And the old usurer, too, now beginning to be obstreperous, China Aster paid him his interest and some other pressing debts with money got by, at last, mortgaging the candlery.

"When next interest-day came round for Orchis, not a penny could be raised. With much grief of heart, China Aster

so informed Orchis' agent. Meantime, the note to the old
usurer fell due, and nothing from China Aster was ready to
meet it; yet, as heaven sends its rain on the just and unjust
alike, by a coincidence not unfavorable to the old farmer, the
well-to-do uncle, the tanner, having died, the usurer entered
upon possession of such part of his property left by will to the
wife of China Aster. When still the next interest-day for
Orchis came round, it found China Aster worse off than ever;
for, besides his other troubles, he was now weak with sickness.
Feebly dragging himself to Orchis' agent, he met him in the
street, told him just how it was; upon which the agent, with a
grave enough face, said that he had instructions from his em-
ployer not to crowd him about the interest at present, but to
say to him that about the time the note would mature, Orchis
would have heavy liabilities to meet, and therefore the note
must at that time be certainly paid, and, of course, the back
interest with it; and not only so, but, as Orchis had had to
allow the interest for good part of the time, he hoped that, for
the back interest, China Aster would, in reciprocation, have no
objections to allowing interest on the interest annually. To be
sure, this was not the law; but, between friends who accommodate each other, it was the custom.

"Just then, Old Plain Talk with Old Prudence turned the
corner, coming plump upon China Aster as the agent left him;
and whether it was a sun-stroke, or whether they accidentally
ran against him, or whether it was his being so weak, or
whether it was everything together, or how it was exactly,
there is no telling, but poor China Aster fell to the earth, and,
striking his head sharply, was picked up senseless. It was a day
in July; such a light and heat as only the midsummer banks of
the inland Ohio know. China Aster was taken home on a door;
lingered a few days with a wandering mind, and kept wandering on, till at last, at dead of night, when nobody was aware,
his spirit wandered away into the other world.

"Old Plain Talk and Old Prudence, neither of whom ever
omitted attending any funeral, which, indeed, was their chief

exercise—these two were among the sincerest mourners who followed the remains of the son of their ancient friend to the grave.

"It is needless to tell of the executions that followed; how that the candlery was sold by the mortgagee; how Orchis never got a penny for his loan; and how, in the case of the poor widow, chastisement was tempered with mercy; for, though she was left penniless, she was not left childless. Yet, unmindful of the alleviation, a spirit of complaint, at what she impatiently called the bitterness of her lot and the hardness of the world, so preyed upon her, as ere long to hurry her from the obscurity of indigence to the deeper shades of the tomb.

"But though the straits in which China Aster had left his family had, besides apparently dimming the world's regard, likewise seemed to dim its sense of the probity of its deceased head, and though this, as some thought, did not speak well for the world, yet it happened in this case, as in others, that, though the world may for a time seem insensible to that merit which lies under a cloud, yet, sooner or later, it always renders honor where honor is due; for, upon the death of the widow, the freemen of Marietta, as a tribute of respect for China Aster, and an expression of their conviction of his high moral worth, passed a resolution, that, until they attained maturity, his children should be considered the town's guests. No mere verbal compliment, like those of some public bodies; for, on the same day, the orphans were officially installed in that hospitable edifice where their worthy grandfather, the town's guest before them, had breathed his last breath.[9]

"But sometimes honor may be paid to the memory of an honest man, and still his mound remain without a monument.[10] Not so, however, with the candle-maker. At an early day, Plain Talk had procured a plain stone, and was digesting in his mind what pithy word or two to place upon it, when

[9] Cf. Orchis' description.

[10] Marietta was famous as the site of ancient mounds, some of which were used for ritual burials and, possibly, sacrifices.

there was discovered, in China Aster's otherwise empty wallet, an epitaph, written, probably, in one of those disconsolate hours, attended with more or less mental aberration, perhaps, so frequent with him for some months prior to his end. A memorandum on the back expressed the wish that it might be placed over his grave. Though with the sentiment of the epitaph Plain Talk did not disagree, he himself being at times of a hypochondriac turn—at least, so many said—yet the language struck him as too much drawn out; so, after consultation with Old Prudence, he decided upon making use of the epitaph, yet not without verbal retrenchments. And though, when these were made, the thing still appeared wordy to him, nevertheless, thinking that, since a dead man was to be spoken about, it was but just to let him speak for himself, especially when he spoke sincerely, and when, by so doing, the more salutary lesson would be given, he had the retrenched inscription chiseled as follows upon the stone.

'HERE LIE

THE REMAINS OF

CHINA ASTER THE CANDLE-MAKER,

WHOSE CAREER

WAS AN EXAMPLE OF THE TRUTH OF SCRIPTURE, AS FOUND

IN THE

SOBER PHILOSOPHY

OF

SOLOMON THE WISE; [11]

FOR HE WAS RUINED BY ALLOWING HIMSELF TO BE PERSUADED,

AGAINST HIS BETTER SENSE,

INTO THE FREE INDULGENCE OF CONFIDENCE,

AND

AN ARDENTLY BRIGHT VIEW OF LIFE,

TO THE EXCLUSION

OF

THAT COUNSEL WHICH COMES BY HEEDING

THE

OPPOSITE VIEW.'

11 See Chapter 16, note 11 and Chapter 39, note 2.

"This inscription raised some talk in the town, and was rather severely criticised by the capitalist—one of a very cheerful turn—who had secured his loan to China Aster by the mortgage; and though it also proved obnoxious to the man who, in town-meeting, had first moved for the compliment to China Aster's memory, and, indeed, was deemed by him a sort of slur upon the candle-maker, to that degree that he refused to believe that the candle-maker himself had composed it, charging Old Plain Talk with the authorship, alleging that the internal evidence showed that none but that veteran old croaker could have penned such a jeremiade—yet, for all this, the stone stood. In everything, of course, Old Plain Talk was seconded by Old Prudence; who, one day going to the grave-yard, in great-coat and over-shoes—for, though it was a sun-shiny morning, he thought that, owing to heavy dews, damp-ness might lurk in the ground—long stood before the stone, sharply leaning over on his staff, spectacles on nose, spelling out the epitaph word by word; and, afterwards meeting Old Plain Talk in the street, gave a great rap with his stick, and said: 'Friend, Plain Talk, that epitaph will do very well. Nevertheless, one short sentence is wanting.' Upon which, Plain Talk said it was too late, the chiseled words being so arranged, after the usual manner of such inscriptions, that nothing could be interlined. 'Then,' said Old Prudence, 'I will put it in the shape of a postscript.' Accordingly, with the approbation of Old Plain Talk, he had the following words chiseled at the left-hand corner of the stone, and pretty low down:

'The root of all was a friendly loan.' "

CHAPTER 41

Ending with a rupture of the hypothesis.

"With what heart," cried Frank, still in character, "have you told me this story? A story I can no way approve; for its moral, if accepted, would drain me of all reliance upon my last stay, and, therefore, of my last courage in life. For, what was that bright view of China Aster but a cheerful trust that, if he but kept up a brave heart, worked hard, and ever hoped for the best, all at last would go well? If your purpose, Charlie, in telling me this story, was to pain me, and keenly, you have succeeded; but, if it was to destroy my last confidence, I praise God you have not."

"Confidence?" cried Charlie, who, on his side, seemed with his whole heart to enter into the spirit of the thing, "what has confidence to do with the matter? That moral of the story, which I am for commending to you, is this: the folly, on both sides, of a friend's helping a friend. For was not that loan of Orchis to China Aster the first step towards their estrangement? And did it not bring about what in effect was the enmity of Orchis? I tell you, Frank, true friendship, like other precious things, is not rashly to be meddled with. And what more meddlesome between friends than a loan? A regular marplot. For how can you help that the helper must turn out a creditor? And creditor and friend, can they ever be one? no, not in the most lenient case; since, out of lenity to forego one's claim, is less to be a friendly creditor than to cease to be a creditor at all. But it will not do to rely upon this lenity, no, not in the best man; for the best man, as the worst, is subject to all mortal contingencies. He may travel, he may marry, he may join the Come-Outers, or some equally untoward school or sect, not to speak of other things that more or less tend to new-cast the character. And were there nothing else, who shall answer for his digestion, upon which so much depends?"

"But Charlie, dear Charlie—"

"Nay, wait.—You have hearkened to my story in vain, if you do not see that, however indulgent and right-minded I may seem to you now, that is no guarantee for the future. And into the power of that uncertain personality which, through the mutability of my humanity, I may hereafter become, should not common sense dissuade you, my dear Frank, from putting yourself? Consider. Would you, in your present need, be willing to accept a loan from a friend, securing him by a mortgage on your homestead, and do so, knowing that you had no reason to feel satisfied that the mortgage might not eventually be transferred into the hands of a foe? Yet the difference between this man and that man is not so great as the difference between what the same man be to-day and what he may be in days to come. For there is no bent of heart or turn of thought which any man holds by virtue of an unalterable nature or will. Even those feelings and opinions deemed most identical with eternal right and truth, it is not impossible but that, as personal persuasions, they may in reality be but the result of some chance tip of Fate's elbow in throwing her dice. For, not to go into the first seeds of things, and passing by the accident of parentage predisposing to this or that habit of mind, descend below these, and tell me, if you change this man's experiences or that man's books, will wisdom go surety for his unchanged convictions? As particular food begets particular dreams, so particular experiences or books particular feelings or beliefs. I will hear nothing of that fine babble about development and its laws; there is no development in opinion and feeling but the developments of time and tide. You may deem all this talk idle, Frank; but conscience bids me show you how fundamental the reasons for treating you as I do."

"But Charlie, dear Charlie, what new notions are these? I thought that man was no poor drifting weed of the universe, as you phrased it; that, if so minded, he could have a will, a way, a thought, and a heart of his own? But now you have turned everything upside down again, with an inconsistency that amazes and shocks me."

"Inconsistency? Bah!" [1]

"There speaks the ventriloquist again," sighed Frank, in bitterness.

Illy pleased, it may be, by this repetition of an allusion little flattering to his originality, however much so to his docility, the disciple sought to carry it off by exclaiming: "Yes, I turn over day and night, with indefatigable pains, the sublime pages of my master, and unfortunately for you, my dear friend, I find nothing *there* that leads me to think otherwise than I do. But enough: in this matter the experience of China Aster teaches a moral more to the point than anything Mark Winsome can offer, or I either."

"I cannot think so, Charlie; for neither am I China Aster, nor do I stand in his position. The loan to China Aster was to extend his business with; the loan I seek is to relieve my necessities."

"Your dress, my dear Frank, is respectable; your cheek is not gaunt. Why talk of necessities when nakedness and starvation beget the only real necessities?"

"But I need relief, Charlie; and so sorely, that I now conjure you to forget that I was ever your friend, while I apply to you only as a fellow-being, whom, surely, you will not turn away."

"That I will not. Take off your hat, bow over to the ground, and supplicate an alms of me in the way of London streets, and you shall not be a sturdy beggar in vain. But no man drops pennies into the hat of a friend, let me tell you. If you turn beggar, then, for the honor of noble friendship, I turn stranger."

"Enough," cried the other, rising, and with a toss of his shoulders seeming disdainfully to throw off the character he had assumed. "Enough. I have had my fill of the philosophy of Mark Winsome as put into action. And moonshiny as it in

[1] See Chapter 36, note 14.

theory may be, yet a very practical philosophy it turns out in effect, as he himself engaged I should find. But, miserable for my race should I be, if I thought he spoke truth when he claimed, for proof of the soundness of his system, that the study of it tended to much the same formation of character with the experiences of the world.—Apt disciple! Why wrinkle the brow, and waste the oil both of life and the lamp, only to turn out a head kept cool by the under ice of the heart? What your illustrious magian has taught you, any poor, old, broken-down, heart-shrunken dandy might have lisped. Pray, leave me, and with you take the last dregs of your inhuman philosophy. And here, take this shilling, and at the first wood-landing buy yourself a few chips to warm the frozen natures of you and your philosopher by." [2]

With these words and a grand scorn the cosmopolitan turned on his heel, leaving his companion at a loss to determine where exactly the fictitious character had been dropped, and the real one, if any, resumed. If any, because, with pointed meaning, there occurred to him, as he gazed after the cosmopolitan, these familiar lines:

> "All the world's a stage,
> And all the men and women merely players,
> Who have their exits and their entrances,
> And one man in his time plays many parts." [3]

[2] See Chapter 38, note 1.

[3] The beginning of Jacques' famous speech on the seven ages or acts of man (*As You Like It*, II, *vii*, 139–142). Jacques' concluding description of the final scene suggests the final scene of *The Confidence-Man*:

> Last scene of all,
> That ends this strange eventful history,
> Is second childishness and mere oblivion.

CHAPTER 42

Upon the heel of the last scene the
Cosmopolitan enters the barber's shop,
a benediction on his lips.

"Bless you, barber!"

Now, owing to the lateness of the hour, the barber had been all alone until within the ten minutes last passed; when, finding himself rather dullish company to himself, he thought he would have a good time with Souter John and Tam O'Shanter,[1] otherwise called Somnus and Morpheus,[2] two very good fellows, though one was not very bright, and the other an arrant rattle-brain, who though much listened to by some, no wise man would believe under oath.[3]

In short, with back presented to the glare of his lamps, and so to the door, the honest barber was taking what are called cat-naps, and dreaming in his chair; so that, upon suddenly hearing the benediction above, pronounced in tones not unangelic, starting up, half awake, he stared before him, but saw nothing, for the stranger stood behind. What with cat-naps, dreams, and bewilderments, therefore, the voice seemed a sort

[1] In Robert Burns' narrative poem "Tam O'Shanter," Tam, after drinking with his crony "souter Johnny" and listening to the souter's "queerest stories," on his way home is pursued by a mad vision of "warlocks and witches," "auld Nick, in shape o' beast," and Death.

[2] The Roman Somnus (the Greek Hypnos), the personification and god of sleep, a brother of Death and a son of Night. Morpheus, one of his sons, caused some dreams; he was "expert in counterfeiting forms, and in imitating the walk, countenance, and mode of speaking, even the clothes and attitudes most characteristic of each man" (Bulfinch).

[3] China Aster had been persuaded by a smiling angel in his dream.

of spiritual manifestation to him; so that, for the moment, he stood all agape, eyes fixed, and one arm in the air.

"Why, barber, are you reaching up to catch birds there with salt?"

"Ah!" turning round disenchanted, "it is only a man, then."

"*Only* a man? As if to be but man were nothing. But don't be too sure what I am. You call me *man*, just as the townsfolk called the angels who, in man's form, came to Lot's house; [4] just as the Jew rustics called the devils who, in man's form, haunted the tombs.[5] You can conclude nothing absolute from the human form, barber."

"But I can conclude something from that sort of talk, with that sort of dress," shrewdly thought the barber, eying him with regained self-possession, and not without some latent touch of apprehension at being alone with him. What was passing in his mind seemed divined by the other, who now, more rationally and gravely, and as if he expected it should be attended to, said: "Whatever else you may conclude upon, it is my desire that you conclude to give me a good shave," at the same time loosening his neck-cloth. "Are you competent to a good shave, barber?"

"No broker more so, sir," answered the barber, whom the business-like proposition instinctively made confine to business-ends his views of the visitor.

"Broker? What has a broker to do with lather? A broker I have always understood to be a worthy dealer in certain papers and metals."

"He, he!" taking him now for some dry sort of joker, whose

---

[4] Genesis 19 describes the lust of the Sodomites for the two angels and its results. See the reference to Sodom in Chapter 29 and the apple of Sodom in Chapter 30.

[5] Matthew 8:28–34 and Mark 5:2–18 tell the story of two men or one man (the stories conflict), possessed by devils and running amuck amidst the tombs. The devils in the men (or man) ask Christ to let them possess a nearby herd of swine; they are permitted to do so, and the swine run into the sea and drown themselves.

jokes, he being a customer, it might be as well to appreciate, "he, he! You understand well enough, sir. Take this seat, sir," laying his hand on a great stuffed chair, high-backed and high-armed, crimson-covered, and raised on a sort of dais, and which seemed but to lack a canopy and quarterings, to make it in aspect quite a throne, "take this seat, sir."

"Thank you," sitting down; "and now, pray, explain that about the broker. But look, look—what's this?" suddenly rising, and pointing, with his long pipe, towards a gilt notification swinging among colored fly-papers from the ceiling, like a tavern sign, "*No Trust?* No trust means distrust; distrust means no confidence. Barber," turning upon him excitedly, "what fell suspiciousness prompts this scandalous confession? My life!" stamping his foot, "if but to tell a dog that you have no confidence in him be matter for affront to the dog, what an insult to take that way the whole haughty race of man by the beard! By my heart, sir! but at least you are valiant; backing the spleen of Thersites with the pluck of Agamemnon." [6]

"Your sort of talk, sir, is not exactly in my line," said the barber, rather ruefully, being now again hopeless of his customer, and not without return of uneasiness; "not in my line, sir," he emphatically repeated.

"But the taking of mankind by the nose is; a habit, barber, which I sadly fear has insensibly bred in you a disrespect for man. For how, indeed, may respectful conceptions of him coexist with the perpetual habit of taking him by the nose? But, tell me, though I, too, clearly see the import of your notification, I do not, as yet, perceive the object. What is it?"

"Now you speak a little in my line, sir," said the barber, not unrelieved at this return to plain talk; "that notification I find

[6] In Book II of the *Iliad*, Agamemnon, commander-in-chief of the Greek forces, tests their disposition by having proposed a retreat to Greece. Not a party to the plan, Thersites, famed for his loquacity and love of verbally lashing kings and heroes, tries in vain to prod the confused Greeks into actually leaving. Later killed by Achilles for laughing at his grief, Thersites became in English drama a stock figure of boastful, railing cowardice. In *Troilus and Cressida*, however, Shakespeare gives Thersites a most incisive kind of cynicism.

very useful, sparing me much work which would not pay. Yes, I lost a good deal, off and on, before putting that up," gratefully glancing towards it.

"But what is its object? Surely, you don't mean to say, in so many words, that you have no confidence? For instance, now," flinging aside his neck-cloth, throwing back his blouse, and reseating himself on the tonsorial throne, at sight of which proceeding the barber mechanically filled a cup with hot water from a copper vessel over a spirit-lamp, "for instance, now, suppose I say to you, 'Barber, my dear barber, unhappily I have no small change by me to-night, but shave me, and depend upon your money to-morrow'—suppose I should say that now, you would put trust in me, wouldn't you? You would have confidence?"

"Seeing that it is you, sir," with complaisance replied the barber, now mixing the lather, "seeing that it is *you*, sir, I won't answer that question. No need to."

"Of course, of course—in that view. But, as a supposition—you would have confidence in me, wouldn't you?"

"Why—yes, yes."

"Then why that sign?"

"Ah, sir, all people ain't like you," was the smooth reply, at the same time, as if smoothly to close the debate, beginning smoothly to apply the lather, which operation, however, was, by a motion, protested against by the subject, but only out of a desire to rejoin, which was done in these words:

"All people ain't like me. Then I must be either better or worse than most people. Worse, you could not mean; no, barber, you could not mean that; hardly that. It remains, then, that you think me better than most people. But that I ain't vain enough to believe; though, from vanity, I confess, I could never yet, by my best wrestlings, entirely free myself; nor, indeed, to be frank, am I at bottom over anxious to—this same vanity, barber, being so harmless, so useful, so comfortable, so pleasingly preposterous a passion."

"Very true, sir; and upon my honor, sir, you talk very well. But the lather is getting a little cold, sir."

"Better cold lather, barber, than a cold heart. Why that cold sign? Ah, I don't wonder you try to shirk the confession. You feel in your soul how ungenerous a hint is there. And yet, barber, now that I look into your eyes—which somehow speak to me of the mother that must have so often looked into them before me—I dare say, though you may not think it, that the spirit of that notification is not one with your nature. For look now, setting business views aside, regarding the thing in an abstract light; in short, supposing a case, barber; supposing, I say, you see a stranger, his face accidentally averted, but his visible part very respectable-looking; what now, barber—I put it to your conscience, to your charity—what would be your impression of that man, in a moral point of view? Being in a signal sense a stranger, would you, for that, signally set him down for a knave?"

"Certainly not, sir; by no means," cried the barber, humanely resentful.

"You would upon the face of him—"

"Hold, sir," said the barber, "nothing about the face; you remember, sir, that is out of sight."

"I forgot that. Well then, you would, upon the *back* of him, conclude him to be, not improbably, some worthy sort of person; in short, an honest man; wouldn't you?"

"Not unlikely I should, sir."

"Well now—don't be so impatient with your brush, barber —suppose that honest man meet you by night in some dark corner of the boat where his face would still remain unseen, asking you to trust him for a shave—how then?"

"Wouldn't trust him, sir."

"But is not an honest man to be trusted?"

"Why—why—yes, sir."

"There! don't you see, now?"

"See what?" asked the disconcerted barber, rather vexedly.

"Why, you stand self-contradicted, barber; don't you?"

"No," doggedly.

"Barber," gravely, and after a pause of concern, "the enemies of our race have a saying that insincerity is the most universal and inveterate vice of man—the lasting bar to real amelioration, whether of individuals or of the world. Don't you now, barber, by your stubbornness on this occasion, give color to such a calumny?"

"Hity-tity!" cried the barber, losing patience, and with it respect; "stubbornness?" Then clattering round the brush in the cup, "Will you be shaved, or won't you?"

"Barber, I will be shaved, and with pleasure; but, pray, don't raise your voice that way. Why, now, if you go through life gritting your teeth in that fashion, what a comfortless time you will have."

"I take as much comfort in this world as you or any other man," cried the barber, whom the other's sweetness of temper seemed rather to exasperate than soothe.

"To resent the imputation of anything like unhappiness I have often observed to be peculiar to certain orders of men," said the other pensively, and half to himself, "just as to be indifferent to that imputation, from holding happiness but for a secondary good and inferior grace, I have observed to be equally peculiar to other kinds of men. Pray, barber," innocently looking up, "which think you is the superior creature?"

"All this sort of talk," cried the barber, still unmollified, "is, as I told you once before, not in my line. In a few minutes I shall shut up this shop. Will you be shaved?"

"Shave away, barber. What hinders?" turning up his face like a flower.

The shaving began, and proceeded in silence, till at length it became necessary to prepare to relather a little—affording an opportunity for resuming the subject, which, on one side, was not let slip.

"Barber," with a kind of cautious kindliness, feeling his way, "barber, now have a little patience with me; do; trust me, I wish not to offend. I have been thinking over that supposed case of the man with the averted face, and I cannot rid my mind of the impression that, by your opposite replies to my questions at the time, you showed yourself much of a piece with a good many other men—that is, you have confidence, and then again, you have none. Now, what I would ask is, do you think it sensible standing for a sensible man, one foot on confidence and the other on suspicion? Don't you think, barber, that you ought to elect? Don't you think consistency requires that you should either say 'I have confidence in all men,' and take down your notification; or else say, 'I suspect all men,' and keep it up."

This dispassionate, if not deferential, way of putting the case, did not fail to impress the barber, and proportionately conciliate him. Likewise, from its pointedness, it served to make him thoughtful; for, instead of going to the copper vessel for more water, as he had purposed, he halted half-way towards it, and, after a pause, cup in hand, said: "Sir, I hope you would not do me injustice. I don't say, and can't say, and wouldn't say, that I suspect all men; but I *do* say that strangers are not to be trusted, and so," pointing up to the sign, "no trust."

"But look, now, I beg, barber," rejoined the other deprecatingly, not presuming too much upon the barber's changed temper; "look, now; to say that strangers are not to be trusted, does not that imply something like saying that mankind is not to be trusted; for the mass of mankind, are they not necessarily strangers to each individual man? Come, come, my friend," winningly, "you are no Timon to hold the mass of mankind untrustworthy. Take down your notification; it is misanthropical; much the same sign that Timon traced with charcoal on the forehead of a skull stuck over his cave.[7] Take it down, barber; take it down to-night. Trust men. Just try the experiment of trusting men for this one little trip. Come now, I'm a philanthropist, and will insure you against losing a cent."

The barber shook his head dryly, and answered, "Sir, you must excuse me. I have a family."

[7] Presumably the sign discovered by the soldier in *Timon of Athens*, V, *iii*, 3–4:

> Timon is dead, who hath outstrech'd his span.
> Some beast rear'd this; here does not live a man.

CHAPTER 43

Very charming.

"So you are a philanthropist, sir," added the barber with an illuminated look; "that accounts, then, for all. Very odd sort of man the philanthropist. You are the second one, sir, I have seen. Very odd sort of man, indeed, the philanthropist. Ah, sir," again meditatively stirring in the shaving-cup, "I sadly fear, lest you philanthropists know better what goodness is, than what men are." Then, eying him as if he were some strange creature behind cage-bars, "So you are a philanthropist, sir."

"I am Philanthropos, and love mankind.[1] And, what is more than you do, barber, I trust them."

Here the barber, casually recalled to his business, would have replenished his shaving-cup, but finding now that on his last visit to the water-vessel he had not replaced it over the lamp, he did so now; and, while waiting for it to heat again, became almost as sociable as if the heating water were meant for whisky-punch; and almost as pleasantly garrulous as the pleasant barbers in romances.[2]

"Sir," said he, taking a throne beside his customer (for in a row there were three thrones on the dais, as for the three kings

[1] In *Timon of Athens* (IV, *iii*, 53) Timon says, "I am Misanthropos and hate mankind."

[2] This chapter plays upon many characteristics conventionally attributed to barbers—their loquacity, their roguishness, and their ability to penetrate, create, and assume disguises. By submitting himself to a barber's intimate examination, the Cosmopolitan suggests he has nothing to hide. On the other hand, the most famous barber of romance, Figaro, is the great master of disguise.

319

of Cologne,[3] those patron saints of the barber [4]), "sir, you say you trust men. Well, I suppose I might share some of your trust, were it not for this trade, that I follow, too much letting me in behind the scenes."

"I think I understand," with a saddened look; "and much the same thing I have heard from persons in pursuits different from yours—from the lawyer, from the congressman, from the editor, not to mention others, each, with a strange kind of melancholy vanity, claiming for his vocation the distinction of affording the surest inlets to the conviction that man is no better than he should be. All of which testimony, if reliable, would, by mutual corroboration, justify some disturbance in a good man's mind. But no, no; it is a mistake—all a mistake."

"True, sir, very true," assented the barber.

"Glad to hear that," brightening up.

"Not so fast, sir," said the barber; "I agree with you in thinking that the lawyer, and the congressman, and the editor, are in error, but only in so far as each claims peculiar facilities for the sort of knowledge in question; because, you see, sir, the truth is, that every trade or pursuit which brings one into contact with the facts, sir, such trade or pursuit is equally an avenue to those facts."

"*How* exactly is that?"

"Why, sir, in my opinion—and for the last twenty years I have, at odd times, turned the matter over some in my mind—he who comes to know man, will not remain in ignorance of man. I think I am not rash in saying that; am I, sir?"

"Barber, you talk like an oracle—obscurely, barber, obscurely."

[3] The three Magi who supposedly brought gifts to the Christ child were supposedly entombed at a cathedral in Cologne. In his journal for December 9, 1849, while in Cologne, Melville records seeing "the tombs of the *Three Kings of Cologne*—their skulls," which were crowned with diadems and on which their names were inscribed in jewels. Sir Thomas Browne gives the history of these relics in *Pseudodoxia Epidemica* (*Vulgar Errors*), Book 7, Chapter 8.

[4] Elizabeth Foster indicates that, quite to the contrary, the Magi are patrons of travelers and pilgrims.

"Well, sir," with some self-complacency, "the barber has always been held an oracle,[5] but as for the obscurity, that I don't admit."

"But pray, now, by your account, what precisely may be this mysterious knowledge gained in your trade? I grant you, indeed, as before hinted, that your trade, imposing on you the necessity of functionally tweaking the noses of mankind, is, in that respect, unfortunate, very much so; nevertheless, a well-regulated imagination should be proof even to such a provocation to improper conceits. But what I want to learn from you, barber, is, how does the mere handling of the outside of men's heads lead you to distrust the inside of their hearts?"

"What, sir, to say nothing more, can one be forever dealing in macassar oil, hair dyes, cosmetics, false moustaches, wigs, and toupees, and still believe that men are wholly what they look to be? What think you, sir, are a thoughtful barber's reflections, when, behind a careful curtain, he shaves the thin, dead stubble off a head, and then dismisses it to the world, radiant in curling auburn? [6] To contrast the shamefaced air behind the curtain, the fearful looking forward to being possibly discovered there by a prying acquaintance, with the cheerful assurance and challenging pride with which the same man steps forth again, a gay deception, into the street, while some honest, shock-headed fellow humbly gives him the wall. Ah, sir, they may talk of the courage of truth, but my trade teaches me that truth sometimes is sheepish. Lies, lies, sir, brave lies are the lions!"

"You twist the moral, barber; you sadly twist it. Look, now; take it this way: A modest man thrust out naked into the street, would he not be abashed? Take him in and clothe him; would not his confidence be restored? And in either case, is any reproach involved? Now, what is true of the whole, holds proportionably true of the part. The bald head is a nakedness which the wig is a coat to. To feel uneasy at the possibility of

[5] A belief supposedly originating in the fact that the priests of ancient Egypt performed ritual shavings.

[6] See Chapter 18, note 8.

the exposure of one's nakedness at top, and to feel comforted by the consciousness of having it clothed—these feelings, instead of being dishonorable to a bald man, do, in fact, but attest a proper respect for himself and his fellows. And as for the deception, you may as well call the fine roof of a fine chateau a deception, since, like a fine wig, it also is an artificial cover to the head, and equally, in the common eye, decorates the wearer.—I have confuted you, my dear barber; I have confounded you."

"Pardon," said the barber, "but I do not see that you have. His coat and his roof no man pretends to palm off as a part of himself, but the bald man palms off hair, not his, for his own."

"Not *his*, barber? If he have fairly purchased his hair, the law will protect him in its ownership, even against the claims of the head on which it grew. But it cannot be that you believe what you say, barber; you talk merely for the humor. I could not think so of you as to suppose that you would contentedly deal in the impostures you condemn."

"Ah, sir, I must live."

"And can't you do that without sinning against your conscience, as you believe? Take up some other calling."

"Wouldn't mend the matter much, sir."

"Do you think, then, barber, that, in a certain point, all the trades and callings of men are much on a par? Fatal, indeed," raising his hand, "inexpressibly dreadful, the trade of the barber, if to such conclusions it necessarily leads. Barber," eying him not without emotion, "you appear to me not so much a misbeliever, as a man misled. Now, let me set you on the right track; let me restore you to trust in human nature, and by no other means than the very trade that has brought you to suspect it."

"You mean, sir, you would have me try the experiment of taking down that notification," again pointing to it with his brush; "but, dear me, while I sit chatting here, the water boils over."

With which words, and such a well-pleased, sly, snug, ex-

pression, as they say some men have when they think their
little stratagem has succeeded, he hurried to the copper vessel,
and soon had his cup foaming up with white bubbles, as if it
were a mug of new ale.

Meantime, the other would have fain gone on with the discourse; but the cunning barber lathered him with so generous
a brush, so piled up the foam on him, that his face looked like
the yeasty crest of a billow, and vain to think of talking under
it, as for a drowning priest in the sea to exhort his fellow-
sinners on a raft. Nothing would do, but he must keep his
mouth shut. Doubtless, the interval was not, in a meditative
way, unimproved; for, upon the traces of the operation being
at last removed, the cosmopolitan rose, and, for added refresh-
ment, washed his face and hands; and having generally read-
justed himself, began, at last, addressing the barber in a manner
different, singularly so, from his previous one. Hard to say
exactly what the manner was, any more than to hint it was a
sort of magical; in a benign way, not wholly unlike the manner, fabled or otherwise, of certain creatures in nature, which
have the power of persuasive fascination—the power of holding another creature by the button of the eye, as it were,
despite the serious disinclination, and, indeed, earnest protest,
of the victim. With this manner the conclusion of the matter
was not out of keeping; for, in the end, all argument and
expostulation proved vain, the barber being irresistibly persuaded to agree to try, for the remainder of the present trip,
the experiment of trusting men, as both phrased it. True, to
save his credit as a free agent, he was loud in averring that it
was only for the novelty of the thing that he so agreed, and he
required the other, as before volunteered, to go security to
him against any loss that might ensue; but still the fact remained, that he engaged to trust men, a thing he had before
said he would not do, at least not unreservedly. Still the more
to save his credit, he now insisted upon it, as a last point, that
the agreement should be put in black and white, especially the
security part. The other made no demur; pen, ink, and paper

were provided, and grave as any notary the cosmopolitan sat down, but, ere taking the pen, glanced up at the notification, and said: "First down with that sign, barber—Timon's sign, there; down with it."

This, being in the agreement, was done—though a little reluctantly—with an eye to the future, the sign being carefully put away in a drawer.

"Now, then, for the writing," said the cosmopolitan, squaring himself. "Ah," with a sigh, "I shall make a poor lawyer, I fear. Ain't used, you see, barber, to a business which, ignoring the principle of honor, holds no nail fast till clinched. Strange, barber," taking up the blank paper, "that such flimsy stuff as this should make such strong hawsers; vile hawsers, too. Barber," starting up, "I won't put it in black and white. It were a reflection upon our joint honor. I will take your word, and you shall take mine."

"But your memory may be none of the best, sir. Well for you, on your side, to have it in black and white, just for a memorandum like, you know."

"That, indeed! Yes, and it would help *your* memory, too, wouldn't it, barber? Yours, on your side, being a little weak, too, I dare say. Ah, barber! how ingenious we human beings are; and how kindly we reciprocate each other's little delicacies, don't we? What better proof, now, that we are kind, considerate fellows, with responsive fellow-feelings—eh, barber? But to business. Let me see. What's your name, barber?"

"William Cream, sir."

Pondering a moment, he began to write; and, after some corrections, leaned back, and read aloud the following:

"AGREEMENT
"Between
"FRANK GOODMAN, Philanthropist, and Citizen of the World,
"and
"WILLIAM CREAM, Barber of the Mississippi steamer, Fidèle.
"The first hereby agrees to make good to the last any loss that may come from his trusting mankind, in the way of his vocation,

for the residue of the present trip; PROVIDED that William Cream keep out of sight, for the given term, his notification of 'No TRUST,' and by no other mode convey any, the least hint or intimation, tending to discourage men from soliciting trust from him, in the way of his vocation, for the time above specified; but, on the contrary, he do, by all proper and reasonable words, gestures, manners, and looks, evince a perfect confidence in all men, especially strangers; otherwise, this agreement to be void.

"Done, in good faith, this 1st day of April, 18—, at a quarter to twelve o'clock, P.M., in the shop of said William Cream, on board the said boat, Fidèle."

"There, barber; will that do?"

"That will do," said the barber, "only now put down your name."

Both signatures being affixed, the question was started by the barber, who should have custody of the instrument; which point, however, he settled for himself, by proposing that both should go together to the captain, and give the document into his hands—the barber hinting that this would be a safe proceeding, because the captain was necessarily a party disinterested, and, what was more, could not, from the nature of the present case, make anything by a breach of trust. All of which was listened to with some surprise and concern.

"Why, barber," said the cosmopolitan, "this don't show the right spirit; for me, I have confidence in the captain purely because he is a man; but he shall have nothing to do with our affair; for if you have no confidence in me, barber, I have in you. There, keep the paper yourself," handing it magnanimously.

"Very good," said the barber, "and now nothing remains but for me to receive the cash."

Though the mention of that word, or any of its singularly numerous equivalents, in serious neighborhood to a requisition upon one's purse, is attended with a more or less noteworthy effect upon the human countenance, producing in many an abrupt fall of it—in others, a writhing and screwing up of the features to a point not undistressing to behold, in some, attended with a blank pallor and fatal consternation—yet no trace of any of these symptoms was visible upon the countenance of the cosmopolitan, notwithstanding nothing could be more sudden and unexpected than the barber's demand.

"You speak of cash, barber; pray in what connection?"

"In a nearer one, sir," answered the barber, less blandly, "than I thought the man with the sweet voice stood, who wanted me to trust him once for a shave, on the score of being a sort of thirteenth cousin."

"Indeed, and what did you say to him?"

"I said, 'Thank you, sir, but I don't see the connection.'"

"How could you so unsweetly answer one with a sweet voice?"

"Because, I recalled what the son of Sirach says in the True Book: 'An enemy speaketh sweetly with his lips;' [7] and so I did what the son of Sirach advises in such cases: 'I believed not his many words.'" [8]

"What, barber, do you say that such cynical sort of things are in the True Book, by which, of course, you mean the Bible?"

"Yes, and plenty more to the same effect. Read the Book of Proverbs."

"That's strange, now, barber; for I never happen to have met with those passages you cite. Before I go to bed this night, I'll inspect the Bible I saw on the cabin-table, to-day. But mind, you mustn't quote the True Book that way to people coming in here; it would be impliedly a violation of the contract. But you don't know how glad I feel that you have for one while signed off all that sort of thing."

"No, sir; not unless you down with the cash."

"Cash again! What do you mean?"

---

[7] Ecclesiasticus 12:16. Mark Winsome had quoted Ecclesiasticus 12:13 in Chapter 36.

[8] Ecclesiasticus 13:11: "... believe not his many words."

"Why, in this paper here, you engage, sir, to insure me against a certain loss, and—"

"Certain? Is it so *certain* you are going to lose?"

"Why, that way of taking the word may not be amiss, but I didn't mean it so. I meant a *certain* loss; you understand, a CERTAIN loss; that is to say, a certain loss. Now then, sir, what use your mere writing and saying you will insure me, unless beforehand you place in my hands a money-pledge, sufficient to that end?"

"I see; the material pledge."

"Yes, and I will put it low; say fifty dollars." [9]

"Now what sort of a beginning is this? You, barber, for a given time engage to trust man, to put confidence in men, and, for your first step, make a demand implying no confidence in the very man you engage with. But fifty dollars is nothing, and I would let you have it cheerfully, only I unfortunately happen to have but little change with me just now."

"But you have money in your trunk, though?"

"To be sure. But you see—in fact, barber, you must be consistent. No, I won't let you have the money now; I won't let you violate the inmost spirit of our contract, that way. So good-night, and I will see you again."

"Stay, sir"—humming and hawing—"you have forgotten something."

"Handkerchief?—gloves? No, forgotten nothing. Good-night."

"Stay, sir—the—the shaving."

"Ah, I *did* forget that. But now that it strikes me, I shan't pay you at present. Look at your agreement; you must trust. Tut! against loss you hold the guarantee. Good-night, my dear barber."

With which words he sauntered off, leaving the barber in a maze, staring after.

But it holding true in fascination as in natural philosophy,

[9] Precisely the sum Frank requested of, and showed to, Charlie.

that nothing can act where it is not, so the barber was not long now in being restored to his self-possession and senses; the first evidence of which perhaps was, that, drawing forth his notification from the drawer, he put it back where it belonged; while, as for the agreement, that he tore up; which he felt the more free to do from the impression that in all human probability he would never again see the person who had drawn it. Whether that impression proved well-founded or not, does not appear. But in after days, telling the night's adventure to his friends, the worthy barber always spoke of his queer customer as the man-charmer—as certain East Indians are called snake-charmers—and all his friends united in thinking him QUITE AN ORIGINAL.[10]

[10] See Chapter 1, note 10.

CHAPTER 44

*In which the last three words of the last
chapter are made the text of the
discourse, which will be sure of
receiving more or less attention
from those readers who do
not skip it.*

"Quite an Original:" A phrase, we fancy, rather oftener
used by the young, or the unlearned, or the untraveled, than
by the old, or the well-read, or the man who has made the
grand tour. Certainly, the sense of originality exists at its highest in an infant, and probably at its lowest in him who has
completed the circle of the sciences.

As for original characters in fiction, a grateful reader will,
on meeting with one, keep the anniversary of that day. True,
we sometimes hear of an author who, at one creation, produces
some two or three score such characters; it may be possible.
But they can hardly be original in the sense that Hamlet is, or
Don Quixote, or Milton's Satan. That is to say, they are not, in
a thorough sense, original at all. They are novel, or singular, or
striking, or captivating, or all four at once.

More likely, they are what are called odd characters; but for
that, are no more original, than what is called an odd genius, in
his way, is. But, if original, whence came they? Or where did
the novelist pick them up?

Where does any novelist pick up any character? For the
most part, in town, to be sure. Every great town is a kind of
man-show, where the novelist goes for his stock, just as the
agriculturist goes to the cattle-show for his. But in the one
fair, new species of quadrupeds are hardly more rare, than in

the other are new species of characters—that is, original ones. Their rarity may still the more appear from this, that, while characters, merely singular, imply but singular forms, so to speak, original ones, truly so, imply original instincts.

In short, a due conception of what is to be held for this sort of personage in fiction would make him almost as much of a prodigy there, as in real history is a new law-giver, a revolutionizing philosopher, or the founder of a new religion.[1]

In nearly all the original characters, loosely accounted such in works of invention, there is discernible something prevailingly local, or of the age; which circumstance, of itself, would seem to invalidate the claim, judged by the principles here suggested.

Furthermore, if we consider, what is popularly held to entitle characters in fiction to being deemed original, is but something personal—confined to itself. The character sheds not its characteristic on its surroundings, whereas, the original character, essentially such, is like a revolving Drummond light,[2] raying away from itself all round it—everything is lit by it, everything starts up to it (mark how it is with Hamlet), so that, in certain minds, there follows upon the adequate conception of such a character, an effect, in its way, akin to that which in Genesis attends upon the beginning of things.[3]

For much the same reason that there is but one planet to one

[1] The first sentence of this book had introduced the founder of a new religion.

[2] The lime-light, an intense white light produced by focusing ignited streams of oxygen and hydrogen on a ball of lime, was invented by Captain Thomas Drummond (1797–1840) and adapted in 1825, at his suggestion, for use in lighthouses.

[3] An allusion to God's command "Let there be light" and his division of the light from the darkness (Genesis 1:2–5). This culminating image makes the original character—here obviously the Cosmopolitan—in the mind of both his author and his ideal reader (who join to produce his "conception") the manifestation of divine and cosmic light in the chaos of night. Thus he embodies the union of white and black, light and darkness, cosmos and chaos.

orbit, so can there be but one such original character to one work of invention. Two would conflict to chaos. In this view, to say that there are more than one to a book, is good presumption there is none at all.[4] But for new, singular, striking, odd, eccentric, and all sorts of entertaining and instructive characters, a good fiction may be full of them. To produce such characters, an author, beside other things, must have seen much, and seen through much: to produce but one original character, he must have had much luck.

There would seem but one point in common between this sort of phenomenon in fiction and all other sorts: it cannot be born in the author's imagination—it being as true in literature as in zoology, that all life is from the egg.

In the endeavor to show, if possible, the impropriety of the phrase, *Quite an Original,* as applied by the barber's friends, we have, at unawares, been led into a dissertation bordering upon the prosy, perhaps upon the smoky. If so, the best use the smoke can be turned to, will be, by retiring under cover of it, in good trim as may be, to the story.

[4] Here the reader is fairly explicitly told his role. If the Cosmopolitan cannot be seen as the embodiment of all, the resulting conflict is chaos; order is possible only if the reader can resolve the apparently opposing principles into a transcendent unity.

CHAPTER 45

The Cosmopolitan increases in seriousness.

In the middle of the gentlemen's cabin burned a solar lamp,[1] swung from the ceiling, and whose shade of ground glass was all round fancifully variegated, in transparency, with the image of a horned altar,[2] from which flames rose, alternate with the figure of a robed man, his head encircled by a halo. The light of this lamp, after dazzlingly striking on marble, snow-white and round—the slab of a centre-table beneath—on all sides went rippling off with ever-diminishing distinctness, till, like circles from a stone dropped in water, the rays died dimly away in the furthest nook of the place.

Here and there, true to their place, but not to their function, swung other lamps, barren planets, which had either gone out from exhaustion, or been extinguished by such occupants of berths as the light annoyed, or who wanted to sleep, not see.

[1] A lamp in which the oil was held in a chamber higher than the wick, necessitating a large lampshade, usually quite ornate. Cf. the revolving Drummond light, the barber's spirit lamp, and China Aster's candles.

[2] God gave precise instructions for making the four-horned altar (Exodus 27:1–2) and for conducting animal sacrifices on it (Exodus 29:12–41). References to the sacrificial uses of the horned altar occur in Leviticus 4:17–18, 8:15, 9:9, 16:18. The horns of the altar also served as a sanctuary (I Kings 1:50–51, 2:28) and as a place to bind animals to be sacrificed (Psalms 118:27). In Revelation 9:13 John hears "a voice from the four horns of the golden altar which is before God." The present horned altar, illuminated by the solar lamp shortly to be extinguished because of its stench, also suggests the temples of Vishnu, which were filled with "the stench of lamps kept continually burning" symbolizing "his GLORY, by horns, imitative of the solar ray" (see *The Wake of the Gods*, p. 185).

332

By a perverse man, in a berth not remote, the remaining lamp would have been extinguished as well, had not a steward forbade,[3] saying that the commands of the captain required it to be kept burning till the natural light of day should come to relieve it.[4] This steward, who, like many in his vocation, was apt to be a little free-spoken at times, had been provoked by the man's pertinacity to remind him, not only of the sad consequences which might, upon occasion, ensue from the cabin being left in darkness, but, also, of the circumstance that, in a place full of strangers, to show one's self anxious to produce darkness there, such an anxiety was, to say the least, not becoming. So the lamp—last survivor of many—burned on, inwardly blessed by those in some berths, and inwardly execrated by those in others.

Keeping his lone vigils beneath his lone lamp, which lighted his book on the table, sat a clean, comely, old man, his head snowy as the marble, and a countenance like that which imagination ascribes to good Simeon,[5] when, having at last beheld the Master of Faith, he blessed him and departed in peace. From his hale look of greenness in winter,[6] and his hands ingrained with the tan, less, apparently, of the present summer, than of accumulated ones past, the old man seemed a well-to-

[3] See the references to stewards in Chapters 3, 7, 9, 18.

[4] See the mock sun (Chapter 29) which accompanies "god Apollo" when he "dispenses the day." See also these two passages from Revelation: "And the city had no need of the sun, neither of the moon, to shine in it: for the glory of God did lighten it, and the Lamb is the light thereof" (21:22); "And there shall be no night there; and they need no candle, neither light of the sun; for the Lord God giveth them light: and they shall reign for ever and ever" (22:5). As J. W. Shroeder points out, this last chapter of *The Confidence-Man* employs many images from the last book of the Bible.

[5] It was prophesied of Simeon that he "should not see death, before he had seen the Lord's Christ." After seeing the infant Jesus, he said that he could "depart in peace" (Luke 2:25-35). This Simeon figure seems to fulfill the Biblical prophecy most literally.

[6] See Chapter 24, note 11.

do farmer,[7] happily dismissed, after a thrifty life of activity, from the fields to the fireside—one of those who, at three-score-and-ten, are fresh-hearted as at fifteen; to whom seclusion gives a boon more blessed than knowledge, and at last sends them to heaven untainted by the world, because ignorant if it;[8] just as a countryman putting up at a London inn, and never stirring out of it as a sight-seer, will leave London at last without once being lost in its fog, or soiled by its mud.

Redolent from the barber's shop, as any bridegroom[9] tripping to the bridal chamber might come, and by his look of cheeriness seeming to dispense a sort of morning through the night,[10] in came the cosmopolitan; but marking the old man, and how he was occupied, he toned himself down, and trod softly, and took a seat on the other side of the table, and said nothing. Still, there was a kind of waiting expression about him.

"Sir," said the old man, after looking up puzzled at him a moment, "sir," said he, "one would think this was a coffee-house, and it was war-time, and I had a newspaper here with great news, and the only copy to be had, you sit there looking at me so eager."

"And so you *have* good news there, sir—the very best of good news."

"Too good to be true," here came from one of the curtained berths.

"Hark!" said the cosmopolitan. "Some one talks in his sleep."

"Yes," said the old man, "and you—*you* seem to be talking

[7] See the "brown farmer" in the last sentence of Chapter 1.

[8] See the man with gold sleeve-buttons.

[9] The bridegroom was a traditional designation of Christ. Christ himself uses this identification, and the image of the bridal chamber, in Matthew 9:15 (also Mark 2:19-20 and Luke 5:34-35). The parable of the bridegroom and the ten virgins (Matthew 25:1-13) is also quite relevant here.

[10] See note 4.

in a dream. Why speak you, sir, of news, and all that, when you must see this is a book I have here—the Bible,[11] not a newspaper?"

"I know that; and when you are through with it—but not a moment sooner—I will thank you for it. It belongs to the boat, I believe—a present from a society."

"Oh, take it, take it!"

"Nay, sir, I did not mean to touch you at all. I simply stated the fact in explanation of my waiting here—nothing more. Read on, sir, or you will distress me."

This courtesy was not without effect. Removing his spectacles, and saying he had about finished his chapter, the old man kindly presented the volume, which was received with thanks equally kind. After reading for some minutes, until his expression merged from attentiveness into seriousness, and from that into a kind of pain, the cosmopolitan slowly laid down the book, and turning to the old man, who thus far had been watching him with benign curiosity, said: "Can you, my aged friend, resolve me a doubt—a disturbing doubt?"

"There are doubts, sir," replied the old man, with a changed countenance, "there are doubts, sir, which, if man have them, it is not man that can solve them."

"True; but look, now, what my doubt is. I am one who thinks well of man. I love man. I have confidence in man. But what was told me not a half-hour since?[12] I was told that I would find it written—'Believe not his many words—an enemy speaketh sweetly with his lips'—and also I was told that I would find a good deal more to the same effect, and all in this book. I could not think it; and, coming here to look for myself, what do I read? Not only just what was quoted, but also, as was engaged, more to the same purpose, such as this: 'With

[11] This is the second passenger with a big book, perhaps what Guinea meant by "a ge'mman wid a big book, *too*."

[12] The agreement between the Cosmopolitan and the barber was dated "this 1st day of April . . . at a quarter to twelve o'clock, P.M." The quotation to which he here refers was made after this. So All Fools' Day is apparently now over.

much communication he will tempt thee; he will smile upon thee, and speak thee fair, and say What wantest thou? If thou be for his profit he will use thee; he will make thee bear, and will not be sorry for it. Observe and take good heed. When thou hearest these things, awake in thy sleep.' " [13]

"Who's that describing the confidence-man?" here came from the berth again.

"Awake in his sleep, sure enough, ain't he?" said the cosmopolitan, again looking off in surprise. "Same voice as before, ain't it? Strange sort of dreamy man, that. Which is his berth, pray?"

"Never mind *him*, sir," said the old man anxiously, "but tell me truly, did you, indeed, read from the book just now?"

"I did," with changed air, "and gall and wormwood it is to me, a truster in man; to me, a philanthropist."

"Why," moved, "you don't mean to say, that what you repeated is really down there? Man and boy, I have read the good book this seventy years, and don't remember seeing anything like that. Let me see it," rising earnestly, and going round to him.

"There it is; and there—and there"—turning over the leaves, and pointing to the sentences one by one; "there—all down in the 'Wisdom of Jesus, the Son of Sirach.' "

[13] Ecclesiasticus 13:

4 If thou be for his profit, he will use thee; but if thou have nothing, he will forsake thee.

5 If thou have any thing, he will live with thee: yea, he will make thee bear, and he will not be sorry for it.

6 If he have need of thee, he will deceive thee, and smile upon thee and put thee in hope; he will speak thee fair, and say, What wantest thou?

11 Affect not to be made equal with him in talk, and believe not his many words: for with much communication will he tempt thee, and smiling upon thee will get out thy secrets.

13 Observe, and take good heed, for thou walkest in peril of thy overthrowing: when thou hearest these things, awake in thy sleep.
See Chapter 43, notes 7 and 8.

"Ah! cried the old man, brightening up, "now I know. Look," turning the leaves forward and back, till all the Old Testament lay flat on one side, and all the New Testament flat on the other, while in his fingers he supported vertically the portion between, "look, sir, all this to the right is certain truth, and all this to the left is certain truth, but all I hold in my hand here is apocrypha."

"Apocrypha?"

"Yes; and there's the word in black and white," pointing to it. "And what says the word? It says as much as 'not warranted;' for what do college men say of anything of that sort? They say it is apocryphal. The word itself, I've heard from the pulpit, implies something of uncertain credit. So if your disturbance be raised from aught in this apocrypha," again taking up the pages, "in that case, think no more of it, for it's apocrypha."

"What's that about the Apocalypse?" [14] here, a third time, came from the berth.

"He's seeing visions now, ain't he?" said the cosmopolitan, once more looking in the direction of the interruption. "But, sir," resuming, "I cannot tell you how thankful I am for your reminding me about the apocrypha here. For the moment, its being such escaped me. Fact is, when all is bound up together, it's sometimes confusing. The uncanonical part should be bound distinct. And, now that I think of it, how well did those learned doctors who rejected for us this whole book of Sirach. I never read anything so calculated to destroy man's confidence in man. This son of Sirach even says—I saw it but just now: 'Take heed of thy friends;' [15] not, observe, thy seeming friends, thy hypocritical friends, thy false friends, but thy *friends*, thy real friends—that is to say, not the truest friend in the world is to be implicitly trusted. Can Rochefoucault [16]

[14] Apocalypse means literally "revealed"; apocrypha, "concealed."

[15] Ecclesiasticus 6:13: "Separate thyself from thine enemies, and take heed of thy friends."

[16] See Chapter 29, note 6.

equal that? I should not wonder if his view of human nature, like Machiavelli's, [17] was taken from this Son of Sirach. And to call it wisdom—the Wisdom of the Son of Sirach! Wisdom, indeed! What an ugly thing wisdom must be! Give me the folly that dimples the cheek, say I, rather than the wisdom that curdles the blood. But no, no; it ain't wisdom; it's apocrypha, as you say, sir. For how can that be trustworthy that teaches distrust?"

"I tell you what it is," here cried the same voice as before, only more in less of mockery, "if you two don't know enough to sleep, don't be keeping wiser men awake. And if you want to know what wisdom is, go find it under your blankets." [18]

"Wisdom?" cried another voice with a brogue; "arrah, and is't wisdom the two geese are gabbling about all this while? To bed with ye, ye divils, and don't be after burning your fingers with the likes of wisdom."

"We must talk lower," said the old man; "I fear we have annoyed these good people."

"I should be sorry if wisdom annoyed any one," said the other; "but we will lower our voices, as you say. To resume: taking the thing as I did, can you be surprised at my uneasiness in reading passages so charged with the spirit of distrust?"

"No, sir, I am not surprised," said the old man; then added: "from what you say, I see you are something of my way of thinking—you think that to distrust the creature, is a kind of distrusting of the Creator. Well, my young friend, what is it? This is rather late for you to be about. What do you want of me?"

These questions were put to a boy [19] in the fragment of an

[17] See Chapter 23, note 10.

[18] See Chapter 1, note 14.

[19] Cf. the "dried-up old man, with the stature of a boy of twelve" (Chapter 20), the various boys under discussion in Chapter 22, and the pale pauper-boy at whom Charlie laughs (Chapter 29). This "little fellow" may be the "very promising little fellow" sold to Pitch by the PIO man.

old linen coat, bedraggled and yellow,[20] who, coming in from the deck barefooted on the soft carpet, had been unheard. All pointed and fluttering, the rags of the little fellow's red-flannel shirt, mixed with those of his yellow coat, flamed about him like the painted flames in the robes of a victim in *auto-da-fe*.[21] His face, too, wore such a polish of seasoned grime, that his sloe-eyes sparkled from out it like lustrous sparks in fresh coal.[22] He was a juvenile peddler, or *marchand*, as the polite French might have called him, of travelers' conveniences; and, having no allotted sleeping-place, had, in his wanderings about the boat, spied, through glass doors, the two in the cabin; and, late though it was, thought it might never be too much so for turning a penny.

Among other things, he carried a curious affair—a miniature mahogany door, hinged to its frame, and suitably furnished in all respects but one, which will shortly appear. This little door he now meaningly held before the old man,[23] who, after staring at it a while, said: "Go thy ways with thy toys, child."

"Now, may I never get so old and wise as that comes to," laughed the boy through his grime; and, by so doing, disclosing leopard-like teeth, like those of Murillo's wild beggar-boy's.[24]

---

[20] See Chapter 23, note 2, on Yellow Jack as the "ge'mman in a yaller west."

[21] In the *auto-da-fe* ("act of faith") of the Inquisition, persons were ritually accused and then punished while wearing robes depicting the grotesque scenes of infernal torments for which they were destined.

[22] See Introduction, p. xxvii, for the boy as Siva.

[23] See Relevation 3:7–8: "These things saith he that is holy, he that is true, he that hath the key of David, he that openeth, and no man shutteth; and shutteth, and no man openeth; I know thy works: behold, I have set before thee an open door, and no man can shut it. . . . ."

[24] Bartolomé Estéban Murillo (1618–1682), Spanish religious painter. *Redburn* (Chapter XLIX) describes "such a boy as Murillo often painted, when he went among the poor and outcast, for subjects wherewith to captivate the eyes of rank and wealth."

"The divils are laughing now, are they?" here came the
brogue from the berth. "What do the divils find to laugh
about in wisdom, begorrah? To bed with ye, ye divils, and no
more of ye."

"You see, child, you have disturbed that person," said the
old man; "you mustn't laugh any more."

"Ah, now," said the cosmopolitan, "don't, pray, say that;
don't let him think that poor Laughter is persecuted for a fool
in this world."

"Well," said the old man to the boy, "you must, at any rate,
speak very low."

"Yes, that wouldn't be amiss, perhaps," said the cosmopolitan; "but, my fine fellow, you were about saying something to
my aged friend here; what was it?"

"Oh," with a lowered voice, coolly opening and shutting his
little door, "only this: when I kept a toy-stand at the fair in
Cincinnati [25] last month, I sold more than one old man a
child's rattle."

"No doubt of it," said the old man. "I myself often buy
such things for my little grandchildren."

"But these old men I talk of were old bachelors."

The old man stared at him a moment; then, whispering to
the cosmopolitan: "Strange boy, this; sort of simple, ain't he?
Don't know much, hey?"

"Not much," said the boy, "or I wouldn't be so ragged."

"Why, child, what sharp ears you have!" [26] exclaimed the old
man.

"If they were duller, I would hear less ill of myself," said
the boy.

"You seem pretty wise, my lad," said the cosmopolitan;
"why don't you sell your wisdom, and buy a coat?"

"Faith," said the boy, "that's what I did to-day, and this is
the coat that the price of my wisdom bought. But won't you
trade? See, now, it is not the door I want to sell; I only carry
the door round for a specimen, like. Look now, sir," standing

[25] Where the PIO man had for "no small period" been in business.
[26] Like the wolf in "Little Red Riding Hood."

the thing up on the table, "supposing this little door is your state-room door; well," opening it, "you go in for the night; you close your door behind you—thus. Now, is all safe?"

"I suppose so, child," said the old man.

"Of course it is, my fine fellow," said the cosmopolitan.

"All safe. Well. Now, about two o'clock in the morning, say, a soft-handed gentleman comes softly and tries the knob here—thus; in creeps my soft-handed gentleman; and hey, presto! how comes on the soft cash?"

"I see, I see, child," said the old man; "your fine gentleman is a fine thief, and there's no lock to your little door to keep him out;" with which words he peered at it more closely than before.

"Well, now," again showing his white teeth, "well, now, some of you old folks are knowing 'uns, sure enough; but now comes the great invention," producing a small steel contrivance, very simple but ingenious, and which, being clapped on the inside of the little door, secured it as with a bolt. "There now," admiringly holding it off at arm's-length, "there now, let that soft-handed gentleman come now a' softly trying this little knob here, and let him keep a' trying till he finds his head as soft as his hand. Buy the traveler's patent lock, sir, only twenty-five cents."

"Dear me," cried the old man, "this beats printing.[27] Yes, child, I will have one, and use it this very night."

With the phlegm of an old banker pouching the change, the boy now turned to the other: "Sell you one, sir?"

"Excuse me, my fine fellow, but I never use such blacksmiths' things."

"Those who give the blacksmith most work seldom do," said the boy, tipping him a wink expressive of a degree of indefinite knowingness, not uninteresting to consider in one of his years. But the wink was not marked by the old man, nor, to all appearances, by him for whom it was intended.

"Now then," said the boy, again addressing the old man.

[27] Cf. the Cosmopolitan's eulogy of the printing press in Chapter 29.

"With your traveler's lock on your door tonight, you will think yourself all safe, won't you?"

"I think I will, child."

"But how about the window?"

"Dear me, the window, child. I never thought of that. I must see to that."

"Never you mind about the window," said the boy, "nor, to be honor bright, about the traveler's lock either, (though I ain't sorry for selling one), do you just buy one of these little jokers," producing a number of suspender-like objects, which he dangled before the old man; "money-belts, sir; only fifty cents." [28]

"Money-belt? never heard of such a thing."

"A sort of pocket-book," said the boy, "only a safer sort. Very good for travelers."

"Oh, a pocket-book. Queer looking pocket-books though, seems to me. Ain't they rather long and narrow for pocket-books?"

"They go round the waist, sir, inside," said the boy; "door open or locked, wide awake on your feet or fast asleep in your chair, impossible to be robbed with a money-belt."

"I see, I see. It *would* be hard to rob one's money-belt. And I was told to-day the Mississippi is a bad river for pick-pockets. How much are they?"

"Only fifty cents, sir."

"I'll take one. There!"

"Thank-ee. And now there's a present for ye," with which, drawing from his breast a batch of little papers, he threw one before the old man, who, looking at it, read "*Counterfeit Detector.*" [29]

[28] Like the "chevalier" in Chapter 1 who is "ex-officio a peddler of money-belts."

[29] Ted N. Weissbuch, in "A Note on the Confidence-Man's Counterfeit Detector," *Emerson Society Quarterly*, #19 (1960), 16–18, points out that innumerable counterfeit-detectors were published periodically all over the country, and that there were also counterfeit counterfeit-detectors, designed to increase the value of worthless money.

"Very good thing," said the boy, "I give it to all my customers who trade seventy-five cents' worth; best present can be made them. Sell you a money-belt, sir?" turning to the cosmopolitan.

"Excuse me, my fine fellow, but I never use that sort of thing; my money I carry loose."

"Loose bait ain't bad," said the boy, "look a lie and find the truth; [30] don't care about a Counterfeit Detector, do ye? or is the wind East, d'ye think?"

"Child," said the old man in some concern, "you mustn't sit up any longer, it affects your mind; there, go away, go to bed."

"If I had some people's brains to lie on, I would," said the boy, "but planks is hard, you know."

"Go, child—go, go!"

"Yes, child,—yes, yes," said the boy, with which roguish parody, by way of congé, he scraped back his hard foot on the woven flowers of the carpet, much as a mischievous steer [31] in May scrapes back his horny hoof in the pasture; and then with a flourish of his hat—which, like the rest of his tatters, was, thanks to hard times, a belonging beyond his years, though not beyond his experience, being a grown man's cast-off beaver—turned, and with the air of a young Caffre,[32] quitted the place.

"That's a strange boy," said the old man, looking after him. "I wonder who's his mother; and whether she knows what late hours he keeps?"

"The probability is," observed the other, "that his mother does not know. But if you remember, sir, you were saying something, when the boy interrupted you with his door."

---

[30] Originally a Spanish proverb: "Di mentira, y sacaras verdad"; apparently first used in English by Francis Bacon, *Advancement of Learning* (1605), II, 18: "Tell a lie and find a truth."

[31] In Chapter 3 Guinea is described as a steer as the drover addresses him as "old boy."

[32] See Chapter 6, note 5.

"So I was.—Let me see," unmindful of his purchases for the moment, "what, now, was it? What was that I was saying? Do *you* remember?"

"Not perfectly, sir; but, if I am not mistaken, it was something like this: you hoped you did not distrust the creature; for that would imply distrust of the Creator."

"Yes, that was something like it," mechanically and unintelligently letting his eye fall now on his purchases.

"Pray, will you put your money in your belt tonight?"

"It's best, ain't it?" with a slight start. "Never too late to be cautious. 'Beware of pick-pockets' is all over the boat."

"Yes, and it must have been the Son of Sirach, or some other morbid cynic, who put them there. But that's not to the purpose. Since you are minded to it, pray, sir, let me help you about the belt. I think that, between us, we can make a secure thing of it."

"Oh no, no, no!" said the old man, not unperturbed, "no, no, I wouldn't trouble you for the world," then, nervously folding up the belt, "and I won't be so impolite as to do it for myself, before you, either. But, now that I think of it," after a pause, carefully taking a little wad from a remote corner of his vest pocket, "here are two bills they gave me at St. Louis, yesterday. No doubt they are all right; but just to pass time, I'll compare them with the Detector here. Blessed boy to make me such a present. Public benefactor, that little boy!"

Laying the Detector square before him on the table, he then, with something of the air of an officer bringing by the collar a brace of culprits to the bar, placed the two bills opposite the Detector, upon which, the examination began, lasting some time, prosecuted with no small research and vigilance, the forefinger of the right hand proving of lawyer-like efficacy in tracing out and pointing the evidence, whichever way it might go.

After watching him a while, the cosmopolitan said in a formal voice, "Well, what say you, Mr. Foreman; guilty, or not guilty?—Not guilty, ain't it?"

"I don't know, I don't know," returned the old man, perplexed, "there's so many marks of all sorts to go by, it makes it
a kind of uncertain. Here, now, is this bill," touching one, "it
looks to be a three dollar bill on the Vicksburgh Trust and
Insurance Banking Company.[33] Well, the Detector says—"

"But why, in this case, care what it says? Trust and Insurance! What more would you have?"

"No; but the Detector says, among fifty other things, that,
if a good bill, it must have, thickened here and there into the
substance of the paper, little wavy spots of red; and it says
they must have a kind of silky feel, being made by the lint of a
red silk handkerchief stirred up in the paper-maker's vat—the
paper being made to order for the company."[34]

"Well, and is—"

"Stay. But then it adds, that sign is not always to be relied
on; for some good bills get so worn, the red marks get rubbed
out. And that's the case with my bill here—see how old it
is—or else it's a counterfeit, or else—I don't see right—or
else—dear, dear me—I don't know what else to think."

"What a peck of trouble that Detector makes for you now;
believe me, the bill is good; don't be so distrustful. Proves
what I've always thought, that much of the want of confidence, in these days, is owing to these Counterfeit Detectors

[33] In the heyday of free banking, otherwise known as wildcat banking,
banks could issue circulatory notes almost at will and counterfeiting
flourished. But since this particular banknote is issued by a Mississippi
bank, it makes little difference whether it is counterfeit or not. In
Mississippi, wildcat banking had gone to the extreme described in
Joseph G. Baldwin's *Flush Times of Alabama and Mississippi* (1853):
almost anyone with a press and some rag paper could crank out legal
tender. Only two of the myriad Mississippi banks survived the bursting
of the bubble in 1837–1838, and the state bonds on which these two
depended were repudiated in 1853.

[34] "The Tartarus of Maids" (1855) is Melville's description of a
factory that makes paper to order; it is a sexual allegory in which the
paper-maker's vats are testicles.

you see on every desk and counter. Puts people up to suspecting good bills. Throw it away, I beg, if only because of the trouble it breeds you."

"No; it's troublesome, but I think I'll keep it.—Stay, now, here's another sign. It says that, if the bill is good, it must have in one corner, mixed in with the vignette, the figure of a goose, very small, indeed, all but microscopic; and, for added precaution, like the figure of Napoleon outlined by the tree,[35] not observable, even if magnified, unless the attention is directed to it. Now, pore over it as I will, I can't see this goose."

"Can't see the goose? why, I can; and a famous goose it is. There" (reaching over and pointing to a spot in the vignette).

"I don't see it—dear me—I don't see the goose. Is it a real goose?"

"A perfect goose; beautiful goose."

"Dear, dear, I don't see it."

"Then throw that Detector away, I say again; it only makes you purblind; don't you see what a wild-goose chase [36] it has led you? The bill is good. Throw the Detector away."

"No; it ain't so satisfactory as I thought for, but I must examine this other bill."

"As you please, but I can't in conscience assist you any more; pray, then, excuse me."

So, while the old man with much painstakings resumed his work, the cosmopolitan, to allow him every facility, resumed his reading. At length, seeing that he had given up his undertaking as hopeless, and was at leisure again, the cosmopolitan addressed some gravely interesting remarks to him about the book before him, and, presently, becoming more and more grave, said, as he turned the large volume slowly over on the table, and with much difficulty traced the faded remains of the gilt inscription giving the name of the society who had presented it to the boat, "Ah, sir, though every one must be pleased at the thought of the presence in public places of such

[35] Unidentified.
[36] Cf. the "Wild goose chase!" of Chapter 3.

a book, yet there is something that abates the satisfaction. Look at this volume; on the outside, battered as any old valise in the baggage-room; and inside, white and virgin as the hearts of lilies in bud." [37]

"So it is, so it is," said the old man sadly, his attention for the first directed to the circumstance.

"Nor is this the only time," continued the other, "that I have observed these public Bibles in boats and hotels. All much like this—old without, and new within. True, this aptly typifies that internal freshness, the best mark of truth, however ancient; but then, it speaks not so well as could be wished for the good book's esteem in the minds of the traveling public. I may err, but it seems to me that if more confidence was put in it by the traveling public, it would hardly be so."

With an expression very unlike that with which he had bent over the Detector, the old man sat meditating upon his companion's remarks a while; and, at last, with a rapt look, said: "And yet, of all people, the traveling public most need to put trust in that guardianship which is made known in this book."

"True, true," thoughtfully assented the other.

"And one would think they would want to, and be glad to," continued the old man kindling; "for, in all our wanderings through this vale, how pleasant, not less than obligatory, to feel that we need start at no wild alarms, provide for no wild perils; trusting in that Power which is alike able and willing to protect us when we cannot ourselves."

His manner produced something answering to it in the cosmopolitan, who, leaning over towards him, said sadly: "Though this is a theme on which travelers seldom talk to each other, yet, to you, sir, I will say, that I share something of your sense of security. I have moved much about the world, and still keep at it; nevertheless, though in this land, and especially in these parts of it, some stories are told about steamboats and railroads fitted to make one a little apprehensive, yet,

[37] This is the voice of the "bridegroom tripping to the bridal chamber."

I may say that, neither by land nor by water, am I ever seriously disquieted, however, at times, transiently uneasy; since, with you, sir, I believe in a Committee of Safety,[38] holding silent sessions over all, in an invisible patrol, most alert when we soundest sleep, and whose beat lies as much through forests as towns, along rivers as streets. In short, I never forget that passage of Scripture which says, 'Jehovah shall be thy confidence.' [39] The traveler who has not this trust, what miserable misgivings must be his; or, what vain, short-sighted care must he take of himself."

"Even so," said the old man, lowly.

"There is a chapter," continued the other, again taking the book, "which, as not amiss, I must read you. But this lamp, solar-lamp as it is, begins to burn dimly."

"So it does, so it does," said the old man with changed air, "dear me, it must be very late. I must to bed, to bed! Let me see," rising and looking wistfully all round, first on the stools and settees, and then on the carpet, "let me see, let me see;—is there anything I have forgot,—forgot? Something I a sort of dimly remember. Something, my son—careful man—told me at starting this morning, this very morning. Something about seeing to—something before I got into my berth. What could it be? Something for safety. Oh, my poor old memory!"

"Let me give a little guess, sir. Life-preserver?"

"So it was. He told me not to omit seeing I had a life-preserver in my state-room; said the boat supplied them, too. But where are they? I don't see any. What are they like?"

[38] Three different Committees of Public Safety played central roles in the French Revolution. The first was formed in April, 1793, and was quickly controlled by Danton. It had complete power except over finance, its agents were everywhere, and it directed a Reign of Terror. The second, run by Robespierre, Saint-Just, and Couthon, lasting for a year, had greater power, more agents, and wider terror. The third, much weaker, took over after Robespierre's fall. There was also a Committee of Public Safety which very briefly exercised control in Vienna during the revolutions of 1848.

[39] Proverbs 3:26: ". . . the Lord shall be thy confidence, and shall keep thy foot from being taken."

"They are something like this, sir, I believe," lifting a brown stool with a curved tin compartment underneath; [40] "yes, this, I think, is a life-preserver, sir; and a very good one, I should say, though I don't pretend to know much about such things, never using them myself." [41]

"Why, indeed, now! Who would have thought it? *that* a life-preserver? That's the very stool I was sitting on, ain't it?"

"It is. And that shows that one's life is looked out for, when he ain't looking out for it himself. In fact, any of these stools here will float you, sir, should the boat hit a snag, and go down in the dark. But, since you want one in your room, pray take this one," handing it to him. "I think I can recommend this one; the tin part," rapping it with his knuckles, "seems so perfect—sounds so very hollow."

"Sure it's *quite* perfect, though?" Then, anxiously putting on his spectacles, he scrutinized it pretty closely—"well soldered? quite tight?"

"I should say so, sir; though, indeed, as I said, I never use this sort of thing, myself. Still, I think that in case of a wreck, barring sharp-pointed timbers, you could have confidence in that stool for a special providence." [42]

"Then, good-night, good-night; and Providence have both of us in its good keeping."

"Be sure it will," eying the old man with sympathy, as for the moment he stood, money-belt in hand, and life-preserver under arm, "be sure it will, sir, since in Providence, as in man, you and I equally put trust. But, bless me, we are being left in the dark here. Pah! what a smell, too." [43]

---

[40] Such stools were actually placed in cabins (for those wishing to avoid going out into the night).

[41] An assertion which may indicate much about his nature.

[42] A special providence is an intervention by God, for the benefit of one or more persons, in the usual operations of natural and historical law.

[43] The smell may be issuing from either the organic world represented by the stool or the celestial world represented by the solar lamp or both; i.e., by man or god or both together.

"Ah, my way now," cried the old man, peering before him, "where lies my way to my state-room?"

"I have indifferent eyes, and will show you; but, first, for the good of all lungs, let me extinguish this lamp."

The next moment, the waning light expired, and with it the waning flames of the horned altar, and the waning halo round the robed man's brow; while in the darkness which ensued, the cosmopolitan kindly led the old man away. Something further may follow of this Masquerade.

The River

Melville's manuscript fragment entitled "The River," discovered with a few pieces of manuscript for *The Confidence-Man* and written on the same kind of paper, deserves reprinting both for its own power and beauty and for its possible relations with *The Confidence-Man*. "The River" uses and explores the same materials: dreams, illusion, the Golden Age, and the Fall; fertility and death; fathers and sons; names, colors, and identity; inanimate, vegetable, animal, and human nature; savagery and serenity; Protean forms; myth and betrayal. And if the vision of the sketch informs that of *The Confidence-Man*, then the very river upon which the Fidèle floats is itself a treacherous masquerader which begins both its treachery and masquerade at the very place where the action of the book begins.

The only previously published complete transcription of the manuscript is the one Elizabeth Foster included in her edition of *The Confidence-Man*. I am deeply indebted to Miss Foster's pioneering job. The various places where my reading differs from hers are all duly annotated. I have taken the liberty of providing punctuation, because Melville often left this task for a later time or for someone else, and clearly did so here.

H. B. F.

As the word Abraham means the father of a great multitude of men, so the word Mississippi means the father of a great multitude of waters. His tribes stream in from east and west, exceeding fruitful the lands they enrich. In this granary of a continent, this basin of the Mississippi, must not the nations be greatly multiplied and blest?

Above the Falls of St. Anthony, for the most part he winds evenly in between banks of flags or thight [1] tracts of pine over marbley [2] sands in waters so clear that the deepest fish have the visible flight of the bird. Undisturbed as the lowly [3] life in its bosom, feeds the lonely life on its shores, the coronetted elk and the deer, while in the watery forms [4] of some couched rock in the channel, furred over with moss, the furred bear on the marge seems to eye his amphibious brother. Wood and wave wed, man is remote. The unsung time, the Golden Age of the billow.

By his Fall, though he rise not again, the unhumbled river ennobles himself, now deepens, now purely expands, now first forms his character and begins that career whose majestic serenity, if not overborne by fierce onsets of torrents, shall end only with ocean.

Like a larger Susquehanha, like a long-drawn bison herd, he hurries on through the prairie, here and there expanding into

[1] Set or growing closely together; thick-set, dense (*NED*). Foster conjectures *through* or *slight*; but the word, though not common, is extremely clear in the manuscript.

[2] Resembling marble. Foster conjectures *marbles* or *marshes*.

[3] Foster conjectures *lonely* or *lowly* both here and for the word modifying *life* in the next clause. The manuscript and the sense appear to me to dictate *lowly* in the first case, *lonely* in the second.

[4] Foster has *form*, but there is clearly a final *s* in the manuscript.

354

archipelagoes cycladean in beauty, while fissured and verdant, a long China Wall, the bluffs sweep bluely away. Glad and content, the sacred river glides on.

But at St. Louis the course of this dream is run. Down on it like a Pawnee from ambush foams the yellow-jacket Missouri. The calmness [5] is gone, the grouped isles disappear, the shores are jagged and rent, the hue of the water is clayed, the before moderate current is rapid and vexed. The opium [6] of the Upper River seems trite [7] in the Lower, nor is it ever renewed.

The Missouri sends rather a hostile element than a filial flow. Longer, stronger than the father of waters, like Jupiter he dethrones his sire and reigns in his stead. Under the benign name Mississippi, it is in short the Missouri that now rolls to the Gulf, the Missouri that with the snows from his solitudes freezes the warmth of the genial zones, the Missouri that by open assault or artful sap sweeps away fruit and field, grave-yard and barn, the Missouri that not a tributary but an under-mine [8] enters the sea, long disdaining to yield his white wave to the blue.

[5] Foster has *calm*, but the manuscript indicates at least *ess* after the *m*.

[6] Foster conjectures *peace, green, prime,* or *dream*. The first two letters are almost certainly *op*; after that my reading is somewhat conjectural, and it is quite possible to read the rest of the word as *ime*.

[7] A conjectural reading. The first letter is *t* or *l* or, less likely, *b*. After two or three strokes which may represent almost any combination of *r, i, n, s, u, e, c,* comes the mark that Melville often makes interchangeably for *t, b,* or *k,* particularly when followed by an *e,* as would appear in this case. There may be a final *s* or *r*. Foster has *broken*.

[8] A conjectural reading. The first three letters are almost certainly *und;* the rest of the word looks something like *erm*. Foster conjectures *outlaw, union,* or *overlord*. *Undermine* has in its favor the precision and accuracy of the image it provides; and this image would be the perfect fulfillment of the preceding image, for the most artful sap is an undermine.

The Library of Literature